PRAISE FO

Fleming's uncanny ability to summon magic from her prose was perfectly tuned to spin up this yarn and put to paper the essence and energy that *is* Music the Gathering."

— PHILLIP DRAYER DUNCAN, AUTHOR OF THE BLADE MAGE SERIES

Music the Gathering: A Most Inconvenient Curse is a fun adventure filled with music and friendship and loyalty and betrayal and magic and fighting. J.H. Fleming has created a world filled with characters that you will hope she returns to again and again.

— JC CRUMPTON, AUTHOR OF *SILENCE IN THE GARDEN*

The Queen of Moon and Shadow is a great start to the series...J.H. Fleming has done an incredible job with world building, creating a living, breathing backdrop to an incredible story of self-discovery, friendship, and self-reliance. HIGHLY recommended!

— DAVID J. GIBBS, AUTHOR OF THE MAD MAGGIE DUPREE SERIES

JACK OF CROWS

J.H. FLEMING

ISBN: 979-8-9879495-2-8

Publisher: Forest Witch Press LLC

Cover Art By: Aaron Moschner

Edited By: Phillip Drayer Duncan

FWP

For Kayla, who has always loved Jack the most.

FOLK SONGS AND FAIRY TALES

I've always loved fairy tales, and was lucky enough to retain that love into my adulthood. The way a tale can cross centuries and continents, morphing and changing over the years, being told and retold by modern authors, fascinates me.

I didn't discover my love of folk songs until I was older, and even then it took me a while to recognize the connection between the two. Like fairy tales, folk songs are passed down through the centuries, changing as they cross time and distant lands.

The two have similar origins, and reside in the same mental space for me: they are echoes of the past, changelings whose shapes depend on the singer or storyteller.

Once I had that realization, I knew I wanted to release a book and an album together—not directly connected, but complementing one another. My new album, *Once Upon A Time*, is both a nod to fairy tales and a collection of some of my favorite folk songs. My new novel, *Jack of Crows*, is not based on any existing fairy tale, but contains fairy-tale elements: witches, curses, animal companions, wild magic, and ancient gods.

May they transport you beyond this world, to a place both familiar and strange...

JACK OF CROWS

JACK AND EVELYN

For countless years, the scarecrow had stood in his field alone, a flock of crows his only companions. None of them had any fear of him. Instead, they perched on his outstretched arms and cawed at the world. Only if a farmer came at them with a hoe would they flee to the treetops. But they always returned.

The scarecrow's clothes had worn away with the weather and passing of years, leaving filthy brown rags in their wake. Two large black buttons served as his eyes, his mouth a twisted grimace. The fields he protected had been abandoned long ago, their farmhouse left to rot in the sun.

The crows were horrible gossips, but they kept off the loneliness, as did the fox who sometimes came by. But he was eccentric and secretive.

And, of course, there was Evelyn.

"I don't know how you stand the crows' infernal racket," the fox said to the scarecrow on his most recent visit.

"They're not all bad," the scarecrow replied. "They keep me sane."

The fox snorted. "More likely to drive you mad. But that's your affair. What about the human kit? Doing well, I take it?"

The scarecrow smiled to himself. Evelyn had started visiting him when she was a child, an energetic little redhead with a vast imagination. The passing years had turned her into a curious young woman, the whole world at her feet. That she continued to visit him, even into adulthood, made him love her all the more. She'd even given him a name, one he had never shared with the fox: she called him Jack.

"She's doing well." Though she didn't visit quite as often as she used to. "What about you? How is life in the forest?"

"Restless. The wolf packs are going to war, and no creature is safe from their fighting. I've considered taking temporary residence elsewhere."

"Surely it's not so bad as all that?"

"Worse every day. But I won't bore you with my troubles."

With that, the fox sprang away toward the village before the scarecrow could protest. Jack didn't mind. He was used to the fox's eccentric behavior.

Jack hadn't always been a scarecrow. At least, he didn't think so. He had memories of being a man once, long, long ago, though the memories were mostly scattered fragments now, too jumbled to make any sense of, let alone a solid past. Often he daydreamed of what it would be like to be human, or even an animal that could move about as it liked. He wouldn't mind being a fox, or a bird; surely flight was something so extraordinary it couldn't be described, only experienced. He never told the fox of these fantasies, though. The fox would only laugh.

More than once he imagined what Evelyn would say if she found not a scarecrow waiting for her in the field, but a man. Would she run? Would she even believe him, if he told her who he was?

If he could be granted a second, just as unlikely wish, it was for Evelyn to be able to hear him, to know that he wasn't a mere scarecrow on a post, but a living spirit with thoughts and feelings. But he may as well wish to be a mage in a tower, for all the good wishing would do him.

"Hello, Jack." Her voice startled him from his reverie. As if he had conjured her with his thoughts, there she stood, her red hair flying in the wind behind her. She looked over her shoulder, as though to make sure she wasn't followed, then sat down in the grass near his post and sighed. She was in her twenties now, with skin pale as the clouds and eyes as clear as the sky. She always dressed plainly, with no fine jewels or accoutrements, but today she held a leather-bound book, thick and ragged from use. She leaned against his post as she opened it and began flipping through the pages. "Oh, Jack, where do I begin? I wish that old prude would have agreed to apprentice me. Save me a lot of trouble. I had to practically steal this book, but I should have it back by nightfall."

The crows returned and perched on his arms, unafraid of her presence.

"What's she got there?" one asked.

"Nothing good, I'll warrant," another said.

"So this is where she snuck off to! Her da wouldn't be pleased to know she was in a hay field with a book."

"How long do you think before she's discovered?"

"Oh, a good while yet. He can't spare to leave the forge for long. I'd be more worried about the old widow, now that the book is stolen."

"Who does the book belong to?" the scarecrow interjected.

The crows paused in their gossip, unsure what to make of him. He'd never actually spoken to them before.

"So you do talk," one finally answered.

"Some say the woman's a mage, but what is that to you?"

"I was just curious," he said, determined to say no more.

"Hmm. Well, it will be interesting to see what will become of the girl."

"Yes, quite interesting indeed."

"That's it!" Evelyn cried, surprising all of them. "Now I'll just alter this slightly..." She closed her eyes as she spoke and twirled her index finger in a circle. The breeze picked up and a small whirlwind of leaves and grass rose into the air beneath her hand. Evelyn opened her eyes, laughing. "It worked, Jack!" she said. "I did it!" She sprang to her feet and danced around the field, spinning and performing more hand movements so that the whirlwind grew bigger and spun around her like a cocoon.

"Magic," one of the crows said. "This one's going to have more trouble than we guessed."

Magic. Evelyn could do magic. He couldn't have been more surprised if someone had told him he'd been born a fox. His Evelyn, a mage? He hadn't even realized she *wanted* to do magic.

When she stopped dancing, Evelyn resumed her seat and looked up at him. "I wish you could speak, Jack. I have no one else in all the world to share my secret with; my father would disapprove, and my mother's long gone, beyond caring what I choose to do. That leaves only my brother and a few distant relatives, but they wouldn't care either way, so long as it didn't affect them." She sighed. "I must be getting back now, but I'll return. Goodbye, Jack. Goodbye, crows!"

"I doubt she'll last till winter," one crow said. "Someone will wise up to her disappearances and follow her, and then all her secrets will be undone."

"I'll give her a month, no more."

Jack watched her disappear across the field, her laughter still echoing in the air, drowning out the omens of the crows.

SHE DIDN'T COME the next day, or the next, and Jack feared the worst. Had she been discovered after all? Was she at that moment enduring some punishment and wishing she were there with him? The crows didn't speak of her, and he dared not ask. When a week had passed, his friend the fox appeared again, sporting new gashes in his red fur.

"Only scratches," he assured the scarecrow. "The battles have grown fiercer of late. How are things with you?"

"Well enough," Jack said. "I'm worried about Evelyn."

"Oh?"

"She hasn't returned. She's practicing magic, you see, and I fear she may have been discovered."

"Magic is a risky business, to be sure."

"Do you think... That is, would you be willing to go to the edge of the village and spy her out? It would ease my mind to know she's all right. I'll owe you a favor, anything you like. Only name it."

The fox considered a moment, then shrugged. "It makes no difference to me. It's safer than walking into a wolf battle."

He bounded off right then, wasting no time. Jack watched him until he reached the edge of the field and disappeared from view. The minutes crawled by, each more unendurable than the last. What he wouldn't give to be able to check on her himself! Finally the fox appeared again, leaping across the field.

"All is well!" he called as he neared. "She is trapped at home, but unharmed."

"Are you sure you found the right person?"

"Positive. A mage is always hard to miss. The magic clings to them, causing a glow. She outshone the sun in these gloomy autumn days, though I daresay she'd give the summer sun a stiff competition as well."

"Where was she when you saw her?"

"Behind her house, chopping wood. Rather skillfully, I might add. From what I could gather, she's under some sort of punishment, but I do believe it will end soon."

"How do you know?"

"I heard the crows talking. Seems you're not the only one with an interest in her."

"You didn't speak to them, did you?" Jack asked, worried suddenly that the fox had told them of his interest.

The fox scoffed. "What do you take me for, a rabbit? I'll return in a week, if the battles permit. Curse wolves and their incessant pack wars."

And with that he was gone, disappearing back into the forest without even a goodbye. But that was his way, and Jack had grown quite used to it. He went back to watching the far edge of the field, hoping he'd soon see a crown of red hair appearing through the tall grass.

THREE MORE DAYS passed before Evelyn returned. By that point, Jack's anxiety had risen dramatically once more, despite the fox's assurances. And then she had come, dancing across the field with the wind in her hair, and at that moment he would've gladly endured endless days of the same agonizing waiting if he knew he'd see her like that again.

"Jack, I'm free!" she cried. "If I had to suffer one more day at home, I swear I would've gone mad. That's what I get for not being more careful, I suppose, but never mind that! Sure wish I still had the book, but I think I remember enough." She raised her hand and twisted her fingers. A gust of wind passed over her, ruffling her dress. She smiled. "It's mostly willpower anyway. So, what should I practice today? Levitation? Or perhaps a scrying spell? I think I remember enough to try that..."

The crows returned, gossiping and cackling.

"She's a persistent one," one said.

"You would think she'd learn her lesson by now. Who ever heard of a great mage being self-taught? Deaths and catastrophes, that's what you hear about the ones with no teachers."

Jack blocked them out, refusing to let them ruin the moment. Evelyn was back.

"I want to travel the world," she said. "Become a master mage, be respected and loved. I suppose that's a lot to ask for, but I won't give up. No matter what my father says. I'm worth more than a few cows and some land."

"Won't she be surprised?" one of the crows said with a laugh. "I don't expect she'll take it well."

"Oh, no, not this one. Drudgery is all she has to look forward to, then the final sleep—"

"Enough!" Jack cried, surprising all of them. Many took flight, thinking some danger had appeared. Unsure what to say, Jack decided to simply continue. "If you don't speak nicely of her, you aren't welcome here."

"What are you going to do? *Scare* us away?"

"I might. I still have a few tricks up my sleeve."

"And why for her? She's not as special as she believes, and she's got a lot less sense than what should be the minimum."

"She's my friend, and this is my field. I'll make the rules, and you can abide by them or find another scarecrow."

The crows mumbled amongst themselves. They no doubt wondered who this bossy scarecrow was, and what had happened to the quiet one they'd become accustomed to.

Evelyn was concentrating again, this time watching a pile of dead leaves with focused intent. After a long moment, a thin tendril of white smoke arose from the pile and she clapped her hands. "Oh, Jack, I've never been so happy! Just think: in a few months' time, I'll have mastered all the basics. Then maybe I can find myself a proper teacher. They say starting off is the most difficult part. But you and the crows will hope and wish with me, won't you? Don't think I haven't seen you following me," she said, addressing them. "I know you like me."

"That's one way of putting it," one said.

"I have to go now." She stood and brushed off her skirt, running her fingers through her hair to catch any stray bits of leaves or grass. "Farewell!"

The crows started to chatter about her as she left, but quickly subsided when they remembered Jack's words. They waited a moment longer, then took off toward the village. Jack watched the path she had taken for several minutes. The sun was sinking earlier and earlier every day as autumn hastened on. The nights would get longer and colder, and then perhaps she'd stop coming, for a while. That had happened before. Or perhaps not. It was still too soon to tell.

THE FOX RETURNED a few days later, looking much better than the last few times Jack had seen him. His coat had thickened, and even had a nice sheen to it.

"I've decided to stay around here for a bit," he said. "The forest is too restless with all the wolves stirred up. How are things with you and your lady?"

"She's not my—"

"I'm joking, of course. Does she still come to see you?"

"Nearly every day. And she's getting much better at magic. I think she has it in her to become a master."

"Too bad humans have to go to school for such things, or risk killing themselves. We animals have it much easier."

"Can *you* do magic?"

The fox cackled. "You won't be getting my secrets that easily. We may be friends, but there are some things you're meant to keep close."

Jack looked down at the fox's shining pelt, at his beady eyes and noble demeanor. Such a creature *would* have magic, or so it seemed to him. "Do you ever wish you were human?"

"Why would I wish *that?*"

"It's just that the humans rule over everything, build advanced machines and houses, and more often than not it's them taking down an animal for food, not the other way around."

"So I should wish to be one so I can eat my kin?"

"No, no, no! I just meant they can do more than we can. More than me for sure. They're free—"

"*We* are free. More so than them, though it may not seem like it. I wouldn't trade a single lifetime as a fox for a hundred lifetimes as a human."

The crows arrived just as the sun started sinking, and the fox slipped off into the woods. Jack listened to the birds' mindless chatter for a bit, but his eyes watched for Evelyn. The sun sank and the wind blew, ever colder and colder. The trees stretched their long shadows across the field, telling each other tales of long ago. Finally, just as Jack despaired of Evelyn coming at all, she arrived, breathless and wrathful. She breathed heavily and paced in front of him, muttering to herself. At last her voice rose and he could make out her words.

"I won't do it! He thinks he can make me, but I would rather die! I am not some piece of farmland to be sold and bought at whim." She faced Jack, her eyes bright and determined. "He intends for me to marry, Jack. Marry some noble's son in a town! I've never met the man, and it seems I won't until the wedding. Can you imagine? I won't do it, but I can't think how to get out of it."

She wrung her hands and turned away again.

"Death is preferable, but I don't wish to die. There is still so much to learn! I can't imagine my intended would approve of my magic studies, but I won't give them up. If I can't marry for love, I won't marry at all." She stopped and looked toward the village, as though she could see her family and divine their reaction to her decision. "I wish you could speak, Jack," she whispered. "I need advice."

"Scarecrows aren't much for advice," a croaky voice answered.

Evelyn turned back around, but there was only Jack and the crows. "Who said that?"

"I did," one of the crows answered. It perched on Jack's outstretched arm, and he could barely see it through his peripheral vision. It was old and hunched, its coat a flat black. It cocked its head at Evelyn and spoke again. "I can help you, for a price."

"How could you help me? Are you a mage in crow form? Is that how you can speak?"

"I am no mage," the crow cackled. "I am a witch. Or I was, in human form. I can still help you, though. All you have to do is switch places with me."

"Switch places?"

"Yes. You would become a crow, and I would become human once more. Crows cannot be forced to marry."

"Don't do it!" Jack said, but Evelyn couldn't understand him.

The crow could, and glared one beady eye at him, but did not comment.

Jack remembered many stories about witches, stories he hadn't realized he knew until that moment, and none of them portrayed such people in a good light. There was something more, too, some important image that wouldn't completely form in his mind. Something to do with an old woman.

"That's all?" Evelyn asked. "We switch places and I'm free?"

"That's all," the crow said. "Do we have a deal?"

Evelyn frowned and touched one finger to her chin, looking at the ground as she paced once more.

"Don't," Jack tried again, but he couldn't make her hear him.

"I can't see any other way," Evelyn said. "I can't run away. My father will find me, I know it. And I don't truly want to die... I'll do it."

Jack tried to move, to scream, anything to stop her, but to no avail.

"Good," the crow cackled. "Just stand there perfectly still, that's a good girl. Now repeat after me: Of my own will, I relinquish my human form."

The spell went on for a bit longer, and Evelyn repeated everything the crow said, oblivious of Jack's unease. When she finished, she cried out and bent forward, clutching her stomach.

"Oh, I forgot to mention it may hurt a little," the crow said. Its voice wasn't so hoary anymore; it was youthful and musical, and the crow was growing. It hopped down to the ground beside Evelyn and cackled again. Evelyn shrank, falling in on herself, her skin and hair darkening and her nose and mouth elongating. The crow grew paler as its size increased, becoming slightly more human with every passing second. Evelyn cried out again and Jack tried once more to move to her side, but he was stuck fast. When it was finally over, a small crow stood in Evelyn's place, flopping about wildly, while next to her a young woman with coal black hair looked on. The girl looked at her hands and touched her face, delight plain in her eyes.

"At last!" she cried, and her voice was soft velvet. She looked at Evelyn still flailing about, then laughed and dashed off across the field without a backward glance.

"Wait, help me!" Evelyn cried, her voice now high and scratchy.

"Don't worry," Jack said. "It will be all right."

"Who said that?"

"Me. Jack."

"The scarecrow?"

"Yes. You can hear me now."

There was no answer for a long moment. Then, finally, Evelyn said, "Have you always been able to talk?"

"For as long as I can remember. I tried to warn you not to do it, but no human has managed to hear me yet."

"I... I see. I can't seem to get my balance. I imagine I'll have trouble flying as well. Can you help me? Or one of the crows?"

"I know nothing of flying. Can any of you help?" he asked the crows. "She's one of you, now."

The crows had remained silent for once, but now they all began speaking together.

"I can help!"

"It's easy, you just—"

"Flying is truly the best part—"

"You made a good decision. Crows are clearly superior—"

"One at a time!" Jack shouted. "She won't get anywhere at this rate."

The crows grew silent again, looking from one to another.

"Malachi shall help," they finally announced.

A young crow stepped out of the flock and landed on the ground next to Evelyn.

"First, let's get your balance." He showed her how to properly stand and shift her weight so she no longer fell over. After a few tries, she managed it, then practiced standing on one foot at a time and hopping about.

"I think I've got it," she said. "Now what?"

He practiced with her for a while as Jack watched. He gazed across the field where the young woman—the witch—had disappeared. There was no guessing where she had gone. Perhaps to the village, if they were lucky. As soon as Evelyn got the hang of flying, she'd need to seek the witch out to get her body back. The witch had to make her human again. She couldn't just leave Evelyn like that.

"Perfect. Just keep practicing," Malachi said.

Jack looked back at Evelyn, who was now fluttering around, rising in the air for short distances. The sun fully disappeared then, leaving only the stars and moon to illuminate them.

"I'll pick up again tomorrow," Evelyn said. "I can't see what I'm doing."

The crows began leaving, heading off to nest for the night. Malachi went with them, leaving Evelyn and Jack alone.

"You can sleep next to my post," Jack said. "There's a lot of grass, and no predators will bother you here."

"Thank you," she said, waddling over to nestle down near his post. She ruffled her feathers and spun in a circle, trying to get comfortable. He imagined sleeping would be difficult, at least at first. For that, he didn't envy her, but he did feel bad. She should be safe at home, warm in bed, not out in the field as a crow. Finally, she got comfortable and settled down to sleep. Jack listened to her faint breathing for a while, then dozed off himself.

LEARNING TO FLY

"Isn't this a grand sight?"

Jack awoke and found the fox sitting before him, staring at the ground near his post. Evelyn was just waking, and she squeaked when she noticed the fox.

"He won't hurt you," Jack assured her.

"So he says," the fox replied. "But we all know he's trapped on that post. He couldn't help you if I chose to attack."

"Will you?" Evelyn asked, her voice small and vulnerable.

The fox chuckled. "Of course not. This is simply too amusing." He moved closer, circling around to get a better look at her. "That's a strong spell," he commented. "It will take a strong mage to break it."

"Who says I want to break it?" Evelyn replied.

"I'm merely stating a fact. Of course, if you enjoy the crow life, who am I to judge?"

"But what about your human life?" Jack asked. "Your family, or friends? What about your magic studies?"

"If I go back, I'll be forced to marry, and I'll lose it all anyway. At least this way I still have my freedom."

"But there are other ways—"

"I'm not going back!" Evelyn shouted. "I'm sorry. I know you're worried for me, but I'm staying a crow. I'll get used to it."

"That's the spirit," the fox said.

Jack didn't respond, worried he'd only upset her more.

"So, what do you plan to do on your first day as a crow?" the fox continued.

"Learn to fly," Evelyn replied. "What was your name?"

"Call me Slade," the fox answered. "Do you have someone to teach you?"

"Well, there was another crow yesterday—"

"Crows aren't reliable. Allow me."

He bent over her and breathed on her. She shuddered and sneezed, then ruffled her feathers and lightly flapped her wings. A moment later, she rose into the air and flew a few feet.

"That's it," the fox said. "Let it carry you. It wants to, but it needs your trust. The magic will help, but you have to let go."

Jack just watched, wondering why the fox—Slade—had decided to be so helpful. He'd revealed two things about himself to Evelyn—assuming he'd given his true name. That was more than he'd ever revealed to Jack. Not that Jack was complaining.

Evelyn flapped her wings again and flew another few feet. Slade followed her and they worked their way across the field. She slowly rose higher and her distances increased until Jack counted several seconds between each landing. Then, in a mighty gush, she flew rose, soaring above them. Jack thought he saw a shimmering trail in the air behind her. Possibly more of Slade's magic. Or the early morning sun.

Evelyn did a circle, and another, then flew off toward the village. Slade shambled back over, looking mighty pleased with himself.

"All it takes is a little coaxing," he said.

"I'm hoping to turn her human again. She's not a crow, no matter what she says."

"Oh, come now. She seems to be enjoying herself. Let her be."

But Jack watched her disappear over the village rooftops and knew he couldn't.

Evelyn returned later that evening, tired and hungry. "I saw all of my neighbors, Jack, and not one of them suspected! I'm well and truly free at last!"

"I'm glad you're happy," he replied.

"Where is Slade? I thought he'd be here."

"He comes and goes. There's no telling when he'll return."

"Well, I hope it's soon. I didn't get to thank him for helping me." She hopped up onto Jack's outstretched arm and preened her feathers. "Everything looks so much bigger. The world is a much grander place, for a crow."

"Just imagine what it must be like for ants."

She chuckled. "I am pretty hungry, though. Crows have different hungers, and I haven't quite figured out what it is I crave."

"Probably bugs. All birds eat bugs, don't they?"

"I'm not sure. I've always thought so, but aren't there some who eat nuts? Fruits? I hope it's not bugs."

"Well, you have to eat something. Why don't you try finding some nuts in the forest for now and worry about bugs tomorrow?"

She nodded and flew silently off into the trees. Jack wished he could search with her. Curse his immobility! He loved watching the clouds and the sky change colors, but he longed for new scenes, for the feel of earth under his feet as he walked.

For warm blood pumping through his veins.

When Evelyn returned, she landed at the foot of his post and nestled into the grass again.

"I'm still not quite used to being a crow," she confessed, "and I'd be terribly embarrassed if I fell in my sleep. I'll spend another night on the ground."

"I don't blame you. I would probably do the same thing."

She took a moment to get settled and then lay still. For a short while there was only the sound of the breeze through the grass and her soft breathing.

"Jack, have you always been a scarecrow?" she asked after a moment.

"I...don't think so. Sometimes I have memories. Human memories, I think. At least, they can't be scarecrow memories. Anyway, it all seems like a dream from long ago. If I was ever human, I've almost forgotten."

"How sad. Perhaps you were cursed?"

"I'm not sure. It's possible, I suppose."

"Why would someone do that, do you think? It seems you'd have to hate someone pretty strongly to cast a spell so powerful."

"You're probably right." Jack tried to remember, but he couldn't imagine having angered someone to that extent. It didn't seem right. Unless he had once been a completely different sort of person. Which was possible, but not likely.

"I still can't believe you've been alive all this time, and I never knew. You watched me grow up, Jack. I told you all my secrets."

"I never told anyone, I promise."

That earned him a laugh.

"It's strange. Like we're complete strangers and old friends at the same time." Her voice grew softer and more relaxed as she drifted off to sleep. Rather than wake her, he settled himself for the night and joined her in the land of dreams.

SLADE RETURNED THE NEXT DAY, just before noon. He carried a stick in his mouth, which he dropped at Jack's post.

"What's that for?" Jack asked.

"Balance," Slade answered.

"Really?" Evelyn said, fluttering to the ground. "This is

perfect. We were just saying last night that I needed better balance."

"I'll carry the stick in my mouth with you perched on the side. You can even practice sleeping, if you like."

"I'll give it a try."

"Why are you being so helpful?" Jack asked, unable to contain himself a moment more. "Not that I'm not grateful for the help, but it's so unlike you. I mean, you've never been so open with me. Why the sudden change?"

"Let's just say it's for the lady's sake and leave it at that, shall we?" Slade said, grinning back at Evelyn.

"When do we start?" she asked, barely containing her excitement.

"We can start now, if you like. If Sir Jack approves?"

"You don't need my approval. Teach her all she wants."

Evelyn hopped on the stick, which Slade had already lifted in his mouth. With that, they stalked across the field at a leisurely pace, Evelyn bobbing happily with every step. Jack supposed she really did seem content. Perhaps she'd have a better life as a crow, and she'd said it was what she wanted. He just couldn't shake the image of her excitement while performing magic. Surely, if it made her that happy, she couldn't just give it up. Could she even do magic as a crow? Slade would know, and maybe if Evelyn did the asking he'd tell her.

The two circled the field three times. Evelyn bobbed a bit deeper than before, then caught herself. As they came back around, Jack noticed that her eyes were closed. She was learning quickly, so no doubt she'd sleep perched on his arm that night. Perhaps she would start living near him. The other crows hadn't returned since she'd transformed, probably unsure what to make of things. They would watch the village, listen for gossip, find out what people thought of Evelyn's disappearance. And the appearance of the young witch, if she'd stuck around.

It was possible the villagers thought the witch was Evelyn, her appearance changed by some spell, but Jack couldn't remember how prevalent magic was among the humans. There were great mages, but how common was it for someone to be enchanted? And if the witch was acknowledged as Evelyn, would her family accept her? Would she still have to marry? Why would she want to pose as Evelyn at all? It would make more sense for her to leave the village and go out into the world to see what it had to offer. At least, he supposed that was what he would do.

Slade and Evelyn came back around and she opened her eyes and hopped to the ground. "I think I have it now," she said. "Thank you, Slade. How can I ever repay you?"

"Oh, I'm certain I can come up with something," the fox said. Jack didn't like the sound of that. "What do you intend to do now?"

"Fly," she said, and with that she was gone, over the field and across the rooftops of the village, until she was just a tiny speck in the sky.

"I suppose you're about to start questioning me again," the fox said.

"You know me so well. If she tried, can she still do magic?"

Slade grinned. "Of course. You use the mind for magic. The body is irrelevant."

That was it, then. With magic, Evelyn could continue being a crow and live a life of freedom and happiness. There was nothing to tempt her back to humanity. Jack sighed, and would've nodded if he could. Everything was just as it should be after all.

THE CROWS RETURNED the next day. Evelyn had already flown out for the morning, and Slade had not appeared. The crows perched along Jack's arms and head, but he didn't mind. He'd actually missed their company.

"How are things in the village?" he asked.

"Tense," one said.

"Quiet," another answered.

"Watchful," said a third.

"So they've noticed Evelyn's disappearance?" Jack asked.

"Noticed? Her father threatened to burn the entire forest to the ground. You're lucky you're still standing here."

"And what of the witch? The dark-haired girl?"

"Everyone's taken with her. She claims she's distant kin to some old couple, and their family's so big they think it just might be true. So they've taken her in, and treat her as their own granddaughter. She has the run of the town, and the eye of every lad younger than forty. Some older."

"It's whispered there's something off about her. Her features are too perfect, her voice too clear and musical, her eyes too discerning. Folks are already whispering of enchantment."

"What exactly do they suspect?"

"Oh, nothing sinister. Just some young woman who's been glamoured to appear fairer than God gave her the right to be. No true harm at all."

"And what of Evelyn? Has her father given up?"

"He's left off the search for now, but it won't last. He'll not rest until he has answers."

"Then he may be searching the rest of his life," Jack said, gazing at the distant rooftops.

"That fool girl," one crow said. "So brash and reckless. She'll destroy her life sooner than find it."

"But it is hers to destroy, if it comes to that," Jack replied, unwilling to let them judge her.

"Who are you to speak? You're just a scarecrow."

"We're not here to talk about me. It's Evelyn I'm concerned about."

"What did she do to deserve such devotion? Surely you can't be in love?"

"Infatuated, more like."

"Be gone, all of you!" Jack shouted. The vehemence in his voice startled them to flight, and he remembered why he was glad for their absence. Despite that, their words struck too close to home. Not that he would ever say anything to Evelyn. He wouldn't risk pushing her away.

For hours he sat alone in the field, watching the clouds move across the sky and the occasional bird fly by. None of them were Evelyn, though. At dusk, Slade returned, sporting some new cuts and matted fur. He sat facing Jack and licked a cut on his foot.

"The war?" Jack asked.

Slade continued to lick his wound. The wolves were getting closer, then, though Jack doubted they'd come into the village. Even with the bloodlust raging, they still feared the humans, and with good reason. They would stop just at the forest's edge, not daring to come closer for fear of being seen.

"I suppose you'll be sticking around here for a while longer," Jack said. "I can't imagine you'll be able to get back through any time soon."

"Perhaps not," Slade said. "Lucky that I have friends here, eh?" He licked his paw one final time, then started in on a place low on his back.

"Can't you use magic to heal yourself?" Jack asked.

"What makes you think I'm not?"

"I suppose it just doesn't seem very magical."

"Would chanting and bright light feel more magical to you?"

"Probably. But I can't do magic, so what do I know?"

"Not much," Slade agreed. "Though if I need knowledge of the movements of the clouds, I'll call on you first."

They sat in silence for a bit, Slade pointedly ignoring him. Jack watched the sky until the sun disappeared behind the distant rooftops, leaving a golden impression in the air. His thoughts wandered and images appeared in his mind's eye of small campfires and a stone cottage, a creek and a watermill, and long brunette hair blowing in the breeze. He didn't know what they meant, so he simply sat and watched. Perhaps he really *had* been human once. There were certainly no mills around here that he could see, but his mind could conjure the image as if it stood in front of him.

"It's going to be a rough night," Slade said, jolting Jack from his reverie.

Jack looked up at the sky, which had darkened with mountainous clouds. Lightning flashed in their depths, followed seconds later by roaring thunder. Slade stretched and took off for the village.

"Good luck," he called over his shoulder just as the first drops began to fall. Jack watched the fox disappear and the rain came down harder and faster. Soon it poured from the sky with the strength of a raging river. The village rooftops disappeared behind a gray curtain and Jack stood alone in the torrent. A rushing wind picked up, blowing him to the side, but his post was buried deep in the earth and he stayed upright. Since he could do nothing but endure it, he allowed his mind to wander back to the stone cottage, and to Evelyn, whom he hoped had found some other shelter for the night.

THE DAWN BROUGHT with it a breeze and a heavy fog. Jack had not yet dried from the deluge and stood dripping as the sun rose higher and the fog began to clear a bit, revealing a land that showed little sign of the storm that had occurred. Slade appeared out of the mist, looking well rested and less bedraggled. Behind him followed Evelyn. Or at least, Jack assumed it was her. None of the other crows had bothered to visit him without the whole flock.

Slade sat on the ground and Evelyn perched on Jack's outstretched arm.

"I never knew a storm could be so violent!" she said. "That seems the right word for it. That awning barely kept me dry. And the thunder!"

"I'm glad you stayed safe," Jack said.

"Just barely. I think next time I'll try to find a barn or something."

"Good idea," Slade said. "Can you imagine having to endure it out in the open?" He cast a cool gaze Jack's way, but Jack paid him no mind.

"You're still enjoying your crow form, then?" he asked Evelyn.

"It's...not bad," she said. "The flying part is nice. The food... Perhaps I'll get used to it. And the freedom is wonderful."

"And your magic?"

"I...haven't tried," she admitted.

"What better time than the present?" Slade said. "Go ahead, try now."

Evelyn ruffled her feathers and then stood perfectly still. A moment later the leaves on the ground rose into the air in a slow spiral. A few seconds more and Evelyn gasped, the leaves falling as she panted. "That was much more difficult than I remember. It felt like it was draining all my energy."

"Magic costs more for animals," Slade informed them. "It's partly due to size, and partly to species, life span, and natural energy. You get used to it after a while."

"So humans have an easier job of it?" Jack asked.

"In some respects," Slade said dismissively. "If they survive the basics, which is almost impossible without a teacher. But they are limited by their lack of perspective and imagination."

"I'll get used to it," Evelyn said in a determined voice. "I have to."

"You *don't* have to," Jack said. "You can still find the witch and get your body back. I hear she's still in the village."

"No. Not while my father is still looking for me."

"Why do you stay here?" Jack asked. "You can go anywhere now. Unless you do hope to get your body back, why not go?"

"Maybe I *will* go," she said. "I'll fly to a distant city and nest in a bell tower and have a dozen crow babies."

Slade chuckled. "Good luck in a city. I may come along just to watch."

"You don't think I can do it?"

"Let's just say I've known too many who venture to the city for a better life. I'm sure you can guess how it ends."

Evelyn balanced on one foot and cocked her head to the side. "I would be fine."

"My dear, even humans have trouble in cities. They are not inviting or comforting places, and even less so to animals. But if you wish to try, I won't stop you."

She didn't answer for a moment, but she put her foot down and ruffled her feathers once more.

"What about another village?" Jack suggested. "Or a town? Somewhere where no one knows you. That's the goal, right?"

"I suppose..."

"City, town, what does it matter?" Slade said.

"You're both just baiting me," Evelyn said. "I can make my own decisions just fine, thank you."

"Obviously," Slade said, his eyes creasing in private amusement. "If you need me, I'll be hunting chickens."

He bounded off toward the village, not sparing them a second glance.

"Sometimes I think we only exist for his amusement," Evelyn said.

"We do," Jack replied. "But I prefer to pretend I don't. It makes for a more pleasant life."

She nodded and looked toward the village in silence. The fog had all but disappeared and the village rooftops were visible once more through the fog.

"Do you miss being human at all?" he asked. "Even a little?"

"Maybe a bit," she admitted. "But if I go back, my father will find me. I just know it."

"Maybe he won't," Jack said. "You won't know unless you try."

"I don't think I can risk it."

"That's your choice, but personally, I think you're letting your fear control you."

She stayed silent a moment more, then asked, "What's it like, always staying in the same place day after day? Don't you get bored?"

"Sometimes," he admitted. "But then I have memories. Or visions, maybe. I'm not sure. And sometimes it's nice to just sit and be."

"If you were able to move, what would you do?"

He considered a moment, then answered, "Travel. See the far-off places the crows talk about."

"Why don't we try it? Make you move, I mean. I probably don't have the strength now, but tomorrow? It may take me several practice sessions, but I think I can manage it. I remember some spells from the book."

"You're welcome to try. Whether or not you succeed, it's kind of you to offer."

She ruffled her feathers again. "I'm getting hungry. I better go find some food."

"I'll be here," he replied.

❧ 3 ❧
FREE AT LAST

"L et me try again," Evelyn said, though it was her seventh attempt at the spell and she had long since exhausted her energy.

"Please don't," Jack said. "It's fine, I'm used to not moving. You can try again tomorrow, if you like."

"But I'm sure I can do it..."

She began the spell once more only to fall over in exhaustion. Luckily, she was already on the ground, so she was unharmed.

"I've lived like this for as long as I can remember," Jack said. "It doesn't bother me. Don't overdo it, okay?"

She was already falling asleep, which was the best way to replenish her energy, so Jack let her doze off. She had done the best she could, and honestly, he was fine with his current state. He had no complaints.

"Persistent, isn't she?" Slade asked, appearing from behind Jack. "I would've guessed she'd give up after the fourth try. Or pass out. But she's resilient, I'll give her that. She'll be up and ready to go faster than you can blink."

"Can you give her some tips or something? She's wearing herself out, and I suspect you could help in some way."

"Perhaps I can. But why should I? Performing magic is tiresome work, and I can think of dozens of ways my energies could be better spent."

"Despite what you say, you keep returning here, and you've shown an interest in helping her. Whatever your reasons, I hope you won't stop now."

Slade yawned with disinterest and stretched out on the grass, narrowing his eyes as he said, "She better rest while she can. The villagers will be up this way soon, and they'll have their dogs with them. Won't want to stick around for that."

"The villagers?" Jack said in alarm. "They're coming here? Why?"

"Not here exactly, but through here. This section of the forest is the only one they haven't searched. Perhaps when they find it empty, her father will finally give up."

"We can hope so," Jack said, looking back down at Evelyn. "I feel bad for him, but it's her choice."

"Well, perhaps if he were more inclined to let her choose her own life, she would not have taken such drastic measures. Or maybe she simply shouldn't be so stubborn. Who can say?"

"I suppose we should wake her. How long till they arrive?"

"No telling. But they were gathering together when I left them half an hour ago."

"Evelyn!" Jack called. "Evelyn, wake up."

She lifted her head and blinked blearily. "What is it?" she mumbled.

"The villagers are coming. They won't recognize you, but they may try to scare you off, or hurt you. It might be best if you hide."

"Villagers? Hide?"

Her voice was still heavy with sleep, so again Jack said, "Hurry! They're coming!"

She fluttered up, looking around and tripping over her feet.

Slade laughed, throwing his head back. "Great job. You've managed to scare and confuse her with minimal effort. You are to be commended."

"It wasn't intentional!" Jack cried.

"What do I do?" Evelyn asked, near panic.

"Hide in the woods," Jack suggested. "Any tree should do."

She flew into the trees and Slade laughed again. "With you around, it'll be a miracle if she survives the winter."

"What's that supposed to mean?"

"Nothing at all," Slade said, walking toward the trees in Evelyn's wake.

Pale gray clouds covered the sky like a blanket, a crisp breeze blowing from over the rooftops, and the scent of smoke permeated the air. It wasn't long before the villagers appeared at the edge of the meadow, many carrying blazing torches. Jack could see them better as they approached: young and old, male and female. No one who wanted to come had been left behind. Some of the children skipped ahead, circling around and laughing to each other, making a game of it. The adults wore grim faces, but they didn't stop the children. They slowed only a little as they neared, many glancing at him in minor curiosity.

"Must've belonged to Old Mason. Should we pull it down?"

"Leave it for the next farmer. They may want to keep it."

"It's an ugly old thing, isn't it?"

"So long as it does its job. No crows, you can see."

"I don't think we're going to find anything. At this point, she's either dead, or she's long gone and doesn't want to be found."

"It keeps the old man happy. Figure we'll search for a bit and head back home."

"Not everyone appreciates the country life. She probably took off for a city. That young Ferah, now, she was made for this place."

"Aye, a regular farmer's daughter. A touch of city, mind you, but it compliments her."

"Strange how she showed up now, isn't it? After all these years."

They must've been talking about the witch. Jack wondered

why she wasn't among them. Afraid to return to the field, perhaps?

The last of the villagers passed him, leaving only the empty field once more. He heard them entering the forest behind him, already calling Evelyn's name. Jack wondered which one was her father, how long the man would search, and if he would continue looking late into the darkness when all others had returned safely to their beds.

W HEN EVELYN RETURNED the next morning, she landed on Jack's arm and sat in silence, staring at the ground.

"Is everything...okay?" he asked.

"Am I a bad person, Jack?"

"Of course not," he quickly assured her.

"I think I am. I watched my father look for me, and it never crossed my mind to go to him, even as he called my name. I was glad he couldn't find me. Even now, I don't want to go back. But I can't stop seeing his face."

Jack didn't say anything. What could he say? Nothing that would be of any help.

"I need to leave this place," she said. "Maybe if I get away, I won't think about it so much."

"Maybe," he said. "Or maybe you could go back. Go home. At this point, he may be so glad to see you that he won't force you to get married."

"You don't know my father," she said just as bleakly as before. "He's the embodiment of tough love. He'll be glad to see me, then pick up as though I never left."

"So...leave, then? Where will you go?"

"Somewhere far away. I wish you could come with me, Jack. You've been a good friend to me. If only I could get the spell to work."

Jack wished he could, too, for the thought of her leaving

while he was stuck there in the field left a cold spot in his heart. Life would be...drearier. Less magical.

"We could ask Slade," he suggested. "I think he can do more magic than he lets on."

"You think so?"

"I'm sure of it."

"Do you know where he is? He disappears sometimes and doesn't come back till it suits him."

"He's probably in the woods."

"I'll go look for him."

She flew off, leaving Jack alone. Cold wind blew across the field, heralding the slow approach of winter. In a few weeks, he expected to see snow on the ground, and the world would don the enchanting dream-like quality of a faery tale. The crows never seemed to notice, and their visits always continued despite the weather. He suspected Evelyn's transformation would change that. Not that he would mind the change; she was much better company than the crows.

He waited only a short while before Evelyn returned with Slade in tow. The fox ignored them both and groomed himself for a minute, only sparing them a glance when he was fully satisfied. "So, what is it you want this time?" he asked. "I know you can't be craving my warm companionship."

"You can do magic," Jack said, deciding to jump right in. "Please grant me the ability to move so I can travel with Evelyn. I will be in your debt."

Slade chuckled in his high fox pitch. "Do you have any idea how great an undertaking that will be? It's one thing to watch a beginner attempt it, but to expend my own energy? And what will I get out of it? I do not see a benefit for me in this."

"But you helped me," Evelyn said. "I don't understand."

"My dear, you are nothing more than a source of entertainment. Spending a little magic here and there is nothing, but what you ask requires much more."

"So it's always about benefit for you?" Evelyn asked. "Is there not one friendly or charitable bone in your body?"

"I don't believe so. I was excluded when those were given out."

"Look, will you help or not? I will owe whatever you wish," Jack said.

"I'm not convinced you understand just how much that will be. But I will accept." Jack and Evelyn sighed in relief and he continued, "I take it you both intend to set off into the unknown? Find a 'better place,' so to speak? In that case, I will go with you. No arguments. That is my first term. If at any time I add a new term and you do not accept, I will reverse the spell and we'll go our separate ways. Agreed?"

"That's not even close to fair," Evelyn objected. "You would leave him—"

"Agreed," Jack said.

"No!"

"Then I'll begin," Slade said.

Evelyn made an annoyed sound and flew off toward the village. Slade closed his eyes to slits and muttered to himself. Jack felt a slight tingle all over his body, but it wasn't uncomfortable. More like a pleasant numbness after spending too long in the cold. It began at his head and worked its way down. When it reached his post, it grew in intensity and warmth, just on the threshold of pain. It didn't last long. A few seconds later, all of it dissipated. Jack tried to move his arm and it bent at his command. His head rolled around and turned from side to side with minimal effort. He swung his legs—yes, Slade had created legs for him—but he was still tied to the post.

"You did it!" Jack cried.

"What did you expect?" Slade asked. "I may not be the nicest chap, but I know magic."

"Can you help me get down?"

"I suppose."

Slade flicked his head and the knots released themselves,

causing Jack to fall forward onto the ground. He landed on his knees and rolled over onto his back, looking up at the gray, cloud-covered sky. It was like receiving a new pair of eyes; everything was fresh and new. He could see the clouds moving slowly, directly above him, and then Slade's face was a few inches from his own.

"Are you going to just lie there all day?"

"It's just...not what I'm used to."

"That will pass. Let's find the crow and be off."

Jack sat up slowly. Why the sudden rush? They were in no hurry. At least, he and Evelyn weren't. He picked himself up on unsteady legs, waiting a moment to gain his balance. He was shorter than he'd expected to be, standing only a couple feet tall. Perhaps that was also the fox's doing. Slade was already walking toward the village, and Jack attempted to run after him only to succeed in falling face-first on the ground. The fox didn't stop walking. Jack picked himself up and tried again.

"Keep close now," Slade instructed when they finally reached the outer walls of the houses. "The last thing we need is for someone to spot you. Stay in the shadows."

Jack obeyed and they crept along, doing more stopping and watching than actual walking. Everywhere he looked, there were new sights and smells, so many that they were hard to keep track of. How could the others stand it? It was enough to make him long for his familiar post, though at the same time it drew him in, daring him to investigate. It amazed him how much he wanted to give in.

They passed non-magical cats and dogs, who barked in panic at the sight of him. There were humans, gardens, homes, stables, barns... They passed so close to them, but were entirely undetected. Slade took him deeper into the heart of the village, which wasn't very large, though for Jack it may as well have been a city. At last they came to a small house on the far side of the village. Smoke rose from the chimney and a few chickens pecked in the yard. Evelyn's father came out of the house, a large, hairy man Jack remembered seeing during the search. He fed the chickens from a sack leaning against the wall of the house, sealing it up tight when he finished. Then he waited a moment, looking toward the village as though expecting someone. Jack and Slade waited, thinking he would go back inside and they'd continue to look for Evelyn. But then her father waved to someone behind them and a young, dark haired woman came into view.

The witch.

"Ferah," Evelyn's father said, smiling. "How kind of you to visit me."

"I can't bear the thought of you here all alone," she said, her voice as smooth and sweet as milk and honey. "Since that daughter of yours ran off, I figure I can serve as a stand in, if you'll have me."

"That's mighty kind of you. I don't think she ran off, though. She may be strong-minded, but she knows her duty."

Jack spotted Evelyn then, perched on a bale of hay behind her father.

The witch smiled and touched his arm. "It's cold, Father, and your daughter has abandoned you. Won't you let me keep you warm?"

Evelyn's father stiffened, his eyes adopting a far-off gaze. "Thank you, Ferah," he said, his voice void of emotion. "Won't you please come inside?"

The witch smiled again, casting a sideways glance back at Slade and Jack. Together, they disappeared inside the house, sending Evelyn into a rage.

"You no-good, scheming *witch!*" she cawed, flapping her wings angrily. She hovered at the door and pecked at it, finally flying off as fast as she could.

"Come on!" Slade said, running after her. Jack followed, doing his best to not fall while also watching for people. He quickly fell behind.

Luckily, he didn't have far to go. Evelyn had retreated just a short distance outside the village. Slade stood near her, watching silently as she flapped about and cursed.

"She's baiting me on purpose. I wish I could change at will! I'd show her."

"Very doubtful," Slade said.

"Where was Mordecai?" she said. "He wouldn't leave Father, not now. He's still too young, anyway." She finally noticed them and rushed over. "Can you change me back?" she asked Slade.

"Alas, that is not one of my talents," Slade said. "We will need a great mage—or another witch. Unfortunately, there are neither in this area."

"Where do we go, then?" Jack asked.

"Into the woods," Slade answered, nodding at the forest. "There are creatures there wiser than me. I suggest we seek their advice."

"Not yet," Evelyn answered. "I need to find my brother. And I want a word with that witch."

She took to the air once more and flew back into the village.

"She's only prolonging the inevitable," Slade said as they followed her. "The witch won't help her."

They found Evelyn perched on the hay bale near her house, eyes focused on the window.

"I don't even want to go back," she said as they approached. "I just want her away from my father."

"That will be easier to accomplish as a human," Slade said.

She noticed Jack and narrowed her eyes. "I wish you hadn't made that deal with him. I don't think it was very wise of you."

"That's how I felt about your deal with the witch," he retorted. "It is what it is."

Her eyes narrowed further for a moment, then she sighed and looked back at the house.

They waited in silence, each keeping their thoughts close and secret. What more could be said? As the sun began to sink, the witch appeared at the window and opened the shutters.

"Well, now," she said. "If it isn't my dear crow friend. And you've brought company. I must say, I'm unprepared to entertain a party. You should've mentioned you were coming."

"I'm not here to play games," Evelyn said. "What have you done to my father? And where is my brother?"

The witch laughed. "Don't worry about your father. He is quite happy, I can assure you."

Evelyn shrieked and flew at the witch, who raised her hand to her mouth and blew, pushing Evelyn back with a thin breath of air.

"None of that, now. I've done nothing but help you, and this is how you repay me? For shame." She glanced at Jack and Slade, one corner of her mouth turning up in a smile. "And what is your opinion, fox? Why are you here?"

"Merely looking after my own interests," Slade said, nodding toward Jack. "Your business is no concern of mine."

The witch chuckled. "Very wise. And you, scarecrow?"

Jack frowned, unwilling to be cowed. "I'm here to support Evelyn, no matter what that may mean."

Evelyn had landed on the ground between them, glaring at the witch and ruffling her feathers. "You still haven't mentioned my brother," she snarled.

"Ah yes, that troublesome boy. Your dear father kicked him out when he wouldn't accept me. No telling where he is now."

Evelyn shrieked again and took to the air, but rather than attack the witch, she flew across the village, back toward the field.

"Hmpf," said the witch, grinning again. "Either of you have anything more to say?"

"No," Slade said, rising to leave.

"I do," Jack said. "Turn Evelyn human again. You managed the spell once, so undo it. Give her back her life."

The witch furrowed her brow. "Why would I do that? Of her own will, she gave all that up. Silly scarecrow." And with that, she closed the shutters.

INTO THE FOREST

They found Evelyn in the field near Jack's post. She didn't acknowledge them, merely paced on the arm posts, back and forth, back and forth.

"Are you willing to listen to me now?" Slade asked.

"Just shut up!" Evelyn cried. "I know what you'll say, and I don't want to hear it! So I screwed up, I get that. It's a horrible situation all around, but what's done is done. I just need to find my brother and free my father, now."

"Well, that can only be accomplished by going into the forest, as I've said before. We only await your consent, milady." Slade dipped his head at the end of this speech, nearly touching the ground.

Evelyn scoffed, but her gaze moved to the trees. "What about predators?" she asked.

"And the wolves?" Jack added. "The war? You always come back looking like you just lost a fight. How are we to survive that?"

"Leave the wolves to me," Slade said. His words did not inspire confidence.

"What about the old woman you stole the book from? Is she a witch as well?" Jack asked.

"Lorna? No, she was a mage. I guess we could go to her—"

"I advise against that," Slade said. "Human mages can't be trusted. They're all too concerned with their Guild. She'd probably turn you in as a *magical wonder*."

"I doubt that," Evelyn said. "I don't think she finished training."

"An incompetent human mage? That's who you want to go to for help?"

"She may still know things," Jack said. "There's no harm in asking."

The fox sighed. "Very well. The two of you go and seek her out. I'll stay here."

"You're not coming with us?" Evelyn asked.

"The two of you are enchanted. That's easily explained to a human. A normal fox who can do magic? I don't need the animal mages after me for revealing secrets, thank you."

Evelyn glanced at Jack, but he just shrugged. What did he know of magic?

"You'll still be here?" Evelyn asked as she fluttered down to land on Jack's shoulder.

"Of course. I'm invested, remember?" he said, nodding at Jack.

Evelyn scoffed again. "How could I forget? Are you ready, Jack?"

"Yes."

"Don't reveal more than you need to!" Slade called after them as they once more crossed the field.

The sky darkened quickly as they made their way back into the village, the clouds conspiring to empty their burdens upon the earth. Jack cleared his throat.

"You mentioned before that she refused to take you as an apprentice. Why was that?"

"She said she didn't have time for such nonsense. But I've seen her casting spells when she works in her garden. I spied on her once and saw her use it in cooking and housework, too. But she claimed she wasn't qualified to teach. She wasn't a full mage."

"Maybe you would've been better seeking out the Guild for training?"

"I know that now," Evelyn said with a sigh. "I should've taken my chances and gone to a city. But it's done now."

"If she isn't able to help us, should we go to the Guild? Maybe—"

"Slade would never agree to that. And as much as I hate to say it, we need him right now. The best I hope for from Lorna is information. Once we're in the forest, *he's* our best hope."

Jack shook his head in frustration. If the fox were just a bit less selfish, he wouldn't mind him so much, but he had a feeling they would regret his involvement.

"I suppose he's helped us both, so far," Jack conceded.

"Why don't you like him?" she asked. "I thought you two were friends."

"I thought so as well, before I could move. But he's shown a side of himself that was hidden before. Yes, he's helpful, but it's for a price."

"He helped me without asking for anything in return."

"Helping you didn't involve much magic," Jack reminded her.

They reached the village and Jack crept along the wall of the closest house, the shadows hiding them from any who might be watching. Evelyn guided him, and several long, cautious moments later, they stood before a little house, a soft orange glow coming from within. Evelyn pecked on the door and they waited, hearing movement on the other side. A moment later the door opened and an old woman glared out into the night, her head turning side to side. She was thin and wore a dirty-looking green dress with a blue shawl. Her gray hair was pulled back loosely into a braid that rested over her shoulder, gray flyaways covering her head.

"Down here," Evelyn said.

Lorna looked down, surprise turning to irritation in the space of a breath. "I should've known," she said. "Come in. Don't want to risk anyone seeing you."

The house was tidy and warm, a large fire blazing against the far wall. A narrow bed sat to the right under a window, and to the left was a long wooden bench with a wicker back, covered in pillows and blankets. Along the wall on either side of the door was a pantry overflowing with herbs, pots, bowls, books, and various other things. It was the only cluttered space in the house. At the end of the bed was a metal birdcage that contained a cardinal. The bird sat very still, watching them intently.

"Have a seat. I have a feeling you're not here for a love potion, and I don't work on an empty stomach. Make yourself comfortable."

They perched themselves on the bench as she went over to a pot hanging above the fire and scooped out some of its contents into a wooden bowl. Tendrils of steam rose into the air and a strong scent of herbs filled the house.

Lorna slurped the broth, sitting on the edge of her bed, and said, "Speak."

"You know who I am?" Evelyn asked.

"Of course. You're the only lass in these parts foolish enough to get yourself turned into a crow."

"Then do you know how to change me back?"

Lorna laughed, nearly choking on her soup. "Girl, I can barely make potions. What makes you think I can do transformation magic? How'd you even get into this predicament?"

"A witch. We made a deal—"

Lorna abruptly put her bowl down on a little table by the bed and stood, hurrying to each window, peering out, and pulling the curtains closed. The cardinal stirred, flapping its wings in agitation. When Lorna finished, she looked at Evelyn with a disapproving eye.

"Don't speak of such powers so lightly. Where did you find her? Where is she now?"

"She was a crow," Jack said.

Lorna glanced at him with raised brow. "You're a curiosity as well. But we'll get to you in a moment. Come then, tell me the full story."

As Evelyn related the tale, Lorna returned to her seat and continued her meal. The old woman nodded now and again, but made no more comment until Evelyn had finished. With a sigh, she placed her bowl on the table and lay back on the bed.

"This is way beyond me," she said, looking up at the ceiling. "Imagine, a witch in these parts, and restored to her youth..." She sighed loudly. "That's something for the Guild to worry about, I suppose. But should I send a warning? They probably won't take me seriously, but at least I'll have done my part..."

She mumbled on, ignoring them as she argued with herself. Evelyn leaned close to Jack and whispered, "I don't think we'll learn anything here."

"At least we tried," Jack whispered back.

"Perhaps—"

"All right," Lorna said, sitting up. "I know for certain I can't do a thing for you with my abilities. The Guild may be able to help. I repeat, *may*. There's no guarantee there. As for you, scarecrow." She fixed him with a studied gaze, brow furrowed. "I see a longing in you. A desire for closure. Do you even remember how you became a scarecrow?"

Jack shook his head. "I remember life in the field. The sky and the crows. Everything else is hazy."

"Lucky for you, the Guild has plenty of experts on memory retrieval. I suggest the two of you seek them out. That's the best I can do for you."

She stood, brushing off her skirt and grabbing a poker to stoke the fire. The cardinal fluttered a moment, then settled down into sleep.

Jack stood, Evelyn on his shoulder. "Thank you," he said.

She waved her arm in a dismissive gesture, not even looking their way.

Their conversation over, Jack turned to leave, the door opening before he'd reached it.

"Keep your eyes open," Lorna called from behind them. "Where witches are involved, you'll need all your wits about you."

The door shut softly behind them and Jack heard the latch click into place. The sun had completely disappeared and a cold wind blew through the village. Evelyn fluttered her wings and said, "That went about as expected. I suppose it was worth the chance, though."

"Doesn't change anything," Jack agreed. "Unless we can get Slade to agree to seek out the Guild."

"Good luck with that."

WHEN THEY RETURNED, they found Slade asleep beneath Jack's old post. Evelyn flew off to find food and no doubt be alone for a while. Jack busied himself by gathering wood just inside the tree line. Mobility hadn't added any other surprises, as far as he could tell. He still had no need for food, and the wind had only the slightest effect on him. Nevertheless, he decided to build a fire. Evelyn might enjoy it, and it gave him something to do. In his life before, he had been satisfied to watch the clouds move slowly across the skies as the light changed. But now he felt the need to move and do things. Gathering wood seemed a good distraction.

Jack had some concerns about what Slade would ask of him, but he tried to not think of it too much. It was too late to go back now, anyway. Unless he wanted to leave Evelyn to travel with the fox on her own, but that was out of the question.

When he had a large bundle of sticks, he began gathering leaves and pine needles and made a small pile. Finding rocks took a bit longer, but finally he had enough to make a small ring around the pile. All that remained was the flame. First he tried rubbing two sticks together. Then he tried rubbing one of the rocks against a stick, but he couldn't even make a spark.

"Allow me," Slade said, appearing from behind him. He twitched his nose and a spark ignited in the center of the pile, creating a small fire that soon consumed the entire thing. Jack added more wood and leaves until he was satisfied it would continue blazing for a while.

"Don't you worry the villagers will come investigate?" Slade asked.

"The children and hunters are always lighting fires. They'll assume that's all it is and leave it be."

"As you say," Slade said dismissively. "It makes no difference to me."

They sat in silence for a while, watching the flame crackle, a small thread of smoke rising into the air. Evelyn returned a short while later, breaking the meditative silence.

"Do you have any idea where another witch may be, or will we figure that out along the way?" she asked Slade.

"There is someone in particular I'd like to find," he said. "An old owl, older than your oldest ancestor, it's said. If anyone knows of magic and the ways of the world—or the locations of witches—he will."

"Is he hard to find, or far away?" Jack asked.

"I'm not sure. I've never met him."

"But you know where to find him," Evelyn said.

"Not really. But how hard can it be?"

"And what of my brother?"

"I'm sure the owl can help with that as well. Just trust me."

Jack shook his head and went back to tending the fire.

THEY LEFT at dawn the next day. Jack stamped out the last of the fire with a rock and they followed Slade further into the trees. Silence and emptiness reigned as far as he could see, but he was beginning to understand that the eyes couldn't always be trusted. Evelyn was eager to be off and continually flew ahead, waiting for them to catch up. When she tired of that, she rode on Slade's back, or Jack's shoulder. They spoke very little. After all, they were all anxious about finding the owl, and tension from the scene with Evelyn's father still lingered between them. Jack hoped it would eventually go away on its own.

The further they went, the more life they found. Squirrels scampered between trees, chittering at them and each other. Birds foraged for food and chirped from branches high above them. Even field mice appeared every now and then, gathering their winter store. Slade didn't bother asking any of them for directions, though Jack thought it a missed opportunity. He followed along silently, willing to trust the fox knew what he was doing.

Around midday, Slade stopped them and whispered, "We're near the land where the wolf packs roam. We'll want to avoid them, so stay as silent as possible."

Jack and Evelyn nodded their understanding. The land sloped upwards and the wind increased, making walking quietly a bit more difficult. Evelyn flew ahead to scout out the land—and to watch for wolves.

"She'll be fine if we run into a pack," Slade said. "She can simply fly away. But you and I will have to keep our heads about us. Let me do the talking if that happens."

Jack nodded in understanding. They reached the crest of the hill and paused to look around them. Trees stood in every direction, blocking most of the view. Evelyn sat at the top of one, seeing much further than they could.

"It's all trees," she said when she rejoined them. "There's a lot of movement to the east—the wolves, perhaps? If we keep our current course, we should avoid them."

"There's a safe land not too far north of here," Slade said. "If we hurry, we should reach it before nightfall."

"I'm going to find some food," Evelyn said. "I'll be just ahead."

She flew off again and they continued down the slope. Jack's sense of balance had greatly improved—he couldn't remember the last time he'd tripped. That was just as well, as it meant he could travel faster. The leaf debris also increased, making it more difficult to avoid causing the occasional noise as they walked. But it couldn't be helped. Near the bottom of the slope, Slade stopped once more.

"Don't make a sound," he whispered. Jack nearly asked why until he saw a bit of movement several feet ahead of them. They stood absolutely still, waiting to see which way the figure would go. For a terrifying moment, Jack was sure it was headed their way. He held his breath until the figure continued east and disappeared from view. "That was too close," Slade said. "A wolf for sure. We will have to be more careful."

Jack only nodded in response, still too nervous to speak. They hurried away from the hill and into a close copse of trees. Most of the grass was still green, though the ground was thick with leaves. Ivy covered many of the tree trunks, and a few autumn flowers broke through the leaf blanket—baby's breath, misty blue, solidago, Queen Anne's Lace, and yarrow, all scattered about.

"These don't look wild," Jack said.

"They're not. We're on the outskirts of Raven's land. He prefers the wild to planted gardens, but he appreciates their beauty in designated areas. Just be sure not to pick any."

"Raven?" Jack asked.

"Evelyn should join us again. It's best if we stay together, especially since we don't know if the wolves respect his boundaries or not."

They paused there until Evelyn came flying back, realizing they were no longer following. "Is something wrong?" she asked.

"We'll need to stick together for a bit," Slade said. "Once

we're spotted, we'll be taken to Raven, and it's best if no one is missing."

"Who's Raven?" Evelyn asked.

"Let's just say the ruler of this area and leave it at that, yes? No point in complicating things."

Evelyn exchanged a confused look with Jack, who shrugged. He didn't have a better answer. They continued through Raven's outer garden and further northward, Evelyn riding on Jack's shoulder. The garden continued for a while, but soon gave way to a wilder landscape. The leaves took over with a vengeance, as though offended at the garden's existence. The three proceeded with caution, watching all directions for the slightest movement. Despite their vigilance, they were still caught unawares.

"Halt!" a voice called.

They obeyed immediately, looking in all directions for the source.

"Wait here for assistance! A representative will be with you shortly!"

The voice came from a small stone gargoyle sitting near the base of a tree a short distance from them.

"Spellwork," Slade said. "We'd better wait. No need to anger Raven and arouse suspicions."

So they waited, though not long. A sparrow flew toward them a few moments later, landing on a branch. "Please follow me!" it said. Then it flew back the way it had come and they hurried to follow it. They didn't speak at all, for fear their words would be reported. Not that they had anything to hide. But better to keep to themselves until they stood before Raven.

They soon reached a small outpost, which was really an old well where several other sparrows were gathered. One sparrow, the biggest of the group, perched on the rim of the well as they approached, while their guide joined the smaller birds.

"What business brings you to Raven's woods?" the big sparrow asked. "And please be aware that everything you say shall be reported to Raven. It's best to tell the truth."

"We are seeking the old owl," Slade answered. "We hoped Raven would know its whereabouts."

"Raven is not a map or guide," the sparrow informed them.

"Nevertheless, that is our only purpose here," Slade said. "If he is unwilling to help, we will be on our way."

"That will be for Raven to decide. You will stay here for the night until Raven deigns to see you."

"Can we not continue now? Surely we can reach his home before evening."

"Raven's words are final. There will be no more discussion on the matter."

The large sparrow disappeared into the treetops and a smaller one—the same as before? Jack couldn't tell—fluttered down and addressed them.

"Please follow me," it said.

They obeyed with no further argument, following it to a small, sheltered area. The tree branches there curved and created a small alcove, covered in ivy and leaves to keep out the wind.

"You will stay here until Raven sends for you," the sparrow informed them. "Food will be brought to you. Do not venture out on your own."

The bird left them alone and Evelyn fluttered to the ground angrily. "Just who is this Raven, and why should we do anything he says? We're wasting time here!"

"Keep your voice down," Slade said. "Isn't it enough that he is the master here? No? Then how about this: sparrows aren't the only animals who do his bidding. Neither are all of his servants birds. Just be glad we've been treated as guests and not as spies."

"Why do the animals serve him?" Jack asked, taking a seat on the ground. "Is he powerful in magic?"

"You could say that." Slade lay on the ground facing them, his legs tucked beneath him. "Have you ever heard the creation stories?" he asked.

Evelyn created a nest for herself using leaves and grass and also lay down. They may as well make themselves comfortable.

"I haven't," Jack answered.

"I've heard the human ones, though I take it you're referring to something different," Evelyn said.

"Correct. Long ago, it is said that the world was created out of nothing. It is difficult to describe nothing, as you can't explain it with your senses. Rather, it's an absence of senses. Everything you see, hear, and experience, was pulled from that nothing. And it is said that a creature named Raven is the one who pulled the world from that senseless state. Now, before you bombard me with questions and statements of disbelief, let me say that it's not certain that this is the same Raven. It could be, or it could be a distant relative. You will get no straight answer from him. It is enough for the animals who serve him that he goes by the name, for even a direct descendant should be accorded respect. And not only that, but the current Raven has abilities and a presence that is beyond the norm of a skilled mage such as myself. He may simply be an anomaly of great talent, but do you really wish to challenge him even if that is the case? A talented mage should be handled with care, no matter his origins."

"If he's so powerful, why not ask him to help me?" Evelyn asked. "If he created the world, surely he can make me human."

"You are welcome to ask him," Slade said. "I would sooner ask the wolves for the time of day, but it is your choice. I prefer to deal with the owl than with him."

"He's not dangerous, is he?" Jack asked.

"He's not of a violent nature, if that's what you mean. But he is certainly capable, if the need arises."

"So long as he helps us, I don't care if he's God himself," Evelyn said. She burrowed deeper into her nest and closed her eyes. "Wake me when food arrives," she informed them.

❧ 5 ❧

RAVEN

The next day, their guide woke them before the sun rose, leading them away from the outpost and further north. In the dim light, it was difficult to make out their surroundings, but it appeared to be trees, trees, and more trees. The ground, however, was most certainly sloping downward. Slade was permitted to create a small hovering ball of light to illuminate their way. No doubt the sparrow was noting for its master that the fox could do magic. It was lucky Slade could, and did, for even with the light, there were a few spots that nearly sent Jack tumbling.

Around the time the sun began to rise, the land leveled out and the company was able to go a bit quicker. No one spoke, not even their sparrow guide, though Jack burned with questions. He was beginning to show signs of wear as well, his pant-ends dirty and his straw feet bedraggled. He would ask Slade to tidy him up —after their meeting with Raven.

The light revealed just what Jack suspected: more trees. He kind of missed his open field with a clear view of the sky. The morning passed and the sun rose higher and Jack wondered if they would keep walking forever until they simply collapsed. At last the sparrow said, "Stop." Before them was another close copse of trees, with another garden just outside of it. "You will speak when spoken to," the sparrow instructed. "If you argue or insult Raven in any way, you will be punished swiftly. If you try to leave without his permission, you will be stopped by every guard in attendance. If you attempt magic without permission, Raven will cut you down with a blink of his eye. Understood?"

They all nodded and the sparrow led them into the trees, landing on the ground and bowing low. Slade followed suit, so Jack and Evelyn did as well.

"Arise," said a voice which could only be described as majestic. It was dual-toned, both young and old, firm and playful, smooth and sharp. Jack lifted his eyes and saw a large raven perched on a great boulder against a backdrop of thick trees. The sun seemed to shine directly on him, as though confirming his importance. "Welcome, travelers," Raven said as they stood once more. "What brings you to my land?"

The sparrow fluttered to the side, joining its comrades.

"We are but three companions in search of the old owl," Slade answered. "We dared approach Your Greatness in the hopes that you would know his whereabouts."

"*Her*," Raven corrected. "You've picked an odd time of year for traveling. The wind grows colder, the nights longer, and the wolves have moved practically to my doorstep. Tell me, what is so pressing that can't wait until the spring?"

"My crow companion is a human, transformed by a witch's spell. We seek to reverse the spell, and we need the owl for guidance."

Raven turned his eyes to Evelyn. "Did you agree to the transformation?" he asked.

"She—" Slade began.

"I was speaking to the crow. Do not interrupt again."

"I did," Evelyn answered.

"Why do you wish to change back? Do you not enjoy your new form?"

"I very much enjoy it. Magic is a little different, but I'm a beginner anyway. I wish to change back to save my father and brother. The witch who transformed me has enchanted my father."

"Enchanted him how?"

Evelyn paused, then reluctantly answered, "I believe she has seduced him to her service."

"And you mentioned a brother. What of him?"

"He and my father quarreled, after I became a crow. My father forced my brother to leave. I believe this is also the witch's influence."

"So, but for the fact that the witch has set her sights on your father—and your brother being outcast—you would continue as a crow?"

"I would."

"Tell me, what drove you to the transformation in the first place?"

"I was to be married against my will."

"This marriage was arranged by your father?"

"Yes."

"You admit you are not obedient, yet you seek to save him. Humans have an odd sense of love."

"I disagree with his plan for my life, but I wish him no harm. He is my father, despite our disagreements."

Slade hissed softly through his teeth, no doubt trying to warn her. Luckily, Raven seemed to take no offense.

"I admire your spirit," he said. "Now tell me, scarecrow, what is your part in this?"

"I am merely a friend," Jack answered. "I possess no magic or special talents, but I will help as I can."

"You have no magic, yet you walk as though born with the ability. How did that come to pass?"

"Slade cast a spell so I could move."

"Ah, yes, our dear fox. Tell me, what is your interest in this affair?"

Slade glanced at Jack and Evelyn, no doubt reluctant to

answer. "I freely admit mine is not the concern of a well-meaning friend. As payment for my services, Jack has agreed to do as I request until I have determined that I have been fairly compensated. At such time, I will leave them to continue their journey."

"This is not your first time traveling near my land. In fact, my scouts have reported seeing you in the land now possessed by the wolves. What is your business there?"

"None. I was merely a traveler, unlucky enough to be caught up in the war."

"More than once?"

"My home is on the other side of the fighting. The escalation of the war has made return difficult for the time being."

"What prompted your travels in the first place?"

"Visiting friends. I am a social creature."

"And you are certain you are not a spy for either side of the war?"

Slade dared to laugh. "Positive. I imagine if I were a spy, I would find better ways to spend my time."

"Undoubtedly. Well, you've given me much to ponder. I shall spend this night considering your words and shall give you my answer in the morning. In the meantime, you shall be treated as guests, though you are not yet free to leave. My servants will see to it that you are comfortable."

Before they could respond, their sparrow guide ushered them away again, leading them to a gently flowing creek not too far away. Jack glanced back, but Raven had already disappeared from view.

"Rest here," the sparrow said. "Food will be brought again soon. You can wander about as you like, but you must stay within sight of the creek. This spot, to be exact."

"Thank you," Jack said. "May I ask, how long have you served Raven?"

"My entire life," the sparrow answered. "Like my father before me, and his before that, all the way back to creation."

"And you're happy?"

"Of course. Raven is everything. Without him, none of us would be here. *You* wouldn't be here."

"Give it a rest, Jack," Slade said, sprawling out on the moss. "We'll be here long enough. You can ask Raven yourself."

"If there's nothing more, I must continue with my duties," the sparrow said.

"Of course. Thank you," Jack said.

The bird flew off and Jack looked around, noting that even the trees seemed to grow in precise patterns here. "Even if he's not *the* Raven, he's powerful," Jack commented.

"That's what I've been telling you," Slade said, both eyes closed and his head resting on his paws. "Best course of action is to play nice, get what information we can, and be on our way."

Evelyn had perched on a low-hanging branch near them so Jack wandered over to her, allowing Slade to nap.

"How are you feeling?" he asked.

"About what you'd expect," she said. "Angry, frustrated, impatient. This waiting is eating me up inside. There's no telling what she's doing to my father, and my brother could be anywhere. He could be dead, Jack."

"Don't think that. I'm sure he's fine."

"But we don't know that. I'm worried I've killed him. My actions caused all of this. His death would be on me."

Her voice caught and she looked away from him, toward the creek. He wished a lot of things, but wishing alone couldn't change anything, so he simply stood with her, offering silent support.

***

THE DAY PASSED with no more word from Raven. They dozed, talked, and ate when food was offered to them. Troubled dreams woke Jack in the dead of night, and though he couldn't remember what visions his mind had conjured, a sense of dread hung over him and he couldn't sleep anymore. Instead, he rose and wandered by the creek, away from their little camp. The water trickled by, offering a gentle lullaby, but its song held no power over him. He started to turn back the other way when a light just ahead caught his eye. He looked back at his companions, both slumbering soundly, then moved quickly through the trees to investigate the source. He had the impression that Raven's land was guarded vigilantly, so he had no fear of encountering danger. The worst that could happen was they'd be angry he'd left the camp. But he would take that upon himself. The light beckoned to him.

As he got closer, the trees withdrew from the creek, but ahead a dark mass loomed, neither trees nor animal. The light shone near the top.

"A stone house?" he whispered as he came closer. Or a ruin. Closer inspection revealed a pile of stones clustered on the ground, a hole in the wall above them. Jack climbed through, tripping over the rubble on the other side, but steadied himself on the wall. The stars shone above, the ceiling gone in that part of the structure. To his left a tower rose, and it was from there the light came. Jack found the path leading up and began to climb, going slowly to avoid tripping again. Somewhere above him someone was humming, deep and sorrowful, a melody to break the heart. At the top, a wooden door separated him from the hummer, cracked open just a little. Jack peeked through, seeing only a rotting bed.

"Come in, little scarecrow," the deep voice said. "You will not be harmed."

Jack froze, cursing himself for leaving the camp in the first place. Maybe there was still time to retreat—

"I said, enter," the voice repeated.

Jack knew that voice, and knew better than to disobey. He pushed open the door. Instead of finding Raven like he'd expected, a large human male sat at a little desk on the left side of the room, writing by the light of a lantern. He was pale, with a dark mop of hair about his head. Then the light shifted and his skin darkened, his hair lightening. His coloring continued to change, and his form, morphing to a bear, a deer, a wolf, connecting him to all species and none. Jack froze again, fearing he'd really messed up. How had a mage gotten through Raven's guards? But then the man looked at him and his fear melted away. There was no mistaking that gaze.

"Yes, it is me," Raven said, his human form solidifying. "I have many forms. Don't be afraid. You're in no trouble."

"I... I shouldn't have left the camp. I'm sorry."

Raven shrugged. "Apology accepted. But it is not so big a deal, for you. Your fox friend, now, he would find himself in a predicament." Raven glanced back at his papers and wrote some more, then put his pen down, stretched, and groaned. "That's enough for one night, I think. How have you enjoyed your stay?"

"It...seems nice," Jack said.

Raven chuckled. "You have not yet seen our hospitality, and in these dangerous times, it is wise to be cautious. But you, I trust. I can see the truth in you, shining like a small flame."

"Th-thank you," Jack stuttered, unsure how to respond.

"It is something to be proud of. Yours is a noble spirit. Not many possess that anymore." Raven stood, nearly touching the ceiling, his long robes draping to the ground around him. He smiled. "The night is young, little scarecrow. Will you fly with me?"

"O-oh," Jack stuttered again. "I...don't know..."

"Have no fear." Raven swept toward him and lifted him gently, placing him on his shoulders. "Hold tight, now." He moved to the window, his body shrinking to fit through the frame, transforming back to corvid form, but larger than before. Then he spread his wings, spanning several feet, darkening the already dark night, and they were airborne. Jack clutched Raven's feathers, watching as the ruin shrank and the trees spread out like a blanket beneath them. The forest extended in all directions, so much larger than he had imagined. All was dark, and then Raven broke through the clouds and millions of stars surrounded them, their crystal light gently illuminating the faces of the clouds. Jack released his grip just a little as Raven's path leveled and he coasted on the wind.

"Few see such marvels," Raven said. "Most rarely think of them. Too focused on what's right before them, on mating, offspring, and food."

The stars seemed to Jack to go on forever, cold and silent and lovely, untouchable and pure. His worries for Evelyn melted away and there were only the stars.

"Do not think I speak only of my own kind," Raven continued. "All species are guilty, human and animal alike."

"You think we should pay more attention to the stars?"

"It's not about the stars," Raven said. "It's about life, about our place in the bigger picture. The stars are merely a reminder."

They descended again, through the clouds, the trees far below. Ahead, trees and clouds alike cleared way, disappearing from view, and there were only stars above and below. Raven swooped low and Jack peeked over his side, wondering if they'd left all the world behind. His own face looked back at him.

"Water," he said.

"This is a land beyond the world, beyond time. It is a place of stars. Memory."

"But...how...?"

"There are many mysteries in the world, little scarecrow. Even the wisest do not understand them all."

Jack questioned no more, instead watching as the pale lights swirled around them, cocooning them in a blanket of black and white. A gentle, deep *hummm* rose on the air, filling the space and rumbling in Jack's chest like a primal sound that spoke to his core, his soul remembering the tune before he existed, when the world was a whisper of a thought and the stars were young. He closed his eyes and let the sound wash over him, filling him with a peace he hadn't realized was absent. Dimly, he became aware that the sound came from Raven. The bird-god sang a love song to the stars, a song of beginnings and peace and beauty. The song went on and Jack sank into it, losing awareness of all else until he entered a dreamless sleep.

JACK AWOKE BACK in their camp, Slade and Evelyn already up and about.

"Finally," the fox said. "We wondered if we would have to carry you to Raven. We've been summoned."

Their sparrow guide appeared again, waiting patiently at the tree line. Jack pulled himself up and the three of them followed their guide back through the forest. The night before played through his mind like a dream. He thought it had been real, but in the light of day, it seemed unlikely, the early morning sun chasing away the magic of the starlight. Jack stole a glance at Evelyn, who flew close beside him, but she was lost in her own thoughts. They entered the clearing again, where Raven and his court awaited their arrival.

"Welcome. I hope you slept well?" Raven said.

Jack searched his face for any acknowledgment of the night before, but he found only polite interest.

"Well, thank you," Slade said. "Your hospitality is above reproach."

Raven turned his gaze on Evelyn. "Here is my decision: though I possess the ability to transform you myself, I do not choose to do so. It is my opinion—"

"But why not?" Evelyn interrupted. "My father is in danger! The witch could—"

"Silence."

The hush that fell over the gathering filled the air like a tangible wave. Raven stared at Evelyn for several moments before continuing. "It is my opinion that you will all benefit greatly from this journey, so I will tell you Siobhan's location. I'll even send a messenger ahead to announce your arrival. However, if word ever reaches me that you have been dishonest with me, my hunters will pursue you to your grave. I can abide much, but not liars. You should also know that a dark Hunter was spotted on my borders this morning, sent by your witch, no doubt. He cannot pass, but it is only a matter of time before he works his way around. I do not need to tell you of your fate, should he catch you."

"That's worrisome," Slade said, eyes squinting as he thought. "We are grateful for the information."

"Yes, thank you for your help," Evelyn added, her demeanor more humble.

Raven nodded and said, "You are free to go."

A sparrow quickly fluttered down to them, indicating they should follow. They complied, not daring to cast another glance at Raven.

"Siobhan the owl currently resides on the edge of Raven's land in a great tree," the bird said. "It is far, but you should reach it within a day or so, if you keep a good pace." At the edge of another garden the sparrow stopped. "Just continue northwest for a day until you see the great tree. You can't miss it. She will be expecting you." When the sparrow left them, they all breathed a collective sigh of relief.

"That went better than expected," Slade said. "We're still on Raven's land, so keep up your best behavior."

"I wish he'd been willing to change me himself," Evelyn said. "That would save me the time and trouble."

"There's a reason I didn't suggest we go straight to Raven for help," Slade said. "This Siobhan should be a bit more useful."

"You haven't asked me for anything yet," Jack commented. "To pay you for your services."

"You think I should?"

"Well, you said your only interest was in me repaying you. So why prolong it?"

"I want it to be worthwhile. I'm not one to squander favors.

Now come along. We're wasting time. Especially if there's a Hunter on our trail."

"What sort of hunter?" Evelyn asked.

"One called forth by dark magic. Do humans no longer tell stories of such monsters? Trust me, we want to be far away by the time it reaches this side of Raven's land."

They followed him with no further questions or arguments. Jack's thoughts wandered, speculating on whether he'd really flown with Raven or if it had only been a dream. Either way, a feeling of peace and hope sat strong within him, and he feared neither witch nor Hunter.

THEY STOPPED when the sun disappeared. Slade could've created a light for them, but he thought it too risky. Instead, they slept till dawn, then continued on their journey. Evelyn had gone into a quiet, introspective state, and Jack decided to leave her be. They stopped only briefly for food, for now that they had a definite goal, Slade drove them on longer and longer. Jack had nearly forgotten about his feet, so the next time they stopped, he asked Slade to fix them, which the fox did with a mumbled reply of adding it to his debt.

Finally, when the sun started to sink and there was no giant tree in sight, Slade cursed. "I suppose we'll have to stop again. Tomorrow we'll go faster, so get as much rest as you can."

Jack gathered firewood, which Slade grudgingly agreed to, and fell asleep soon after the fire was lit, dreaming of cottages and watermills again. The long brown hair from before made another appearance, this time connected to a person, though she faced away from him. He tried to call to her, but his voice wouldn't work. His legs also refused to budge, rooting him to the ground only a few feet away from her. He awoke with a start and saw Evelyn resting near the fire, which had shrunk to a few embers. She gazed into it, her mind far away.

"What are you thinking?" he asked.

She blinked slowly, then looked up at him. "My brother. He's still just a kid. He can't survive on his own."

"Do you have any family he could've gone to? Friends?"

"My family is scattered. We have no strong feelings for one another, so it's unlikely he sought any of them. Friends... It's possible. I just worry he took off to find me all on his own."

Jack could think of nothing to say to that, so he sat next to her and placed one arm gently around her. She sighed and rested her head against him. The next thing Jack knew, Slade was nudging his side, saying, "It's time to go."

He got up and put out the remains of the fire. As promised, Slade kept a quicker pace, but Jack managed to keep up. It helped that his feet were whole again. Evelyn resumed her quiet flight and Jack's thoughts wandered to the Hunter. If the witch had sent it, it must be trying to stop them. And if Slade's concern was anything to go by, it wouldn't ask them nicely.

Within a couple hours, they saw the great tree ahead of them, towering above all around it by several feet. A carpet of red, orange, and yellow leaves surrounded its trunk, but many still clung to its branches, not willing to relinquish their hold just yet.

Slade ran ahead, not caring how fast they followed. "The end at last," he said. "Hurry. Let's find the owl."

Jack and Evelyn summoned another burst of energy and followed him. He stood at the base of the tree, which would take several humans to surround, and called up, "Hello! Is anyone home?"

"Not very polite," Evelyn commented. "What if she's sleeping?"

"Then we'll wake her up. Do you really want to sit here all day waiting on her?"

None of them wanted to do that, so Jack joined Slade while Evelyn flew upward, searching for Siobhan's nest. Their shouts and Evelyn's search soon produced her, a great horned bird, who had in fact been sleeping. She followed Evelyn back down and stared at them bleary-eyed.

"I figured you'd have the decency to wait until this evening." Her voice was croaky like an old woman's.

Slade quickly apologized. "We simply couldn't wait any longer," he said. "Every moment counts, after all."

"Well, spit it out. The sooner you leave, the sooner I can get back to sleep."

Slade explained Evelyn's situation, ending with their meeting with Raven and the subsequent journey to her.

"Well, your story matches," she said when he finished. "Smart. But I'm afraid I've got some bad news for you." She began picking through her feathers, seeming to forget her guests entirely.

"Yes, what?" Slade prompted.

Siobhan glared at him and picked through her feathers a moment longer. When she finally finished, she said, "Witches use a very specific type of magic, and by the sound of it, the one you dealt with was under some spell herself. So the only one capable of breaking it is another witch, preferably the one who cast the original spell."

"Where can we find another witch?" Evelyn asked. "I didn't think they were too common."

"They're not, thanks to the Guild. But that makes finding the right one much easier." The owl began picking her feathers again, producing a silver coin a moment later. "Aha! Now, I'll use this to locate your witch for you. Unfortunately, you will have to do something for me as payment."

"All right, name your price," Slade said.

"The wolves have an artifact that can channel large amounts of magic. It's a storm-eater. Bring it to me and I will consider your debt paid in full."

"The wolves? But that's suicide! We'll never make it back!" Slade said.

"Those are my terms. Take them or leave them."

Slade cursed and started to argue when Evelyn said, "I'll do it."

"What?" Slade said. "Are you insane?"

"It's my choice, my quest," Evelyn said. "You're only along for Jack's sake. If you wish to stay behind, I understand. But I'm going."

Siobhan laughed. "Foolish girl, walking into danger so willingly. But I suppose that's how you got into this situation in the first place. I'll even tell you which side has the storm-eater. If you hurry, you can be there and back in a matter of days."

"I won't be part of this," Slade said. "This is not worth dying over. It's tough enough getting through as an innocent bystander. How do you think you'll survive if you try leaving with something of theirs?"

"It doesn't matter," Evelyn said. "I have to try."

"Are you able to provide some sort of protection?" Jack asked the owl. "An invisibility spell or armor or something?"

"Of course, but that will cost extra."

"What happened to helping others out of the goodness of your heart?" Evelyn asked.

"That only happens in faery tales, and sometimes not even then. You have my terms. The choice is yours."

"I'll take them," Evelyn said. "And we won't accept any extra protection."

"You're on your own, then," Slade said. "I'll go no further, and Jack isn't either. I didn't waste my energy just for him to be torn apart by wolves before I'm paid in full."

"No, I'm going with her," Jack said.

"Not a chance. I forbid it. If you try, our deal is off. You'll be stuck here, unable to move."

"Just how is that beneficial to anyone?" Evelyn asked. "If you're going to do that, you may as well let him go. Either way, you wouldn't be paid."

"That's a valid point," Siobhan said. "At least by letting him go, there's a chance you'll be compensated."

"I don't need your advice," Slade said. "My decision is made. Now Jack, what will it be?"

The scarecrow looked helplessly between the three, all eyes on him. If he chose Evelyn, he'd be stuck and wouldn't be able to help her anyway. But if he chose Slade, could Evelyn forgive him? She'd be by herself, and the Hunter was still out there. Unless he could find some way to get away from Slade...

"Why can't I pay off my debt now?" he asked. "Isn't there something I can do?"

"Nothing," Slade said. "Quit stalling, straw man."

Jack looked between them again and made the hardest decision of his life. "I'll go with Slade," he said.

THERE WAS a hushed moment of shock at his words. Evelyn looked as though someone had just killed her best friend, and Slade smiled as if he'd been given a gift he greatly desired.

"Jack," Evelyn said. "Why—"

"I can't help you if I'm stuck here," he said.

"You can't help me if you go with him, either!" she cried. "How can you just abandon me? We could find a way to make you walk again."

"You can't guarantee that," he said.

"Very true," Slade said. "It's actually a very complex spell. I'd be surprised if you were able to cast it with even five years of study."

"I would have been able to," Siobhan said, "had he chosen the young lady. But he's made his choice, and that is that."

Evelyn glared at both of them and said, "Just go! I never want to see you again!"

"But Evelyn—"

"Go!"

Slade turned without another word, heading northwest. Jack stayed another moment, trying to think of anything he could say to make it better. There was nothing. So he followed Slade, leaving Evelyn behind with the owl.

"I'm glad that business is over," Slade said. "You made the right decision. And no more worrying about the Hunter, thank the gods. Now we can focus on more important things."

Jack tuned him out. He could still see Evelyn's hurt face, the anger in her eyes as she turned away from him. He had to make it better, but how? What could he do to get away from Slade and keep his mobility?

"We should head directly to Alibeth," Slade continued. "It's a large city, but we won't venture far. Just to the outskirts. I have a friend there who owes me a favor."

"Are all of your 'friends' in your debt?" Jack asked.

"Most," the fox admitted, taking no offense.

"What's a storm-eater?" Jack asked, his curiosity overpowering his frustration for a moment.

"There are several different types of magical artifacts in the world, and you can gauge their power by the category they fall under. A storm-eater is one of the most powerful types, eclipsed only by a death-bringer. Someone really should retrieve it from the wolves, who will no doubt do horrible things with it. But it doesn't have to be us."

Jack looked back once more, still able to see the great tree in the distance. He thought he could make out the owl and the crow. The land sloped downward again and even the tree was soon lost to his view. He sighed and turned his gaze forward, hoping he hadn't made a mistake.

6

ALIBETH

Hours turned into days, until a week had passed. Had Evelyn already gone to the wolves' land? Had she been captured? The uncertainty gnawed at him, and he fantasized of pouncing on the fox and beating him unconscious, then running wildly back to find Evelyn. His rational mind knew it wouldn't work, but he had no better solution. The trees simply went on and on, and Slade was ever vigilant.

"We shouldn't be too far away now," Slade announced when they climbed yet another hill. "Alibeth is just on the other side of this hill, across a field or two. We should be there by sundown."

From the top of the hill, Jack saw the shining city in the distance, sprawled out across the ground like a child's play area. Travelers and wagons and horses filled the road leading into the city, its streets full of constant movement.

"I suppose we're not using the main entrance?" Jack asked.

"We could hide in a wagon. But no, the human entrance would be a bit difficult to pull off. We'll take the side entrance." Slade hurried down the hill, calling back, "We still have a way to go before we actually get there. Let's close the distance, shall we?"

Jack followed at a slower, more reluctant pace. Could he even find his way back to Evelyn on his own, now? Surely in the city he could at least give Slade the slip. But what then? Before they approached the outer wall, Jack asked the fox to fix his feet once more. He needed shoes, or some sort of shield that would protect them from wear. Slade would certainly tire of his requests, with time.

A small hole in the wall, hidden by bushes and too narrow for humans—except for perhaps a young child—served as their entrance into Alibeth. Slade and Jack slipped in quite easily. Jack half expected there to be guards of some sort, but they passed unchallenged. Smells accosted him from every direction the moment they squeezed out the other end: bacon, chickens, feces, horses, sweat, flowers, hot coffee, vegetable soup, pigs, and many things he'd never smelled before. He wanted to cover his nose and take a deeper whiff at the same time. Sounds, too, accosted his ears: hawkers crying their wares, parents calling their children, footsteps on the cobblestones, wagon wheels, horses clopping along, animal noises, laughter, food sizzling and boiling. He felt he could merely stand in one spot for days on end and pick apart the sounds and smells and not be bored in the slightest.

Slade allowed him a brief glance at their surroundings before ushering him behind a row of barrels. "You're going to have to keep close," the fox instructed. "We don't have far to go, but it's easy to get turned around. And whatever you do, avoid being seen by the humans. The last thing we need is an uproar."

"Can you not change me into some sort of animal?" Jack asked as Slade turned to leave. "I mean, if I were a dog, no one would look twice at me."

The fox laughed. "That would require even more energy than your mobility cost you. I'm not even sure I could do it by myself. No, you'll simply have to keep to the shadows and be extra vigilant."

The barrels ended after only a short distance, and the fox darted behind a wagon that stood a few feet further on. Jack paused at the edge of the barrels, watching the people pass by. None of them glanced his way, but it would only take one. He looked around for anything he could use as a cover and spotted a wet, crinkled newspaper lying just at the edge of the street, around the side of the last barrel. As quick as he could, he snatched it up, then draped it over himself. With a deep breath, he ran across the gap and joined Slade behind the wagon, then waited for any shouts or cries of alarm.

Nothing.

"Well done," Slade said. He turned and hurried on, darting behind every hay bale, trash bin, and storage crate he could find. Jack followed along at a much quicker pace with the help of the newspaper, but he still paused before every crossing, just to be sure.

Finally, Slade turned down a side alley, crates and barrels cluttering the space and creating all sorts of hiding places. With the sun sinking and no lights illuminating that particular alley, the shadows hid them quite well all on their own.

"It's just a bit further," Slade said.

Jack considered sneaking off. With the fox focused on the alley, his absence wouldn't be noticed right away. He had grown accustomed to using the newspaper for cover and could make his way fairly quickly back to the side entrance and be out of the city before the fox realized his quarry had fled. Almost he turned to run when Slade said, "Manus, you old rat, good to see you! How is the missus? Jack, come along and meet my friend here."

Jack stepped forward in defeat. He would just have to find another opportunity, that was all. A large rat sat next to Slade, its fur dark and matted. It was nearly the size of a healthy full-grown cat. It twitched its whiskers and narrowed its eyes.

"How do you do?" it said, its voice high-pitched and possessing a wheezing quality that grated on Jack's senses.

"This is Jack," Slade said. "Jack, this is Manus. He owes me a favor, so we're here to collect on that. Manus, dear friend, do you have the item I requested?"

Manus rubbed his paws together. "Yes and no," he said.

"What do you mean?" Slade demanded. "Either you have it or you don't. Which is it?"

"I did have it, I did indeed. But then *he* came and took it. Without so much as a penny of payment! Flat out robbery, I tell you."

"Who took it, Manus? And your answer better be a good one, or it's your neck."

"Olivarion von Liebowitz. None other than the dreadlord himself, I swear. How do you expect me to stand up to him, and all those lackeys he brings along? I should say my debt's been paid twice over, for all the trouble this has caused me."

"Yet now I'll have to go through a lot more trouble to get the item that, by rights, I should be getting from you. I can't call that a fair trade, Manus. I'm afraid you'll have to pay off your debt some other way."

"But that's not fair!"

"Neither is me having to steal what's mine back from Olivarion, but such is life. Don't worry. I'll find some other way you can be useful. Something even you won't be able to botch up."

Slade pondered a moment, mumbling softly to himself. Manus cursed and scratched at his matted fur. Jack couldn't blame him. Slade was a cold businessman.

"This will require some careful planning," Slade said. "We shall have to stay here for the night. Manus, is the closest shelter still in the garden district?"

"It is," the rat said, scowling.

"Good. Let's be off, Jack. Send my regards to the missus, Manus. I'll send word soon." Out of the rat's earshot, Slade said, "That bumbling blockhead. This should've been a simple pickup. Oh, well. Looks like we get to have a bit more fun. I suppose you've never heard of the dreadlord we're about to tangle with. He's well known in Alibeth, and rumors of his ferocity circulate to other cities. Olivarion von Liebowitz is a cat of great power, not only in magic, but in politics and intimidation. He rules an entire district, some say the entire city, and the word is that the other district lords are mere puppets under his control. I think that may be more than rumor, but what do I know? We need the fire-tamer, so we can't simply walk away. I spent far too long tracking it down."

"What *is* a dreadlord?"

"Oh, just a glorified term for a strong mage who also happens to have a league of followers. Nothing special."

"And a fire-tamer?"

"Another type of magical artifact. Not near as strong as a storm-eater, but powerful enough."

"Do you have a plan?"

"None, but I'm sure I'll come up with something this evening. Let's go!"

Slade dove back into the city streets and the game of dash and hide continued. Jack didn't have much experience with cats, much less a dreadlord, so he hoped Slade came up with a good plan. As the sun disappeared, the crowd thinned, everyone going home or finding some form of lodging for the night. It made their travel much easier, especially as they now took several more turns and were forced to cross streets that would've been impassable during the day. New denizens emerged from the shadows, humans and animals alike, that preferred the night life to the bustling day. They took no notice of the fox and scarecrow.

Bright lights hovered above, illuminating the roads and casting long shadows. Likely there was a chapter of the Mage's Guild in the city. Jack wondered if the humans could see the magic aura Slade had spoken of before, and if so, he was curious how the animals avoided detection. Evelyn would've found it fascinating. The thought of her pricked his conscience, so he watched those around him instead: lanky, narrow-eyed men and women and thin, skittish animals. Their desire to go unnoticed equaled Jack's.

"We're in luck," Slade said. "At the shelter, we'll have a chance to rest and hear the local gossip. We may discover something useful."

"Why don't you free me already? We both know I should be with Evelyn. She could die because of your stubbornness."

"And here I was thinking we were getting along swell. Really, Jack, you should forget about her. She's going to certain death, and your presence wouldn't change that a bit. It's not like you could scare the wolves. Not even the crows feared you."

"That's not the *point*," Jack said, barely containing his anger. "I should be there with her. It's your fault I'm not."

The fox rounded on him, pushing him up against a wall and lifting him in the air with a twitch of his nose. "I'm the reason you're not still on that damned post," he said. "You'd do well to remember it. You chose to come with me, in case you've forgotten. So stop complaining or I'll seal your mouth shut."

Jack only glared, though a dozen retorts crossed his mind. As the fox lowered him, he considered searching the city for another mage, one who would grant him mobility without forcing him into bondage. Surely he could find *someone*. They continued on with no more conversation.

Jack didn't remember the rest of the journey, too lost in his thoughts. When Slade stopped beside a rundown warehouse, Jack nearly ran into him.

The fox moved around the door, touching his nose to various parts of the wood, which glowed brightly at each touch and dissipated again. After the final one, the door unlatched itself and slid open two feet. Slade slipped inside and Jack followed. A yellow light at the end of the large room cast the only illumination. Crates towered high on either side of the room, abandoned wares left for the rats. Muffled conversation echoed from beyond the open door on the far side. They reached it quickly, passing through a short hallway that turned right and opened again to another large room, though smaller than the first. A dozen or so animals filled the room, mostly dogs and cats, but also a few birds and mice. A few acknowledged them with a nod of their heads and conversation resumed.

More crates of varying heights lined the room, padded with blankets, clothes, and other human castoffs, providing makeshift beds atop them and on the ground.

"Find a spot and make yourself comfortable," Slade advised. The fox approached one of the dogs as Jack looked about the room for an empty bed. A few animals glanced his way, full of curiosity. He found a place atop a small crate and climbed up, preparing to listen to the conversation around him until he fell asleep.

"Have a run-in with the Guild?" a voice asked very near his ear. Jack glanced up to see a small jay perched on the crate just above him to the right.

"Because I'm a scarecrow, you mean? I don't actually know. I've been this way as long as I can remember."

"It's some sort of spellwork. Are you here to see the Guild and have them remove it?"

"No. I'm actually not sure why we're here. My companion has business and I'm obliged to follow."

"Ah, your fox friend. I've seen him around before. Always up to some scheme or another. I'm Doran, by the way."

"Jack."

"Have you known him long?"

"We're really just getting to know each other."

The jay chittered. "Be careful. He's a crafty one, from what I've heard."

"I heard a story once," a cat on the other side of Jack said, "concerning the friend of a relative of mine. Your friend had entangled himself in the affairs of the Guild somehow, over some book or trinket. My relative's friend acted as a go between and was blamed when the item ended up missing. The fox, of course, had an alibi, but the whole thing was a little too convenient. The cat nearly lost her home because of it."

"When was this?" Jack asked.

"Oh, a few months ago. The excitement has died down a bit now, but she'll not be pleased to hear he's back in town."

"We don't plan to be here long," Jack said. "At least, I don't think so."

"How did you end up with him?" the jay asked.

"He helped me and now I'm in his debt," Jack said, thinking it better to keep the details to himself.

"Typical," the cat said.

"It will only require two or three of your number, no more!" Slade said, voice raised.

"It's too risky," the dog answered. "You've been gone too long, friend. His power has grown, and grows more every day. Even the Guild is wary of him."

"Have all of you turned to cowardice?" Slade asked, glancing around the room.

"If the dreadlord's involved, yes," the dog said.

They lowered their voices once more and the cat said, "Sounds like they're speaking of Olivarion. You're not involved with him, are you?"

"We may soon be," Jack admitted.

"You should run," Doran advised. "Whatever debt you owe the fox, it's not worth the trouble you'll find."

"I'll keep that in mind," Jack said. "Enough of me. Why are the two of you here? Are there shelters like this elsewhere?"

"It's warmer than sleeping outside," the cat said. "The city is my home. Tomorrow, I'll probably be in a different shelter— they're scattered all about. Beats finding lodging in Underbeth."

"Under—?"

"Same for me," the jay interrupted. "Tomorrow, I plan to take my chances with the Guild. What with life becoming more dangerous every day, it'd ease my mind to have a bit of protection."

"Protection from what?"

"Everything. The dreadlords especially. Olivarion's in power now, and that's bad enough, but what if one of the others makes a play for dominance? Then it's all-out war. You can't be too careful, nowadays."

"I agree," the cat said.

Before Jack could ask any more questions, the arrival of someone new distracted the room. Jack peered like the rest of them and spied Slade walking through the door. Only it wasn't Slade, because he was still standing below, looking at the door with all the rest. The new fox swished its tail and studied them.

"Don't let the party stop on my account," it said—clearly female. Her voice was higher than Slade's, and a bit scratchy. Slade's fur looked downright shabby next to her glossy coat. "We meet again," she said.

"Nadya," Slade replied. "I thought you were heading south. To 'seek your fortune,' wasn't it?"

She swished her tail again and walked past him, stopping before a bed on the floor already occupied by a large dog. The dog looked up at her, then stood and moved away. The female fox lay down. Slade approached her and they continued a whispered conversation.

"Who is that?" Jack asked.

"Not someone you want to tangle with," Doran replied. "This shelter is less welcoming by the second."

"Is she a dreadlord?"

The cat snickered. "Hardly. Just an unscrupulous sort. Much like your own fox friend."

The jay took to the air. "Good luck," he said. "You're going to need it."

He flew out of the room, along with a few other animals.

"Is she that bad?" Jack asked the cat.

"I've never met her, personally," the cat admitted. "Just heard rumors. Still, better to be safe than sorry." The cat settled himself in, closing his eyes and mumbling, "Good night."

Jack looked about, keeping to himself as small groups around the room whispered and pointedly did not watch the two foxes. Eventually, Slade withdrew and found his own bed. Nadya lay down and twitched her nose. Immediately the fire extinguished itself. No one protested.

"I HOPE YOU'RE WELL RESTED," Slade said the next morning. "There's no telling what will happen today."

They had slipped out of the shelter early in the morning when most were still sleeping. Not many humans were up and about, but Jack kept to the shadows anyway. They traveled back through the maze of the city, the fox barely speaking a word to him. Finally, Jack could take it no longer.

"Who is she?" he asked.

Slade glanced back at him with a questioning gaze. "Who?"

"The female. The one from last night."

Slade shrugged and turned away. "No one you need concern yourself with."

"But—"

"Let's call her an old friend and leave it at that, shall we?"

He bounded across an alley before Jack could reply. Jack sighed and followed. It didn't matter, he supposed.

"We're nearly there," Slade announced after several more twists and turns. "With luck, he won't be expecting us, but you never know."

"I suppose we'll see his guards before we see him, just like with Raven?" Jack asked.

"Most likely. Only Olivarion won't be as just as Raven. In fact, you may as well prepare yourself for the worst, because we won't be leaving without a great fuss."

"What is the plan?"

"That would be telling, wouldn't it?"

Jack sighed in acceptance. Perhaps he should've stayed with Siobhan. At least then he'd be free of Slade, and Evelyn wouldn't hate him. Also, he wouldn't be walking into what was most likely a highly dangerous situation.

Except that wasn't quite true, either. There were the wolves to consider, after all. His worry for Evelyn increased.

"Stay very quiet, now," Slade whispered, crouching low near the opening of another street crossing. "We're about to cross into Olivarion's district, and this will go much more smoothly if we're not spotted. Keep close, and do exactly as I say."

Slade dashed out and then under a table along the street. Jack followed as fast as he could only to have Slade rush off again across the cobblestones and behind some empty crates. Another alley opened before them and Slade peeked into it cautiously, not daring to show his whole face around the corner. He pulled back after mere seconds.

"There are five guards this way. With time, I could come up with a passable story, but time is not on our side. We shall have to ascend to the rooftops."

"The rooftops? How do you suggest I climb up there? And how will we cross the gaps between buildings?"

"Leave that to me. And keep your voice down. Do you want us to be caught?" The fox dashed off back down the street, stopping next to a metal pipe hanging from the roof and reaching all the way to the ground. "Marvelous, isn't it?" Slade asked. "Quite new, and only the wealthy possess them. Lucky Olivarion made his headquarters in this district, eh?"

"What is it?" Jack asked.

"It directs water into a grate in the street to avoid flooding when it rains. I'm sure with time every house will have them. We'll climb here and work our way back to the alley."

With that, he jumped onto the pipe, his paws clinging to it like a cat as he scampered up. No doubt magic played a large role in his effortless movement, but the effect was quite impressive.

Once at the top, the fox peered back down at Jack and said, "Wrap your arms around the joints and try climbing. I'll do the rest." Jack did as instructed, expecting to slide back down, but he ascended nearly as quickly as Slade had. All he had to do was reach for the next handhold and he practically floated to the top.

"There, now. Quite simple, no?" Slade said once Jack reached the top. "Come along now. We've still got a ways to go."

The wooden roofs made it easy to get a firm footing. Luckily it hadn't rained recently, or Slade might've turned around only to see Jack go sliding back down to the street. The scarecrow suspected the fox was still using magic to keep his balance. Any bit of extra safety was welcome, in his opinion. Whenever they reached a gap between houses, Slade used his magic to boost their jump. At Jack's turn, he hesitated for a long while before gathering the courage to make the leap. It was one thing to trust that the fox would help him across, and quite another to actually put it into practice. He made the jump without trouble and they continued on.

They turned at the next gap and followed the roof along the alley, keeping as quiet as they could. Slade wouldn't even allow a whisper. A few more turns and Jack heard an angry voice saying, "What do you mean, you lost him? How do you lose a fox in a city? I will not accept any more of your excuses. Find him. *Now.*"

Slade motioned Jack closer and together they peered over the edge and down into the alley, which was illuminated by a few glowing balls of yellow light, as well as two fire pits on the ground. On a pile of crates topped with several fluffy red cushions sat a cat as large as a dog. Short, dark gray fur covered its body, and a much smaller cat knelt before it on the ground. After a moment it rose and scurried away down the alley. The longer Jack looked, the more cats he spotted. They filled the small space: behind crates, in windowsills, atop barrels. All eyes stared at Olivarion, for the large cat could be none other than he.

"When that sniveling rat informed us that the fox was on his way here, I expected him to be caught swiftly," Olivarion continued. "And to make it that much easier, he travels with a scarecrow! Is there no one here who can manage to spot two such conspicuous beings? Shall I be forced to search for new, more capable felines to serve me?"

"No sire," many cats answered.

"Be off, then!" Olivarion commanded. "And do not return until they are found." The alley emptied of nearly every cat, leaving only Olivarion and a few personal retainers. Slade motioned for Jack to follow him and they sneaked around the edge toward Olivarion's throne. The large cat rubbed his eyes with one paw and sighed loudly. "You can come out now. I know you're up there."

Jack and Slade froze, but it did no good. The cat looked right at them.

"Come down," he said. "I will not kill or harm you...for now. I wish to talk first."

Slade stood and looked down at the dreadlord, discarding the pretense of secrecy. "We can see and hear you just fine from here," the fox said.

"No, no, no, that won't do at all." The cat waved his paw and his guards scurried up to the roof from several directions. "You can come down of your own will, or my guards can bring you down, but come down you shall."

The cats advanced on them, two to Jack's left and three more on the other side of Slade. For a moment, Jack thought the fox would stand and fight, but then Slade laughed and jumped off the roof, descending slowly to the ground. Invisible hands lifted Jack and pulled down, and a second later they stood before the dreadlord. The guards began their descent.

"If you knew we were there, why not let your lackeys stay and witness our defeat?" Slade asked.

"They needed to be taught a lesson. Clever of you, to use the rooftops to approach. You will not find it so easy next time, I assure you."

"I hope there won't be need for a next time. I have no issue with you, other than the possession of my property. Surely we can come to some sort of arrangement and then we'll be out of your hair."

"The item you seek is of great value to me. I'm afraid there will be no 'arrangement' to be found. You understand, I'm sure."

"Unfortunately, no. I spent much too long tracking it down."

The two glared at one another, neither willing to budge. Jack felt as though there were an invisible argument going on beneath the vocal one, and it was unclear which side was winning.

"Whatever are we to do?" Olivarion asked. "It seems we are at an impasse."

"What if I could offer you something better?" Slade asked. "Some item of far greater power?"

Olivarion laughed. "Why would you do that? No one gives up something of great power for something of lesser ability."

"I would. And I assure you, it's no trick. However, I will need the fire-tamer in order to retrieve the more powerful item: a storm-eater. You can cast whatever spell or insurance you can think of in order to ensure my honesty."

The great cat considered for a moment, probably not entirely convinced of the fox's honesty. Jack wondered the same thing, for Slade's offer made no sense to him. But he could ask questions later.

"I will consider your offer," Olivarion said. "In the meantime, you will stay here. I will give you my answer this evening."

The remaining cats stepped forward, ushering them further down the alley where a small hole disappeared into one of the buildings. Jack glanced back at the dreadlord, but the great cat's attention had turned elsewhere. One of the guards entered the hole, the second one indicating they should follow. They quickly complied, crawling through a short distance and emerging into a room full of boxes and crates stuffed with food and wine. Floating balls of light illuminated the space, and a lovely warmth permeated the room. A wooden staircase leading up to a closed door served as the only other exit, muffled voices drifting down from the other side. The second cat emerged from the hole and stopped just in front of it, preventing their exit.

"You can rest over there," the first cat said, pointing to a large pile of blankets, clothes, and pillows. "You can eat anything you find, but only in small quantities. We do not wish to be discovered by the humans of the house."

"Of course," Slade answered. He proceeded to inspect the crates of food as if the cats weren't there at all. "Pity you don't eat, Jack," he said. "There's quite a lot here to tempt the taste buds."

"I'm sure," Jack answered. He moved closer and whispered, "What exactly are you doing? Is this part of your plan?"

"I'm looking for breakfast," Slade answered. "And yes, it is. We will wait here until Olivarion accepts my offer, then we will be on our way to complete our end of the bargain. Simple as that."

"And if he doesn't accept?"

"Let's not dwell on that now, shall we?"

The fox continued perusing the contents of the crates, so Jack made himself comfortable in the nest of blankets. Slade made small talk with the guard-cats, his manner unworried and even playful.

"I say, have you tried the sausage links?" he asked. "Simply divine."

7

THE MAGES' GUILD

Someone shook him roughly awake and Jack grudgingly opened one eye. A cat stood over him, shaking him again when Jack didn't get up. "You've been summoned," the cat said. "You must come."

He groaned and rose. Slade dozed a few feet away. "What about him?"

"Olivarion will deal with him later. It's *you* he wants now."

He could've asked why, and meant to, but held his tongue. The dreadlord would speak with him no matter his opinion on the subject. Jack followed the cat, leaving Slade resting undisturbed. They crawled back through the hole, emerging into a now empty alley.

"This way," the cat said, taking a path to the right which led even deeper into the maze of streets.

"Where are you taking me?"

The cat didn't answer. The sky had turned a lovely shade of blue, the sun high and void of clouds far above them. He saw no other animals, but he once more heard human voices and the murmuring bustle of the city at noon. Now and then a window opened and a woman aired out a sheet or clothing. A voice, lifted in song, drifted on the air. Finally the cat stopped before a blank wall and motioned Jack over.

"Stay close to me," he said. "It's less jarring that way."

Before Jack could ask what he meant, the cat stepped forward, pulling Jack with him. They smacked into the wall... except they didn't, pressing forward until they broke through, the wall flexing like the sail of a ship. Jack stumbled forward and would've fallen if the cat hadn't held him.

"Easy, now," he said. "The worst is over."

Jack had never seen anything like the place that now sat before him. It was clearly created by magic, but he couldn't begin to imagine the amount of power required to form it. A large patio sat on an island surrounded by clear blue water. Ten feet or so behind it, a small cliff towered over them, water pouring down from every side. The patio was made of white marble, and smooth columns stood in an even circle around it, supporting a ring higher up and open in the middle so the sky was clearly visible above. In the middle of the patio was a large red divan, and atop the divan sat Olivarion. Jack looked back the way they had come and saw only trees, the water forming a swift stream and cutting through them. Gentle birdsong filled the air, but no birds were visible.

"Leave us," Olivarion said. His escort bowed and withdrew, disappearing at the edge of the island. "Convenient, no?" the dreadlord asked. "A private paradise in the middle of the city. Few know it even exists."

"Why show me?"

"I have a feeling you won't reveal my secrets. Do you even remember how to get here?"

"No," Jack admitted.

"There you are, then. Come, sit down and relax."

Jack hesitated, but figuring there was no point resisting, he approached the divan and sat down. Olivarion watched him with an amused smile. "I'm positively dying to know: how did you end up with that fox? He's not the friendliest sort."

"He did me a favor," Jack answered. "Now I'm in his debt."

The dreadlord laughed. "Not an enviable position. You must know I can't give up the artifact he's after. It's much too valuable."

"I don't care one way or another," Jack said. "I'd prefer to not even be here, but I have no choice in the matter. Unless you can free me? If you can do all of this..." He gestured to their surroundings. "Then you can do the same magic he can. Probably more."

Olivarion shook his head. "Don't misunderstand, little scarecrow. I have no desire to help you. I'm curious to see what becomes of you, that I'll not deny. If ever that curiosity wanes, I'll abduct you and sell you to the mages." He laughed at Jack's shocked expression. "You're safe for now. Oh, this is too amusing! I shall have to get a scarecrow of my own. Are you actually any good at scaring crows? Do you have any special abilities?"

"Not that I know of."

"Pity. Imagine a scarecrow who could change his appearance to become more fearsome, or who wielded some horrible weapon or magic to terrorize his victims. It's truly a shame you have no magic. Missed opportunity, I say."

Jack shook his head in confusion. "Why am I here?"

"To entertain me, of course. I can't be expected to make important decisions without a bit of fun, can I?"

Jack opened his mouth to reply and only then realized the scenery had changed. The sky had darkened to a stormy gray and the trees had completely lost their leaves, their trunks black and gnarled. Worst of all, the water had lost its clear blue shade, a stream of blood now surrounding them and disappearing into the dark forest. Jack stood in alarm and Olivarion laughed again.

"Don't like my sort of magic, do you?"

Jack could only watch as twisted faces appeared in the bark of each tree, skeletal grins and empty eye sockets watching them. Something rippled beneath the blood, and dark shapes dashed overhead, gone before he could get a clear look. Olivarion sat unmoved.

"Stop toying with me!" Jack said. "You've had your fun. Either say what you really want or let me go."

The dreadlord grinned and everything went back to the way it had been before. Rather than sit back down, Jack stayed standing. The two regarded each other silently a moment, then Olivarion asked, "Are you afraid of me?"

"Afraid? I'd be a fool if I weren't. But no, not in the way you think. I'm afraid you'll interfere with my own desire, the same way Slade has done. I fear you'll inflict some horrible fate on me just as I've freed myself of all debt. If you killed me, I'd only be sorry I didn't have more time."

"You do not fear death, then?"

"I'm not sure if I *can* die. So I don't think about it. But I suppose if anything lies on the other side, it's a mite better than anything here."

"And if it isn't? If it is indeed a hell, or worse, nothing at all, what then?"

"I'll worry about that when I come to it."

Olivarion regarded him a moment, eyes squinted in thought. Finally, he smiled. "I like you, scarecrow. You're foolish, but honest, and that can't be said of many anymore."

Jack stayed silent, catching the echo of Raven's words in Olivarion's.

"Go back to your friend," the dreadlord said. "I will call for you both in a few hours."

On cue, his escort appeared out of thin air and motioned for Jack to follow him. He hesitated, looking back at the dreadlord, but Olivarion had looked away, lost in his own thoughts. Jack followed the cat, feeling only a slight pressure in the air before the alley once more appeared around him. Neither spoke as the guard took Jack back to where Slade was kept. He couldn't understand why Olivarion had displayed such power to him. To intimidate him? What would that accomplish? He was still musing about it when they reached the cellar.

"Well?" Slade said as Jack crawled in. "What did he want?"

"I think he was trying to scare me."

Slade regarded him with narrowed eyes. "You're not foolish enough to lie to me, are you?"

"What? No. Why would I lie?"

The fox shrugged and lay back down. Jack almost told him about Olivarion's magic, but kept it to himself. Slade probably knew. Olivarion was a dreadlord, after all. By definition, they were strong. Instead, he lay back down, arms behind his head as he stared at the ceiling. Sleep wouldn't come, leaving him alone with his thoughts.

OLIVARION CALLED for them later that evening. They met in the alley once more, the dreadlord's guards spread out along the ground and on the rooftops above. Jack and Slade stood before him in silence, unsure what to expect. Olivarion wasted no time.

"I have thought about your proposal and decided I cannot simply part with so powerful an artifact on the promise that you will return with a greater one. Here, then, is *my* proposal: you will retrieve a spell book from the Mage's Guild for me. I do not care how it is done. If you can do this by tomorrow evening, you may use the fire-tamer in pursuit of this storm-eater."

"What spell book am I looking for?" Slade asked.

"*The Descent of Alexander Crimmons.* My agents have been unable to secure it, or even locate it, but I know the mages have it."

Slade sighed and looked at the ground, as if he would find some answer amidst the dirt and leaves. But they were tight-lipped, keeping their secrets close. "I will do this," he finally said.

"Excellent. Then I will see you tomorrow evening." The dreadlord rose and twitched his nose, instantly disappearing.

Slade snorted, murmuring, "Show off." He turned to go and Jack scrambled after him.

"Wait! We're going tonight?"

"Why not? We've wasted enough time lazing about most of the day."

None of Olivarion's guards moved to stop them. They reached the end of the alley and the fox strode out into the street. Jack paused a moment, looking about for any humans.

"Besides," Slade continued, "most of the mages will be asleep. It's the perfect time for theft."

Not a soul moved on the street, so Jack followed the fox, who hadn't slowed.

"Just like that, we're heading to the Guild?" Jack asked. "You were so resistant to it before. What's changed?"

"Well, I have proper motivation now," the fox answered. "I'm willing to risk a little danger if the reward is great enough. I'm not sure how long I'll need to locate the book," he continued, seemingly talking to himself. "I'm sure they'll have protective spells, so not only will I need a tracking spell, but also one to disarm the wards in place..."

Orbs hovered above, casting only the slightest light on their path. Far away, Jack heard the sound of laughter and music. The city had emptied of life, congregating at some distant point. So long as it helped them go unnoticed, Jack was glad for it.

"I could always summon a construct, distract them a bit—"

"What's a construct?" Jack asked.

Slade glanced back at him with an annoyed huff. "A creature composed of various parts, brought together in a new shape to serve a temporary purpose."

"What does it do?"

"Whatever I command it to do."

Jack thought about that as they continued, increasing their speed to a jog. Slade turned streets with little thought, the path imprinted on his heart. The distant laughter grew louder.

"What is that noise?" Jack asked.

Slade didn't slow. "Festival. It's the Harvest season, and most humans celebrate with food, dancing, and games. It'll go on for weeks. You can join them later. We have work to do."

Jack asked no more questions, but he watched as an orange glow ahead and to his left grew bigger, the sound increasing with it. The village back home had a similar celebration that lasted for a week, but of course he'd only experienced it from a distance. Curiosity urged him to explore further, but he resisted and obediently followed the fox. A few more turns and the festival fell away behind them, lost in the labyrinth of streets. A hazy mass loomed ahead, rising above them several hundred feet, gray and silent and still. Jack stopped, trying to make it out in the misleading light of the orbs: pointed towers, narrow walkways, windows reflecting moonlight and clouds.

"It's the Guild castle," Slade said, noticing he'd stopped. "You'll see it up close in a moment. Come on."

"Why are there no lights?" Jack asked as he followed.

"Festival," Slade replied. "But there may still be a few mages inside sleeping. We'll have to be careful."

"Do you know where to look for the book?"

"No, but I have a few guesses. Just stay close."

As they moved closer to the castle, carved stone buildings soon replaced the wood, the streets themselves cleaner and better cared for. More patches of green appeared, revealing small gardens and flowering trees in a city that had all but forgotten nature. A large courtyard sat just before the castle gate, empty and quiet, the gentle splash of the fountain the only sound. The excitement of the festival couldn't touch that place, leaving only silence and stillness. Slade strode straight to the front entrance, stopping a couple feet away and motioning for Jack to stay back. A bright light appeared around him, cocooning him in a fiery glow. When he released the magic, the light shot forward in a wide arc, covering the width of the castle and rising above its tallest tower until the whole building was engulfed. Slade lifted one paw and the giant door creaked open.

"Hurry!" the fox said.

Jack slipped through the crack a moment before the door shut behind him. They stood in a vast hall, pillars running along both sides of the room, doors hidden in shadowy recesses. A balcony circled the hall, and large banners hung from the ceiling. Slade paused only a moment, casting a series of spells in quick succession. Items from the edges of the room flew toward them —chairs, candles, vases, paintings—all swirling together into a large beast with flaming candelabra for eyes. The next spell created another burst of light, green and smoky, which darted away from Slade and through a door to their right. The final spell caused a crystal web to attach to every wall, pillar, door, and window. It stretched across the floor and ceiling, solidifying in seconds. The beast roared and dashed across the room, chasing transparent human-shaped figures that had appeared.

"Let's go!" Slade said, dashing after the green trail.

Jack stumbled after him, tripping as the floor shook from the thundering of the beast. Dark corridors greeted them, lit by a few wall sconces and the light of the trail. In the dim light, Jack could make out doors in each hall, all shut to them. Further down the hall, the trail rose, ascending a winding staircase illuminated by a shaft of moonlight.

Slade dashed toward it, up and around, and Jack followed. The steps rose and rose, winding around and opening once more on a series of branching hallways and connecting rooms. More wall sconces and ghostly portraits of mages of the past lined the corridors, and now and again Jack saw stately furniture standing guard in empty rooms. But there was no time to investigate further. The trail snaked through the halls, twisting and turning so often that Jack was quickly lost. As they turned yet another corner and prepared to ascend another set of stairs, a thought struck him and he stopped. Slade continued on, oblivious that Jack no longer followed. Jack watched as the fox disappeared to the next floor, leaving him alone in the dark. The trail quickly dissipated, taking its guiding light with it. A room lay open on his right, another further down to his left. Behind him, more doors stood open invitingly, awaiting an occupant. Or someone curious enough to explore them.

He didn't know much about mages, except what he knew about Slade, but animal and human mages were different, it seemed. Perhaps he could find one more inclined to help him. With the festival going on, there was little chance he would find one that night, so he entered the room on his right and waited just within the doorway until his eyes adjusted. The dim light from the wall sconce in the hallway wasn't much help, but another sconce perched on the opposite wall inside, and a small candle stood to the left on the bedside table. A large four-post bed sat to the left, empty, except for an abundance of pillows. A dark shape that may have been a dresser stood against the wall on the other side of it. On the right, just beside the wall sconce, were several large bookcases overflowing with books. Jack moved further into the room and nearly ran into a round table that sat near the bookcases, a few large tomes open on its surface. In the corner beside the door was another shadowy shape, but he couldn't begin to guess what it was. He was sure he'd never seen anything like it before.

There was no point shutting the door, for if Slade came looking, a closed door would alert him to check the room. So Jack circled around the bed and hid in the darkest corner, between the dresser and another nightstand he hadn't spotted before. The candle and the wall sconce flickered gently, and the distant rumblings of the beast served as a soft lullaby, soothing him to sleep. As he dozed off, a thought struck him: what was there to stop Slade from using a seeking spell to find him?

"I DON'T THINK he's dangerous."

"You can't be too careful. We were attacked last night; we have to be on our guard."

"We weren't really *attacked*. We were robbed. And no one was hurt, so it's not the same thing."

"You really feel safe when someone simply walked in here, created a construct, stole a valuable book, and left a scarecrow in your room? You're either brave or a fool, Miriel."

Jack cracked one eye open, soft morning light greeting him. The room had taken on a rosy glow, and the enticing scent of baking apples filled the air. A middle-aged woman sat on the bed, her brown, frizzy hair falling to her shoulders and a pair of spectacles resting on her nose. She wore a plain green gown and a star and moon pendant around her neck. Next to her sat a snow white cat with bright green eyes. Both watched him.

"He's awake!" the woman said, her voice identifying her as Miriel.

"Why are you here?" the cat demanded.

"I need help," Jack said, standing. He stepped toward them, but an invisible barrier stopped him. He lifted his hands against it, feeling a smooth surface extending around him and ending flush with the wall.

"Sorry about that," Miriel said. "Arnica insisted."

"With good reason," the cat said.

"I don't blame you," Jack said. "I'm surprised you can understand me. Do all mages know animals can speak? I'm guessing I'm not the strangest thing you've encountered."

"Many know," Miriel answered. "The apprentices learn with time and experience, unless they come to us already knowing because of their gifts. But you're certainly an oddity. I wanted to examine you while you slept, but Arnica advised against it."

"We still don't know why he's here," the cat said. "Why *are* you here, by the way? If you need help, why did you sneak in? Who created the construct? Where is the book?"

Jack shrugged helplessly. "I came here against my will, honestly. I was indebted to a fox and managed to escape while he went after the book. I don't know where he is now. But he was taking the book to Olivarion."

Miriel sighed and Arnica narrowed her eyes. "Who was this fox?" the cat asked.

"He called himself Slade," Jack said, seeing no reason to protect the fox.

The woman and cat looked at each other. "Could be him," Miriel said.

"Likely," Arnica agreed. "And he took it to the dreadlord?"

Jack nodded.

"That's not good," Miriel said. "Lirelin won't be pleased."

"He needs to be dealt with anyway," Arnica said.

"How did you escape?" Miriel asked Jack.

"When we reached this floor, my companion was so focused on finding the book, he didn't notice when I slipped away."

"He may be back for you, then," Arnica said. "Unless you're lying. He could've left you behind as part of some grander scheme."

"You don't really think that," Miriel said, frowning at the cat. "I sense no deception in him."

"Might want to use the stones, just to be sure," Arnica said.

Miriel rose and crossed the room to the corner behind the door. Jack tried to peer over the bed to see what she was doing, but he wasn't tall enough. Arnica watched him, as though at any moment he would break through the invisible shield and attack them.

A moment later Miriel said, "He's telling the truth."

Arnica sighed and lifted one paw in the air. "Very well," she said.

A force like a gust of air pulled Jack forward and he landed on the floor, the barrier gone. He rose to his feet. "Thank you."

"You're not off the hook yet," Arnica said. "You were with that fox, so you're just as responsible for the theft. You'll have to be judged."

"Oh, come now," Miriel said. "He's as much a victim as us. I'm sure he didn't want to come here and cause trouble."

"Why do you need help?" the cat asked again. "If you're wanting us to hide you from the fox—"

"No, no," Jack said. He spread his arms. "The fox gave me the ability to move. He may reverse the spell at any moment, now that we're separated. That's why I didn't escape sooner. I was afraid he would leave me, immobile, in some alley, or in the forest. But you're a mage. Can you grant me mobility? I don't want to worry about him anymore."

Miriel crouched in front of him, pity in her eyes. "Oh, you poor thing. I don't know any spells like that... Though maybe one of the other mages does. But I don't think it would do any good right now. You can already move."

"How is it you can speak in the first place?" Arnica asked. "Is that a spell as well? And why are you so small? I thought scarecrows were supposed to be human-sized."

"I...don't really know," Jack admitted. "I sometimes have these dreams, only I'm a man in the dreams. Someone may have cursed me, but... I just don't know."

"Let's find out," Miriel said, picking him up.

Jack had never been carried before, at least not by anyone who knew he could speak, and certainly not in many years. It was an odd feeling, and Miriel walked very quickly. Arnica moved to the other corner of the bed to follow them. Miriel set him down on the round stone table behind the door. A wooden spear rose from the center, ending at about the same height as the bedposts. Swirling designs covered the surface of the table, and the edge was rimmed with small holes, green pieces of ribbon looping through them. He peered over the edge and saw that each ribbon was covered with multiple colored beads, all varying shapes and colors so that no ribbon was the same length. On the other side of the table were several smooth, round stones of green, gold, white, and a single black. Miriel gathered the stones and tossed them once more upon the table, then bent over to read what they had to tell.

She studied them for a moment while Arnica and Jack waited

in silence. Jack stole a glance at the cat, but the feline's eyes stayed fixed on her mistress. Jack took the moment to look around the room again, which was much more inviting in the light of morning. He could see more books, and discovered they reached all the way to the ceiling. A narrow stepladder rested against the end of one case.

A green blanket with swirls stitched in black thread covered the bed, and a small washstand and mirror stood near the door, which was closed at the moment. Of course it would be. They wanted to interrogate him in privacy, before turning him over to superiors.

"Hmm. Strange," Miriel said.

"What is it?" Arnica asked.

Jack peered at the stones spread out on the table, but he didn't see anything special in them.

Miriel rested her chin in her hands, her elbows on the table. "You, sir, are under a strong enchantment. But it doesn't resemble any magic I've encountered before, and I've studied every branch in existence."

Arnica narrowed her eyes at him again. "And you don't remember anything? That sounds suspicious to me, scarecrow."

"I promise, I remember nothing. But..."

"But?" Arnica prompted.

Jack sighed. "There's only one thing I can think of, but I'm no expert."

"Well, out with it," Miriel said.

"Is it possible I'm cursed by...a witch?"

The mage and cat looked at each other, Miriel's eyes wide. "Why would you have that idea?" she asked.

"Witches haven't been seen in hundreds of years," Arnica said. "If you know about one, you need to tell us."

Jack looked back and forth between them, unsure how much he should reveal. He didn't want to bring Evelyn into it, but if the mages could help...

"A friend of mine was cursed by a witch recently," he said. "If mages didn't cause my enchantment, that's the only other magic I can think of." *Excepting powerful bird gods.* But he wasn't about to get into that.

"Cursed how?" Miriel asked.

"Where is the witch now?" Arnica asked at the same time.

"She was turned into a crow," Jack said. "Last I saw the witch, she was in a village several days' travel from here. I don't know if she's still there."

Miriel rose, rubbing her chin and pacing. "This isn't good. Lirelin will definitely have to be told about this."

"Think for a moment," Arnica said. "We don't know for sure that there's a witch. We don't want to cause an uproar. Everyone's still searching for the intruder, and Lirelin is buried in things to do. We would do better to find out for ourselves about the witch and *then* go to Lirelin, once we have hard evidence to present to her."

"You want us to go by ourselves to search out a *witch?*" Miriel asked, mouth agape and eyes wide in horror.

"Why not?" Arnica said. "We don't have to confront her. Just spy on her."

"Do you have any idea what she could do if she caught us?"

"Look, are you a mage or not?" the cat retorted.

"I can't face down a *witch*! I could barely defeat another mage. I excel in the *study* of magic, and the divination arts. You know that."

"Why not seek her out from here?" Jack asked. "If you can read things about people, surely you could find her."

Miriel shook her head. "I've never met her in person, so I can only guess at what I'm looking for. I also have no idea how far away she is. The more precise information I have, the better the magic works. As it is, it would be like finding a specific leaf in a forest. In the dark."

"Isn't it worth it to try?" Jack asked.

"No, she's right," Arnica said. "It's better if we seek her out in person. And you're coming with us."

"Me? Can you at least help me first? Turn me human, or something? My fox friend may return for me at any moment."

Miriel shook her head, lips pressed in a thin line. "I have no idea what sort of magic is on you, whether witchcraft or something else. But I'm not able to touch it. If your fox friend comes back, I will do what I can to stop him."

Jack sighed. It was better than nothing.

"We'll need to prepare immediately," Arnica said.

"But Lirelin... She expects everyone to help look for the intruder."

"And we've figured out who it is," Arnica said. "Now the trail leads to something even more pressing, and we have to follow it. By going, we're helping to prevent this sort of thing from happening again."

"What about Olivarion?" Jack asked. "Don't you need to get the book back?"

"We'll have to deal with the dreadlord later," Arnica said, jumping to the floor. "Next to a witch, a cat mob is nothing."

BY NOON, the two were completely packed and ready to go. Miriel had tossed a single spare dress and several books in her bag, then thought better of it once she picked it up. She reluctantly put a few books back on the shelves and sighed. "If only storage magic wasn't so draining," she said. "The problem is you have to maintain it. Before you know it, you're completely exhausted and can barely manage a simple light." She gathered her stones and placed them in a small blue pouch, then put that in the bag as well.

Arnica had left the room to scout their path, but she returned now and shut the door softly behind her. "We have a clear road for the moment, but it won't last long. We'll need to go quickly."

"I'm sorry about this," Miriel said, gently lifting Jack. ."We need to hide you until we're out of the city." She stuffed him in her bag and secured the top, plunging him into darkness, except for the pinpricks of light that shone through the fabric. "Be quiet, now," she said.

He felt her moving, but soon his only concern was avoiding bumping the books. The edges dug into his side and other uncomfortable places, and the stones clicked together and made for an uncomfortable pillow if he happened to rest against them. He struggled to pull the dress out from beneath the pile, but it was stuck fast, and Miriel soon patted him and said, "Still." He obeyed and resigned himself to an unpleasant trip.

Time dragged on. When he saw pinpricks of sunlight shining through the tiny holes, he sighed in relief. At least they had managed to make it outside the castle. Now they just had to get out of the city and he could be free of the bag.

They hadn't gone far when Miriel suddenly stopped, jostling him roughly, and Arnica hissed.

"Good evening, mage," a voice said.

He'd heard that voice before, but where?

"What do you want, fox?" Arnica asked.

A chuckle. "The scarecrow, of course."

It wasn't Slade, that was for sure. Another fox...?

Of course. Nadya, the one from the shelter. It had to be.

"What scarecrow?" Miriel asked.

"Don't play dumb. We both know you've got him stowed away in that bag of yours. Now, hand him over and we can all be on our way."

"What's your interest in him?" Arnica asked.

"That's my business. Are you going to cooperate, or shall I have to use force?"

Miriel shifted the bag and Jack fell over. A loud *bang!* filled the air and Miriel shifted again, then ran. Jack tried to lie as flat as possible, but he rolled back and forth, hitting into her books. More small explosions sounded all around him. Something hit the bag and he fell, landing on the ground on top of the books, an edge ramming into his back. He turned over and crept to the opening, lifting it just a little to peek out. Miriel stood in front of him, the fox a few feet away. He started to crawl out, hoping he could escape before either noticed him, but Arnica pounced on him from behind.

"Where do you think you're going?" she hissed.

Nadya sent a whirlwind of dirt and leaves at the mage, knocking her off her feet and into the wall of a building. Miriel cried out and Arnica ran over to her, abandoning Jack. He scrambled out of the bag and ran down an alley, but he'd only gone a few feet when something heavy knocked him down from behind.

"Come along, little one," Nadya crooned, picking him up by the scruff of his neck. She looked back at the mage and cat and Jack saw Miriel begin to rise. Then the air popped and fizzled and the alley disappeared.

8

BARGAINING CHIP

Gray. Gray all around, above, below, side to side. He and the fox flew at dizzying speeds through the gray, but there was no way to tell where they were or where they were going. Nadya held him tightly, and they moved so quickly he couldn't move his mouth to ask a single question. Then, just as quickly, there was another *pop!* and the world returned, color and sound rushing back all at once. They were still within the city, or within *a* city, but Miriel and Arnica were nowhere to be seen.

She set him down and said, "Catch your breath. Travel like that can make you sick if you're not used to it."

He swayed a moment, then plopped down on the ground and lay back, watching the distant clouds pass slowly by. Everything spun, but lying down helped. He heard her moving about, but he didn't have the strength to turn his head, or do anything except lie there.

His mind raced through all the reasons she could possibly want him, but only one made any sense: he was a bargaining chip. She would trade him, either to Slade or Olivarion, or possibly the mages. He thought and thought, searching for any way to escape, but nothing came to mind. With her magic, he wouldn't get far.

After another moment, she nudged him. "Up now. We have people to see."

He rose to a sitting position, but the world didn't tilt quite so much, so he stood to his feet and looked around. They stood in a courtyard, a fountain splashing a few feet away. Small pots of shrubs and flowers sat scattered about, and a few lounging chairs rested under awnings that lined the buildings. No humans in sight.

"You can enjoy the scenery later. Walk. Now."

She nodded her head in the direction of a side alley, so he sighed and went ahead of her. "I'm not of any value," he said. "Don't waste your time. Let me go."

"I'll be the judge of that," she said. "That trickster will want you, no doubt, and the dreadlord. And your mage friends, I'm sure. But they'll have to pay a steep price to get you back."

"Why?" he asked. "Why go to all this trouble?"

"A girl's gotta make a living," she said. "I can't get by on my good looks alone."

Jack said no more. She led him through a labyrinth of alleys, moving ever deeper into the city until the buildings clustered together, hiding the way back. Even if he somehow escaped, he had no idea which way to go.

Nadya spoke a word that slipped across his mind before he could grasp what it was, and he felt the tingly sensation of magic around him. At the next turn, a small group of humans stood speaking together, and there were more further on, but not one so much as glanced their way. He stopped at the mouth of the alley, but Nadya nudged his back.

"They can't see or hear you. Walk."

He did, peering at the humans nervously as he passed them. Dogs and cats lounged in windowsills and on porches, but they didn't acknowledge the pair, either. Jack mused that their initial entry to the city would've been much easier if Slade had known such magic. Unless the fox preferred to conserve his power, or hide his abilities. It was impossible to tell with him.

"How did you and Slade meet?" he asked.

"Slade? Is that what he's calling himself now? Better than some of his past choices, I suppose. You could say we're old friends."

"What does that mean?"

"We've done a few jobs together. Had a fling for a bit. We're both too headstrong for anything lasting. More often than not, lately, we've been on opposite sides of the fence, so to speak. Go up the stairs to your right. We've arrived."

Jack looked at the building she indicated, a structure of dark gray wood two stories high. A couple of creaky steps led to the door, where Nadya spoke another magical word. The door creaked open obediently to a surprisingly bright entrance hall. They entered and the fox shut the door behind them. Wooden floors and walls greeted them, and a bright glow permeated the air. It seemed that a shaft of sunlight lit every room, reaching spots it shouldn't have been able to touch. No sconces lined the walls, which left magic as the only explanation.

The hall continued straight ahead, a stairway on the right wall, and a sitting room to the right of that. Portraits of serious-looking people decorated the walls beside paintings of forests, rivers, and mountains. A large oval mirror perched on the left wall above a small square table with a vase of yellow flowers atop it. Nadya nudged him down the hall, preventing him from exploring. Further down, another door stood open, this one leading back outside. Jack entered the private garden, taking in everything in an instant: a shady tree, flowers climbing the walls, a stone birdbath, a wooden bench, and at least a dozen cats.

"Here's the one I told you about," Nadya said as the cats looked at them.

"He's a scrawny thing," one said, a sleek black female standing near the tree.

"His size wasn't part of the deal," Nadya responded. "You can trade him to whomever you please. My part's done."

"Of course. Clendon will have your payment on the way out."

The fox slightly dipped her head, winked at Jack, then retreated back into the house.

Jack looked back at the gathering of cats, wondering if they would take him to Olivarion next. The leader studied him with narrowed eyes, as if she hadn't quite made up her mind about him. The others waited in silence.

"What can you do?" she finally asked.

"You mean magic?" Jack asked. "Nothing. I'm just a scarecrow."

"Yet several powerful persons in this city would pay highly for you. So I ask you again: what can you do?"

Jack swallowed, not liking the tone her voice had taken. "I don't lie," he said. "I can do no magic. I am indebted to the fox Slade, and Olivarion had half a mind to trade me to the mages. The mages I've met want to use me for their own purposes. Are you going to give me to Olivarion?"

The cat laughed. "Give? No. If he wants you, he'll pay for you. Though perhaps it would be better to take you straight to the mages. Their pockets are deep."

"Who are you?" Jack asked. If she wasn't with Olivarion, did that mean she was another dreadlord?

"I'm called Sitara. Tell me of this mission for Olivarion. The mages had a bit of excitement overnight, I'm told."

Jack glanced at the other cats present, but none seemed too interested in him. Not like the guards Olivarion kept. He took a seat on the ground, eliciting a smile from Sitara.

He told her of the fire-tamer Slade wanted, and the book Olivarion had sent them after.

"What is he planning?" she wondered aloud. "He must have some goal in mind. He wouldn't go to all this trouble just to stick these items in a chest."

"I wouldn't know," Jack said. "What are you going to do with me?"

Sitara smiled. "I haven't decided yet. Come," she said, rising, "there's no need for imprisonment or chains. You are a guest. Let's have some entertainment."

The other cats rose as well, but they waited for him to follow their leader before moving. She went back inside, down the hallway, and up the stairs. Jack climbed up behind her, leaving the others on the ground floor. She entered a room at the end of another short hallway. Jack stopped in the doorway, impressed by the sight: a long table sat in the middle of the room, covered in so many books, test tubes, taxidermy animals, and potted plants that the table top couldn't even be seen. Shelves stuffed with more books and instruments lined the walls, and more potted plants covered most of the wooden floor. Large windows covered the wall directly across from the door, overlooking the garden. A single chair sat next to the table.

"Like it, do you?" Sitara said.

Jack shook himself and stepped further inside. "I've never seen anything like it. Is it yours?"

"It belongs to a mage friend of mine. She has quarters at the Guild as well, so I'm free to use it when she's away. You should see the workrooms they have there."

"You're connected to the Guild? Then why—"

"I said I have a friend in the Guild, not that we were partners. What I do in pursuit of my own interests is my affair alone."

"I see. Just what are your interests? What do you hope to gain out of all of this?"

She jumped onto the chair and then onto the table, walking gingerly between the items. Her gaze darted back and forth, searching. "I aim to replace Olivarion," she said.

"That's an ambitious goal. Then you can do magic, too?"

"I can," she said. "Though, word of advice: don't go around asking if someone can do magic. Not everyone wants to reveal their secrets."

"I'll remember that. But you should know Olivarion is pretty powerful. I've seen some of the things he can do."

"I have patience," she said. "All it takes is time and perseverance." She found whatever she was looking for and jumped back to the chair, then to the floor. In her mouth was a silver pouch, which she dropped in front of him. Its contents clicked together on impact. "Open it," she said. "I'm going to demonstrate a bit of *my* magic." Jack dumped the contents on the floor. Several stones fell out, similar to Miriel's, only these were purple, blue, silver, and a single black. "Stand back," Sitara said.

Jack obeyed and she crouched over the stones, reading their hidden message. She studied them for a long while, giving no indication of how long it would take. Finally, Jack wandered over to one of the shelves, examining the various objects upon them. A few jars of some mysterious white floating object sat tucked away in different spots, blending in to their chaotic surroundings. If he didn't know any better, he would guess they were organs. He shook his head. Most likely they *were* organs. He was in a mage's workroom, after all.

"Hmm. Interesting," Sitara said.

"What is it?"

"Seems there's more to your story than you let on." She looked up at him with a piercing gaze. "Care to share?"

"Not really," he said. "It doesn't change the fact that I have no magic or abilities. I'm little use to you except in trade, and I still question that."

"Yet the stones tell me you were traveling with another companion. A bird? And you were seeking someone."

"It's true," he admitted. "All of it. But it doesn't change anything. I can't help her while I'm here."

"Help her how? Indulge me, please. It's curiosity, you know."

He sighed. He didn't see how Evelyn had anything to do with Sitara's goals, so perhaps it would be fine to reveal a little bit.

"She's under a curse. We were seeking a way to break it when we were separated."

"But the stones say you left of your own free will."

"I did. Sort of. My other companion, the fox, gave me no choice. I was in his debt."

"Then you tried to run away to help her again."

He nodded. "Yes. That's the long and short of it. I'd much rather be on my way back to her, but I keep finding myself being captured by one faction or another."

Sitara laughed. "Such is luck sometimes." She gathered the stones and scooped them back into the pouch. Jack felt more despondent than he had at any point in his journey thus far. It seemed he would never reach Evelyn again, no matter how hard he tried.

"Well," Sitara said, standing. "Now that—"

The house shook and a small explosion echoed from the bottom floor.

Sitara dashed to the door, leaving the pouch on the floor. "Stay here," she said over her shoulder. The door closed behind her, the lock clicking into place. Another explosion shook the building and Jack retreated to the far corner of the room, near the window. There was distant shouting, wounded cries, and the *thumping* sound of battle magic being thrown back and forth. It went on for several minutes before stopping suddenly, plunging the house into silence. Jack waited, listening for any sound of movement, any cry for help, but he heard nothing.

The urge to creep down and see how things stood fought with his desire to find a way to climb out the window and escape. The window seemed the better option, and he was just about to reach for the latch when he heard the sound of footsteps on the stairs. He froze, his instincts telling him to hide, run, get away, do anything but stand there and wait for the person to reach him. But he couldn't force his feet to move. The footsteps came closer and then the lock clicked and the door opened. Jack backed up against the wall, expecting to be spirited off once more to some other mage.

Slade entered the room and looked around, spotting him a

moment later. "There you are," he said. "I've had a devil of a time tracking you down. Never thought a scarecrow could get into so much trouble in a city. Let's be off. Olivarion is waiting."

Jack stood still a moment longer, not quite believing this turn of events. Sitara's words echoed in his mind. *Such is luck sometimes.* Resigning himself to his fate, he crossed the room and followed Slade out the door.

Pictures, vases, and broken furniture littered the house, the bottom floor a ruinous mess. Cats lay sprawled everywhere, all unconscious.

"They're not dead," Slade said, reading the worry on his face. "I'm not a killer," he added.

"I didn't say you were."

"You thought it." Slade spoke a word like Nadya had and a tingle crept up Jack's arms. Then they stood outside once more, the humans and other animals still mingling about. As before, none acknowledged them, though whether that was Slade's doing or some lingering magic of Nadya's, Jack wasn't sure. He guessed the former. Perhaps, given the circumstances, the fox was willing to expend more magic. The brief magical battle had been completely contained and unnoticed. "How did you get lost in the first place?" Slade asked. "I warned you to keep up."

"I just got lost," Jack said, not knowing what else to say. He couldn't tell the fox he'd purposely run away.

"I see. And what did Sitara want with you?"

"She planned to trade me. To whom, she hadn't yet decided."

"And you didn't reveal any of our secrets?"

"No," Jack said automatically, not even pausing to consider what the fox might mean by 'our secrets.'

Slade nodded and they continued on, leaving the alley and returning to the labyrinth of the inner city.

"Nadya did this...fast travel thing. We were in one place, and then we were in some gray place, and then we were here. Can you do that, too?"

Slade grabbed him, pulling him into the shadow of a stack of crates, and whispered, "When did you see her? What did you say? Speak!"

"Sh-she found me," Jack said. "Then she did some sort of magic and we traveled, just like I said. Then she brought me to Sitara. We didn't talk much, I promise."

The fox studied him a moment, likely deciding whether or not to believe him. Jack was just glad he couldn't read minds. And he wasn't about to bring up the situation with Miriel and Arnica. Finally, Slade released him and they continued on their way.

"To answer your question, it's none of your business. Not everyone likes to flash their magic around, revealing their abilities. Plus, it expends energy. So if I did have such magic, I would have two good reasons for not using it."

"Understood," Jack said. He asked no more questions on the journey, afraid he would inadvertently reveal more than he wished. As soon as they were clear of the inner city, Slade spoke another word and the tingle vanished.

"We're no longer hidden by magic. It's back to the shadows for us."

Jack sighed but didn't complain. If he were a mage, he supposed he would want to conserve power as well, but it was terribly inconvenient. Through the maze they went, dashing and darting in and out of hiding places, avoiding the gaze of humans and the attention of other animals. A few times, Slade started to enter an alley only to dash off in another direction. A glance back revealed a human, or a dog, or sometimes a cat. Slade took no chances. Jack didn't recognize anything, which reinforced his despair of ever escaping and finding his way on his own. Maybe once they were clear of the city, he could figure out how to get back to Evelyn.

"We're nearly there," Slade finally whispered. "Remember, best behavior."

They turned another corner and Jack spotted the dreadlord in the distance. He frowned, hardened his nerve, and followed Slade down the alley.

❧ 9 ❧

A FAIR TRADE

The guards ushered them into Olivarion's presence without affording them even a moment to announce themselves. The dreadlord sat exactly where he'd been when they'd last seen him, only he appeared more content with himself, as though he'd just enjoyed a deep sleep and a large breakfast. Slade's stomach rumbled in response, echoing in the alley.

"Do you have the book?" Olivarion asked.

His gang filled every available sitting space, all eyes on the pair.

Slade twitched his nose and a blue leather-bound volume appeared in the air between them. It floated to the dreadlord, coming to rest on a box beside him. Olivarion opened it and leafed through a few pages, his smile widening.

"Excellent," he said. "You have proven yourself trustworthy. I will lend you the fire-tamer for your next task. With one added condition: two of my guards will travel with you. If at any time you attempt to break our deal in any way, not only are they trained fighters who will not hesitate to attack you, but they will immediately send word back to me so that on the chance you manage to escape, I can send reinforcements. I shall also put a tracking spell on you so you can be found no matter where you go. Best to be prepared for all possibilities, eh?"

"Indeed," Slade agreed.

"If you are successful and return the storm-eater to me, then the fire-tamer is yours. Do we have a deal?"

Slade nodded. "I am amenable to these requests. If there is nothing further, shall we start right away?"

"Yes," Olivarion agreed. "You may go. But the fire-tamer shall remain with my guard. If you need to make use of it, very well, but it shall not leave their sight. Understood?"

"Perfectly."

"You have until one week from today to return with my artifact. If you do not, I will consider you in contempt of our agreement and our contract void."

The guards ushered them away, the eyes of the other cats following them to the mouth of the alley.

"I thought that went fairly well," Slade commented when they neared the bustling street once more. "Believe me, it could have gone much worse."

"If you say so," Jack answered. "Just where is this super powerful item you spoke of? Is it another storm-eater? And why are you willing to give it up?"

"It's a short way south of here. I don't anticipate the journey will take more than a couple of days. We'll make the switch and be back well within the time limit."

"This way," one of the cats said, ushering them into an open grate. "This will make travel much faster."

Jack scowled at the opening, but he didn't see that he had much choice. He had no doubt that Slade would leave him there in a heartbeat if he refused, immobile and useless. Down they descended, onto a little shelf of stone just below the opening. A narrow walkway extended to either side, disappearing into the darkness. Straight ahead was a drop off that ended in a stream of foul-smelling liquid.

"Mind if I make a little light?" Slade asked. A ball of yellow light appeared before either cat could answer. They made no protest, so the party continued, following one of the pathways further into the tunnel.

Jack walked as carefully as he could, having no wish to slip and fall into the nastiness below. They zigged and zagged for several minutes, occasionally passing more grates overhead. Finally, the cats stopped them below another grate, one scampering up to peer out before motioning them to follow.

"Quickly," he said.

They emerged into the daylight, just behind a stack of boxes. A hole leading outside the city sat a few feet away, and in another minute they were through and back outside.

"We'll circle around a bit," Slade said, heading south of the city so as to avoid the road. They plodded along in silence, still a bit uncomfortable with the new additions to their group. Or at least, that's how Jack felt. Once they had gone far enough to cross the road and disappear into the forest on the other side, Jack asked the cats their names.

"Elwin," one said.

"Dariel," said the other.

"Jack," the scarecrow said.

"And I'm the princess of Alibeth. Can we please continue?" Slade said.

"That's Slade," Jack offered. "You get used to him."

"I need something to eat," Slade announced. "I'll be half a moment."

He disappeared into the trees, leaving Jack alone with the two cats. With nothing better to do, he sat on the ground and rested his head on one hand. "I don't really want to be here, either," he told the felines. "I was traveling with a friend, and would much rather be with her. It's just that I owe Slade, and he won't let me go until my debt's paid."

"Why don't you leave now?" Elwin asked.

"Wouldn't that be breach of contract?" Jack asked. "With Olivarion, I mean?"

"As I recall, the deal was made with the fox. So long as he stays within the contract, it is valid. But you are free to come and go as you choose."

Once more Jack's thoughts argued amongst themselves. His instincts told him to flee, to put as much distance as he could between himself and the fox. He would find Evelyn, beg her forgiveness, and then help her find a way to become human once more. Then again, what was the point? Slade had found him once already, and it was likely he would do so again. But the thought of Evelyn facing the wolves all alone gnawed at his mind.

Slade returned and the moment passed. Jack lagged behind the others, barely able to force himself to take another step. He felt more wretched than he ever had. Nothing he had done had turned out quite like he'd intended. If it weren't for Slade constantly turning around to make sure he was still following, Jack would've seriously considered simply stopping and refusing to move another step.

"Keep up, now," Slade called back to him.

No, he'd have to come up with a better plan that that. The fox was too watchful. Not for the last time, he thought of his post back in his field, miles and miles away now. If he could get back to that village, he thought he could live a long and happy existence merely sitting and watching the clouds move across the sky. Traveling was not his favorite pastime. At least, not in the current company, and not to the destinations they had so far set. Perhaps a nice visit to a coastal village? He couldn't remember ever having seen the ocean.

Unbidden, he began to daydream once more of the cottage of his vision. The water wheel turned slowly, and the water flowed noisily down a rock-filled stream, disappearing into the distance. A woman with long brown hair appeared in the doorway, waving to him. He tried to wave back only to find his arms tied to his side, preventing even the slightest budge. He was seated on a chair, moving away from the woman—was he on a wagon?—and she grew smaller and smaller as he was taken down the hill and around a corner. He cried out in the daydream, but he couldn't hear his own words.

"Are you all right?" Dariel asked.

"I'm fine," he answered. "Why?"

"You cried out as though you were in pain," Elwin answered. "Did you step on a sharp rock or something?"

"Oh, sorry. I wasn't paying attention. Won't happen again."

Slade watched him with narrowed eyes, keeping his thoughts to himself. The land rose again and Jack made an effort to keep up with the group. Perhaps if he kept Slade happy, the fox would grant him his freedom sooner, and then he could be on his way to Evelyn. He couldn't help her by trudging behind and daydreaming.

He didn't think much of the dream, either. There was no telling what it meant, and what was the use in speculation? Perhaps it was some sort of memory, but what could he do about it? Nothing. If it was in fact the past, it was done and over anyway and best left where it was.

Slade stopped again only when the sun began to sink. "This is as good a place as any," he said. "I'd like to start again first thing in the morning."

Jack sat down beside a tree trunk while the others searched for food. He thought of the crows who used to come visit him and wondered what they thought of his absence. They had not witnessed the spell that had allowed him to move, nor had he seen them after. Very likely they thought some human had pulled him down and done away with him. They wouldn't know what to think if they could see him walking around, conversing with dreadlords and bird gods and very likely walking into yet another mess.

When the cats returned, Jack decided to talk with them further. After all, he had nothing better to do, and they would be traveling together for a while.

"What made you join Olivarion?" he asked. "Is he a good leader?"

"Everyone serves Olivarion," Dariel said. "We were recruited when we were just kittens. The strongest and bravest are chosen to be part of his guard. The rest are given other jobs within the community based on skill. He takes care of us, which is more than can be said for some of the past rulers we've heard of."

"So you enjoy your life as his guard?"

"Of course," Elwin answered. "He's not cruel by nature, though he can be stern and cold. I would serve him even if I hadn't been raised in his service."

"Same here," Dariel said.

As the darkness deepened, the wind blew stronger than ever, and they huddled close together for warmth as they settled in for the night. Jack didn't remember dreaming.

THE TRAVELED for almost a whole day before Slade finally said, "It's just ahead! We'll need to come up with some sort of plan, and I'll need to use the fire-tamer now."

"You mean you don't have a plan yet?" Jack asked.

"Somewhat. A general idea, anyway. Now, come closer, please. And the fire-tamer, if you will?" he asked the cats.

Jack moved closer and Elwin produced a small white item, hidden the gods knew where in the folds of his fur. Slade picked it up and held it aloft: a mouse skull.

"Perfect!" he cried. "Now, stand very still, Jack. This will only take a moment."

Jack did as he was told, trying to limit even his breathing. Slade mumbled to himself, bringing the skull down in a wide arc around Jack. His voice grew louder as the arc circled back around, the words in no tongue Jack had heard, finally ending in a shout as the circle was completed.

Jack felt himself stretch and grow until he stood several feet higher than the fox and cats.

"There," Slade said. "What do you think?"

"Impressive," Dariel said.

"Creative," Elwin offered.

Jack looked down at himself, his body transformed into something large, brown, and furry. "What did you do?" he asked.

"I cast a temporary transformation spell on you. You are now a young bear, just past the cub stage. Old enough to fight and be useful, but not so big as to be uncontrollable."

"Oh. And this will help us how?"

"Just wait and see. Come along now. I need to scout to figure out just the right place to make our appearance."

Elwin cleared his throat.

"Oh, how silly of me," Slade said, handing the skull back. "Off we go!"

He moved quickly through the trees, stopping often to peer around a trunk or bush. The others did the same. Voices drifted on the air, deep, growly voices that snarled and snapped at one another. They reminded him of something, but he couldn't quite put his finger on it.

"This way," Slade whispered, dashing off to the east.

The voices grew louder and louder until suddenly Jack remembered.

"The wolves!" he said.

"Shh!" Slade called back.

"You're going after the storm-eater the wolves have? The same one the owl wanted Evelyn to steal for her?"

"Keep your voice down!"

But it was too late. They had been heard, or spotted, for the voices were moving in their direction.

"Hello, there!" Slade called. "Get close to me now!" he whispered back at them. "Do exactly as I say!"

They did as commanded and stopped next to Slade, who was sitting and waiting on the advancing wolves. They didn't have to wait long. Dozens soon appeared from between the trees, all gray and white, fangs bared. They formed a tight circle around the group, leaving only a small space that was soon filled by a large gray wolf approaching alone. His fur held more white hair than the rest of the pack, especially around his snout, and he walked as though unafraid of anything.

"Hail Brusius," Slade said. "I have returned."

"So I see," the large wolf answered. "Are you ready to fulfill your part of the bargain?"

"I am," Slade answered. "Although, I would like to suggest a substitute. I'm sure you haven't failed to notice the strong young bear I've brought along."

Brusius turned his eyes to Jack, studying him in silence. "You propose the bear take your place?" the wolf asked.

"I do," Slade said with a nod.

"And your cat companions? What of them?"

"They are chance companions, nothing more. We are on our way back to Alibeth. I insisted on a stop to fulfill my bargain with you."

"Can he do magic?" Brusius asked.

"No, but as I'm sure you can see, he can more than make up for that with strength."

Brusius flicked his head at Jack and two wolves left the circle to inspect him. They sniffed and prodded, and Jack wondered just how long the transformation would hold. If Slade's trick were discovered, the large wolf would not be happy. But then, why should he go along with it? He didn't want to go with the wolves. He opened his mouth to reveal the ruse when Slade whispered, "Do this, and your debt is fulfilled."

Jack scowled at the ground. Of all the lousy schemes! If his position with the fox had ever been in question, it was no longer. A pawn to be bartered off whenever convenient, that's all he was. He vowed that he would never fall into the debt of another creature, if he could help it. The price was simply too high.

The wolves completed their inspection and nodded at their leader.

"He is acceptable," Brusius said. "We will take him on trial. If he performs to our satisfaction, our bargain is complete. If not, well, you will have to fulfill it yourself. Agreed?"

"Completely," Slade said.

"Be off, then. You are going to Alibeth, you say? I shall send a messenger in three days' time. You shall know then if your young bear has performed to our liking or not."

Brusius turned, walking away from the circle. The wolves ushered Jack to follow them, leaving Slade and the cats behind. He turned to catch a last glimpse of them, but the wolves closed in, blocking his view. Then they prodded him from behind and he nearly fell, so he kept his eyes forward and continued walking. He wondered again how long the spell would last, and what the wolves would do to him when it failed.

BEAR STRENGTH

The wolves took him to a large clearing where they had set up camp. A few rocky overhangs provided shelter from the weather, but these were reserved for the more important among them, generals and captains and the like.

Jack hadn't realized there were so many wolves in the world, and he'd still only seen one side of the war. Many looked his way as he passed, but none spoke. They took him to the far side of the camp where a small cave opened into the rock. Jack entered, brought up short a few feet inside by a sheer rock wall that prevented further movement. Pale light illuminated the space enough that he could see the three walls, and that no other way out existed. That left only the entrance, which three wolves guarded.

"You will stay here," one said. "We will bring you food and allow you out to do your business. Otherwise, you will not leave unless called for."

"Don't worry," another said. "That won't be long."

Two of the wolves turned away from him, watching for anyone approaching the cave. The third stood facing him, silently noting every movement in case he decided to attempt an escape.

Jack sat down and considered his options. He had all the time in the world to think now, so he might as well make use of it. Even if the wolves decided he was worthless, he no longer owed anything to Slade. The fox would have to agree with that, since he hadn't put conditions on the deal. He'd simply said, *go with them and your debt is fulfilled.* So, one less thing to worry about. The next and more pressing issue was how long exactly the spell would last. If it suddenly wore off in front of all the wolves, there was no telling what they would do. Go into a fit of rage at the deceit? Would they take it out on him and tear him apart? Or if it happened here in his prison, would the guards try to keep it quiet? They would let Brusius know, no doubt, but would the chief then destroy him for good measure?

The best thing would be to somehow get away so that when that moment came, they didn't connect the scarecrow to the bear. Then he could leave unmolested, for they would simply overlook him.

Next was the issue of finding Evelyn. That thought brought him up short. She had been heading straight for the wolves when last he'd seen her. Had she already come and gone? Was she captured, or dead, or—

The not knowing was enough to drive him mad. He would simply have to look for her when they allowed him out, and keep his ears open.

THE WOLVES LET him out twice that day. He pretended to be a normal bear, hiding behind a bush to do his "business," then returned to his little cave. They also brought him food, which was a bit more difficult to fake. Although he was temporarily a bear, he suspected it was only his outer appearance that had changed, for he still felt no need for food. He took only the smallest bites of the berries and fish, chewing and pretending to swallow and carefully spitting them out when the wolf guarding him chanced to look away for a second, which wasn't often. Finally, Jack simply rolled over with his back facing the exit so that he didn't have to feel their eyes quite so much. He stayed that way until the afternoon, when Brusius finally called for him.

"Come along," the wolves said. "You've been summoned."

They took him from the cave and ushered him back to the main clearing, where several wolves fought. No, trained. Their attacks stopped short of delivering actual wounds. Other wolves watched, sometimes barking orders or commenting on their strategy or form. Brusius sat atop a rocky overhang looking down at the training ground. He nodded when Jack was brought forward.

"Now it's your turn to show your skill," he said. "You will join them after the next break. Are three wolves too many for you to handle, or do you prefer more?"

Jack swallowed nervously. "Three is enough."

Brusius nodded in response. "I, too, was exposed to war at a young age. Fighting is all I have ever known, but I understand your fear. I remember all too well the sleepless and painful nights of my early years. But those nights will make you stronger, I promise you. And when you are as old as I am, you will look back and be grateful."

The fighters below ended their session and the wolves prodded Jack to descend to the field.

"Good luck," Brusius called after him.

They placed Jack in the middle of the clearing, three young wolves forming a circle around him. The others kept back in a wider circle, all eyes watching. If he were capable of sweating, it would've dripped from his brow in streams. He watched the wolves nervously, turning slowly to be sure they hadn't moved in to attack.

Then, like a storm breaking, the three leaped at once. Jack dove between their legs, which sent one flying into the air. The others turned quickly to attack again and he instinctively swiped to keep them back. They snarled and snapped, pushing him from all sides so that he barely had a moment to think. He cried back at them, in terror and frustration, and also because he hoped it would intimidate them, at least for a moment. How long they continued in that way, he didn't know, but he knew he couldn't keep it up for long. His legs weren't even completely used to walking long distances yet, let alone ready to support him through a battle.

Just as as his legs buckled, ready to collapse, the wolves backed off. On the rocky ledge, Brusius stared down at him, his eyes narrowed. The three guards approached again and ushered him away, back to his cave.

"You'll get used to it," one said. "And your skills will improve. Those natural instincts will kick in, and then it will all be easy. Just give it some time."

Jack didn't answer. All he wanted was a nice long rest and for there to be no wolves when he woke up so that he could be on his way. He hoped he would dream of the cottage and the woman again, but only darkness awaited him.

THE NEXT DAY proved to be a near exact repeat of the previous day. They took him to the clearing and forced him to defend himself against three young wolves. Then, just to make it more interesting, they added a fourth. Whatever magic Slade had done, it held up, for Jack still appeared to be a bear, and his counterattacks and defenses held all the strength of that species. Before they let him go for the day, they added a fifth wolf into the fight. That nearly broke him, but Brusius stopped the skirmish before it went too far.

He nodded at Jack and the guards prodded him up the path to their leader. "You will join the real battle now," the great wolf told Jack. "If you try to escape, every wolf on the field will follow you, not only those on our side. Our enemy is even more merciless, and will kill you just for the sport of it. Fight well and you will be rewarded. I'm sure you would like better sleeping arrangements and more freedom, hmm?"

"Yes," Jack admitted.

"Now is your chance to earn it. You'll leave with the troops at sundown under the command of Captain Peras. I have high hopes for you."

The guards took him back to his cave, back to the hours of waiting. Panic started to set it. It was one thing to defend himself against three wolves who weren't really trying to hurt him. It was quite another to be surrounded by wolves who were all intent on ripping his throat out. How would he be able to tell which side was which? What if he attacked the wrong side and they thought he was a traitor, and then both sides tried to kill him? There were so many things that could go wrong, not least of which was the chance that the spell would fade amidst the heat of battle. And he still hadn't heard even a whisper of Evelyn.

When they finally brought him out to transport him to the battlefield, he was more dejected than ever. His shoulders drooped and his feet dragged on the ground, and he couldn't bring himself to even look at his guards. They carried him along all the same, reluctant or not. They had a war to fight.

Jack realized that he didn't even know what all the fighting was about. He could very well be walking to his death, and he wouldn't even know why he was dying. This struck him as quite funny and he began to laugh, long and loud, despite the looks the wolves gave him. Let them think he was a hysterical bear. It made no difference to him.

They placed him at the end of a battalion of wolves three columns thick, all facing a lone black wolf. His guards stood on either side of him, with one behind. Without a word, the black wolf turned and walked away from the clearing, the battalion following obediently. Jack lumbered along, his laughter subsiding to the occasional chuckle now and again. Who would have imagined he'd be disguised as a bear on his way to a wolf battle? The crows would've talked about it for months.

Uphill and downhill they went, across streams and paths, until he heard wolf voices ahead in the distance. Bile rose in his gut and threatened to spill out of his mouth, but he managed to keep it in check. He determined he would get through it, no matter what he had to do.

"Halt!" the black wolf commanded, its voice that of a female. She turned to face them. "I understand not all of you came willingly, and even those of you who did may be scared out of your minds right now. I have been there, and I know the fear that eats at you. But you must fight it! Ignore the instinct that tells you to flee, and forget your home and loved ones. They are a weakness here. To survive, you must fight with your entire being. I cannot promise that you will all live to see home again, but I can promise that those who lose their nerve will be struck down with no mercy. Be brave, fight well, and die gloriously."

She glanced at Jack, only for a moment, but it was enough for him to harden his resolve and set his eyes firmly on the path before them. He would not die here.

"Forward!" the captain yelled, leading the charge through the trees. Many wolves howled in response, all surging forward with fangs bared. Jack howled with them, plunging through the underbrush and right into the thick of the fighting. There must've been hundreds of wolves, fighting in every direction he turned, all gray and brown and black and white. Jack followed the wolf directly in front of him, looking for any indicator of which side was which. But the wolf attacked another that was similar in build and coloring, and there didn't seem to be any special markings on it. Jack swung at the creature, telling himself it was him or it, and the wolf staggered sideways from the blow. Another attacked him from behind, its fangs sinking into his arm. He swung his arm about, throwing the wolf into a tree, where it fell to the ground and whimpered. All semblance of control vanished. Wolves attacked from every side, and he spent more time defending than worrying about injuring the right group.

A lifetime passed on the battlefield, where all that existed was "attack" and "defend." He almost believed he actually was a bear, and threw off attackers left and right. Wolves fell around him, both the enemy and his own battalion, though he still couldn't completely tell them apart. He thought he recognized one of his guards, but couldn't be sure. Captain Peras called her battalion to her from atop a small boulder, fending off attacks from below at the same time. Jack rushed to reach her side, his instincts screaming for him to obey and survive. He had almost reached her when a group of wolves attacked him from the side, knocking him to the ground and rolling him over. He rose and flung them all away with a few swipes of his paws. The remainder attacked again and he struck them down one by one until finally all lay wounded and still before him.

By that time Captain Peras had disappeared, and though he searched in all directions, he couldn't find her. Much of the fighting had stopped for the moment, and many eyes turned to him.

"The general will be pleased with this one," one wolf said. "We should take it prisoner and present it to him."

"Better to kill it now," another said. "Don't want it turning on us in our sleep."

They were all from the enemy side. He didn't know what had happened to the soldiers he'd been with, if they were all dead or if they'd left him behind.

"I won't turn on you," he said. "You can take me willingly. But I will not die today."

"You'd turn on your comrades?" the first wolf asked.

"They are not my comrades; they are my captors. I want nothing more than to go on my way unhindered."

The wolves laughed.

"I'm afraid that won't be happening," the first said. "To the general with him."

The wolves circled him, daring him to attack. Resigned, he followed where they led.

THE CAMP APPEARED much like the first one, only it sat in a little dell a good distance away from the fighting. Jack could tell no difference between the wolves he'd left and the wolves that were now before him. Like the first time, all eyes turned to him, only most regarded him with clear suspicion.

They took him up a rock path on the far side of the dell, between large boulders and sparse trees. At the top, another boulder jutted out a short way over the dell. A white wolf sat alone, looking down at those gathered below.

His new captors shoved him to a kneeling position, then knelt beside him until the white wolf turned. "Rise and report," he said, his voice as deep as what a god's must be.

"We've captured one of the enemy," one of the guards said.

"Is that so?" The white wolf approached him, looking him up and down. "What do you have to say for yourself?" he asked.

"I am merely a captive in this war," Jack said. "I have no desire to be here, on either side."

"Yet you fought with all the ferocity of someone who has an interest in the outcome."

"I only fought to survive. It was my hope that my service would be enough to gain my freedom."

"Yet here you are, a captive once more." The wolf paced back to the edge and looked down again. "Will you fight for me as fiercely as you did my enemy?" he asked.

Jack looked at the wolves around him, knowing he had no choice in his answer.

"Yes," he said.

"Good. You can begin by helping with the cleanup. You are dismissed."

The wolves led him away again, back toward the battlefield.

"What is this war even about?" he dared to ask.

One wolf looked at him incredulously. "You really were a captive, weren't you? This is the war of the Succession, the battle to decide who will take the place of High Wolf."

"And the candidates? The great leaders, I take it?"

"You guessed right. The rightful heir is our commander, Ardel, but his younger brother Brusius challenged him. That's what started this whole mess."

"No more talking," another wolf called from ahead of them. "We're approaching the field, and you never know when they'll launch a surprise attack."

They all hushed obediently, walking as quietly as they could upon the leaves. The trees cleared and then they were back on the field, strewn with the bodies of the dead and wounded. The events of the day caught up with Jack and he had to stop and put his head to the ground, taking deep and slow breaths. Some of the wolves laughed at him, but they didn't force him to get up right away.

The faces of the wolves he'd attacked flashed before his eyes, but they'd changed. They were no longer snarling and snapping. They were pleading, begging him to spare them. Mercilessly, he'd struck them down, laughing as he did so, revealing himself for the monster he was. But no, he wasn't a monster, or even a bear. He was a scarecrow. He shouldn't even be here. He cursed Slade and the circumstances that had brought him to that moment. If he ever saw the fox again, he'd—

But no, that wasn't him, either. He wouldn't look for the fox, and if he ever came across him, he'd pretend he didn't know him. Yes, that was the best course of action.

"You all right?" one wolf asked.

Jack looked up and took one final deep breath.

"Yes," he said.

"Come along, then. We need all the help we can get."

Jack joined them, moving the bodies of the dead into a pile at the edge of the clearing and helping the wounded to the other side, where they would be escorted back to camp. The wounded of the enemy side were mercifully put to death, rather than taken as prisoners. Jack did his best to not look at their faces, for if he did, he feared he'd lose the last of his nerve and bolt then and there, and to hell with the consequences.

❧ II ❧

REUNITED

When they finally allowed him to return to camp, the sun was sinking low in the sky, though only a few hours had passed since he'd left for battle. It seemed like he'd been clearing the field for a lifetime.

Captain Peras's lifeless form had peered up at him from behind a boulder, her eyes staring at a world beyond his sight. He'd never thought the death of someone he'd met in passing would affect him so much, but he'd choked up as he rolled her out into the clearing with the rest. It could've been him, or Evelyn, or even Slade, the old devil.

Then they showed him to his bed for the night, which was a nest of pine needles beneath the overhanging branches of a tree. Better than a cave, at any rate. Only one wolf stood guard over him, but exhaustion enveloped him so completely that he responded only with groans and grunts when the wolf addressed him. He was already falling asleep.

They woke him the next day, the guard shaking him roughly. Once again he hadn't dreamed, at least not that he actually remembered. Then his guard spoke, banishing all other thoughts. "It's time to fight."

Jack groaned internally, but forced himself to get up. They

placed him with another battalion, much like the first one, and took him to another battlefield. Only birdsong and soft morning light greeted them, but the sounds of the enemy soon reached them through the trees. Their captain instructed them to hold their position as they waited for the other side to arrive.

When the opposing wolves finally appeared between the trees, their faces weren't twisted in snarls and grimaces, as Jack had expected. Instead, each wolf held a single white flower in its mouth. The captain set out to meet them, and the other wolves stopped as their own captain proceeded to the center of the clearing.

"It's a truce flower," the wolf next to him informed him. "It doesn't mean the war's over, but it allows a brief time for discussion, with neither side attacking."

"What do you think this is about?" Jack asked.

"Probably you," the wolf answered. "I'm sure Brusius wasn't happy to hear about your capture."

The two captains conversed for a few minutes, keeping their voices low, their faces betraying no emotion. Then they parted, each heading back to his respective company.

"There will be no bargaining," their captain said. "Prepare for battle!"

The wolves fell into a long formation, ushering Jack to the side. Then they charged and the wolves howled and thrust Jack once more into the thick of battle, only on the opposite side this time. Even after his experience clearing the field the previous day, his instinct to survive remained strong, propelling him forward to do what was necessary to survive. This time, however, the arrival of scouts cut the battle short. "Humans!" they cried. "Approaching on foot, barely a league away!"

The armies separated as though forced apart by a rushing river.

"Back to camp!" many cried, fleeing into the trees.

Jack began to follow, then realized it was a perfect opportunity to escape. He only had to flee in another direction, away from the humans and wolves alike.

"This way," a wolf called to him, pausing for him to follow.

Reluctantly, he followed, knowing he would regret it. *Fool,* he berated himself. *If you don't take action, you'll stay a captive for the rest of your life.*

In the camp, Ardel issued orders from his perch above the dell while the other wolves rushed to obey his commands. His guards guided Jack into a narrow fissure in the rock, just large enough for him to squeeze through. Further down, it widened into a small room about the size of a human shed. He sat down and waited for whatever would happen next.

"Who's there?" a voice said.

He froze, thinking his ears had deceived him, but a moment later it came again.

"Is someone here?"

There was no mistaking it. The voice was Evelyn's.

"Evelyn?" he said. "Is that you?"

"Jack? What are you doing here?"

"Getting myself into more trouble. Where are you?"

"Against the far wall. They've tied my legs up and I can't get them undone."

Jack walked carefully to the further side of the room until he found her. He could barely see her lying on the ground, a thread keeping her legs tied together.

"They caught me just as I started to fly off with the storm-eater," she said. "What about you?"

"It's a bit of a longer story. Can it wait until after we've gotten away?"

He focused on getting the knot undone, using his claws and teeth as gently as he could. A pull there, a twist here, and the ropes fell away. She fluttered a few feet into the air, landing near Jack.

"You have no idea how good this feels! They've had me trapped down here for four days."

"Let's be away quick," he said, heading back to the entrance.

"Surely you don't think I'm going with you?" she asked. "I appreciate what you've done for me, but I can't just forget that you left me to fend for myself. You chose that fox over me, and I'm still upset about that."

"We don't have time for this right now," he said. "The wolves could be back at any moment."

"We don't have time for anything. Like I said, I'm not going with you."

"Do you realize what I've gone through to get back to you? The only reason I went with Slade was so that I would be able to move. I've been trying ever since then to get back to you. I would've been helpless just stuck on the ground."

"The owl would've helped you."

"I didn't know that at the time, and anyway, how can you say that for sure? Very likely I'd be in her debt as well, and I'm quite through with being in anyone's debt, thank you! At least now I'm free to go where I will, no debts owed."

"Slade released you?"

"He traded me to the wolves. Like I said, it's a long story. Apparently he owed them. He made a bargain and they took me instead."

"Why were they willing to do that?"

"Well... You can't really tell in this light, but Slade put a spell on me. I don't look like a scarecrow at the moment."

"What are you, another wolf?"

"Just wait until we're out in the light, you'll see."

"I'm still upset, Jack."

"Look, I'm sorry, okay? I thought I was doing the right thing and it all fell apart on me. I watched every moment for a chance to sneak away and find you, but I always waited too long. The one time I did get away, I was captured pretty quickly and traded off from one party to another, just to end up once again with Slade. I'm here now, and I want to help."

"Prove it."

"You're a stubborn ass, you know that?" he said.

He sneaked back up to the opening and peered out. Evelyn flew up behind him, landing on his shoulder.

"You look like a scarecrow to me," she said.

He looked down at himself. She was right.

"It must've worn off. I looked like a bear, and I could fight like one, too. Good timing for it to go, I guess. Can you imagine what would happen if I changed during a battle?"

"You were in a battle?"

"Later," he said. "Looks like the coast is clear, for the moment. Come on!" he dashed over to a nearby bush, waving for her to follow. She did a moment later, looking around for the wolves.

"Where is everyone?" she whispered.

"They spotted some humans and everyone scattered. If we hurry, we can get away before they return."

"I'm not leaving without the storm-eater. I've come this far, and now is as good a chance as any."

"Do you even know where it is?"

"Yes, it's in a cranny up on the ledge, where the leader sits."

Looking around one more time, they crept up the little pathway leading to the ledge. But someone else arrived before them.

"Here it is," a voice said. "Just as I suspected." Jack peeked around a boulder and saw three human males, one holding something in his hand. "One storm-eater, as promised."

Jack knew that voice: Slade, that scheming devil. He must've used the fire-tamer to change their appearances.

"Let's go before they come back," one of the others said.

They turned to descend the path and Jack quickly hid behind the boulder, Evelyn close beside him. He put a finger to his lips and waited until they had passed by.

"That was Slade," he said. "He's in disguise, and he's got the artifact you need."

"Let's go after him, then! What are we waiting for?"

"He's got two guards with him, strong fighters. I don't think he'd willingly give it up, and they wouldn't let us leave with it anyway. Not alive, at least."

"What do we do, then? I need it to get Siobhan's help."

"I know. But... What if we went to the Guild instead? Perhaps they'd be willing to help us. Let's at least get away from this area first. I need to think for a bit."

"A pox on your thinking! Maybe the Guild can help me and maybe they can't. I don't have time to speculate about it. I'm going after them."

She flew off and Jack cursed, then followed. He kept a watch out for any of the wolves, but not one showed itself. Leaving the dell, he strode into the forest with every intention of yelling at Evelyn for being so stubborn. He didn't have to go far, for she had caught up with the group and flew back and forth overhead, diving at Slade.

"Stay back!" he yelled. "I'm giving you fair warning. Do *not* make me harm you."

"You're a liar and a cheat!" she yelled hysterically. "You know I need it! Don't you ever think of anyone but yourself?"

"No," he responded.

The others swiped at her, and one nearly managed to knock her out of the air. Slade finally had enough and sent a blast of air her way, knocking her into a tree. She hit it hard, falling to the ground in a dazed stupor.

The three watched her for a moment, then turned away.

A blast of lightning struck the ground just in front of them and they jumped back several feet. They looked at the sky, which hovered blue and innocent overhead. Another blast struck the ground and Slade cursed.

"Show yourself!"

The wind picked up, blowing leaves off the ground and swirling around the three. Jack used the distraction to rush to Evelyn's side, gently picking her up and cradling her in his arms. She looked around in confusion.

"What's happening?"

A blurry figure darted out of the trees, crashing into Slade and knocking him to the ground. For a moment, the blur became visible, a fox holding something aloft. Then it dashed away and the storm of leaves subsided, leaving Slade cursing again.

"After her!"

His companions rose and they followed as quickly as they could. Jack hesitated, knowing Evelyn would want him to follow as well, but she still hadn't gotten her bearings. He went in the opposite direction, hoping to find a safe place where they could rest and talk.

ONLY WHEN THEY had left the wolf-infested lands far behind them did Jack finally stop. Evelyn woke on the way, and though she was angry, she didn't have much energy to argue. He set her down in the roots of a tree near a creek and told her everything that had happened since he'd left her by Siobhan's tree, leaving nothing out. She frowned when he got to the part about the battles.

"You actually participated in that?"

"I didn't have a choice. It was that, or be killed. Or be locked up again until I was willing to fight."

"Still. I can't imagine you fighting anyone."

"I hope I never have to again, but I may not get that luxury. We need to figure out how we're going to get the storm-eater from Nadya. Or Slade. Or Olivarion, if it somehow gets back to him before we can swipe it."

"Tell me about him again." Jack repeated all he knew about the dreadlord. Evelyn pondered a moment, saying, "It sounds like it would be better to get it from Slade before he makes it back to the city. Otherwise, we'll have a lot more trouble to deal with. You said this female fox is a strong mage as well?"

"Yes. I'm not sure of the extent of her abilities, but she did some pretty impressive magic while I was her captive. She may be just as difficult to go up against as Olivarion."

They made plans for a while longer, finally deciding the best course would be to head back to Alibeth and wait for Slade. Or Nadya, but Jack hoped it wouldn't come to that. He couldn't see that encounter going well.

"I'm exhausted, and I'm sure you're not much better," he finally said. "Let's call it a night."

She agreed and they curled up to sleep beneath a low-hanging tree, Evelyn snuggled up next to his side. But as tired as he was, Jack couldn't sleep. Something niggled at the back of his mind, drawing his gaze to the surrounding forest. He could almost believe he saw something moving in the shadows. He nearly got up to investigate when a host of birds exploded out of the trees, shrieking in fear. A herd of deer soon followed, eyes wide in panic. He stood, watching them pass and looking back toward the shadows, fear urging him to flee. His instincts told him he didn't want to meet whatever pursued them.

"Wait!" he called out. "Take us with you!"

One of the deer looked back, started to run again, then thought better of it and returned for them. "Hurry!" she said, bending down. Jack lifted Evelyn and climbed atop the deer's back. No sooner had he sat down than she was running again, swiftly gaining on her companions. Jack glanced back, seeing a large shadowy form engulfing the forest behind them.

"What is that thing?!" he cried.

"Hunter," the deer said.

They spoke no more and Jack buried his face in her neck, clutching her and Evelyn as firmly as he could. Evelyn woke and wiggled out of his arms enough to glance back, but she said nothing and fell back asleep in his arms. The rhythm of the deer's run soon had Jack nodding off as well, his exhaustion growing too strong for him, despite his fear of whatever pursued them. The last thing he remembered was the splash of water as they crossed a creek.

⁂

WHEN THEY WOKE, a brown face with large dark eyes peered down at them. Jack sat up quickly, startling Evelyn awake. He lifted an arm to defend himself, but the face backed away.

"So sorry," it said. "I didn't mean to startle you."

With a better perspective, Jack saw that it was the young deer from the night before. They were in a small clearing surrounded by pine trees, alone. For a moment, the three just stared at each other before Jack broke the silence.

"How long were you watching us?"

"Only a couple minutes," she said. "I've never seen a scarecrow away from a farm before. Especially not one that could move. You're so tiny."

"What was that thing last night?" he asked.

"Hunter," she said. "Haven't heard that word in years, but they're still remembered among my people."

"What is it?" Evelyn asked.

"An evil creature created by a witch. It seeks its prey relentlessly, destroying any creature in its path. We got away by crossing the stream. They don't like water."

Jack remembered that Raven had mentioned a Hunter. He'd almost forgotten it. "We'll have to remember that," he said. "We're grateful you returned for us."

"I couldn't leave you for the Hunter. I wouldn't be able to live with myself."

"Maybe you can help us further," Evelyn said. "Have you seen a fox and two cats pass through the forest? Or maybe three humans?"

"Oh, I wouldn't know about the humans, I always keep my distance. No foxes or cats, either."

"Are we going the right way to Alibeth?" Jack asked.

"It's not too far from here, if it's the city life you want. I never go there myself."

"Would you be willing to do us one more favor?" Evelyn asked. "We're in a terrible hurry, you see, and we need to get to Alibeth as soon as possible. Is there any way you'd be able to give my friend a ride? I can fly fast enough on my own, but he's forced to go a bit slower, having to rely on straw legs and all."

"I don't know about that. I avoid cities as a rule. I just don't think I could."

"We would be extremely grateful," Jack added.

"And I will personally be in your debt," Evelyn said.

The deer thought a moment longer, clearly not convinced. But in the end she said, "Oh, I suppose I could. I won't go near the city, though. Just to the tree line and no further."

"Whatever you can do is appreciated," Jack said, standing and climbing atop the deer's back as she knelt.

Once he had a firm hold, she darted through the trees, quickly leaving the clearing behind. Evelyn flew alongside and the land rolled by beneath them. Other creatures scurried out of the way as the deer passed, many chattering angrily at them. Another deer joined in after a while, and another, all running alongside, enjoying being alive. As they neared the city, the other deer went their own way, having no wish to go to that human-infested place. At least an hour must have passed, but it seemed only minutes, and then they stood at the end of the forest, looking down on Alibeth sprawled out below them. The deer panted heavily as she knelt to let Jack down.

"Here you are," she said. "I've brought you as far as I dare."

"Whatever can I do to repay you?" Evelyn asked.

"Nothing," the deer said. "I'm not the kind to keep track of a debt. My philosophy is to do good to others, and the world will see to it that I'm treated in kind."

"If only everyone took that stance," Jack said, thinking of everything he'd been through.

"You're a kind soul," Evelyn said, doing the best she could to hug the deer. Her wings made it awkward, so finally she settled for a nod and a wink. "You never did tell us your name," she said.

"Islei," the deer said. "If you're ever back this way, do come find me."

"We certainly will."

She dashed back into the forest, the trees soon engulfing her.

"My life would be a lot simpler if she had been the one to get me off of that post," Jack said.

"True. But if that were the case, we would likely still be prisoners of the wolves. I've never been to a city, you know."

"You can see all of them once you're human again."

"Do you think Ferah sent that Hunter?"

"Likely. Remember how Raven mentioned there was a Hunter on his borders? I bet it's the same one."

"Do you think it will follow us into the city?"

"There's only one way to find out."

12

UNDERBETH

Jack figured Slade would use the same entrance into Alibeth as before, and he found it again easily. The only thing left to do was wait.

"You're sure they'll come this way?" Evelyn asked.

"Positive," Jack said, but in truth he was only mostly sure. Who knew how many other secret entrances there were into the city?

The bustle of the streets echoed over the wall and through the tunnel, enticing Evelyn, who kept peering through the tunnel.

"Sounds interesting," she said. "Just think of all the shops!"

"There are quite a few," Jack agreed. "That I saw, anyway, what with the dashing and hiding. We'll have to return once you're human."

She pulled back from the tunnel and took to the air, flying above the wall to get a better look. After a moment, she hurried back. "They're coming!" she said.

Jack looked toward the forest, not seeing anything at first, but a moment later a fox appeared, followed by two cats and another fox. The earth in front of Nadya erupted, rocks jutting up to block her path. She dodged around them, aiming straight for the side entrance. Jack moved to stand just in front of it, hoping to at least slow her down. He had no doubt she would move him with magic, but the second it took her to do so, perhaps Slade would catch up.

Evelyn flew into the melee, diving at the female fox and dodging the rocks that continued to rise from the ground. The cats both gained bursts of speed, coming up alongside the fox and closing on her, leaving her no way to dodge. This forced her to stop when another rock jutted up in front of her, but as Slade closed in behind, she jumped atop the rock. She lifted one paw as though about to do her own magic when one of the cats leaped at her from the side, catching her off guard and knocking her to the ground. Slade jumped on her. A brief struggle followed, and then Slade dashed out of the pile and raced for the entrance, the cats following. Nadya lay unconscious on the ground behind them.

Jack stood his ground. Evelyn flew down to join him and they waited. A moment later, a blast of wind too powerful to be natural knocked them to the side. Jack managed to see Slade and the cats pass by them without even a glance their way before he succumbed to darkness.

WHEN HE CAME TO, Evelyn was already awake, pacing the ground nervously.

"You're awake!" she said. "I was afraid—"

"I'm fine," Jack assured her. "Slade got through, I guess. How long have I been out?"

"Maybe half an hour? Nadya's gone. Probably slipped through before I woke."

Jack glanced toward the field, seeing plenty of new rock formations, but no fox. He groaned. "Looks like we're going up against Olivarion, then."

"I don't see how," Evelyn said. "We couldn't even stop Slade. How are we going to steal from a dreadlord?"

"We'll have to use more cunning," Jack said, flopping back against the ground. "No more head-on meetings."

"No objection to that."

Slowly Jack rose and dusted himself off. "We better move. Olivarion probably has the storm-eater by now."

He crept through the tunnel and sneaked along behind the crates and barrels to avoid being seen. Evelyn simply flew over the wall and perched on the rooftops as he traversed the streets. Before long, he realized he had a problem. The first time he'd been there, Slade had been his guide, but this time he had to rely solely on memory. He thought he could remember how to get to Manus, if the rat still haunted that part of the city, but he had no idea how to reach Olivarion. He thought of seeking out Miriel and Arnica again, but even if he somehow managed to find them, they'd probably want to go after Ferah immediately. Better to finish with Olivarion first.

After diving behind another stack of crates, he waved for Evelyn to join him. She finally noticed his gestures and glided down, landing on the ground next to him.

"What is it?" she asked.

"I think I'm a bit lost," Jack admitted. "I don't have Slade to lead me this time. We should probably find some sort of guide."

Evelyn shrugged. "If you say so. I'm having a great time simply looking at everything. Did you see all those shiny necklaces back there? They sparkled in the sun like gold!"

"I'm afraid I missed that. Up ahead there should be a rat named Manus, down some side alley. Slade took me to him the last time we were here, but I got the impression they weren't the best of friends. He may be able to help us, or at least point us in the right direction."

"Just let me know once you've found him. I'm going to look at the shops some more!"

She flew back to the rooftops as Jack hurried along the

street. He managed to find another newspaper, which helped
him to go a bit faster, but the journey still seemed much longer
than the first time he'd been there. When the alley suddenly
opened up beside him, he merely stood and stared at it for a
moment before recognizing it and hurrying inside.

"Hello!" he called, not wanting to hide his presence and rouse
suspicion.

Evelyn landed next to him. "So where is this guy?"

"Not sure. Manus? Are you here?"

"Who's asking?" the rat asked, appearing from inside a crate,
his mouth full.

"Good afternoon," Jack said. "You may not remember me,
but—"

"You're that scarecrow who followed that no-good fox
around!" the rat cried. He started to scurry away, but Evelyn
quickly blocked his path

"Please, just listen," Jack said. "I'm no more friendly with
Slade than you are. Maybe we were friends once, but he's done
nothing but use me since we began our travels. Needless to say,
we are no longer traveling companions."

"Easy for you to say. I'm sure he sent you here, planning to
trick me so he can get revenge. What would you have done in
my place? If Olivarion had found out that I knew of the fox's
intentions and hadn't said anything, he would've had my head!"

"I understand, and I don't blame you," Jack said. "We're not
here for you, or for Slade, really. My friend needs to see Olivarion, that's all, and I don't remember the way. Can you help us?"

Evelyn glanced at him, but didn't speak. She didn't expect
him to tell the complete truth, did she? The rat would send word
to Olivarion faster than they could leave the alley. Likely he
would tell him anyway, but at least the message wouldn't alarm
the dreadlord.

"No one just speaks with Olivarion," Manus said. "There are
procedures to follow."

"Slade did it."

"He's an exception. The rest of us have to follow the rules."

"Nevertheless, we need to see him. If we have to go all that way just to make an appointment, so be it, but we need to get there."

The rat looked back and forth between them for a moment, his nose twitching. "Fine," he said. "I'll tell you the way. But if this is some sort of trick, Olivarion will have your head, he will."

"No trick," Jack promised.

The rat dropped to the ground and grabbed a shaved wooden stick, food residue still clinging to it. He began to draw on the ground with it, marking their location with a big X.

"You can't go directly to him, so you'll need to go to Underbeth. That's the hidden city for us non-human types. Built in the old city ruins."

He drew some more, marking their path to Underbeth's entrance.

"Go to The Mottled Hairpin. That's the main office, so to speak, but it's also an inn and a tavern. You can even buy some nice baubles if you're so inclined," he added, glancing at Evelyn. "Anyway, ask for Hammy. He's the go-to for anything related to Olivarion. He can get you an audience."

Jack studied the drawing a moment longer, setting it to memory. "You've been more than helpful," he told the rat. "Thank you."

"Ah, don't mention it, I help people all the time. 'Helpful Manus' they call me, handing out wisdom left and right with no thought of payment."

Evelyn rolled her eyes and Jack asked, "What do you want in return?"

"I want that no-good fox to leave me alone! I've more than paid back my debt, and it's time he held up his end of the bargain and left me be."

"I'm afraid I can't do anything about that," Jack said, shaking his head. "Is there anything else you desire?"

"Well... Perhaps," Manus said, squinting and rubbing his hands. "Just a moment."

He scurried back to his crate and disappeared inside. They heard the scuffle of paper and items being moved. A moment later the rat returned holding a small bundle wrapped in cloth and tied with a thin cord.

"There's a young lady rat who works at The Mottled Hairpin. Goes by the name of Druselda. Give this to her and we'll call it even."

Jack took the bundle and stowed it in his shirt pocket. Hadn't Slade said something about a missus? Or was Druselda the same missus? No matter, not his business.

"We will deliver it," he promised. "Thank you."

Manus disappeared into his crate and Jack studied the drawing one more time before they headed back to the alley entrance.

"You handled that very well," Evelyn said. "Although I don't know what good an audience will do."

"We're not actually going to the audience," Jack whispered back. "But Manus will report that's all we wanted, and Olivarion will think nothing of it. Plus, now we know the way, sort of."

They dove back into the street, this time following the path imprinted in Jack's head. Underbeth lay just below the surface of the human city, built in the ruins of the old human town from centuries before, if Manus was to be believed. With that sort of place, why did Olivarion keep his headquarters in the human part of the city? Something to do with intimidation? Maybe it helped his reputation and kept the other animals in check. Jack wouldn't put it that sort of thing past him.

They finally found the entrance just under the humans' noses: a narrow alley leading to the back entrances of shops and restaurants, a hole in the wall much like the one Jack remembered from his first meeting with the dreadlord, and then down and down they went. The tunnel must have been a drain at one point, for it was circular and smooth, made of some sort of stone. It went more or less straight all the way down, though not too steep that they lost their balance. Evelyn gave up trying to walk, having a hard time finding purchase on the stone, and clung to Jack's shoulder.

After a short time of utter darkness, Jack saw a light ahead, which inspired him to quicken his pace. When they emerged from the darkness, they found a city much like the one they had just left, only animals of every kind filled its streets, completely void of humans. Cats and dogs appeared more than any other species, but Jack also saw rats, squirrels, several species of birds, raccoons, moles, mice, rabbits, and many others, in every direction. The humans had left the buildings just as they were. There was even a cobbled street left over, and some few plants that bloomed without sunlight. Balls of light floated all over the city, giving it the appearance of twilight.

No one noticed their sudden arrival. The end of the tunnel opened out of a wall along one of the many streets, and there were several more in various places. Many entrances to Underbeth existed, and more creatures arrived every minute.

When anyone did notice them, they stared at Jack. An enchanted scarecrow was not something they were used to seeing. No one was curious enough to approach them, though, so they passed unhindered through the streets. At first they merely walked, taking in as much as they could. Nearly every shop had been reopened, with animal shopkeepers in place of humans. Observation revealed there was even some form of currency in the shape of clay coins with a cat's paw imprinted on them. Jack assumed the paw was Olivarion's, until he remembered there were other dreadlords in the city. Unless Slade was right and Olivarion controlled them all. Excepting Sitara. Either way, it seemed to Jack that the cats were the main power, while the dogs served as the guard force. Many sat at street corners simply watching the passersby, and they all wore a cord around their neck with a clay pendant. Jack couldn't get close enough to see what was on the pendant, but he supposed it marked them as officials.

"I've never seen so many animals, even as one myself," Evelyn said. "How are they not discovered?"

"I don't have the faintest idea. My guess is they have scouts or some other position whose only job is to watch for approaching humans. That's what I would do, at any rate."

"Where do you think this Mottled Hairpin is?"

"If it's as important as Manus claimed, we shouldn't have to look long."

They walked in silence for a while, looking at everything around them. Many of the shops that had remained closed were those that carried items specific for humans, such as clothing. But others were open that surprised him, such as jewelry stores and accessories. Evelyn hurried over to look in their windows. Birds and human females alike seemed to like shiny things, in his experience.

The bells of Alibeth tolled out the hour, echoing down to Underbeth as a faint but reliable signal. They would need to find the inn soon, and a place to sleep for the night. If they needed those coins to buy a room in the inn, very likely they'd be sleeping in a park, or in some alley.

"Let's hurry," he called to Evelyn.

She followed him silently and they continued down the street. They passed several other streets that branched off perpendicular to theirs, but Jack only spared them a cursory glance. Fewer animals traversed those roads, making him think they were lesser thoroughfares.

A couple more blocks proved him right. Up ahead, a sign hung over a doorway proclaiming The Mottled Hairpin. Several creatures stood outside, talking and laughing amongst themselves. Jack and Evelyn hurried inside, careful to get out of the way of those leaving, and paused just within the entrance. It looked exactly like a human inn, only with animals everywhere instead of people.

"Go in or move out of the way!" someone behind them called.

Jack quickly apologized and they hurried over to the bar. He had to climb up on the stool, which Evelyn merely perched on, and they waited for the bartender to spare them a moment. The bartender was a cat, white with brown spots, and he hurried from customer to customer with practiced ease.

"What can I get you?" he asked, finally standing on the bar before Jack.

"A few things, actually," Jack said. "Am I right in guessing that a room requires a few of those clay coins I've seen?"

"You guessed right. They're not so hard to come by as they may seem, but you may have some difficulty at this time of the evening."

"Where would I be able to get some? We're still not quite sure how long we'll be here, and I'm guessing they'll be needed."

"Right again, sir. You'll want to speak with Hammy about that. He's just left for the evening, but he'll be back first thing in the morning. His office is upstairs and to the left at the landing."

"Wonderful. You've actually answered my second question. Now, for the last. Can you tell me where I can find Druselda?"

"Ah, sure. She's right over there waiting tables. Let me know if there's anything else you need."

They turned away from the bar and looked around for the female rat. Jack jumped down to the floor.

"When did you get all these fancy manners and proper speech?" Evelyn whispered. "I don't remember you being so bold before."

"It...just sort of came to me," he said. "I've been having flashbacks, or visions, and those combined with my recent adventures have given me a new perspective, so to speak."

"You sounded like you belonged here."

He shook his head with a laugh. "The only place I belong is in my field."

They spotted the rat and caught her just as she turned away from a table.

"Excuse me," Jack said.

"Oh!" she said at the sight of him. "What new devilry is this?"

"Devilry indeed, but that's irrelevant. Are you Druselda?"

"I am. Who's asking?"

"I have something for you from Ma—"

She grabbed his arm and pulled him behind her, up the stairs and around the corner so they were hidden from the customers below. Quite strong, for a little rat. Evelyn fluttered up behind them, having lost her perch at the sudden movement.

"You were saying?" Druselda asked in a whisper.

"I have a package for you from Manus," he said, adopting her whisper. He pulled the little bundle from his pocket and handed it to her.

"Thank you," she said, her tone much kinder. "How can I repay you?"

"Don't wo—"

"We need a room for the night," Evelyn broke in. "We're new to the city and have no means to pay for lodging."

"That's easily fixed," Druselda said. "There are a few empty beds at my house, and you're welcome to them. You'll have to wait here until my shift ends, which I'm afraid will be a few hours. Can't stay here, though."

"We understand," Jack said. "And we're grateful."

She hurried back down the stairs and Evelyn gave Jack a grin as they followed. "And you were about to tell her we didn't need anything."

"That was smart thinking."

They turned to head back down the stairs, but an open door caught Jack's eye. It was dark within, but he could just make out shelves and books. Evelyn noticed his hesitation and followed his gaze.

"What is it?" she asked.

"I was just thinking I wish we could browse through those books. There might be some about magic in there. Maybe something about how to lift your curse."

"Let's take a quick peek!"

Before Jack could respond, a ball of light appeared, floating in the air above Evelyn's head.

13

THE MOTTLED HAIRPIN

"I think I'm getting better at this," Evelyn said.

"Have you been practicing?" Jack asked, staring up at the hovering ball of light.

"No," she admitted. "I kind of let it slide, what with all the traveling around."

He glanced over his shoulder, half expecting Druselda to return and admonish them for lingering.

"I do miss my hands for reading," Evelyn said.

"You'll have them back soon."

"You know, it's not really about my father anymore, or even my brother. Sure, I don't want that witch working her spells on them, but that used to be my only motivation. I didn't mind remaining a crow, otherwise. But now..." She paused, looking at all the books and then back at Jack. "I actually miss my body," she continued. "I miss eating hot food, and snuggling under blankets next to a fire while snow falls outside. I miss having arms to grab and hold things and perform simple tasks like turning a page. I miss talking with other humans. Not that the animals haven't been kind, because they have, for the most part. It's just a different world."

"I understand," Jack said. "It's an adjustment for me, too,

believe me. For the longest time all I did was sit in my field and watch the clouds float by. And I still miss that, simple as it may seem. I even miss the crows, sometimes."

That made her laugh. "You must've thought I was a real brat," she said.

"Well..."

"You admit it! And I was. I only wanted to study magic, nothing more. Not so bad in itself, but I let it take me too far."

"You're not saying you should've married that man, are you?"

"No, but I should've found another solution, as you said. A coastal village doesn't sound too bad right about now."

"And miss out on all of these adventures? Never. Those villages will be there till the end of time. How many humans can say they've experienced even a tenth of what you've gone through?"

"True, but—"

"And if you'd simply left, I probably would still be sitting in that field, only imagining what you were getting up to."

"Isn't that what you want?"

He shrugged. "I'm fine with how everything's turned out. The wolf part was horrible, but the rest hasn't been too bad."

She performed a quick search of the upper shelves while he took care of the lower. There were a lot of books on science, literature, and history, but whoever the human owner had been, apparently they weren't fans of magic.

"No luck," Evelyn said.

"Me, neither. We could always go to the Guild. They'll have plenty of magic books, I'm sure. I remember Miriel had quite a few."

"Do you really think they would help us? You said they were pretty keen on going after Ferah. I guess that's a good thing, but what will it mean for me?"

"I don't know," he admitted. "Maybe they could make her undo the spell?"

"That's a pretty big *maybe*. With my luck, they would simply go after her with no thought for me. What if they can't even make her reverse it? I could end up stuck as a crow. I can't risk that, Jack. I don't think I want to go to them unless we have no other choice. I wouldn't mind taking a look at their books, though. Maybe they have something on witches that could help us."

"I don't doubt it."

They skimmed the titles a moment longer, then gave it up and headed back downstairs. Nearly every table was occupied, but they snagged an empty one and settled in to wait. Evelyn's gaze drifted to the patrons around them while Jack found himself nodding off, the excitement of the day finally catching up with him. He drifted back to his dream world, back to the cottage with the brown-haired woman. He was sitting at a table this time, watching her move about the kitchen like a mage in her study. Every now and then she turned and he saw her mouth moving, but no sound could be heard. He moved closer, trying to read her lips, but she was speaking so fast that he couldn't keep up. She pointed at the doorway over and over until finally he went outside just to see what she was talking about. Armed men grabbed him from either side, tying him up and tossing him on a cart. The house and the water wheel grew smaller as it pulled away, and the woman stood in the doorway, waving.

He woke with a jump, startling Druselda, who had just approached.

"Gave me a fright!" she said. "Sorry for the long wait. We can be off, now."

The tavern was nearly empty. How long had he slept? He stood, following the rat like a sleepwalker onto the streets of Underbeth, Evelyn perched on his shoulder.

⁂

WHEN JACK AWOKE, he couldn't remember where he was or how he had gotten there. A quick look around revealed Evelyn sleeping in a nest of blankets and pillows in an armchair. He lay in a bed covered with thick wool blankets, with a view of a peaked wooden roof. He stood and looked out a square window next to the bed and saw the streets of Underbeth below, already filled with animals of all shapes and sizes.

The bells of Alibeth began to toll, announcing half past eight, so he roused Evelyn and together they left the little room and descended a flight of stairs, entering a large family room. Five rats greeted them, all seated atop a large human-sized table.

"Hope you slept well," Druselda said. "Breakfast is ready, if you'd like to take a seat."

Evelyn complied by perching at the end of the table while Jack examined the other half of the room, which contained a couch and a few armchairs.

"He doesn't eat," Evelyn said behind him.

"Lucky bastard," one of the rats said. "Saves a fortune a year, I'm sure."

"I wouldn't know," Jack replied, taking a seat on the couch. "I suppose I would, if I worked."

"What do you do, then?" another rat asked.

"For most of my life, my only job was to scare crows, and I wasn't paid for it. Just recently I've gotten into the adventure business, and I'm afraid it hasn't paid any better. Besides, what would I do with money? It's better off where it is, I figure."

"You'll need some if you plan to stick around Underbeth for any length of time," Druselda said. "The Watch will hurry you along if they find you sleeping in the streets. You may not need food, but you seemed tired enough to me."

"All the more reason to see Hammy," Evelyn said.

"Dear Hammy," a fourth rat said. "Olivarion's bootlicker. If you want my advice, you'll forgo that particular appointment and leave the city altogether. No point in looking for trouble where there is none."

"We'll keep it in mind," Jack promised.

The fifth rat carried a plate of food across the counter and jumped onto the table, the conversation ceasing as everyone filled their belly.

Jack went back to examining the room, which still contained the portraits of its long-dead previous human owners. He opened his mouth to comment, then closed it just as quickly. It was no business of his.

When Evelyn had finished, Druselda kissed her family goodbye and took the crow and scarecrow back to the streets.

"Thank you so much for taking us in," Jack said.

"My pleasure. Besides, you've done me an even greater favor. And thank you for not mentioning Manus to my family."

The thought hadn't crossed Jack's mind, but he thanked the gods he had kept his mouth shut. No telling what conversation that might have started.

Druselda guided them back through the streets, which was just as congested as the previous day. They took a few turns Jack didn't remember from the previous night and soon stood once more before The Mottled Hairpin.

"My shift doesn't start till this evening, so I'll be off back home now. Good luck to you both!"

She disappeared back into the throng while Jack and Evelyn once more entered the inn. Fewer customers sat around the bar and at the tables, but a short line trailed up the stairs. Jack took his place at the bottom and they settled in to wait.

"How long do you think we'll be here?" Evelyn asked. "In Underbeth, I mean."

"Depends on how soon our...audience...is," Jack answered, casting a glance at the raccoon in front of him. "Maybe a few days. Perhaps as long as a week."

Evelyn sighed. "I was afraid of that. At least we can take in the sights while we're here. I'm sure there are many things to see in the city."

"All of which likely cost money," Jack responded. "We might have better luck in Alibeth."

"Ooh, we *could* go back there, couldn't we?" she said.

"We'll see. Let's find out when our audience is first."

The line moved slowly forward, and none of the other animals so much as glanced their way. Still, Jack didn't dare speak of their true intentions. There was no telling who would drop a word in Olivarion's ear.

Around midday, they finally reached the top of the stairs. Several of the doors stood open, but it seemed their line led to a single office. A moment later they stood at the front of the line and a voice called, "Next!"

Jack hurried down the hall to the open door, which was just across from the library. Inside, a large dog with droopy eyes and jowls sat behind a desk. He used magic to write a note on a piece of paper before looking up at them.

"Well, this is an odd sight," he said. His voice had a creakiness to it that spoke of age, but his eyes were kind enough. Not what Jack expected of someone who worked for a dreadlord. "Whoever enchanted you did an excellent job," the dog continued, "although your feet could use a little touch up. Now, what can I do for you?"

"We seek an audience with Olivarion," Jack said.

The dog laughed. "So you're the duo that old rat spoke of. I'm sorry to say that the lord is not currently accepting any more audiences. He is booked through to the end of the year."

"Surely you can squeeze us in somewhere?" Evelyn asked. "It's a matter of some urgency."

"It always is. But please, do go on."

"It's my enchantment," Jack cut in, not giving her the chance to reveal their real quest. "I'm afraid of it wearing off, and I've heard Olivarion is the most powerful mage in these lands. If anyone can ensure that I will continue to be mobile, it's him. If we have to wait until the new year, well, I do not think I shall be able to attend, unless someone can carry me."

"Find someone to carry you, then," Hammy said. "As I've said, the lord is booked."

"He probably doesn't have the power anyway," Evelyn said. "I mean, it's a pretty great spell. Surely no one but a master could cast such a thing."

"You're probably right," Jack said. "Sorry to waste your time," he added to the dog as he stood to go.

"You're doubting Olivarion's powers?" Hammy said, raising one paw to stop them. "Let me be the first to say that the lord ranks among the most powerful mages in the land. Why, he constantly increases his personal collection of magical artifacts to boost his power further, making him nigh indestructible."

"What sort of artifacts?" Evelyn asked.

"Oh, this and that," Hammy said. "Nothing the non-magical need worry about. But between you and me, he recently acquired one vastly superior to any other in existence, as far as we know. It would be a grave folly of yours to doubt his power with that in hand!"

"How does he even find such things?" Jack asked. "Surely, with his busy schedule, he doesn't go out looking for them. Do others bring them to him so willingly?"

The dog leaned in a bit further. "The most recent was promised to him," Hammy said, "by a fox of questionable character. Olivarion got a smaller artifact out of the deal, too. I heard it caused quite a ruckus with the fox. Apparently it wasn't part of the bargain." The dog leaned back, adopting a formal air once more. "All the more reason to be completely honest and open when dealing with authorities. That fox probably reneged on his part of the deal. Now, I can fit you in just after the first of the year, but I simply cannot promise any sooner than that."

"Will you at least mark us down for a sooner slot in case someone else cancels?" Evelyn asked.

"That I can do. Where shall I send notice of such an event?"

"Put The Mottled Hairpin for now. We'll let you know if that changes," Jack said.

"Very well." The dog made more notes on the paper with a wave of his paw. "Is there anything else I can do for you today?"

"Yes, actually," Jack said. "We are new to the city, and I was told to come to you about those clay coins I keep seeing. I'm afraid we'll need them if we're to stay here till the end of the year."

"Quite right." Hammy got up and rummaged around in a drawer at the far end of the desk. "Every visitor who seeks it is given a small stipend to get him started, then he's on his own. There are plenty of places around the city needing workers. You need only look." He handed Jack a small bag, which jangled with coins as he took it.

"Thank you. You've been more than helpful."

"Good day." Hammy went back to writing and Jack and Evelyn hurried out. There was an arrow posted on the wall, instructing them to leave by the other end of the hall. This they followed and soon found a stairway that took them back to the common room of the inn.

"Now what?" Evelyn asked as Jack led her outside.

"We need somewhere we can speak freely," Jack said. "Would you like to visit a park?"

She nodded her agreement and they entered the ever-growing crush of animals. They hadn't noticed on the first day, but there were maps posted on a few of the street corners with the locations labeled. They found the closest park and followed the path to the entrance, only a few streets away. It was relatively empty at that time of day, so they entered and began following a trail that circled it, Evelyn perched once more on his shoulder. The trees were long since dead, deprived of the sunlight they needed, but several mushrooms had thrived, many growing to outlandish proportions. The magical lights floating above created a gloomy, surreal mood that was surprisingly appropriate.

"Obviously we're not waiting till the new year," Jack said.

"I guessed as much."

"I just needed an idea of what we were up against. Also, Manus would've sent word by now, and it would look odd if we didn't follow up on our end."

"So, what? We launch a sneak attack, steal the storm-eater, and make a break for it?"

"Basically. But did you notice what Hammy said?"

"He said a lot of things."

"He mentioned Slade. And it sounded like Olivarion broke his end of the deal. The fox probably isn't too happy right now."

"So what? After all he's done, I'm glad things went south for him."

"But think about this: Olivarion broke his end of the deal, keeping both artifacts and leaving Slade with nothing. Now Slade is out there, probably plotting a way to get what he considers rightfully his. Why shouldn't we be a part of that?"

"Surely you're not suggesting we join up with Slade again?"

"Only temporarily. At least until we get the storm-eater. And I've thought of someone else who would be only too happy to steal from Olivarion."

"Not that female dreadlord! She tried to use you!"

"But now she'll have a reason to work with me. Plus, with Slade involved, she'll have a tougher time turning on us. We'll just need to enlist Slade's help first."

She sighed and didn't answer right away.

"Come on, Evelyn," Jack said. "You have to admit he has a mind for strategy."

"That he does," she admitted, each word said with reluctance. She sighed again. "All right. Where do we look for him?"

14

BACK TO THE FOREST

The lunch crowd filled the common room of The Mottled Hairpin, but Jack and Evelyn managed to find a seat at the bar as they waited for the bartender. A few minutes later, the cat once more stood before them.

"It's the duo from yesterday," he said. "How did it go? Did you speak with Hammy?"

"We did," Jack answered. "Now I'm afraid we have another question to ask you. We've heard that a friend is in town, a fox who goes by the name of Slade. Do you know where we might find him?"

The cat laughed. "I know of him, but I can't say I've ever heard anyone call that scoundrel a friend. He never stays in the city long, and almost never comes to Underbeth. My guess is he's already long gone."

"Thank you," Jack said. He left a coin on the counter and re-entered the pulsing streets.

"We'll just have to track him down in the forest," Evelyn said.

"Easier said than done. But it's that, or attempt it on our own. I don't trust Sitara if Slade isn't with us."

Evelyn flapped her wings in excitement. "I have an idea. But we'll need to get back to the forest first."

THEY LEFT Underbeth with barely a backward glance. It was fairly easy to find a tunnel that lead back to Alibeth, and soon they were once more crossing its streets in the shadows. Evelyn flew high above the city to get their bearings and instruct Jack in which way to go. On a whim, he made one more stop to ask Manus if he'd seen Slade, but the rat either refused to come out, or wasn't at home. Probably for the best. Didn't need any sort of report getting back to Olivarion.

Once they were free of the city, they raced for the forest, laughing at the joy of being free and in the open air. The trees took them in like a parent long separated from its child, and for a moment they simply sat in silence and enjoyed the quiet calm. The sun was sinking fast, so they made camp right where they were, not bothering with a fire. Evelyn scavenged for food while Jack gathered some pine needles for a bed.

As he waited, he watched the sky change colors and remembered when that was all he used to do. He hadn't had much time lately for such things, but sitting there, he realized he missed it fiercely. Perhaps if everyone made time for simple pleasures, they would treat each other more kindly. Not that the city animals had been bad. They had been helpful, and hadn't required a favor in return. But they had their currency, which was along the same lines.

Evelyn finally returned, already yawning.

"I've been thinking," he said.

"Hmm?"

"Once you're human again, and go off to see the world, will I just return to my field? I suppose it's really up to me, but I haven't given it much thought before now."

"I thought you'd travel with me," she said. "At least, I assumed."

"A young woman traveling with a scarecrow? I suppose I'd have to pretend to be inanimate."

"It wouldn't be all bad. Out in the wild, you could move all you wanted, and if we stayed at an inn, you could move about my room to your heart's content."

"Hmm. Still seems a bit stressful."

"We could think of it as a game. How many people can we fool, or how long can you sit still? I'm sure we could come up with something."

"Perhaps," Jack said. "You wouldn't be able to understand me anymore, though."

"You said Miriel understood you. Surely once I'm better at magic I can manage it. There may even be some sort of spell to help it along."

He nodded, already drifting off to sleep.

He stood in the cottage again, but the scene was different this time. The woman was sitting by a fire, sewing and unaware of his presence. He looked around the room, at the furniture and decorations, which were sparse. A bed sat against the far left corner, just behind the woman. There was another chair across from her, empty. To the right was a little kitchen, with a table and a smaller fire pit for cooking. Vegetables, fruit, and bread overflowed from the shelves. He took a step toward her and she looked up at him, her mouth moving but her words inaudible. He spoke back, but his words were also lost. It only occurred to him then how silent everything was, the crackle of the fire, the sound of her sewing, his footsteps on the floorboards. She spoke again, laughing.

Jack woke with a start, but didn't disturb Evelyn. He stood quietly and wandered away from their camp to a little stream that flowed nearby. The sun was barely peeking over the distant hills as he sat on the ground and watched the water dash over the rocks.

His dreams hadn't bothered him before; he merely thought of them as the creations of his subconscious mind, or perhaps a memory from long ago. But their frequency was beginning to concern him, and he wished he knew how to make them stop.

Maybe he'd been human once, and maybe not. He didn't see how it made much difference now.

"Jack?" Evelyn called from behind him.

"Coming," he called back. He sat a moment longer and watched the water. There was no need to worry her. They were only dreams, and the two of them had more important business to attend to.

He walked for hours, sometimes with Evelyn perched on his shoulder, other times with her flying ahead to scout the way. "We never spoke about my idea," Evelyn said just after they had set off.

"Oh?"

"I have a plan for getting Slade to help us, just in case he refuses. He always has his own schemes."

"Go on."

"There have only been two creatures he's shown any fear or respect toward, one being Olivarion."

"Who cheated him and likely inspires revenge. Who was the other?" Try as he might, Jack couldn't remember anyone else Slade was afraid of.

"Raven," Evelyn said.

"Ah, you're right," he said, recalling their encounter with the bird. "Well, what do you propose? We seek Raven's help?"

"It's worth a try, right?"

He agreed it was, so they set off in what they hoped was the direction of Raven's land. Late in the morning, they heard a rustling just ahead and muffled voices. Evelyn flew back to join Jack and they approached slowly together.

"I don't know what you're so worried about," a voice said. "The war is over. No one's going to attack you, I promise."

"But what about those scouts we saw?" another voice asked.

"They're looking for something. I don't want to run into them if I can help it."

"Even if we did, they wouldn't worry about the likes of us."

Two adult raccoons and three babies came into view, plodding along through the trees. "I'm going to speak to them," Jack whispered. Evelyn nodded in response. "Excuse me," Jack said, coming forward so they could see him.

The raccoons froze, probably half expecting him to be a wolf. Relief shone in their eyes when they saw he was not what they feared.

"This is a strange sight," one raccoon said, the male of the duo. "A scarecrow and a crow traveling together. Didn't do a very good job scaring it off, did you lad?" The raccoon laughed, its voice still a little shaky from fright.

"Oh, he tried," Evelyn said. "But it takes more than a twisted grin to scare me."

"Quite right," the raccoon said, chuckling.

"We heard you mention the wolf war just now. Was I right in hearing the fighting is over?" Jack asked.

"Yes, the white wolf finally cast down his brother and took his place as High Wolf. The land is safe to cross once more."

"Or so we hope," the female raccoon added.

"The white wolf. That would be Ardel?"

"Yes. You know something of the fighting?"

"Just a bit. We're merely hoping to cross the land safely and swiftly. Raven's land is our destination."

The raccoon brightened a bit at that. "Oh, is it now? You're a tad off course, if you don't mind my saying so. You'll need to head a bit further to the east."

"Thank you," Jack said. "Safe travels to you and your family."

The raccoons nodded in response and continued on their way.

"He didn't say how far it was," Evelyn said once they had started off again.

"I'm sure we'll reach it before too long. I just hope Raven's willing to shield my feet once more. They're getting a bit ragged again."

They didn't cross the path of any other animals, although they heard and saw them from a distance. Mostly squirrels or mice, going about their lives with no worry about wolves or foxes or magic.

The hours passed with little excitement, until a slight tingling spread from the bottom of Jack's feet to the top of his head. He stopped and looked around, thinking it had to be some creature casting magic on him. But he saw no one. He followed Evelyn again and the tingling grew stronger, so he stopped once more, only to be knocked to the ground from behind.

"Fly!" he yelled to Evelyn.

"Do calm down," the attacker said. "You're in no danger."

The weight on his back lifted and he rolled over, looking up to see Nadya smiling at him.

"You!" he said. "Why did you attack me?"

"Oh, come now. If I wished to attack, I could've done so and you'd be captured now. But as you can see, that's not the case."

"What do you want?" Evelyn asked, fluttering down to land on the ground beside Jack.

"I'm curious. When I first met you," she said to Jack, "you traveled with 'Slade,' I believe you called him. I assumed your interest was only in his service. But then you attacked me for the storm-eater and tried to stop Slade as well. Why?"

"That's none of your business," Jack said.

"I could bind you now," she said. "Or better yet, remove Slade's spell and leave you here immobile. Would you like that?"

"Why are you so cruel?" Evelyn asked.

"I'm not cruel. Merely practical. Now, you were telling me your story?"

Evelyn scowled and said, "We need the storm-eater to trade to the owl, Siobhan. If we do that, she'll help us find a witch."

Nadya's eyes widened. "Why in the world would you want to do that?"

"To make me human again. Does that satisfy you?"

The fox stood, swishing her tail. "It does. For now. Though I must hear the rest of this story, sometime."

She glanced behind them into the forest, standing perfectly still, her ears perked up.

"Do you attack and demand answers from everyone you meet in the forest? Is it some sort of amusement for you?" Jack asked.

"Quiet," Nadya whispered. She knelt by Jack, her body magically growing larger, and said, "Get on, hurry!"

"Why?" Evelyn asked.

"Hunter," she said.

Jack saw, far away, a darkness spreading between the trees. He cursed and climbed atop the fox. Immediately, she bolted, Evelyn flying alongside.

"Why are you helping us?" Jack asked as she ran.

"I'm looking after my own interest," she called back. "Hold tight now!"

She leaped over rocks and climbed hills, dodging trees and scaring other animals into flight. Finally, they came to a creek and she dashed over, stopping and catching her breath on the other side. Jack looked back and saw no sign of the darkness behind them. He slid to the ground and studied the fox as she shrank back to her normal size.

"We're grateful," he said. "But why did you do that?"

She panted a moment more, then said, "Slade thwarted my plans. If you succeed, you'll be thwarting his. Any little blow to him is worth supporting."

"What happened between you two?" Evelyn asked.

"We've taken different paths. Have to look out for ourselves, after all. Good luck to you."

She turned to go and Jack called, "Hey, wait! You're just going to leave us here?"

"I just saved you from a Hunter. If anything, I should be asking for some recompense, but I'm not going to do that. This time. Farewell."

She bounded away into the forest and Jack and Evelyn watched her, standing beside the creek in silence.

"Well," Jack finally said, "at least she didn't try to kidnap me again."

"There is that," Evelyn agreed.

ANOTHER SUNDOWN and Jack was just preparing to find a place to stop for the night when a voice called out, "Halt!"

They obeyed immediately, looking around for the speaker. Then Jack laughed and looked down to find another stone gargoyle, marking the border of Raven's land.

"Looks like we made it," he said, sitting on the ground to wait.

"Now let's just hope he helps," Evelyn responded.

They didn't wait long. A sparrow flew up a few minutes later, saying only, "Follow me!"

This they did, and before long they once more passed lovely autumn gardens and green grass that hadn't been informed that spring was long past. There were many more animals going about their business than there had been in the surrounding forest, which spoke well of Raven's rule. They passed a large pond that Jack hadn't seen the first time, and on its surface floated several large white swans and many smaller ducks and geese. Balls of light floated up into the air all around them, illuminating the land as the sun disappeared for the evening and the stars made their appearance.

"Raven will receive no other visitors today," the sparrow informed them. "Because you have been here before, you will be staying in the flower suite. This is reserved for those who are trusted and deemed friends of Raven."

Evelyn's eyes widened at that and Jack merely shrugged. He supposed they'd made a good impression the first time. The sparrow took them to a thick cluster of trees and ushered them to pass through the overhanging branches.

They gasped when they broke through to the other side. Flowers covered every available inch of ground, and the trees formed a canopy over their heads that blocked the wind, opening at the very top in a small hole that revealed the stars and a sliver of moon. A couple of glowing balls of light floated above their heads, and several fireflies began their pulsing glow just above the flowers.

"It's like a faery tale," Evelyn said. "I've always imagined this is what a faery's home must look like."

"Close," the sparrow said. "Although faeries are much less likely to allow mortals to visit their secret homes."

"You mean they're real?" Jack asked.

"Naturally. None in these parts, I'm afraid, although we occasionally receive a visitor now and again. Is there anything I can get you before I leave?"

"Nothing, thank you," Evelyn said.

The sparrow nodded and disappeared through the branches again. Jack sat on the ground and watched the fireflies, then looked up at the stars far ahead. "I could get used to this," he said. "Much better than any place in Underbeth."

"Do you think the fireflies do Raven's bidding, or do they just happen to be here?" Evelyn asked.

"I wouldn't be surprised to learn the wind serves him," Jack answered, lying back on the ground with his hands behind his head.

Evelyn settled down in a bed of baby's breath and heaved a contented sigh.

Jack watched the stars a bit longer, not willing to surrender to sleep just yet, or the dreams he was certain would come. He barely noticed when sleep finally took him, and his rest was dreamless.

THE SPARROW CAME for them shortly after daybreak, bearing a twig of blackberries for Evelyn. When she had finished, he bade them follow once more and they left the flower suite behind.

Animals everywhere went about their business, gathering and planting and tending and rushing off with this or that message or errand. The sparrow took them up a small hill and down the other side, where the largest pond Jack had yet seen filled the dell before them. Several weeping willows bordered its rim, and more swans and ducks and waterfowl swam across the cold surface. The sparrow led them directly to one of the weeping willows, bowing as he entered its hanging strands.

"Welcome," Raven said. The large bird sat perched on one of the lowest branches, his eyes on the pond before him.

The sparrow bowed again and left them alone.

"Good morning," Jack ventured, unsure if he was supposed to immediately state his business or wait for Raven to speak.

"You do not travel with your fox companion," the bird said, his eyes never leaving the water.

"We had a bit of a falling out," Jack said. "But that is why we have come to you. We wish to find him again."

"Oh?" The old bird turned his eyes to them and Jack felt exposed, as though Raven were reading all his secrets in his eyes. "Please, tell me what happened after you left my land."

They related their story to him. Raven listened quietly until they got to the point where Jack chose to go with Slade.

"Well, now," he said, nothing more.

Jack continued, recounting his first trip to Alibeth and the encounter with Olivarion, then the subsequent encounters with Miriel, Arnica, Nadya, and Sitara. When he reached the part about the wolves and his bear transformation, Evelyn took over, telling of her journey alone and meeting up with Jack again. Jack finished the story from there, ending with their trip back to Raven's land and their most recent encounter with Nadya.

"And now here you are, once more seeking my help," the bird said. Several sparrows appeared, bearing a large leaf filled with several varieties of berries and nuts. They placed these at Raven's feet and he nodded them away, sighing. "Nothing against the food, but sometimes you simply crave a little meat, no?" He didn't wait for an answer, just proceeded to eat in front of them without saying another word. Evelyn's stomach rumbled as he finished, but he took no notice.

"I would like to finish our conversation this evening," he said, extending his wings. "I will need time to consider your tale. For now, the hunt rises within me. Please do as you will until then." He rose into the air and flew over the pond and into the trees on the far side. Jack and Evelyn rushed out and watched him disappear, then stared at each other in confusion.

"If you'll come with me." Another sparrow appeared and led them back down the other side of the hill. "There is plenty of food, and you are free to sample any of it. Just be back here before sundown." Then the bird left them alone, and for a minute they just looked around at all the animals passing by without a glance their way.

"Guess I'll find something to eat," Evelyn said, taking to the air herself. "Those berries weren't very filling."

Jack nodded and wandered back to their suite, finding it empty and quiet. It looked less ethereal now, although the light spilling in from the opening high above did suggest some enchantment. He lay down and dozed off, wondering if Raven would choose to help them, or if they'd be sent out once more to fend for themselves.

❧ 15 ❧

THE HAWK MAGE

W hen they met with Raven that evening, the old bird was noticeably more jolly and talkative. They sat once more beneath the willow tree, the sun quickly sinking.

"I have thought long about your tale, and I've come to a decision," Raven said. "I *will* help you. But when you're finished with him, I want the fox brought to me. I don't feel he was entirely truthful in his intentions, and I shall hold him accountable for it. I shall send my best mage with you, not only to ensure your success, but to bring the fox to me when all is over. I know you'll have more urgent business on your mind, and I need to guarantee my desires are also met."

"Send anyone you please," Jack said. "We're grateful for the help."

Raven nodded to someone behind them and a great hawk appeared, landing on the ground just before them.

"I am Caerla," she said.

"Caerla will lead your quest from here," Raven said. "At least until the fox is apprehended."

"Is there anything we can do to repay you?" Evelyn asked.

"Actually, yes," the old bird said, a hint of laughter in his voice. "The next time you come through my land, let it be only to visit. It gets tiresome, with all my visitors wanting this or that."

"I think we can promise that," Jack said. "Though if we're successful, one of us will be human."

"Human or animal, it's the soul that matters. I'll see to it that you are let through regardless."

"Thank you," Jack said, bowing. Evelyn followed suit.

"We will leave immediately," Caerla said, leaving Raven's presence after a quick bow. Jack and Evelyn followed behind, glancing back once to see the old bird watching the water again. The sun sank behind the trees, its final rays casting the sky in a golden light.

Caerla led them away from the willow, avoiding the hill that led back down to the dell. Jack and Evelyn followed, waiting for her to explain the next step, but she remained silent. Soon the sky turned a deep shade of blue, quickly changing to the blue-black of night, and still they went on.

Finally, Evelyn could take it no longer. "Excuse me," she said. "How much further tonight?"

"The night is better for casting the spell we need," the hawk said. "Just a bit further."

They asked no more questions and the land rolled by beneath them. Jack wondered if the rest of his life would be nothing but endless travel through forests and cities, always close but not quite reaching his goal. It was a disheartening thought. Then he glanced at Evelyn, who was flying just ahead of him. She hadn't ridden on his shoulder once since they set out, likely because the hawk had flown the whole way. At least, that was his guess for why she'd chosen to fly.

"We'll stop here," Caerla finally said, landing on the top of a large boulder. "You, girl, you have some talent with magic?"

"Just a little," Evelyn said.

"Come over here."

Evelyn obeyed, landing next to the hawk on the stone.

"We will combine our energies to cast this spell. You've done such a thing before?"

"No," Evelyn admitted. "I'm still just a beginner. What will the spell do?"

"It will take us directly to the fox. It isn't difficult. Just close your eyes and imagine filling a large cauldron with clear water."

Evelyn closed her eyes and Jack sat against a tree, barely able to see in the dark. But then, so long as it worked, he supposed he didn't have to see.

"Now picture yourself lifting the water out of the cauldron by magic, and thrust it toward me. That's it, just a bit more..."

A bright white light burst into life around the two birds, illuminating the entire hillside. Jack jumped to his feet in surprise, unable to look away. Both birds glowed with the light, their eyes tightly shut as Caerla chanted the words to invoke the spell. All at once the light shrank into a tiny, brightly glowing ball floating between them. It hovered only a moment before zipping off through the trees.

"Hurry!" Caerla said, flying after it.

Evelyn fluttered after her, followed by Jack, who ran as fast as he could. He soon fell behind, but he could still see the ball flying ahead of them, so he followed that.

"Hurry, Jack!" Evelyn called back.

Try as he might, he soon lost sight of the ball as well. His feet were falling apart beneath him, making even a slow jog a struggle. He was forced to stop and walk, the night pressing in around him. The distant hoots of hunting owls reached his ears, the soft scurrying of mice and squirrels, or perhaps some other creature of the night. Already he was so tired, his eyes drooping closed as he walked. Only the fear of being unable to find Evelyn and the hawk again kept him moving forward. He didn't notice when he finally passed out in exhaustion, for in his dreams he followed them still.

WHEN THE FIRST trills of the morning birds flew into his ears, Jack woke in a panic. He had fallen behind! He rose to dash off in the direction he thought they'd gone when someone asked, "Where are you off to?"

He paused, really looking around for the first time. There sat Caerla and Evelyn, watching him in amusement.

"We thought we'd let you sleep," Evelyn explained. "You were so tired."

"How did... I mean, you had gone so far ahead. I thought for sure I'd lost you."

"Caerla returned for you and carried you by magic."

"But what about the spell? Did you find Slade?"

"Indeed we did," the hawk answered. "He's dozing just over there." She flicked her head to the side and Jack followed her gaze, spotting the fox sound asleep beneath a tree. "He's bespelled as well. Don't worry, it will take magic to wake him. Quite a fierce fighter, but still no match for me."

Jack merely stared in wonder, then sank back to the ground, laughing. "Wonderful. All that's left then is to get the help of Sitara, then off to Olivarion, then return the storm-eater to Siobhan."

"So it seems," Caerla said. "Shall I wake him now?"

"Might as well."

Jack stood, noticing that his feet had also been fixed while he slept. They felt stronger than ever, as though he could walk all the way to Alibeth and back home again and not feel the slightest wear.

Caerla waved one wing over Slade and he blinked his eyes open, looking around blearily. He laughed when he saw them. "I might have known," he said. "So you've caught up with me. What now? You'll extract your vengeance and go on your merry way?"

"No," Jack said, walking closer. "What you did to me was cruel, not to mention what you did to Evelyn by refusing to help her, and then going after the very artifact she needed. But it's behind us now. It's done, and I am no longer in your debt. However, I believe we can still help one another."

"How do you figure that?"

"We heard what Olivarion did to you," Evelyn said.

"Oh? And I suppose you'd like to offer your help?"

"Not exactly," Jack said. "He has something all of us want. Evelyn still needs the storm-eater for Siobhan, and I'm sure you would like the fire-tamer you sought for so long."

"Go on."

"We join together and take both of them."

"A nice idea, but just how do you think we will succeed? You've already seen he is more powerful than me, and with those two artifacts, he'll be untouchable."

"That is where I come in," Caerla said.

"And you are?"

"One of Raven's mages," Jack said. "His most powerful, in fact."

Slade regarded the hawk with new respect. "Really? How did you manage to get Raven's help?"

"We told the truth," Evelyn said.

"There's one other we'd like to ask for help," Jack said. "She has a keen interest in seeing Olivarion fall, and with all of us working together, we can see it come to pass."

"Who are you speaking of?"

"Sitara. With her followers added in, there's no way Olivarion can guard against all of us."

"Now, will you help us or not?" Evelyn asked.

The fox regarded them all in turn, then yawned widely. "Why not?" he said. "All my other plans have come to naught. I may as well come along. I would so love to see Olivarion outsmarted for a change."

"Then let's be on our way," Caerla said.

"Not so fast," Slade said. "So far we've gotten by with not sharing our plans and waiting until the last moment to reveal them. If we're going to do this, we need to be completely honest and open with one another. What exactly will we do? What happens if we are separated, or one of us is captured?"

"Very well," the hawk said. "Let's plan, then. Do you have any suggestions?"

"None," the fox said. "Though I'm eager to hear yours."

"I think we need some sort of diversion," Evelyn said. "Perhaps Sitara can help with that. But we'll need to know exactly where he keeps the artifacts."

"That I do know," Slade said. "The alley where we first met him has several secret exits. Follow the right one and you find his true headquarters, his home, if you will. That's where we'll find them, if they aren't on his person. I doubt he carries both continuously, though."

"And you know which path to take?" Caerla asked.

"I do. But go on, what sort of diversion shall Sitara employ? Or what if she refuses to help?"

"In that case, Caerla can act as Raven's messenger," Evelyn said. "Surely that would be important enough to bypass the regular channels?"

"If you're referring to that sniveling hound that calls himself a secretary, then yes, that would be important enough to bypass him."

"Then she can go straight to Olivarion while we snatch the artifacts."

"That's it? That's your idea?" Slade asked. "You do realize he will have magical wards, not only to sense the presence of trespassers, but also around the artifacts themselves? Do you know your way through the streets of Alibeth well enough to escape? And even then, do you not think he'll have some sort of tracking spell tied to them that will lead him straight to you out in the forest?"

"It's a good start," Jack said. "And you haven't come up with anything. If Sitara helps and provides the distraction, Caerla and you will both be free to handle the magical aspect. Caerla, is there anything we can do about wards or tracking spells before going in?"

"I can cast a masking spell that will veil our true intentions until we have left the city," she said. "Even if a ward is tripped, he will not come after us until we are well within the trees once more."

"And what then?" Slade asked. "Run for our lives?"

"With the fire-tamer in hand," Evelyn said, "I'm sure you could cast a spell of your own to break whatever link he has with it. By that time, Caerla's part will be done and she'll be eager to return to Raven. Why not go with her and let Raven shield you until Olivarion's wrath has died down?"

Jack smiled at Evelyn's quick thinking. Make it seem like Slade chose to go to Raven, rather than being summoned. The hawk didn't say anything about that part of the plan, making it seem as though she gave her silent agreement.

Slade considered a moment more. "Olivarion *wouldn't* dare go up against Raven, no matter how angry he was. And by then I'm sure I could come up with something to get rid of the tracking spell. Very well, I will agree to this. It will mean avoiding Alibeth for the rest of my life, but I consider that no great loss. When do we start?"

"Now, if you're finally ready," Caerla said.

They all nodded their agreement and the birds took to the air.

"Listen, Jack, no hard feelings about the wolf thing, yes?" Slade asked as they followed behind. "I knew you would figure out a way to escape. You're very resourceful, for a scarecrow."

"I'll take that as a compliment and put the matter behind us, then," Jack said. "But you won't catch me in your debt again."

"I wouldn't dream of it," the fox said. "Besides, you are much too valuable as an ally."

"Now you're just flattering me."

They continued through the forest, heading for Alibeth yet

again and hopefully for the last time. They didn't notice till hours later that they were being followed.

Evelyn was the first to see them during one of her flights back to check on Jack. "Wolves!" she said, flying higher into the air. Jack and Slade turned just as the wolves charged, their cover blown.

"Stand back!" Caerla commanded, flying ahead of them as she cast a spell that created a thick white cloud between them and the wolves. "Keep going! I will meet up with you in the city. Go!"

Slade took off, stopping when he saw Evelyn and Jack still standing there. "We need to hurry," he said, his body growing larger the way Nadya's had. "Jack, climb atop my back. We'll go faster that way. Evelyn, fly!"

"Flight is useless," one of the wolves snarled through the cloud. "The High Wolf summons you, fox! And the crow! You will answer immediately!"

As soon as Jack had a firm hold, Slade rushed off through the trees, Evelyn close at his heels. Jack glanced back once to see Caerla casting another spell to keep the wolves at bay. Slade jumped a fallen tree and Jack nearly lost his seat, so he clung tighter and turned away from the hawk. More wolves appeared on either side of them, and Slade cast what spells he could while running. Evelyn joined in as well, and great flashes of blue and green light burst on all sides, knocking the wolves back, at least temporarily. Jack buried his face in Slade's fur as the fox picked up speed. The last thing he wanted was to fall off and be caught by the wolves again. They wouldn't treat a scarecrow with the same respect they had a bear.

Snarls and growls followed close behind them, but the fox kept just ahead. He was darting through the trees now, zigzagging his way to the end of the forest, casting more spells as fast as he could run.

And then they burst into the bright sunlight and the wolves' growls fell further and further behind them. Jack lifted his head to see Alibeth ahead once more. Looking behind, he saw the wolves stopping just at the tree line. They wouldn't dare enter the human city. Slade slowed his pace and Evelyn came to rest on Jack's shoulder.

"We made it!" she said. "For a minute there, I wasn't so certain we would."

"Let's just hope the hawk joins us soon," Slade said. "Without her, we'll have to come up with a new plan."

16

CONSPIRATORS

They decided to wait outside the city. The sooner Caerla found them, the sooner they could be about their business. But hours passed and she didn't come. Soon it was long past midday and the fox grew restless.

"If she doesn't show soon, I won't be joining you," he said. "I'm willing to risk going against Olivarion with a powerful mage at my side, but not with you two and that sorry excuse for a dreadlord. No offense."

"We still have to try," Evelyn said. "We certainly can't do this without you. I'm even willing to be in your debt, but you must stay."

Slade smirked. "You have nothing I want," he said. "Unless perhaps you succeed and become human. That would be another story. But there's no guarantee that will happen."

"You're just going to leave us here?" Jack asked.

"The way I see it, you have a pretty good life ahead of you. Evelyn's used to being a crow now, and that spell on your feet will likely last for years. You two could travel, or make a nice living in Underbeth. Or join the Guild. No need to go up against dreadlords. Evelyn can study magic and become the master she's always wanted to be. There are more willing teachers in the animal world than in the human one, after all, and the Guild has both. They're always looking for more animal mages to join their side. Besides, I'd like to keep living for several years to come. No point in throwing it all away now."

"And your fire-tamer? What of that?" Evelyn asked. "You're willing to throw away all the time you claim you searched for it?"

"It's regrettable, but not worth my life," he said.

"What if we went back for Caerla?" Jack asked. "Would you stay if we could find her again?"

"My guess is the wolves have her by now. But yes, I would consider it, if she were with us."

"We can't, Jack," Evelyn said. "They nearly captured us before."

"But if they've caught Caerla, we'll need to go back for her anyway. We can't leave her with them."

"You'll need to decide soon," Slade said. "I'd really rather be on my way than sit here while you argue about it."

"I'm going back," Jack said. "I'll go alone if I have to."

"Nonsense. I'll come with you," Evelyn said.

"And I suppose I'll just sit here and wait for you, yes?" Slade asked.

Jack cursed. "We can't leave him alone. He'll run off for sure."

"You just love making things difficult, don't you?" Evelyn accused the fox.

"It does make life a bit more colorful, yes."

"I'll go alone, then," Evelyn said. "I'll have a better chance of freeing her than you will."

Jack wanted to argue, but he couldn't think of anything to say. Instead, he glared at the fox, wishing they didn't need his help.

Evelyn was just preparing to take off when Jack spotted something emerge from the forest, speeding toward the city.

"It's Caerla!" Evelyn said. She rose into the air to meet the hawk, who changed her course to head for them.

A minute later she landed next to them, her feathers sticking up in many places.

"What happened?" Jack asked. "Were you caught?"

"They were more persistent than I thought. Raven needed to know about this turn of events, so I had to find a messenger. It look me a bit longer than I anticipated."

"We're glad you're all right," Evelyn said. "We were worried."

"No need. Let's get on with it, shall we?"

Slade made a 'hmpf' sound, but made no further comment. As he and Jack entered through the side entrance, Evelyn and Caerla flew over the wall. "We'll need to avoid being seen by any of Olivarion's servants," Slade said, "including Manus, the filthy traitor. This will make our route much more difficult and winding."

"Lead the way," Jack said.

Once inside the city, the fox led them in the opposite direction of what Jack was used to. Shadows filled the streets with the setting of the sun, providing numerous hiding places. Few people prowled the night, and still the fox led them at a crawl. Not until the last ray of light had completely disappeared, leaving only a few magic balls of light to illuminate the way, did Slade quicken his pace. In the dark, they could easily be mistaken for a cat or dog, so no one should give them a second glance.

The two birds followed overhead, their eyesight much keener than the fox's and scarecrow's. They wound through the streets, letting the darkness deepen and the residents of the city seek their beds, animals included. Finally, Slade stopped. The birds landed beside them and he whispered, "We're here. I'll let you do the talking. I'm sure she has no great love for me."

The houses loomed above them, shadowy shapes whose windows reflected the moonlight. Jack stepped forward and knocked on the door. They waited a few moments, hearing the soft padding of someone moving about. A second later, the door opened and a bleary-eyed cat looked out at them. Another mage, no doubt.

"What do you want?" he asked.

"We'd like to see Sitara," Jack said.

"Do you have any idea what time it is?" he asked. "Her lady-ship has taken to her bed. You'll have to come back in the morning."

"I'll see them now," Sitara said, appearing out of the darkness behind him. "Thank you, Shanden."

The guard cat left and Sitara opened the door wider for them, ushering them inside. "Come in," she said. The group entered and Sitara created a ball of light to hover over them, providing a soft glow. "Please have a seat in the parlor. I'll be with you in a moment."

They followed her instructions while she hurried up the stairs, leaving them with another glowing ball in her absence. Jack and Evelyn perched on one sofa chair and Slade and Caerla sat on the couch. A fireplace sat dark and empty on the back wall, a stool and harp next to it. Potted plants stood in the corners, tamer than the ones Jack had seen upstairs. A moment later, Sitara returned, jumping on a love seat near the door.

"What can I do for you?" she asked, looking around at all of them. "Surely you're not here to attack me again. Knocking on the door would be an odd way to go about it."

"We came to seek your help," Jack said.

She laughed. "Why would I help you? Your fox friend injured many of my companions and cheated me out of a beneficial transaction."

"If you can put aside your differences and work with us, we've thought of a way for all of us to get what we want."

"Go on."

"Olivarion has an artifact we need," Jack continued, indi-cating himself and Evelyn. "He also has one Slade wants. With your help, we can steal them with little trouble."

"And what do I get out of it?"

"The loss of these artifacts will weaken Olivarion. He'll be less able to defend against future attacks."

Sitara nodded in understanding. "Your offer is tempting. What about the hawk? What's her part in this?"

"I follow the orders of my master. For now, that involves helping them achieve their goal. I will use my magic to steal from the dreadlord."

"You don't fear his wrath?" Sitara asked.

"I fear the wrath of my master much more."

"And who would that be?" the cat asked.

"What does it matter?"

"Will you help us, or not?" Jack interrupted.

She looked at each of them for a long moment, keeping her thoughts to herself. Jack was suddenly sure she would refuse, that they'd have to find another way to distract Olivarion, but then she nodded. "I will. To see Olivarion fall... That is a goal I can get behind. He has held this city for far too long. But we will do nothing tonight. You may sleep here, if you wish. Tomorrow, we will plan."

"Thank you," Evelyn said.

"Do not mistake me; I do this for my own interests. After we've stolen the artifacts, our companionship ends and you are on your own. Understood?"

"Perfectly," Jack said.

She rose, bade them goodnight, and disappeared back upstairs.

"I hope this works," Slade said. "That one is more likely to turn on us than help."

"And you're not?" Caerla asked.

"I have no reason to wish any of you harm. If Olivarion falls, many of my problems will be over."

"Let's get some sleep," Jack said. "I'm sure we'll need as much rest as we can get."

SITARA TREATED them to a gourmet breakfast the next morning, ushering them into a large dining room already laden with food. Sausage, bacon, ham, fruit, baked bread, all was there for them to enjoy. While the others ate, Jack asked Sitara about strategy.

"Do you think you and your followers can provide the distraction? Slade and Caerla can handle the magic aspect while Evelyn and I steal the artifacts."

"What sort of distraction do you have in mind? I won't put my people in danger, so attacking is out of the question."

"What about offering an alliance?" Evelyn said.

"You mean as his consort?" Sitara asked derisively.

"It's only a ruse," Caerla said. "And if it fools him, where's the harm? It only proves you're smarter than he is."

"But still," the feline said. "The thought of offering myself to him..." She shuddered.

"Do you have a better suggestion?" Jack asked.

"At present, no. But let's speak more of this after breakfast. Perhaps a full stomach will make for better ideas." The others finished their meal while Jack returned to the parlor. He sat on the stool by the harp and gently ran a finger across the strings, creating a soft utterance of notes. Waiting gave him a chance to think. He had set out to help Evelyn, but his adventures on his own had opened his eyes to another issue. Being traded from one powerful being to another had created a sense of helplessness in him. They couldn't even complete their first task without the help of others. But if he were human...

Miriel's words echoed in his mind. His enchantment, the one that made him a scarecrow in the first place, hadn't been created by a mage. The only other magic users he knew of were witches. Why shouldn't he see if the one they sought could make him human, too? He didn't even want to think of what the witch would want in return, but surely it wouldn't hurt to ask.

Visions of traveling the world with Evelyn—both of them human—filled his head, and he imagined all the places they'd visit:

the coast, distant cities, perhaps even other countries. The world would be open to them. He smiled to himself. The world was already open to them, but Evelyn wouldn't be happy until she'd stopped Ferah. That meant becoming human, and honestly, Jack agreed that it was the best course to follow. It just made their task more difficult.

The others appeared at last, resuming their seats from the night before. Jack joined Evelyn on the sofa and Sitara cleared her throat.

"I'm willing to offer myself to Olivarion in order for this to work. However, I will expect a reward."

"Is seeing Olivarion defeated not enough?" Evelyn asked.

Sitara just glared at her. "This is my pride we're talking about."

"I will ask my master to reward you," Caerla said. "Will that suffice?"

"And if he refuses?"

Jack sighed. "Then I will be in your debt." Even saying the words was difficult, but he saw no other option.

Sitara nodded. "This is acceptable. Now, let's talk timing."

"Would not sooner be better?" Evelyn asked.

"One might think so. But I happen to know that Olivarion plans to attend the festival tomorrow night. His security at his headquarters will likely be high with him absent, but with two mages, that's surely no problem for you."

"It will be fine," Caerla said.

"How do we know he won't have the artifacts with him?" Evelyn asked.

"Not likely," Slade said. "At least, not both at once. My guess is he may carry the fire-tamer with him, but the storm-eater he'll leave guarded, to be used only in special situations. But if we can snatch that one, taking the fire-tamer will be simple. Especially if we allow Caerla to use it."

"Won't there be humans at the festival?" Jack asked.

"Leave that to me," Sitara said. "It will be my people who will be in danger. If all goes well, the four of you will be busy at his headquarters, far from the crowd."

"What of an escape plan?" Caerla asked.

"With the storm-eater in hand, none should be able to stand against us," Slade said. "We can cast a sleep spell on them, or invisibility on ourselves. Or both. Perhaps a misguided tracking spell to put any pursuers off the scent."

"And if we're separated?" Jack asked.

"We meet outside the city," Evelyn said. "At the side entrance."

"And what of me?" Sitara asked. "What of my reward?"

"I will return after I have reported back to my master," Caerla said. "You will have your reward then."

"And how can I trust you'll return? I would think some sort of collateral should be left behind. I have to look out for my own interests, after all."

Jack glanced at Evelyn, but she only shrugged. "What would you consider fair?" he asked.

"Hmpf. Perhaps one of the artifacts should stay with me. Or one of you, until the hawk returns."

"Leave a powerful item with you?" Slade scoffed. "Not a chance."

"We have to do *something*," Evelyn said.

"Then why don't you stay with her?" the fox retorted. "Or are you in too much of a hurry? Surely with the storm-eater in hand you won't be in any danger."

"We can't stay around here," Jack said. "It's too close to Olivarion."

"I can take the storm-eater with me, and Evelyn can stay with you," Caerla said to Sitara. "That way any tracking Olivarion uses will lead away from the city. We'll retrieve Evelyn when I return with the reward. Is this acceptable?"

"I'll stay as well," Jack said.

"That may not be wise," Sitara said. "Olivarion knows you.

He may just as easily cast a spell to track *you*. Best you get away from the city as fast as possible."

"I won't leave Evelyn again," he said.

"It's okay, Jack," Evelyn said. "We don't have much of a choice this time. You'll return with Caerla and we'll be on our way."

"But—"

"She'll be fine," Sitara said, rising. "Now, I have to make plans with my own people. You are free to roam the house. Enjoy the workshop or the garden. Be cautious if you go into the city, though. Best to stay out of sight for as long as possible."

"Agreed," Slade said.

Sitara left them and Slade rose and headed for the door, calling, "I'll be back soon," over his shoulder.

Jack shook his head, sighing. Evelyn fluttered to the top of the harp, examining the tuning pins and neck.

"Wonder who plays that," Caerla said. "Surely not the cat."

"She mentioned a human mage companion," Jack said. "She stays at the Guild most of the time."

"You think she'll show up while we're here?" Evelyn asked. "Bet she'd have a lot of questions."

"Possibly," Caerla said. "But doubtful, considering the festival and the recent theft at the Guild. I've dealt with human mages. She'll likely be gone till midwinter."

Jack shrugged. "Doesn't make much difference to us. Do you want to see the workroom? It's pretty interesting."

"I'll remain here," Caerla said.

Evelyn flew to Jack's shoulder. "Let's go."

They left the hawk in the parlor and Jack climbed the stairs to the second floor, where every door was closed except for that of the workroom. At the sight of the plants, Evelyn gave a cry and flew ahead. Jack found her on top of the table, sorting through the numerous things that covered it.

"This is amazing!" she said. "So many books, and there are herbs and tools! I wish I had a workroom like this."

"You may, one day," Jack said. "You can join the Guild when this is over. I bet you'd advance quickly."

She laughed. "Think so?"

"Positive."

"Doubtful. But your faith in me is encouraging. I wonder..." She studied one of the open books on the table, then glanced about until she found what she wanted. "Aha!" she cried, picking up a black candle from the tabletop. "Let's give this a try."

"What are you doing?"

"I'm going to attempt some magic. It's been a while."

Jack laughed. "Running all about the world doesn't leave much time for practicing magic."

"And we've only explored this little area of the world. Just think what else may be waiting out there!" She held the candle aloft, still studying the book, then turned her wings just so, eyes closed in concentration. Immediately, a flame sprang up on the wick, blazing green. Evelyn opened her eyes and cried out in joy. "It worked!"

Jack clapped. "See? A natural."

"Let's try another."

She moved on to another spell, and another, and though she didn't always get them right, she always got some sort of reaction, which was a start. After about an hour and a half, she stopped, finally tiring.

"I should've run away to the Guild, rather than become a crow," she said, nestling down on a discarded scarf on the table. "I could've learned so much already."

"And miss out on meeting dreadlords and a god? Never," Jack said.

She laughed. "I suppose there's that. And I'm glad you're with me. I guess things haven't turned out *too* bad. I still worry about Mordecai, though."

"We'll find him."

"I hope you're right."

She dozed off, too exhausted to keep her eyes open a second

longer. Jack watched her a moment, then climbed atop a chair to look at the contents of the table for himself. There didn't seem to be any order to the setup, but perhaps that was intentional. You never knew with mages. Finally, he gave up trying to make sense of it and found a book from one of the shelves and settled himself down to read.

THEY DIDN'T SEE Slade again until the next morning. Jack asked what he'd been up to, but the fox gave no explanation. Typical. Sitara encouraged them to rest as much as possible, claiming they'd need all the strength they had, but Jack felt restless. He couldn't just sit anymore; he had to *do* something.

He went out into the garden alone and tossed pebbles against the tree. The wind blew above the buildings, whistling down into the garden, causing more leaves to flutter to the ground. Jack frowned. Winter was coming on fast. If their search took too much longer, they'd be traveling in snow, and there was no telling how Caerla's spell would hold up on his feet. Not to mention how it would affect Evelyn. She'd never experienced winter as a bird.

Caerla joined him a short while later. "You're thoughtful," she observed.

"A little worried, yes," he admitted. "Many things can go wrong."

"You must have faith," the hawk said. "All will be well."

"Will you tell me about Raven? How did you come to serve him? And where did you learn magic? If you don't mind, that is."

"Not at all." She perched atop the bench, situated to so she could see the door and the windows above them. "Raven taught me all I know," she said. "For as long as I can remember, he has always been there, first as a father figure, then as a teacher, and now as master."

"Do you have family?"

"The other birds, they are my family. All creatures who serve him are my family. That is our way."

"So what about the magic? Was it difficult to learn? And what about...other places?"

"Other places?"

"Places not in this world."

Jack almost hadn't brought it up, half believing he'd dreamed the star-filled sky, the smooth water, and the peaceful flight on Raven's back.

"I do not understand you," Caerla said.

"Forget it. It doesn't matter."

"Magic is what it always is: turbulent, unpredictable at times, stubborn. It is its nature. If you do not love it, you will never bend it to your will."

They sat in silence, listening to the muted sounds of the city beyond the walls. From within the house, a voice rose in laughter. It was peace, for a moment, even if it was false.

"It's time to go." Sitara stood in the doorway, her tail swishing back and forth. Jack and Caerla rose.

"Let's finish this," the hawk said.

THE CITY TRANSFORMED, lights and colors morphing before their eyes into something foreign and strange, but enticing. Many humans passed them wearing masks and elaborate costumes to celebrate the festival. After they had passed by, the group moved, traveling together for a time until Sitara stopped them and announced it was time to part.

"We'll continue to the festival. Be quick. And don't forget your promise." She aimed the last at Evelyn, who nodded.

Caerla cast a spell over them so they could pass unnoticed and they raced toward Olivarion's headquarters. Around one corner, they nearly ran into a man who had begun the celebration early. He stumbled about the street, slowly weaving his way in the direction of the festival. Slade snickered but made no comment.

Many of the costumes sparkled in the light of the hovering discs and the stars far above: birds and mammals, fish and reptiles, and even stranger—scarecrows, ghosts, faeries, and other denizens of the spirit world. They leaped and sang and laughed on their way, and Jack almost wished he were going with them.

"Almost there," Caerla said, stopping near an alley.

"You distract the guards out here," Slade said. "We'll retrieve the storm-eater."

"It's likely heavily spelled," Caerla objected. "And you'll need extra shielding once there. It makes no sense to split up now."

"I'm strong enough to do this," Slade said.

The hawk tutted in disbelief.

"I do not reveal my full strength often," the fox confessed. "Waste of energy, and then my enemies know my limits. Better for them to underestimate me. But for this, I will not hold back."

The hawk didn't look convinced, but she said, "I'll cast another masking spell over you as added protection. But if you get into trouble, I won't be able to reach you right away."

"We'll be in and out," Slade said.

"I'll give you ten minutes, no more. Even I can't distract them for longer than that. I'll meet you outside the city when we're through." The fox nodded and Caerla began her spell. She moved her wings in precise patterns, humming, and finally said, "It is finished. Hurry!"

Slade dashed around the corner, Jack close behind him, Evelyn perched once more on his shoulder. Caerla kept back, waiting for any sign of Olivarion's guards. They crept down the same alley where Jack had first met the dreadlord, only from a different direction. Every few feet, Slade stopped and listened, but never heard any sign of movement. Without a word, he stopped before a grate in the side of a building, holding one paw to his mouth to indicate silence. Then he cast a spell of his own before lifting the grate, which made not a sound. He let them enter first, closing the grate carefully behind them once he was also inside. A tunnel extended in front of them, ending far ahead where a faint glow of light could be seen. When they finally reached the end, they peeked down into a large living room, a single candle burning to illuminate their surroundings. Several cats stood guard on the ground, on couches, and near the doors.

Slowly Slade opened the grate and stepped out onto a shelf below, motioning for them to follow. From there, he cast another spell, though Jack couldn't begin to guess what its purpose was meant to be. "Stay up here," the fox instructed in a whisper. "We'll need to get away quickly, and this is our best way out." Then he jumped to the floor, walking among the cats without drawing the least attention to himself. At one end of the room, two cats stood before a small chest, which sat on a table. Slade aimed straight for it.

"It's so bright," Evelyn said. "So many spells on it... I hope Slade can get through it."

The fox reached it, moving behind the cats and casting another spell, this one creating a soft light that quickly extinguished itself. The chest opened a moment later and the fox carefully retrieved the contents, closing the lid before the guards noticed it had opened. Just as he turned to rejoin them, a voice echoed throughout the room.

"Well, now. What have we here?"

17

THE STORM-EATER

The cats immediately stiffened, adopting battle stances as they looked about the room. Nadya stepped out of the air, dropping her spell and glaring at the cats, daring them to attack her. Many hissed, but they stood their ground, waiting for her to make the first move.

She swished her tail in amusement. "You have something I want," she said to Slade.

"All here is Olivarion's," one of the cats answered, thinking she spoke to them.

"Good luck," Slade answered. "You're out of your league, Nadya. Don't make me do something I won't really regret."

"Empty words. You wouldn't touch me."

"You dare oppose Olivarion?" one of the guards asked. They circled her, pressing closer with every second.

"I won't have to do anything to you. You're doing it to yourself," Slade answered. He dashed back along the wall, aiming for the shelf.

Nadya sent a blast of magic—like a pillar of light—after him, which just missed his tail and exploded against the wall. The guards immediately leaped for her, but she cast them all back with another spell. Slade jumped up the shelves, reaching the top and yelling, "Go! Go!"

Jack and Evelyn hurried back through the grate, Nadya's voice echoing up to them. "Thieves! Idiots! They're getting away!"

Slade quickened the pace, practically pulling them out of the tunnel and rushing down the alley. Another explosion of light burst behind them and Nadya's cries echoed up the tunnel, alerting more guards to the danger.

Slade dashed ahead, running through the streets at dizzying speeds, taking sudden turns to throw off pursuit. Jack followed as fast as he could, and Evelyn flew ahead, keeping an eye on Slade while making sure Jack didn't fall behind. Finally, she got the fox to stop and allow Jack to climb aboard his back—after once more changing his size—but then he was off again, barely waiting for Jack to get a firm grip.

There was movement behind them, something following them in the dark. The next time they passed a light, Jack looked back to see several cats chasing them. Whatever spells had protected their group had worn off.

"Take the skull!" Slade commanded. He flicked his head and the storm-eater fell into Jack's hands. A cat skull. "Touch it to my back! Quickly!"

Jack complied. Slade chanted and a white fog descended around them, shielding them from sight. The fox laughed and turned to meet their pursuers.

"Are you crazy?!" Evelyn cried.

Slade roared and a strong wind blew toward the cats, knocking them back several feet. He chanted again and his body changed and grew, two more tails sprouting beside his, a blazing fire kindling in his eyes. He roared again and fire mixed with the wind, burning any who continued their pursuit.

Jack watched with a mixture of shock and fear. Was this Slade's power, or the storm-eater's? Evelyn fluttered above in a state of panic and anxiety. Neither of them had seen anything like this.

Then out of the fire a figure appeared, walking through the flames unscathed. A bright bubble of light surrounded her, and her eyes also blazed with an inner fire. She spoke in a voice unlike anything Jack had ever heard, like the sound of the turning of the earth, or of the collision of clouds, her words lost in the rumble. He shuddered involuntarily.

Slade's muscles shifted and Jack jumped off his back, shouting in alarm when the skull stuck to the fox's back, absorbing into his body a second later. Then Slade leaped and Nadya met him in the air, both snarling and snapping, the fire surrounding them both. It was more terrifying than anything Jack had seen in the wolf war. Why the leaders hadn't used the storm-eater in battle was beyond him. But then magic was always more complicated than it seemed. All of them were walking proof of that.

Nadya knocked Slade to the ground, closing in to latch onto his neck, but he rebounded and propelled her backward. A moment later, he knocked her into the side of a building so hard that when she landed on the ground, she didn't get up again. He stood there, growling and waiting, but Nadya didn't rise. Finally, the flames dispersed and he slowly shrank, resuming his true shape. He looked at Jack with an amused smile.

"One more stop," he said.

"That wasn't the plan!" Evelyn cried.

"I was promised my fire-tamer!" Slade snapped. "And I don't trust Sitara. Do you wish to give me the storm-eater? I will happily keep it if that is your desire. Either way, I will take what is mine, and Olivarion will know he cannot renege on a deal with me so lightly."

Jack and Evelyn exchanged a glance, but Jack could think of nothing to stop the fox. He shrugged. Evelyn huffed in exasperation, but made no further protest. Jack resumed his place on

Slade's back and they dashed once more through the city, this time aiming straight for the light and noise of the festival.

SLADE CAST another spell over them as they neared the streets bordering the festival grounds. Evelyn rose in the air, watching from above as Slade entered the pressing crowd, weaving in and out of legs with hardly a stop. Shouts and laughter and music filled the air, leaving hardly any room for thoughts. Nothing else existed during the festival. Revelers swayed, children squealed, and constant movement and excitement and merriment filled the air. The further they pressed in, the more jubilant the celebration became. Revelers danced and leaped about in front of them, forcing them to go around or be trampled. Humans roamed in every direction. How would Slade find Olivarion in the press of people?

Finally, the crowd cleared just a little, and there he was; the dreadlord sat atop a dais next to an aged human male upon a throne. A slightly younger female sat on his other side, both humans dressed in elaborate costumes that denoted royalty. Slade didn't even slow his pace. He dashed straight up the dais, leaving Jack watching from the ground, out of the way of the revelers. Evelyn hovered overhead. Sitara sat just behind Olivarion, speaking to him from behind, though Jack couldn't make out her words.

Slade dashed by Olivarion like a gust of wind, passing to the left of Sitara and off the dais again. The cats shivered a moment, but gave no other sign that they'd noticed anything unusual. Slade picked Jack up on his way back, growing in size and tossing Jack onto his back with little effort, and hurried off again through the crowd, the fire-tamer secured. A few more moments passed before they heard the commotion: shouts and curses and a few screams. Jack glanced back and saw the human king standing, shouting something to the crowd that was lost in the noise.

Olivarion had climbed to the very top of the throne, his narrowed eyes roaming over the people.

"Hold tight!" Slade said.

Jack obeyed, hoping Evelyn was able to keep up with them. Finally, they broke through the edge of the crowd and dashed off into the mostly-empty streets, the noise of the festival growing fainter.

"He'll send his guards after us," Slade said. "We'll have to drop the shield sooner or later. Let's see if we can make it outside the city, eh?"

The fox quickened his pace, flying over the streets like a cool breeze. Soon they squeezed through the side entrance once more and leaped out into the empty fields surrounding Alibeth. Still Slade didn't slow, keeping his lightning speed until they reached the trees. Only then did he stop and allow Jack to climb down.

"What about Caerla?" Evelyn asked. "We're supposed to wait at the entrance."

"It's too dangerous," Slade said. "She'll have to find us here, or in the forest. Olivarion's guards may not be able to see us, but they'll guess which direction we've gone. And Nadya may be up and about now."

"What about Sitara?" Jack asked.

Slade ignored the question, panting heavily for a moment. "If that hawk isn't here in ten minutes, I'm going on without her."

Jack sat on the ground against a tree and Slade produced the storm-eater, handing it over without hesitation. Jack tucked it in his jacket pocket.

When Caerla flew up a few minutes later, she glided beside the tree line until she spotted them and landed.

"We've roused the hornets' nest," she said. "Olivarion will likely send his entire army after us, and he won't wait until dawn."

"What are we waiting here for, then?" Slade asked. "Let's be off!"

"What about my promise?" Evelyn said. "I have to go back."

"Go if you want," Slade said. "Though you'd be much smarter to run as far as you can and never return."

"We cannot stay here," Caerla said. "You'll need to decide quickly."

Evelyn sighed, looking back at the city with regret. "We don't even know if she's safe."

"I'm sure she's fine," Slade said. "I'm much more worried about the fox and the cat army likely not too far behind."

"We can come back later," Jack said. "We'll make it up to her. And Caerla will return with her reward. I'm sure she'll explain what happened."

"That I will," the hawk promised.

Evelyn sighed again. "Fine, let's go. But I feel horrible about it."

"Are you coming with us to Raven's land, or continuing on your own?" Caerla asked. "It will be far safer if you come back with us. Raven can grant you safe passage to Siobhan."

"We'd like to, but we've waited so long already," Jack said. "And the wolves are still searching as well. And the Hunter. I'd like to avoid them if possible."

"We appreciate everything you've done for us," Evelyn added. "Will you make sure there's no tracking spell on the storm-eater before we part?"

"Of course." Caerla examined the item carefully, then cast her own spell, which caused the skull to glow brightly for a moment before returning to normal. "It is done."

Slade cast a similar spell over the fire-tamer and said, "That will throw them off a bit."

"We cannot tarry any longer," Caerla said.

"Good luck escaping," said Slade. "You're going to need it."

"Come visit soon," Caerla added. "Raven will be waiting."

With that, the fox and hawk dashed off into the trees, leaving Jack and Evelyn once more alone.

"No time to rest," Jack said. "We'd better be off, too."

"Right."

"Unless you know how to make a shield with this thing?"

She laughed. "Maybe someday. I wouldn't trust it right now."

They headed south along the tree line for a while, until it curved around and proceeded east. Then they plunged deep into the trees, keeping their southward path. Hours passed in silence until the sun began to rise once more and they found a shallow hole in a cliff face to hide in and rest. Evelyn examined the skull as she settled into a makeshift nest, saying finally, "Who thought to create such a thing? It's ugly and disturbing. A cat skull. How repulsive."

"As long as it's what the owl wants, it can be as repulsive as it likes," Jack said.

"You're right," she said, settling down to sleep.

"I'll stay up and keep watch," he said. "You rest."

But she was already dreaming.

THEY SET off again a few hours later, Evelyn still bleary-eyed. Jack felt his exhaustion catching up with him, but they couldn't stop, not now. After another few hours of travel, Evelyn called another halt and asked to see the skull.

"I may be able to cast some small illusion spell to hide us," she said. "Not sure how effective it will be. But worth a shot, right?"

Jack didn't argue, just watched the forest around them for any sign they were being followed. He placed the storm-eater on the ground and Evelyn stood before it, one wing barely touching it as she closed her eyes. She began to hum the way Caerla had when casting the masking spell, but it was a different tune. A moment later the skull began to glow with a pale blue light. She opened her eyes and cocked her head.

"Well, that's not exactly what I had in mind," she said.

"What did you do?"

"I'm not sure. We should probably keep moving, though, just in case it didn't work."

He gathered up the storm-eater again and they took off. The land rose, giving way to hills,, and they crossed more streams than Jack had in all his travels thus far. Luckily, with the new spell on his feet, he didn't worry so much about them falling apart, but he was still careful.

As the evening drew nearer, his eyes began to droop more and more. "I need to find a place to rest," he said. "I've been up for over a day. I can't go on anymore."

"Maybe there's another hideaway nearby. Be right back."

She flew ahead to look down the other side of the hill they were climbing, hurrying back a moment later. "You're in luck!" she said. "There's a little village just down the other side. It should have plenty of places to hide."

He hurried the rest of the way up and looked for himself. A few people moved about far below, but it seemed they were all going indoors for the night. The wind picked up, its cold breeze announcing winter close at hand. For a moment, Jack pictured them traveling through the snow, him buried under deeper and deeper drifts. They would need to finish their quest before then, or even the spell on his feet likely wouldn't keep him from falling completely apart.

Smoke rose from many chimneys as they descended the hill and stole through the trees. Evelyn spotted a barn behind one of the houses, so they made for it rather than sneaking through the village itself. Once inside, the neighing of several horses greeted them, but none of the animals spoke to the duo. Jack found a bed of hay just inside, away from the horses and the risk of being stomped. He was already asleep before Evelyn had a chance to land.

THE DREAM WAS the same as before, but this time Jack could hear the woman's words.

"You can't expect me to live in these conditions," she said. "I won't do it, Alex."

"Martha, please," he was saying, "just wait a bit longer."

They were seated across from each other near the fireplace, but Jack's mouth was moving against his will. He was merely a spectator, witnessing something that had already passed.

"So you keep saying," she said. "How long? Do you think I'll wait another year while you attempt to get on your feet? I could've married an earl's son, but I chose you, though the gods know why."

Alex rose and turned away from her, pulling the door open roughly.

"That's right, run away," she said. "Just like you always do! That's all you're good for, running away from your problems."

He slammed the door shut behind him and walked out into the cool dark. The water wheel spun on incessantly, taking no notice of his anger. After taking a few deep breaths, he decided to take a walk in the forest, the only place he ever felt at peace anymore. But the door opened behind him just as he entered the trees.

"You're going to regret this!" Martha called from behind, searching the dark for him. "I can't sit back and do nothing!"

"Then do something!" he called over his shoulder. He was already within the canopy of trees, ignoring her shouts and threats. In the forest, he could pretend he was the only person in the world, and the only sounds he heard were those of startled animals as he disturbed their slumber.

Jack was carried through the man's eyes, feeling the anger and uselessness that he'd let build within him. But as he walked further, those emotions dissipated until there was only the cool breeze and the gentle night sounds. The man walked for a long time, passing hours easily amidst the trees before finally sighing and heading back home. The cottage was dark when he returned, the woman already snuggled tight in the bed. Silently, Alex removed his shoes and outer garments and climbed in beside her, hesitantly wrapping one arm around her. She barely moved, adjusting herself in her sleep, but didn't stir. Soon the man was falling asleep too, dreaming of riches he didn't have, all for a single smile from her lips.

WHEN JACK awoke, Evelyn was nowhere to be seen. The horses moved restlessly in their stalls, but still spoke no word to him. He carefully left the barn and searched the sky, but didn't spot her anywhere. He considered waiting for her to return, but they should leave as soon as possible, which meant he needed to find her quickly. He sneaked out of the barn and across the field to the edge of the village, which was just beginning to stir.

Jack hid behind barrels and bales of hay, keeping an eye on the rooftops as well as the passing humans. Finally, he spotted her stealing a bite from a meat pie left to cool on a windowsill. "Evelyn!" he called.

She turned at his voice and swallowed quickly, then flew over to meet him. "Just getting some food in my belly. Are you ready to go?"

"Yes. I was worried for a minute."

"No need. Let's be off."

"Too late for that," another voice said.

A familiar cat approached from around the corner of a house.

"Elwin?" Jack asked.

"Never thought I'd see you again, after your fox friend sold you to the wolves."

Jack slowly backed away, keeping the cat firmly in his sights. "I'm glad you made it back all right. You never know, with Slade around."

"Oh, we can handle the fox. Where is he, by the way? I'm sure he's the one who orchestrated this little scheme."

"He's gone," Evelyn said. "On his way to Raven's land. Maybe even there already."

She alighted on Jack's shoulder once more as he drew closer and closer to the end of the house and the edge of the field.

"How unfortunate," Elwin said. "For you, I mean."

More cats appeared, both behind and ahead of them. Jack thrust the storm-eater at Evelyn and said, "Fly!"

She hesitated a moment, fumbling to get a firm grip on the skull, then flew high above the rooftops, leaving him alone with the cats. They charged all at once, many trying to swipe her out of the air. Jack ran in all the confusion, ducking and dodging between them and out into the open village. A few humans looked their way and he quickly hid behind a wheelbarrow, then he ran again as fast as his legs would carry him. But even with enchanted feet, he was still no match for the cats.

Several of them pounced on him from behind, knocking him firmly to the ground and keeping him there. Elwin approached, looking down at him with a shake of his head.

"This could've been much easier for you. All you had to do was hand over the artifacts and we would've let you go."

"You can at least be honest with me," Jack said, trying to keep his mouth out of the dirt. "We both know Olivarion wouldn't just let us walk away without some sort of punishment."

"Too true, I'm afraid. It's a pity; Olivarion could've used someone with your spirit. Oh, well." They lifted Jack and dragged him back into the alley between two houses. "Find the crow," Elwin commanded. "And make it known that if she doesn't surrender, I can't guarantee the scarecrow's safety."

"You don't have to do this," Jack said.

"Of course I do," Elwin replied. "Olivarion commands it."

18

THE HARVEST DANCE

They tied him up and hid him on the other side of the barn. Jack hoped Evelyn had gone on without him, but he feared her better nature would win out. The cats had toyed with him, ripping off a few buttons of his jacket and loosening threads that connected his arms and legs to the rest of his body. Only two cats stayed to guard him; the rest searched for Evelyn.

Jack considered talking with his guards, of trying to convince them to let him go. After all, he could help in the search, right? But he shook that off as futile. They were all too loyal to their master. So instead he focused on loosening the ties that bound him. Very slowly he moved his wrists, just a bit here and there so the cats wouldn't notice. They watched the surrounding forest, not paying attention to him. They didn't even speak to one another, simply kept silent watch, with an occasional glance back at him.

A little more maneuvering and Jack was sure he could move one hand up and down, just a little bit. It was a start. He could hear the distant sounds of the village, the people awake and bustling around now, and the horses in the barn behind him moving restlessly in their stalls. The sun rose higher and still he sat, barely moving his hands. Around midday, he was certain he had one hand free and was just preparing to loosen the other when a small group of screaming children ran around the edge of the barn toward the forest. When they saw the cats, they ran at them, still yelling wildly, and the cats bolted.

Jack sat absolutely still, doing his best to appear like nothing more than an average scarecrow.

"Eh, what's that?" one of the boys said, pointing in Jack's direction.

The children hurried over, five of them in all, and one of the girls picked him up. "It's a little scarecrow," she said. "Look, his arms are tied."

"Wonder what he's doing back here," one of the boys said. "He's scrawny, isn't he?"

"And short."

"We should stick him on a post in the field," the girl said. "Then see if he really scares the crows away."

They carried him back to the village with shouts and squeals, happy to be young and alive and free. Jack saw only the ground passing by, his current captor holding him by his back. He didn't dare lift his head to see their destination.

"There!" one said. "That'll do."

The earth spun as they turned him around to face the sky, then pressed his back firmly against a piece of wood.

"I found more string," one of the girls said.

Then they bound his legs together against the wood, followed by one arm.

"It's my turn!" one of the boys said. "You got to do the other arm!"

"I can tie better than you. He'll just fall off if you do it."

"Will not!"

They tugged at his arm, wrenching it back and forth as their argument escalated. Then, with a loud ripping sound, his arm broke free and flew into the air as the boys lost their balance and fell to the ground.

"Now look what you've done!"

"It was your fault!"

"Was not!"

"Let's just get him on the post!" one of the girls interrupted. "We can still tie the arm on. Maybe the crows won't notice."

The other children edged the two scowling boys out of the way and continued their ministrations, tying his detached arm onto the post next to him. He couldn't feel the tear, or any pain at all, and thank the gods for that. But it still dismayed him that they hadn't been more careful. It was his arm, after all, and how could he help Evelyn with only one?

Satisfied with their work, the children lifted him into the air and carried him back to the open fields around the town. They dug a shallow hole about midway between the village and the forest and stuck the post down into it.

"He's an ugly fellow, ain't he?" one of the boys said.

"Especially now with only one good arm," one of the girls said.

"That was Tom's fault."

"Was not!"

"Do you think any crows will come?"

"If he's a good scarecrow, they should all stay away."

"But then how will we know if he works?"

They argued a bit more until one girl said, "We should use him in the Harvest Dance tonight. If he survives that, surely he can scare away a few crows."

The children agreed with this logic, leaving Jack sitting on the post as they hurried back to the village. Fear rose within him in a way it hadn't in all of his travels so far. Humans were destructive by nature, and the girl's words implied that whatever they had in store for him wouldn't be pleasant.

He watched the village, looking for any sign of Evelyn or the cats, but he saw only humans. He tried wriggling his wrist, but the children had bound him tightly. The clouds passed by overhead in their slow, familiar pattern of gray and white, and a chill wind blew down from the north. He sighed in frustration and resigned himself to waiting. It was almost like he'd never left home, had never left the field he'd occupied for so long, only now he had a view of a village. Despair poked at him, nudging him closer and closer to the edge, until he almost believed his journey was over. He would remain on that post for the rest of his days. Or at least until that evening when the children retrieved him for the Harvest Dance. Perhaps the end would come soon, if that was indeed his fate. He hadn't realized how exhausted he was, how tired of running across the land with barely a rest.

Then he thought of Evelyn and a small seed of hope blossomed once more in his breast. At least he'd done what he could for her.

He drifted in and out of consciousness, dreaming of wolves surrounding him and snapping at his feet, of witches casting spells over him to ensure he never woke again, of Evelyn transforming into a giant bear, of a flaming fox flying over a sea of stars. Raven appeared in his dreams, warning him of evil faeries and bird women. When he woke, the gray clouds had gathered and darkened. Still no sign of Evelyn or the cats.

He felt eyes on him and looked to the side, spotting a small bird seated on the post. It cocked its head at him in confusion.

"You can move," it said.

Jack just nodded.

"How odd. Where'd you come from? Never seen you before."

"I was passing through," Jack said. "The children caught me and tied me up."

The bird cheeped in disapproval. "How are you able to move? Are you a mage?"

"I was enchanted by one," he said. "But I can't do magic."

"Pity. You'd probably be free by now."

"Probably," Jack agreed. "Is there anything you can do to help me?"

"Maybe I could pull at the cords," the bird said.

"Anything would be helpful."

The bird set to work, pecking and pulling at the twine, but only managed to loosen a few ragged pieces. He kept at it until the sun sank low in the sky and Jack spotted the children at the edge of the village once more.

"Better be off," he said, nodding at them. "Thank you."

"Sorry I couldn't do more," the bird said.

"Maybe you can. Send word to Raven. Tell him we're in a bit of trouble, if he's willing to help. My name's Jack."

"That I can do," the bird said. He took to the air as the children raced up, shouting and laughing.

"Be careful!"

"He's going to look great!"

"I bet he'll scare even the Autumn King!"

Together they lifted his post out of the ground, carrying it above their heads back toward the village. Music drifted from somewhere ahead of them, some stringed instrument playing a lively tune. The smell of smoke filled the air, growing thicker the closer they got. Voices rose in conversation, song, and laughter, all the sounds of the festival in the city echoing in the open air of the country village. Then they pushed him up, his view of the sky changing to a view of a clearing in the village where a large bonfire blazed and the people danced about. They passed around food and drink and pulled each other into the dance, no one sitting idle for long.

They placed Jack right before the bonfire, the flames warming his back. The adults clapped and patted the children on the heads.

"Where'd you find him?" one man asked.

"Next to Neri's house," a girl answered.

"He's ugly as death," a woman said. "And a little small, don't you think?"

"He's perfect," the man responded. "A perfect nemesis for the Autumn King."

A cheer went up behind him and a new dance began. The man pulled the woman into it and the children shouted and danced their own version, not quite together but not quite alone. The constant movement had Jack looking back and forth, struggling to take it all in. He expected at any moment to be lifted and tossed into the fire, or forced to battle some god-like creature. Too many faces and voices swirled around him and he had no way to escape, no way to block them out.

Then a face appeared in the crowd, leaping about with excessive energy. Red, orange, yellow, and brown leaves covered his body, his eyes round and black. The leaf man danced among and between the dancers, inspiring them to higher energy.

The Autumn King.

Closer and closer he came, working his way to Jack slowly, leisurely, the way autumn does to winter. Any moment now they would grab him, force him to battle, and he couldn't begin to guess the outcome. Then the Autumn King was before him, dancing his wild dance, and someone lifted him up from behind, jumping him around in a mock-dance to rival the leaf man's. A space cleared around them, the people pausing their own celebration to watch the two. The music swelled and the Autumn King danced with even greater energy until finally Jack, the "nemesis," was forced to yield. His human carrier dipped the post, forcing him to bow in defeat.

Then the music stopped and a loud voice cried, "What shall be done with the enemy?" The speaker was the first man, the one who'd said he was perfect and had held his post through the dance.

"Death!" some called.

"Burn him!"

"Rip his straw out!"

The man stood to the side of Jack, holding the post with one hand, and raised the other for silence. "The people have spoken! Death shall be his punishment!"

The crowd cheered.

A second later, Jack soared through the air, the bright stars high above in the endless sky, singing their song of beauty and peace. Then they withdrew, fleeing from him as he was pulled down and engulfed in flames.

Then he was lifted again and pulled away from the fire, a small portion of it going with him, still burning. When he landed on the ground a moment later, a bucket of water appeared above his head, emptying its contents over him. This repeated a couple more times until the flames snuffed out and he watched the steam from his body rise into the air. The noise of the celebration continued, but was more distant.

HE FELT NOTHING.

No pain, no heat. He didn't feel his body or clothing catch fire, and for a moment he thought he had cleared the flames and landed on the other side. But he heard the crackle and pop as his straw body burned. Rather than feel afraid, he had a clear, soothing vision of his dust ascending into the air to join the stars. It seemed a fitting end.

Then he was lifted again and pulled away from the fire, a small portion of it going with him, still burning. When he landed on the ground a moment later, a bucket of water appeared above his head, emptying its contents over him. This repeated a couple more times until the flames snuffed out and he watched the steam from his body rise into the air. The noise of the celebration continued, but was more distant.

"You're lucky I was there to save you. If not for me, you'd be a pile of ashes by now."

Jack smiled, or tried to. His mouth didn't want to work quite right. But he knew that voice. "Hello, Nadya. What are you doing here?"

"Saving you, apparently." Her face peered over him and she shook her head and sighed. "You're even more of a sight now. All black and shriveled on both sides. It didn't quite engulf you completely, but it was only a matter of time."

She unbound him, the ropes disintegrating at her touch. Then she reattached his arm with a twitch of her nose and helped him sit up. It was more difficult to move, but he managed.

"Have you seen Evelyn?" he asked. He looked around. They were in a narrow side street just a short distance from the celebration. No one looked their way.

"We're shielded, for now," she said, following his gaze. "And no, I haven't seen your friend."

"Well, I'm grateful for your help, whatever your reason for being here."

She swished her tail. "I was following you," she admitted. "When you split with Slade and the hawk, I followed them for a while. Had to make sure he got what was coming to him. But after they reached Raven's land, I headed back. Got here just in time to see those kids carry you from the field to the Harvest Dance."

"Why follow me?"

"We've been useful to each other," she said, walking away from the dancing and nodding for him to follow. He did so, slowly. "Besides, I'm beginning to grow quite fond of you."

"I see." If he just kept moving, it wasn't so bad. Maybe Raven could do something, even if he had to carry the scars forever...

"Where is it you're headed?" Nadya asked.

"Siobhan, the owl. But I have to find Evelyn first."

"Any idea where she is?"

"No. The last I saw her, she was being chased by Olivarion's guards."

Nadya clicked her tongue. "That doesn't bode well. If they caught her, they'll be heading back to Alibeth."

"But I don't see how that could've happened. She can fly. They shouldn't have been able to touch her."

"Magic," Nadya said. "Olivarion would've made sure his guards had whatever magic trinkets they could carry, no matter how weak."

"Then what's the point of any of this?" Jack said, throwing up his arms in exasperation. He heard something rip, but without being able to feel it, he wasn't able to tell where it came from.

Nadya glanced sideways at him. "Don't tell me you're giving up."

"No, but—"

"The way I see it, you just have to steal her back and be on your way. You have a storm-eater, so taking them on should be no problem."

"But *I* don't have the storm-eater. And even if I did, I can't do magic."

They reached the end of the village and crossed the field, the forest a shadowy expanse in the distance.

"Lucky I'm here, eh?"

"But why should you help me? I can't keep relying on others to get me out of predicaments."

"Oh? Then how do you plan to get her back?"

"I don't know... Maybe I'll offer a trade or something."

She stopped, forcing him to halt and look her in the eye. Jack shrank back.

"Why can't you just accept my help? Not only am I a mage, but I am offering to help you freely. You're a bigger fool than I thought if you're going to turn that down."

Jack held both hands up in a gesture of peace. "I'm sorry. Free help just isn't what I'm used to. I do appreciate it."

"Hmm."

They continued on, the forest growing larger in their sight until they once more entered its sheltering canopy. Crickets chirped in the distance and cicadas sang their nightly song. They didn't go far before Nadya called a halt and forced him to lie down beside a large tree.

"I'll do what healing I can while you sleep," she said. "We'll leave at first light."

Jack didn't argue. Only when he was nearly asleep did he realize she was giving orders like she was in charge. For some reason that made him smile.

HE EXPECTED to be stiffer the next morning, but his limbs moved a bit more easily, if still not quite how they used to. It was a small price to pay, all things considered. In the morning light, he could see his arms and lower half, which were completely black on the outside. The line stopped abruptly before reaching his middle, for which he had Nadya to thank. He couldn't imagine what his back must look like.

"About what you'd expect," she told him when he asked. "We could find you new clothes. Perhaps steal from a child. Theirs should fit you."

"I'll deal with it," Jack said.

She shrugged. "Suit yourself. I'm going to try a tracking spell."

"I got the impression you had to know what you were looking for pretty well for that to work."

"I may not be close to your friend, but Olivarion's guards are plenty familiar to me. I could perform this spell in my sleep."

She blinked slowly and raised both paws in the air, clapping them together and giving a short bark, then a shimmering trail appeared, silver and sparkling, snaking through the trees. She smirked at Jack, simultaneously growing in size.

"How about that?" she said.

"Impressive."

"Apprentice stuff. Let's go."

He climbed atop her back and they were off, flying through the trees in a mad dash. Jack hoped with all his might that the cats hadn't made it back to the city yet. The trail wound up hill and down hill, over rocks and under ledges, always extending further in the distance. The further they went, the more he despaired that they would have to return to the city and go head to head with Olivarion. The thought scared him.

"The trail's thinning. Look!" Nadya said. "That means we're close. Hold tight!"

She picked up speed, forcing Jack to clutch her fur tighter or risk being thrown to the ground. He closed his eyes and rested his head against the back of her neck, thinking it must be the closest thing to flying.

Suddenly the fox stopped, halting behind a tree while Jack

carefully climbed down and peered around the trunk. The cats stood sprawled out before them, eyes focused on something to the side.

"What are they—"

Nadya cursed. "Stay here!"

She dashed into the midst of them, spotting Evelyn before Jack did and scooping her from the guard who held her. He didn't even put up a fight, his eyes riveted just like the others. Nadya raced back and then Jack saw it: the darkness spreading across the ground, up the trees, engulfing everything in its path. The cats stood entranced, unable to look or move away. When the darkness reached them, it passed over them slowly, almost reluctantly. Then all at once they howled, attempting to flee even as their bodies stiffened, grayed, and crumbled to ash. The cats who hadn't yet been touched shook off their stupor and fled in all directions.

Nadya reached Jack and scooped him up as well, passing Evelyn off to him. The crow was unconscious, her legs and wings bound with twine. Jack held her close to his chest and clutched Nadya's fur with his free hand, leaning down as far as he could to make up for the less-secure grip.

The fox ran even faster than she had before, enhancing her speed with magic and sending spells behind her to slow or hinder the Hunter. Jack risked a look back and saw a man-like shape within the blackness, leisurely walking after them. Except every so often the man *shifted* and wound up closer to them. And it seemed he was gaining ground.

"We have to hurry!" Jack yelled.

"What do you think I'm doing?!" Nadya yelled back.

Jack closed his eyes again, not wanting to watch as the shadow man came closer and closer. Questions of whether or not he could die fled his mind; he knew the Hunter would destroy him.

Then Nadya stumbled on a hidden rock and rolled, sending Jack and Evelyn flying. He lay on the ground for a moment, a canopy of leaves over him, the sun gently filtering down. He rose as fast as he could and scrambled for Evelyn, who lay a couple feet away. Nadya still lay on the ground, moaning softly.

"Run!" she said, lifting herself as much as she could. "There's a creek just a little further ahead. Run!"

"But—"

"Run!"

The Hunter moved closer again and Jack fled, Evelyn clutched in his arms. He saw the creek and dashed for it as fast as his burned body would allow him. He nearly stopped when Nadya screamed, but he pressed on, through the fear, through the guilt and anger and sorrow, then through the water and to the other side.

19

SOUTH

For a long time, he lay on the ground, too shocked and angry and afraid to move. Evelyn continued in her stupor, blissfully unaware of what had happened. After a while he finally looked back across the creek, but no sign of the shadow remained. It would not approach the water. Nadya had also disappeared without a trace, and for a moment a cry caught in Jack's throat, demanding release, but he suppressed it. Crying wouldn't get them anywhere.

Jack sighed, lifted himself up, and unbound Evelyn. He decided then that he would seek out Ferah and demand justice for what she'd done, not just to Evelyn, but to all the animals who had been caught by the Hunter. They would be avenged.

Finally Evelyn stirred, groaning as she stretched her wings and legs. "Jack?" she said, squinting.

"I'm here." His voice wasn't quite right. Too soft. Hollow.

"What happened?" She blinked, adjusting to the light.

He choked on the words, unable to tell her the fox's fate.

"Where are the cats?"

"We were rescued," he managed. "The cats are gone."

She opened her eyes fully and took in his damaged appearance with a gasp. "Oh, Jack. What happened?"

"I'll be all right. Where's the storm-eater?"

"Hidden. It'll be safe for now. Please, talk to me. Tell me."

So he did, relating everything from the moment he was captured by the children to their flight across the creek. Evelyn looked back the way they'd come as if she expected Nadya to appear from behind a tree at any moment.

"Why would she do that?" she said. "Why risk her life in the first place? I don't understand."

"I think the fall injured her. She couldn't get away in time. As for why... I don't know. She mentioned a fondness for me, but I took that as seriously as if Slade had said it. Maybe she wanted to use me again." He shook his head. Even that didn't feel right, but he had no other explanation. It didn't matter now, anyway.

Evelyn shook her head, sighing. "I didn't mean for this to happen," she said. "Any of it. I just wanted to be free."

"It's not your fault," Jack said, wrapping one arm around her. "It's Ferah's. And we will make sure she pays."

Evelyn nodded and fluttered into the air, hovering just above him. "We better retrieve the storm-eater and be on our way. There's no telling when the Hunter will find a way across."

Jack nodded and they took off, looking carefully all around them in case the cats returned, or the Hunter reappeared. They backtracked until they reached the village once more. At the edge of the field, Evelyn flew to the top of a tree and returned with the skull. Jack took it and hid it once more inside his jacket, carefully securing it so it wouldn't fall. His limbs still moved stiffly, but he managed.

They plunged into the forest, hoping they would reach the owl without further mishap. They would make the journey to the second witch after that, and Jack shuddered to think how long that trip would take. The end was still so far.

"I wish we could rest a bit," he said.

"You want to stop?"

"No, I mean really rest. The end of the journey. No more

travel, no more running, no more death. Haven't you had enough?"

"Yes," she said, her gaze straight ahead.

"I miss my post. The simple days, the gossipy crows. The slow movement of the clouds across the sky. Easy to appreciate them now when we're constantly on the run."

"You didn't have to come with me."

"That's not— I'm trying to say I long for it to be over. Not for the journey to not have happened. Just for the end. The only good thing out of all of this is being able to help you."

"And what about you, Jack?" she asked, looking down at him. "What will the end mean for you?"

He sighed, looking up at the gray sky between the leaf canopy, the flutter of autumn leaves as they released their grip on the branches.

"Well, I know a lot more about the world than I used to. I've fought and run and escaped and endured more than I ever dreamed on my post back home. If anything, this journey has opened my eyes. Made me wiser, I hope."

"Wise enough to not travel with an enchanted young woman next time?"

He laughed softly. "Never that."

They continued in silence, each lost to their own thoughts. A family of mice appeared away to their left, then a lone squirrel overhead, more and more animals appearing until they were all around, each going about their day with no thought of witches or shadowy death. That such a peaceful world still existed was a welcome surprise.

They descended another hill and came across a herd of deer, grazing on grass that had no right to be as green as it was. A few looked up at them, but other than a raised brow here and there, they were ignored. Jack and Evelyn were pressing on when one of the deer said, "Jack? Is that you?"

"Islei?" he said, recognizing her a moment later. "It's good to see you again."

"What happened to you?"

"It's a long story."

"Are you here to see Raven?"

Jack looked around at all the animals, the greenness of the grass. Of course. Raven's land.

"We're actually on our way to Siobhan."

"You're a bit turned around, then," she said. "You're on the outskirts of Raven's land, so you don't have too far to go. But it's that way." She nodded her head to their right.

Jack sighed. "Thank you. We appreciate it."

"Do you want a ride? I can get you there faster."

"I hate to ask."

"It's no trouble. Really."

She knelt down and allowed Jack to climb up. Evelyn had to help him, and the minute he was secured, Islei took off. Evelyn flew close by, zipping through the trees in pace with the deer. The land rolled by beneath them and Jack closed his eyes, remembering the sound of Nadya's scream, and the stark silence after.

WHEN NEXT HE opened his eyes, Islei slowed to a trot, panting heavily. "This is as far as I can go," she said. "The tree is just ahead, in the next clearing."

"How can we repay you?" Jack asked.

"You know better than that," she said, kneeling to let him off. Evelyn hurried to help him and he secured the storm-eater again once he was firmly standing.

"We are very grateful," Evelyn said.

"It was my pleasure. It isn't right, folks mistreating each other the way they do. Seems the norm nowadays. I do what I can to counter that."

"I can't thank you enough. Take care of yourself, Islei," Jack said.

"You too. Good luck!"

She darted away into the forest, setting a more leisurely pace for herself. Jack and Evelyn turned together and crossed the remaining ground to the great tree. The sun's last light cast long shadows across the ground, heralding the arrival of evening.

"Hello!" Evelyn called once they reached the foot of the tree. "We're back!"

A moment later Siobhan glided down on silent wings, landing on the last branch and regarding them with narrowed eyes.

"Ah, so you've returned," she said once she recognized them. "It took you long enough."

"We ran into a bit of trouble," Jack said.

"I'm surprised to see you again, scarecrow. What happened to your fox companion?"

Jack struggled for words until he remembered she was talking about Slade. "We've parted ways. I am free of my debt to him and can now help Evelyn as I please."

"How noble. Do you have the storm-eater?" Jack produced the cat skull and held it out to the old bird. She took it with one great claw and held it up before her eyes. "Yes, this is it," she said. "Good. You've kept up your end of the bargain. Now I will help you break your curse."

Evelyn sighed in relief, leaning forward to see what the owl would do.

She produced a silver coin and waved one wing over it. It glowed blue for a moment and she leaned toward it, as if it would speak to her.

"There is a powerful witch named Igraine who lives on the outskirts of a deserted village a day's journey south of here," she said after a moment. "You will need a witch to break a witch's spell, and she is the most powerful in this area. She may ask for some sort of payment in return for her services, but that will be for her to say. Find her and you will find the means to become human once more." The coin stopped glowing and Siobhan looked at the skull again, snatched it up in her beak, then took to the air. "Good luck with your journey. And take care not to deal with witches, if you can help it. Happy endings aren't found where they're involved."

Then she disappeared back to the top of the tree without even giving them a chance to reply.

"Thank you!" Evelyn called after her, but the great bird didn't respond.

"Well, it looks like we're in for more walking," Jack said.

"Let's get a good night's rest first. I can't have you collapsing on me again."

"Ahem."

They turned at the sound, startled, and found the last person they expected.

Slade.

"You!" Evelyn said.

"Yes, it's me."

"Are you here to get revenge on us?" Jack asked.

The fox chuckled. "Hardly. I'm here to help you. And by the looks of you, straw man, you could use all the help you can get."

"Why would you help us?" Evelyn asked. "You've caused us nothing but trouble since we met you."

"Well, part of it has to do with my penance. Raven commanded me to do what I could for you without asking for anything in return. So. Here I am."

Jack furrowed his brow. "Raven sent you?"

"The same. You sent for help, didn't you? Oh, and you'll be glad to know Sitara is taken care of. The hawk returned with apologies and rewards and all is forgiven."

"I was worried about that," Evelyn said.

"Now then, you've delivered the storm-eater to the owl. What's our next destination?"

"Just a moment," Jack said. "I don't know that we want to let you just join back up with us. You could be lying."

Slade smirked. "You're right. I could be. But consider this: I haven't asked for anything from you. You can refuse my help if

you like and I'll return to Raven and find another way to atone.
Or you can move past your doubt and we can be on our way.
Which will it be?"

"Since when do you do Raven's bidding?" Evelyn asked.

"That's the thing: when gods, or even extremely powerful
mages, demand something of you, it's unwise to refuse them.
Not to mention unsafe."

Jack and Evelyn exchanged a glance, neither completely
convinced.

"Give us a moment," Evelyn said. "We need to speak in
private."

Slade rolled his eyes, but he moved far enough away that they
could speak without him overhearing. Unless he used magic, but
there was nothing they could do about that.

"What do you think?" Evelyn asked.

"He *is* a powerful mage, and he's right, he hasn't asked for
anything. I did send a bird to ask Raven for help. If Raven sent
him in response to that, I think we should let him come along.
At least for a while."

"I really don't want to go traipsing all around the countryside
anymore, Jack. He complicates things. I want to go straight to
the witch and undo the curse."

"I know, I know. And we will. Something in my gut just tells
me we should give him a chance."

She frowned, sighed, and said, "I hope you're right."

Jack waved Slade back over and the fox said, "So, you've
decided?"

"We have. You can come with us."

"Oh, goody. Lead on, straw man."

THEY FOUND shelter beneath a blackberry bush that night and
woke the next morning feeling refreshed and ready for the new
journey before them. As they set out, Evelyn began a whistling

song, belying her excited mood. Jack was glad one of them was cheerful. Despite the fox's words, his thoughtful expression betrayed he'd rather be anywhere else than traveling with them.

The land changed quickly as they left the owl's tree behind them. They soon came to the edge of a cliff, a narrow rushing river flowing far below, and they had to search for another way down, which took several hours. By the time they got down to the river, they had to find some way across, which required going much further downstream and out of their way. When Siobhan had said it was a day's journey, Jack supposed she'd meant by flight. Ahead of them were more mountains reaching toward the sky, hiding whatever path led through them.

"I'll scout ahead," Evelyn said. "There's no need for us to wander around any longer than we need to. You two stay here and make camp and I'll find the way through. Then we can start off in the morning."

They didn't argue. Jack was too frustrated with the unexpected difficulties, and the fox's silence just brought up more questions. The owl could at least have warned them about the mountains. When Evelyn finally returned, the sun had already disappeared behind the peaks, its final rays dancing across the sky high above. They settled in for the night once more, hoping it would be the last one before they reached the witch.

THE NEXT DAY, Evelyn led the way, directing them up a narrow path that Jack would've expected to end at a cliff's edge. But up it continued, up and around until finally it opened to more forest that continued up and up to the top of the mountain.

"It should be a bit easier from here," she said. "At least until we get to the other side."

About halfway to the top, Jack had to stop and rest. The climb had drained more of his energy than he'd expected, though

Slade seemed unaffected. Again Evelyn scouted ahead, returning
this time with better news.

"It's not too far to the top now, and I can see a village in the
distance on the other side. But climbing down may be a bit
difficult."

"Do you know any floating spells?" Jack asked the fox. "Or
maybe a shrinking spell? I can't imagine you'd want to carry me
down a mountain."

"I remember a floating spell from a book," Evelyn said. "If I
could just hold it, gravity should pull you down gently."

They looked to Slade for an answer.

"I may know one or two," he said. "Though I admit, I'd like
to see Evelyn do this one. She'll never grow as a mage if she
doesn't practice."

"We're in a bit of a hurry," Jack said. "No offense, Evelyn. But
I think I'll wait until you've mastered that one before trying it
out."

"I can work on it now," she said. "If Slade agrees to
advise me?"

The fox shrugged. "Makes no difference to me. You'll need
plenty of practice, though. May take a whole day. Maybe two.
And that's just to get you comfortable enough to cast it."

"Are you sure you want to wait that long?" Jack asked Evelyn.

"Well... Don't get me wrong, I want to learn. But you're right.
The sooner we do this, the better."

Slade shrugged. "Suit yourself. But remember, any chance to
practice magic is invaluable. You're passing up an opportunity."

"And what about the Hunter?" Jack asked. "What if he
catches up with us while she's practicing?"

"You mean the one Raven spoke of? We haven't seen it even
once, so more than likely it's already returned to the witch."

For a moment Jack just stared at the fox, then remembered
Slade hadn't been with them any of the times they'd been chased
by the Hunter. He didn't know.

"We've seen it," Evelyn said.

"It's killed people," Jack added. "It caught up with us when Olivarion's guards took Evelyn captive. They just...crumbled to dust. Slade, it... It took Nadya."

The fox scoffed, looking between them as if waiting for one of them to laugh and give the joke away. But when neither did, he frowned. "You're serious."

Jack nodded.

"She... She's dead, then?"

Their expressions must have confirmed it, for Slade looked away and blew out a huff of air. He was silent for a long moment, and Jack wondered if he should try to comfort him. He hadn't been sure how the fox would take it.

"Well, this is unexpected," Slade finally said, his voice catching. "No more heists. No butting heads, no witty conversations. I thought... Well, it doesn't matter what I thought. It's over now."

He stood and shook himself.

"I'm sorry, Slade," Evelyn said. "I'm guessing you knew her a long time?"

"Like I said, it doesn't matter. Let's move on if you don't want to try the magic yourself."

He started to walk on alone and Evelyn glanced at Jack, then called, "Wait! I'll try it. You're right. Any little bit helps."

The fox looked over his shoulder and flicked his head for her to follow.

While they wandered off to practice, Jack set about making camp. He still thought they should press on, let Slade float him down, and be done with it. But it was Evelyn's choice, he supposed. He would respect it. If the Hunter showed up, though, he hoped the fox would step in to help them get away.

Jack's dreams that night were filled with new images. He imagined a witch identical to Ferah, sitting in a cottage and waiting for them to arrive. She stirred a giant cauldron filled with a glowing green liquid, and all around her on the shelves and furniture were hundreds of animal bones. She laughed as Jack and Evelyn entered, ushering them to the boiling pot and urging them to peer into its depths, just a bit closer, closer...

He woke with a start to the quiet night, Evelyn and Slade sleeping a few feet away. The moon shone bright and close, illuminating innocent trees and shrubs, nothing more. He went back to sleep with a deep sigh of relief, this time resting without dreams.

EVELYN PRACTICED magic all the next morning, and had been since before Jack awoke. He stretched and yawned as he watched her and Slade, just within the trees a few feet away, but they didn't notice. Evelyn's focus and will were bent to a small twig that floated above her in the air. Slowly it rose and fell, moving only slightly as the breeze attempted to toss it to and fro. Finally, she let it float to the ground.

"Good job," Slade said. "Now let's take it a step further."

They turned to Jack.

"It's your turn," Evelyn said.

Jack swallowed uneasily. "Don't you think you ought to practice some more?"

"I could keep practicing for the rest of my life, but it would only waste more time," she said. "Are you ready?"

"...Yes?"

"Come on, then," Slade said.

"You'll need to stand," Evelyn added. "Close your eyes if it makes you feel better. And try not to move too much."

Jack obeyed, staying as still as he could, his eyes firmly shut. With each movement, he expected to rise suddenly in the air, his legs swinging as panic set in. But it didn't come. After several moments passed, he opened his eyes to ask when she intended to start only to find that she and Slade were several feet below him. He looked down in amazement, which quickly turned to panic as he rose ever higher. He shut his eyes once more, pretending he stood firmly on the ground. The fear slowly subsided. Couldn't he feel the solid earth beneath his feet? Surely Evelyn had already lowered him.

"I'm going to return you to the ground now," she said. "You're doing great, just continue to not move."

He stubbornly refused to open his eyes again. How they were going to manage this down the side of a cliff was beyond him.

"You can open your eyes now," she said.

He did so, finding himself, gratefully, on the ground.

"You were wonderful," Evelyn said.

"A perfect test subject," Slade added.

"I'll need to try it again while flying," Evelyn said. "I'm sure you'll want to repeat it a few times, too. Just to be sure."

Jack collapsed backwards onto the grass. "Try as many times as you like," he said. "I just need to rest for a moment."

"ARE YOU READY?" Evelyn asked.

"As ready as I'll ever be."

They had practiced several more times, mostly with Evelyn hovering in the air while Slade watched silently. They stood before the edge of the cliff now, looking straight down to the tops of the trees far below. It wasn't that he was afraid of heights. He just had no desire to break into multiple pieces; at least, not any more than he already had.

"Don't worry," Slade said. "If anything happens, I am right here to catch you. You will be fine."

Jack nodded and closed his eyes once more, knowing the experience would be better if he refrained from opening them at all. He could hear Evelyn take to the air and settled in for a long wait. After all, it would take quite a while to reach the bottom. To distract himself, he thought about his village and field they'd left far behind. Although he missed it still, he no longer wished he were back there, though in many ways it would be simpler if he were. But his experience in the most recent village with the children and revelers had satisfied that longing. He'd never been quite so relieved as when Nadya had unbound him, freeing him to move as he pleased once more. It drove home that his life had changed, and he couldn't go back to life in a field again. At least not without a struggle, both physically and mentally.

Knowing he probably shouldn't, Jack cracked one eye open to a tiny slit, just to see how much progress they had made. The treetops loomed a great distance below, though the mountain just before him now towered much higher overhead. He quickly shut his eyes again as the fear began to rise. Patience, that was the key.

"Hang in there, Jack," Evelyn said from somewhere just above him. "It won't be much longer, I promise."

He hoped she was right and not just trying to comfort him. He could imagine all sorts of scenarios, all ending with him plunging to the ground, hitting every tree as he fell. He took this as further incentive to keep his eyes closed.

"You're going to maneuver through the trees now," Slade said.

He didn't answer, didn't even feel the slightest change to his body. Evelyn had really come a long way, even without a teacher. What else would she be able to accomplish with the guiding hand of a master? Something thin brushed his leg, bending gently and giving way as he passed. Then another, followed by one less flexible.

"Sorry," Evelyn said. "These branches grow thick together."

He felt himself shift, turning to the right as the descent continued. The breeze picked up, violently jerking him to the left, and then, like a line snapping, he was falling, hitting a few branches that slowed him just a little. He opened his eyes to see the ground rushing closer and prepared himself for impact when he was jerked again, back this time, then floated the remaining feet to the ground.

"I've got you," Slade called.

"Are you all right?" Evelyn asked, fluttering down to land

beside him. "It got away from me. I'm so sorry, Jack. I know that's no excuse."

"It's all right," he said, taking deep breaths and spreading himself out on the ground.

Slade floated down a moment later with no visible effort that Jack could see.

"Very good," the fox said. "Ready to move on?"

20

THE WITCH

The forest ended at last, the land opening on a wide field, dark buildings in the distance. As they approached, the earth rumbled and erupted, giant hedges appearing and reaching toward the sky, blocking their path. The trio jumped back, Jack falling to the ground. For a long moment they simply stared, unsure what to make of it.

"What do you think it is?" Evelyn asked.

"Obviously magic of some sort. The witch?" Jack said.

"Who else would it be?" Slade said.

"You think she wants to keep us out?" Evelyn asked.

"Possibly," the fox said.

"I'm not going back," Evelyn said. "I've come this far, and it will take more than shrubbery to scare me away."

The hedges extended to the left and right, all the way to the edge of the field. Evelyn flew above them and away, and when she returned she said, "It surrounds the village. I saw a lone house far away on the other side, but even if we tried to go around the hedges through the forest, we'd find the path blocked."

"Is there an entrance?" Jack asked. "Should we start climbing?"

"There's a small opening around to the left. The whole thing looks like a maze."

"What are we waiting for, then?" Slade said.

They trudged to the opening, which wasn't too far compared to how far they'd come already. Evelyn hovered above them, guiding them through the twists and turns. A whistling wind echoed through the passages, now growing louder, now softer again. At first Jack ignored it, but as it slowly grew closer it began to grate on his nerves.

"What is that noise?" he asked.

Evelyn rose higher, squawking in surprise before descending once more. "There are dark shapes!" she said. "Coming from behind. They're not the Hunter. I don't know what they are, but they're getting closer." She rose again, descending just as quickly. "They give me the creeps. Come on!"

She darted ahead, Jack and Slade running as quickly as they could behind her. Up and down, around and around they went, never seeming to get any closer to their destination, and still the whistling grew nearer. At times Jack thought he could see them emerging from the hedges on either side, darkness seeping into and through the leaves, closing in to trap them. They didn't seem to bother Slade. Evelyn didn't look back, just flew ahead with increasing speed, slowly leaving them behind. For a terrifying moment Jack thought she would disappear and imagined himself abandoned, overcome by the darkness.

Then blackened buildings stood before them as they burst through the other side of the maze. Jack collapsed and looked back, worried that the darkness would chase them out of the maze as well. But even though the leaves slowly blackened and withered, the darkness stayed at the edge of the hedges, filling every inch with its dark cloud until that was all he could see.

Evelyn landed beside him, breathing heavily. "I guess she doesn't like visitors," she said.

"Let's hope that's the only thing we'll have to worry about," Slade said.

They turned to face the town, which rotted under the gray sky like a carcass. The buildings had obviously suffered fire damage at some point, not a one of them unscathed. Deathly silence reigned. The whistling had stopped, and not even the true wind blew through the streets. The air sat heavily upon them as though with a physical presence. Every step required a great effort of will, their minds struggling against some invisible barrier. They hadn't even passed the first row of houses when the rumbling began. The ground beneath them shook and the houses swayed on their unstable posts.

They continued their trek, hoping to get through as quickly as possible, until the soil in front of them erupted upward and a giant hand emerged, the fingers wiggling above the rooftops. Whatever it was lifted itself, revealing another arm, and then a monstrous head resembling some great beast with tusks and fur and yellow eyes. Its fur was the color of dead leaves, and its head was covered with a mane of straw-like hair. As it pulled itself from the earth, it moved its head from side to side and sniffed, as though searching.

"We need to go, now!" Slade said.

Jack struggled to move through the dense, invisible web. Evelyn wasn't having any more luck than he was, her wings moving so slowly she appeared to be swimming. Even Slade seemed to be having some difficulty. The beast lifted its legs free of the earth and stood to its full height, far above the tallest trees. Then it turned in a circle, unaffected by the web that had ensnared them, and began to sniff again. When it turned its head in their direction, it stopped and took deeper breaths, then howled to the sky and stomped their way.

"Do something!" Jack cried.

"I don't know what to do!" Evelyn yelled back.

"Blast it with fire, pull its feet out from under it, or hold it in the air until we've passed, but do something!"

"We'll do it together!" Slade said. "Follow my lead."

Evelyn looked about in panic, then nodded and struggled to

concentrate. Slade said a few words and she repeated them, falling into a rhythm. The giant came closer, its eyes alighting on them. It howled again and reached one large hand in their direction. Slade and Evelyn finished the spell with a shout, a burst of light shooting toward the giant from their chests. As it impacted, the light split into several smaller strands, surrounding the creature and squeezing tight, binding its arms to its sides. It howled in anger, shaking from side to side, until it lost its balance and fell backwards to the ground.

The earth shook again as it landed, breaking the web that encased them so that they could move freely once more. Jack and Slade ran between the buildings as the giant thrashed, causing more rumblings. Many of the houses collapsed on themselves and dust filled the air, making it difficult to see more than a few feet in front of them.

"Stay close!" Slade yelled. Evelyn flew beside them through the streets, but she alighted on Jack's shoulder a second later, gripping tightly. A town square opened before them, an enormous hole in the ground in the middle of it from where the giant had emerged, and they crossed the space as fast as they could, not daring to look back. They didn't notice that the doors and windows of the buildings were opening.

JACK THOUGHT he could see the end of the village ahead of them, which meant they were drawing closer to the witch. He tried to run faster, wishing to put the monster as far behind them as he could. When the ground rushed up and smacked him in the face, he lay there for a moment, confused. As he lifted himself again, he saw Evelyn a few feet away, also struggling to stand.

"What happened?" he said.

Then he looked behind him and saw what he had tripped over.

On the ground lay a human skeleton, its hand stretched out into the street where it had crawled through the open door of a house. Then, to Jack's horror, it started to move, turning its head in his direction as it pushed itself up on bony hands and arms. Its mouth opened and snapped at him, its teeth clicking together with a horrible crunching sound. He scrambled away and stood to his feet, picking up Evelyn and following Slade away from the horrible sight.

Evelyn wriggled free and perched on Jack's shoulder once more as they dashed through the streets. The air was clearing, but the giant still thrashed occasionally in the distance, sending up more clouds of dust. What concerned Jack more was the skeletons emerging from every door, some tumbling through windows and splattering on the ground only to pull themselves back together and stand. They all shuffled toward the trio, who did their best to avoid the outstretched arms and snapping jaws. The end of the village was just ahead, if only they could make it a bit further...

Something grabbed Jack's foot and his face met the ground once more. This time Evelyn jumped into the air as he landed and Slade sent a burst of flame at the skeleton who had snagged Jack's ankle. It released him and he was up again, running for all his might. They dodged the remaining skeletons and burst clear of the village, the witch's cottage across another small field at the edge of the tree line.

All at once the thrashing stopped.

They looked back and the town was just as it had been when they'd first seen it, no skeletons, no darkness, no hedges. Jack assumed the giant had also disappeared, but he wasn't willing to go back to check.

"Do you think it's safe to go on?" Evelyn asked, looking toward the witch's cottage.

"Even if it's not, we have nowhere else to go," Jack said.

"Onward," Slade said.

Evelyn nodded in agreement.

Together they started across the last field, watching the ground around them for any new monstrous creations. None appeared. The sky darkened with every passing moment, though Jack wasn't sure if it was truly growing later, or if it was more of the witch's doing. How long they'd struggled through the maze and the town was anyone's guess. With magic involved, the passing of time could have been distorted, especially when the one doing the magic was a witch.

A light shone through the window of the cottage, and smoke rose from the chimney, swirling into the air like no natural smoke should. They slowed as they drew nearer, unsure what waited for them on the other side of the door. After the horrors they'd just escaped, Jack really wanted to rest and calm his nerves. He would even let Evelyn float him through the air again if only he could put off opening the door for just a bit longer.

But Slade approached it and there was nothing else to do but follow. The fox lifted his paw to knock, but before he could, a deep voice from the other side said, "Enter."

The three exchanged a look and Slade whispered, "Be on your guard. We have no idea what to expect."

Jack grabbed the handle and pushed the door open. The first thing he noticed was the smells; they were unlike anything he'd ever experienced, even in the city. Scents of hundreds of herbs and flowers and vegetables assaulted them from every direction. The sources of the smells were all around him, on shelves and hanging from the ceiling and covering every available surface: flowers and roots and clippings, even covering much of the floor and stacked in piles here and there.

The door shut behind them, but Jack still didn't see anyone. There seemed to be a bed to the left, also covered in herbs, a large mound piled just beside it. A great black cauldron sat in the middle of the room, the only thing that wasn't hidden beneath a pile of nature. The fireplace behind it blazed with a roaring fire, its crackle the only sound in the room.

"Where is she?" Evelyn asked.

"I don't know," Jack said. "You'd think after all the trouble of keeping us away she'd be waiting to kill us herself."

Evelyn narrowed her eyes at him and he shrugged.

"Please show yourself," Slade said.

For a long moment, nothing happened. Evelyn opened her mouth to speak when the large mound by the bed began to move, rising up as the witch emerged from beneath it. A chair revealed itself behind her, many of the roots and flowers falling into it. The witch herself was an old, bent crone, her hair white and haloing all around her. She looked at them with milky white eyes, her mouth turned down in a grimace.

"What do you want?" she asked, her voice deep and scratchy.

Jack stayed silent, deciding to let Slade or Evelyn answer.

"Are you Igraine?" Evelyn said. "I need your help. I've come a long way, and—"

"Spare me," the witch said. "I'm not in the business of helping people. Why do you think I went to such lengths to keep others away?"

"But I'm not a crow, I'm a human. You're the only one who can change me back."

"Too bad. Whatever happened to change you in the first place, you probably deserved it. Now leave me alone. If you're not gone in half a minute, I will kill you."

"Please," Jack said. "She just—"

The witch moved with lightning speed to his side, so close he had to lean backwards.

"And what do you want, little straw man? Hmm? You've come a long way for the sake of another. But a man is a man, no matter what other form he takes. Deep inside, though you won't admit it to yourself, you only have your own interests at heart. You should've left her to her fate and saved yourself the trouble."

"That's not true!" Evelyn said. "He's been a good friend to me. We have both gone through hell to get here, and we're willing to do whatever you ask if you'll help me."

The old crone turned to Evelyn. "I don't care if you sacrificed everyone you love to stand before me. Get. Out. Your time is up."

"Please, madam," Slade said. "Hear the girl out."

"And what do you want, clever fox? Oh ho, you're the most selfish of all here. Only helping to gain your freedom, eh? Is that the way of it?"

Slade didn't answer.

"You witches are all the same!" Jack cried. "Selfish, evil crones who do no good to anyone!"

"What do you know of witches?" the witch hissed, getting in his face once more. "I could set a fire deep in your belly with a blink of my eye and you would be ash before your friends could so much as flap a wing or paw to save you. Do not tempt me, straw man! You've wasted enough of my time already."

"Let's just go," Evelyn said.

Jack's stomach churned. All of the time they'd spent, the struggles they'd faced... He couldn't just let that go to waste. But the witch scowled at him and there was nothing else he could do.

"We probably would've been better off attacking the first witch," Jack grumbled as they turned to leave.

"What witch would that be?" the crone demanded. "I'm the only one for hundreds of miles."

"I guess you overlooked this one," Evelyn said. "She's the one who changed me. She was a crow when we met, and now she's human while I'm stuck like this."

The witch grew very still and quiet. Jack could almost believe she'd turned herself into a statue, if it weren't for the subtle rise and fall of her chest.

"Where was this witch? What did she look like?"

Her voice was so soft Jack almost didn't hear her.

"What do you care? You're not helping us," he said.

She closed in on him again, their faces nearly touching. She smelled of cinnamon and earth. "Listen to me very carefully," she said. "I don't give one whit about you and your friends here, but

I care a great deal about that witch you mentioned. Now speak quickly or I'll burn the rest of your body."

"She looked like a young woman," Evelyn said. "Long dark hair, perfect features. Goes by the name of Ferah. She was in my home village, northeast of here. Only a few days' worth of travel."

The witch sighed as if in pain and began to pace. "Yes, that's her," she whispered. "Different name, but there's no way around it. Well, well. Seems she's escaped her net, for a bit."

"You know her?" Slade asked.

"She's my sister."

Evelyn and Jack exchanged a look. Better to that leave alone. "So...you still won't help?" Evelyn asked.

The witch chuckled. "Don't think for a moment that I'm helping *you*, but her fate must be dealt with. My only interest is keeping her bound for all eternity. The terms of the release from the curse required a willing human, and though you may have been at one time, you are certainly not now. Your deal with her is therefore null and void. She would've known the moment your heart changed, so she is attempting to bend the rules. I must remind her of her place."

"Dreary thoughts to have about your little sister," Evelyn said.

"Older. Don't let her looks fool you."

"So you'll switch them back?" Jack asked.

"Not so fast. A sacrifice is required to set things right. And there are ingredients to be gathered."

"What sacrifice?" Evelyn asked.

"Ingredients?" Jack said.

The witch wandered over to a shelf and pulled a book from beneath a pile of dried flowers. She blew the dust off the cover and opened it, running her finger down the page. "No, no," she muttered. Finally, she turned back to them, crying, "Here! In order to switch the bodies back, a few things are required. *Tears of stone to bind her body, blood of leaves to bind her magic, breath of the dead to bind her soul.* Find these things and I can recast the spell to bind her in crow form."

"Why not do it yourself?" Slade asked. "You cast the spell in the first place, didn't you?"

The witch scowled at him. "Do not provoke me, fox. She would still be bound if not for this crow. She freed her. She should be the one to gather the items."

"I'm fine with that," Evelyn said. "I know it's my fault. But where do we begin to look?"

"That is none of my concern," the witch said, resuming her seat in the chair. "Return here once you've found them."

"Wait a second!" Jack said. "Your sister sent a Hunter after us. Can you get rid of it?"

The witch cackled. "I could. But where's the fun in that?"

"You realize we'll never complete your task if the Hunter takes us," Slade said.

The witch just waved a hand. "No matter. Then I will do it myself. Good luck."

All at once they were swept out of the house in a gust of magic and found themselves standing outside once more, the light of the fire within glowing in the gathering darkness.

❦ 21 ❦

ONWARD

They walked for a long time without speaking. By silent agreement, they skirted the village, choosing instead to walk through the dark woods where only the normal sounds of nocturnal animals could be heard. An almost palpable mood of frustration and defeat settled over them. Jack felt especially bad for Evelyn: to come so far, only to be sent off in another direction.

They stopped, still not speaking, and settled in for the night right where they were. Jack couldn't get comfortable; rocks and twigs pulled at his clothes when he turned, the wind blew almost constantly, and he kept imagining the Hunter coming upon them while they slept, their bodies dissolving right where they lay.

The next morning, Slade said, "So, the visit didn't go as expected. That's life. The way I see it, you have a couple options. You can give up, resign yourself to life as a crow, and leave your family to their fates. No more witches, no endless travel, no getting involved with dreadlords or mages or wolves. End of story. Or you can continue. Find the items the witch mentioned, bring them back, and hope that's the last thing asked of you."

"That's no choice," Evelyn said. "How can I not go on?"

"And what of the Hunter?" Jack added. "He won't stop pursuing us."

"You're decided, then?" Slade asked.

Evelyn nodded.

"Very well. Which way shall we go, my lady?"

She looked about hopelessly, not knowing where to even begin.

"What about Raven?" Jack asked. "He's helped us so far, and I think he's taken a liking to us. If anyone knows where to find these things, it will be him."

"Or the owl," Evelyn said. "But I'd rather not ask her. Her last errand was a lot more trouble than I anticipated."

"We may not have a choice, if Raven is no help," Slade said.

"Let's ask him first," Evelyn answered.

They continued their journey, not quite so crestfallen as when they'd started the previous night. Jack pondered the witch's riddle as they walked. None of the items made much sense. *Tears of stone to bind her body, blood of leaves to bind her magic, breath of the dead to bind her soul.* But what did that mean?

When they reached the mountain, Slade floated Jack up before he had a chance to ask if Evelyn should do it again. Jack closed his eyes as he rose higher, resigning himself to never growing used to the experience. Slade followed a moment later, Evelyn having already flown up, and they proceeded down the other side of the mountain. The journey down that side didn't seem to take nearly as long, but perhaps that was merely the absence of anticipation, of the end they'd striven so hard for.

"I've been thinking," Slade said after they'd walked for a few hours. "What if the ingredient list isn't as impossible as it seems? After all, this is a witch we're talking about. They love to make things unnecessarily difficult. It's probably a few simple items that she's chosen to describe in a mystical fashion."

"You're probably right," Jack agreed.

"But then what could they be?" Evelyn asked. "I've racked my brain and can think of nothing."

"Two liquids and air," Slade said. "That can only be so many things."

"Not when magic's involved," Jack said. "I'll feel better about it once we've asked Raven."

The land sloped upward, leading them along a path Jack didn't remember encountering. Were they going a different way?

"Best way is the straightest, right?" Slade said when Jack mentioned it.

"I suppose," Jack answered.

"We want to avoid the owl anyway," Evelyn added.

When they reached the top of the hill, Jack thought for a moment they'd climbed above the clouds. Patches of fluffy whiteness dotted the landscape below them, contrasting with the gold and orange and red of the leaves. But it was only the reflection of clouds in a vast lake.

"Ah, perfect," Slade said. "There's a bit of magic I want to try, and this will provide just what I need."

"What are you going to do?" Evelyn asked.

"A scrying spell. I'll teach you. I'll need to find something bowl-like, though."

The fox searched on the bank, picking through the rocks and limbs for something suitable. Jack and Evelyn joined him. It seemed better to help him and complete the task faster than to waste time while he combed the sand alone.

Their hunt took them further around the right bank where the forest thickened again and the land once more descended. The sun shone every now and then through the gray clouds, speckling the ground in scattered light. It was easily the most beautiful place Jack could remember seeing, except for perhaps Raven's land. For a moment he imagined living there on the shore, maybe in a little wooden cabin with large windows. Maybe he could find some way to be human too, and then—

"Aha!" Slade said, lifting a piece of wood high over his head. "I've found one!"

Evelyn and Jack returned to his side as he dipped the wood in the lake. The water formed a little pool in a depression in the wood, and Slade set the whole thing on the ground between them and motioned for Evelyn to lean closer.

"What I'm about to do requires an extreme amount of concentration," he said. "I'll need both of you to be as silent as possible, but I want you to watch closely, Evelyn. You'll need to try it for yourself."

"You want me to try it, too?"

"Of course. Are you training to be a mage or aren't you?"

She had no answer for that, so Slade motioned for silence and then bent low over the pool, staring into its depths as though it held all the secrets in the world. He chanted words in an unknown tongue, his eyes never leaving the pool, then passed one paw over the water slowly. Jack leaned closer as an image appeared, but it was difficult to make out, like looking through a fog. Slade spoke again and the image cleared, revealing a close view of the bottom of a tree. Flowers grew around it and the grass was a rich green, but the leaves in the treetops were the colors of autumn.

"Raven's land," Jack said.

"Yes," Slade answered. "It seems that is indeed our destination. Now you try, Evelyn. Most of it is in your mind, but the trick is to hold your goal firmly in your thoughts while chanting the words of the spell. Go ahead."

The image in the pool cleared, once more reflecting nothing but the gray clouds overhead. Evelyn mimicked Slade's posture, leaning far over the pool and staring intently at the water. She repeated the words, stumbling a little, but he corrected her. She tried again, watching with focused gaze, but nothing happened. Again she tried, and again, her words growing more clipped and deliberate as her frustration showed. Finally, Slade called a halt.

"It's a good start," he said. "This is a difficult thing to do, so don't be discouraged. All you need is practice." He left the wood sitting there and walked across the sand toward the trees. "Excuse me a moment," he said. "I'm quite famished."

"I am as well," Evelyn admitted. When Slade was out of earshot, she added, "It's strange, having him be so helpful. It's almost like he's a different person."

"I feel the same way," Jack said. "It's...odd."

"You think it's just Raven's influence? Nothing more?"

Jack glanced toward the forest where Slade had disappeared. "It's possible. I know he was friendlier once, before his own goals got in the way. Unless it was all a ruse. At this point, I'd say just about anything is possible."

Evelyn laughed. "Well, that was really helpful."

Jack shrugged. "I honestly don't know. If we're basing his behavior on what we know of him, I'd say he's only doing this to get himself out of trouble. But I could be wrong." Under his breath he added, "I hope I'm wrong."

"I'm going to look for food, too," Evelyn said. She flew off between the trees, leaving Jack alone on the shore. A bird flew high in the distance, the only other sign of life. Jack watched it a moment, following its trail as it whirled back toward the mountain behind him. He turned with it, spotting a path leading up and up. He glanced back at the forest, but seeing neither Slade nor Evelyn, he decided to follow it. At least for a short distance.

Rocks slid out from under his feet, and the path alternated between stone and dirt. But it was fairly straight, and ahead he could see where it snaked through a small copse of trees. He hurried over the last stretch of land to reach the trees, loving the silence and stillness of the place. It reminded him of his post, and though he had no real desire to go back, the similarity was comforting. It had been a pleasant life, for the most part.

He picked a particularly large tree and lay down beneath its branches, the red and orange leaves fluttering gently down. Far away an echo of thunder rumbled across the land, announcing the coming of rain. Jack sighed and closed his eyes, burrowing deeper into the roots and leaves at the tree's base.

Dimly, he thought he should probably go back down soon so

Evelyn and Slade wouldn't wonder what had happened to him. But his little nest was *so* comfortable.

The whispers began some unknown time later, just the faintest breath of air, then a little louder as the voices came closer. Blearily, Jack creaked one eye open, but saw no one. He resumed his nap and the whispers began again, a little louder this time. He sat up, groaning, wishing they could stay in the same spot for a few days and just rest. Looking all around, he thought he could see something moving far away to his right, almost behind him. He watched a few moments more and then was sure of it: *something was moving*.

Likely it was just another animal, going about its business with no thought or care for the doings of mages or witches. Nothing was more probable, but he couldn't look away. He had to *know*.

Carefully, he stood and crept along between tree trunks, deliberately staying out of sight, just in case. The whispers grew gradually louder until he could finally make out a few words.

"I told you we shouldn't have come this way."

"We're not lost. I know exactly where I'm going."

"That's what you said the last time, right before we ended up on the edge of that cliff."

"That was different."

"How?"

"It just was. I really wish you would trust me."

Jack could see them, now, one figure blending in with the landscape, the other standing out in white. The white one was small, some sort of animal, and Jack was almost positive he had heard their voices before.

"Why can't you just admit we're lost? We're never going to find the witch if we keep wandering around in circles. We should stop. I need to consult the stones."

The small one sighed. "Fine. But we're wasting time."

He saw them, then, the tall figure bending over the ground as she pulled a pouch from beneath her green cloak and cast the contents on the ground. The white figure—a cat —sat nearby, clearly unhappy, her tail swishing about in the air.

"Well?" the cat asked after a moment.

"Just...hang on a second, Arnica. I need to concentrate."

"Come on! They're going to say the same thing they did last time; we're on the right path. We just need to keep going."

He knew them, now: Miriel and Arnica from the Mages' Guild.

"Aha!" Miriel said, lifting her head and pointing a finger at the cat. "I knew it! We're off course. We need to go back that way." She pointed to their left, further up the mountain or perhaps beyond.

Arnica swished her tail. "We have to go around the mountain, Miriel," she said reasonably. "Unless you want to climb to the peak and dash down the other side?"

The mage sighed and gathered her stones. "We really should've waited for Lirelin. We're both out of our depth here, whether you care to admit it or not."

Jack decided he'd heard enough and started to back away, but his feet on the leaves and hidden twigs echoed in the still air and the mage and cat looked around at the sound.

"Who's there?" Arnica called.

Jack cursed himself.

"Probably just an animal," Miriel said.

"Perhaps. We shouldn't risk it, though."

Miriel secured her stones and the two searched the surrounding trees. Jack couldn't figure out how to get away unseen, so he sighed and stepped out from behind his tree.

"It's just me," he said. "No need to be alarmed."

The mage and cat stood frozen a moment, eyes wide.

"You!" Arnica finally managed.

"We thought we'd never see the likes of you again," Miriel said. "What happened to you?"

"And how'd you get away from that fox?"

"It's a long story," Jack said, his heart twisting at the mention of Nadya.

"What are you doing out here?" Arnica asked. "Isn't it dangerous for you?"

"It's actually pretty safe," Jack answered. "Much better than the city, in my opinion."

Arnica scoffed. "I doubt that."

"What are you two doing out here?"

They exchanged a look and Miriel said, "Looking for the witch you mentioned. She still needs to be dealt with, but with you gone, it was up to us to find her. So, here we are."

"Well, it's brave of you, I'll give you that," Jack said.

"Will you join us?" Arnica asked. "You know where she is. The journey will be over a lot sooner with you along."

"I can't," Jack said. "I have...other things I need to do."

"What could be more important than stopping a witch?" Arnica asked.

"I'm helping a friend," Jack said.

"Funny. I don't see any friends."

"They're probably looking for me now. They went to find food and should be back any moment. I really can't keep them waiting." Jack turned to leave and ran straight into an invisible wall. He turned back around and Miriel shrugged.

"Sorry," she said. "We really need the help."

"I agree. It will be...easier, with the scarecrow," Arnica said.

"Are you taking me captive?" Jack asked.

"Soliciting your help," Miriel said.

"By force," Arnica added.

"What about my friends?" Jack said. "I can't just leave them. Please, you have to let me go. If we help my friend, the witch will be taken care of, too. I promise."

But they weren't listening to him. Miriel opened her pack and Arnica trotted forward and nudged Jack toward the mage. The opening yawned wide and the cat pushed him forward, the invisible wall preventing him from going in any other direction.

"Please," he tried again.

But it was no use. The cat pushed him into the sack and the mage closed and secured the top and all was darkness.

"WE HAVE to let him out sometime."

"He'll try to run the minute we open that thing. Better to leave him in there and let him exhaust himself."

"But how can he help us if we just leave him tied up all the time?"

The debate had gone on for at least half an hour. Jack sat in the darkness of the bag, trying to avoid Miriel's stones, and her books, and the other items she'd brought along with her. He worried what Evelyn and Slade would think. Surely they couldn't believe he'd abandoned them. Not after all they'd gone through.

"We'll leave him in there at least until tomorrow," Arnica said. "That should give him time to calm down."

"I need my stones. And my books. I really don't think he'll be much of a problem. Especially if I keep a barrier up."

"You need all your strength for when we confront the witch. You can't waste it on things like this."

"I won't try to run away," Jack said.

Silence.

Then the sound of someone walking and Miriel's voice close to the bag saying, "What was that?"

"I won't try to run away," Jack repeated, a little louder this time.

"As if we can believe him," Arnica said.

"I think we can," Miriel replied.

The whole bag was lifted and a small speck of light grew larger and Jack was pulled out into the deepening evening twilight. He didn't know how long he'd sat in that bag, but there was no way Slade and Evelyn hadn't noticed his absence by now.

Miriel turned him around to face her. "Will you take us to the witch?" she said.

"I will," Jack said. "But please, listen first—"

"We know, we know," Arnica interrupted. "You want to help your friend. We get it. But this takes precedence."

"Let me finish!" Jack said.

"We can at least hear him out," Miriel said.

Arnica sighed loudly.

"Go on," Miriel said, looking back at Jack.

He paused a moment, then said, "My friend was transformed by the witch. But we've found a spell that will get her body back. If we can cast it, the witch will be cursed again as a crow. If your goal is to 'take care of her,' or whatever it is you plan to do, surely she'll be easier to deal with once she's enchanted."

Miriel glanced at Arnica, who didn't look convinced.

"I think it sounds like a good plan," Miriel said, looking back at Jack.

"What spell?" the cat asked. "Where'd you find it?"

"It's kind of a list of ingredients," Jack said. "We...found it in a book. *Tears of stone to bind her body, blood of leaves to bind her magic, breath of the dead to bind her soul.* If we can gather all of that, she'll be bound."

Miriel frowned, brows furrowed as she pondered. "What does that even mean?" she said.

"Sounds like an impossible list of nonsense," Arnica said.

"It's not, I swear!" Jack said. "It will work. Yes, we have to figure out what it means, but you're a mage, aren't you? Surely you guys have books on witches?"

Miriel glanced at Arnica and back at Jack helplessly. "I'm not sure," she said. "I've never studied witches, personally. The little I know is that their magic is unusual and they're extremely dangerous. Other than that, I'm quite in the dark."

"Did the book not explain it?" the cat asked. "Where'd you get it, anyway? And where is it now?"

Jack shook his head. "It didn't explain, and I'm not sure. The book was lost during our travels. But what about the items? Do they sound similar to any magical items you know of?"

"No," Miriel said. "They're so twisted in mystical nonsense that they're unrecognizable. I don't have a clue what they could be."

"Face it, scarecrow," Arnica said. "There's nothing we can do for your friend. The best we can hope for is to stop the witch and make sure she doesn't curse anyone else."

"My name's Jack," he said. "And you're wrong. The spell will work."

"Hmm," Miriel said. She closed the bag and kept Jack under her arm, taking him with her as she sat on the ground beside Arnica. They had gathered a pile of leaves and twigs as kindling, and as she sat, Miriel used magic to start a fire. "Much better," she said, extending her hands to the flame.

"I think we should silence him," Arnica said. "It's no use arguing with him; he's dead set on this quest of his. If we're to have any peace—"

"I know, I know," Miriel said. "Don't think I haven't thought of it. But you have to admit, it *is* interesting."

Arnica laughed. "Right. Sure. Whatever you say."

"I could refuse to help you," Jack said. "Or I could lead you astray so that you'd never find the witch. Have you even considered that I could be lying about the whole thing? Why would you take off on a wild chase and take people captive based only on something someone said?"

Arnica hissed. "You better not be lying, scarecrow."

"He has a point, though," Miriel said. "We did believe him pretty quickly. Why should the spell be any different?"

"Because that spell is nonsense!"

"And the chances of there really being a witch are pretty good?" Jack asked.

"You're here, at least, even if you were lying about your friend," Arnica said.

"I think we should give him the benefit of the doubt," Miriel said. "Come on, Nica. Surely there's no harm in that. If he's right, it will make confronting the witch *much* easier. I, for one, would like any help I can get."

The cat scowled and curled up closer to the fire, glaring at Jack. "I still don't like it. But you do what you like, Miriel. If he tries to trick us, I'll pull his straw out. Maybe I'll burn the rest of his body for wasting our time."

Miriel frowned and shook her head. "You will do no such thing. We are not brutes, Nica. You've been spending too much time with those cousins of yours."

"It's not my fault they threw in their lot with the dreadlords."

"True. But I know you, and I know you're better than that."

"Hmpf," the cat said.

She closed her eyes and Miriel positioned Jack in her lap so that they were facing each other. She put her fingers to her lips and whispered, "Quiet now. Let her sleep."

Jack obeyed, sitting and listening to the crackle of the flames, the call of distant birds, the whistling of the wind through the leaves. He half hoped that Slade or Evelyn would notice the light of the fire and come to investigate. Surely the mage was no match for the fox. He played out the encounter in his mind, imagining all the ways Slade would dispatch the pair and smuggle him off into the night—

"She means well," Miriel said, still whispering. "She just doesn't like to take chances. We've encountered too many disappointments."

"I can't blame her," Jack said. "After everything I've been through, I sympathize."

"It's not that I don't want to help your friend, because that sounds like a good thing to do, and it's brave of you to go to so much trouble. But we have priorities to think of."

"I get it," Jack said. "Really."

"Good."

She poked the fire with a stick and hummed to herself. The sounds of crickets, cicadas, and night birds echoed through the

trees, adding a background to her song. She placed Jack beside
her on the ground and continued poking the fire. He looked up
at her, then at the surrounding forest, then back at her again.
But he couldn't bring himself to run, not with her being so trust-
ing. And he really didn't want to end up in the sack again. So he
sighed and leaned back against the log, falling asleep with her
voice in his ears.

AN UNEASY ALLIANCE

"I've been thinking," Miriel said. They were still breaking down camp. It had rained during the night, but they had been protected by an invisible shield, the ground surrounding them completely dry. The mage curled her hair behind her ear and squinted at Jack. "Maybe we *should* find your friend. Another set of eyes won't hurt, and I suppose your friend knows the witch's whereabouts just as well as you."

For a moment, Jack could think of nothing to say, the words swirling in his head so that he couldn't grasp on a single idea without saying the whole of it. Finally he managed, "Thank you. Yes, my friends can help. I have two around here somewhere who must be worried sick about me by now."

"Are you sure this is a good idea?" Arnica asked. She kicked more dirt on the fire and glared at Jack, as though she could read his thoughts.

"I don't think there will be a problem," Miriel said. "He's behaved himself so far."

"But can we handle two more creatures?"

"They will cooperate, I promise," Jack said.

Arnica ignored him and waited for Miriel's answer.

"I believe so," the mage said.

The cat studied her, finally sighing and saying, "I suppose that'll have to be good enough. I don't like it, though. We have the scarecrow. Why waste our time?"

"You never know," Miriel said. "Anything can happen out here." She picked Jack up so that he was eye level with her. "I'm going to let you walk on your own," she said. "You'll be on an invisible leash, but if you try to run, I'll put you back in the sack. I really don't want to do that, but if you don't give me a choice—"

"It won't come to that," Jack said.

"Fair enough."

She set him down and he stretched his arms and legs. Miriel secured her pack on her shoulder while Arnica watched the surrounding wood.

"I guess I'm leading the way?" Jack said.

"You got it," Miriel said. "We'll look for your friends first, then see if we can figure out this spell business."

He nodded and started back toward the lake. The gray clouds covered every inch of sky, forcing the sunlight to filter down through a thick haze. For a moment, Jack worried it would snow. That was just what they needed. He found the path fairly quickly, and from his high vantage point, he looked down on the forest, but saw no sign of Slade or Evelyn.

They climbed down carefully and in silence. Whatever the two were thinking, they kept it to themselves. At the bottom, Jack looked around once more. Nothing.

"Are either of you trackers?"

Arnica snorted. "I can track mice fairly well."

"I'm afraid I'm useless," Miriel said, shaking her head. "I could possibly manage a tracking spell, but it's really not my area. My stones could at least point us in the right direction."

"We may need them," Jack said, looking around again.

"If we can't find your friends, we'll go on without them," Arnica said. "We can't waste time."

"She's right," Miriel agreed. "Sorry, Jack. We can give you half an hour, no more."

"We'll find them," Jack replied. "I'm sure of it."

He strode into the forest, searching for anything that might tell them which way Slade and Evelyn had gone. Not that he was any sort of tracker, but he'd seen others do it often enough that he knew there were signs, if only he could read them. That broken twig? That smashed leaf? That scatter of pebbles? Any of them could be signs of Slade's passage.

After several minutes of looking, he groaned in frustration and took to calling as loud as he could. "Evelyn! Slade! Where are you?" Pause. Silence. Scuffle of animals. Bird calls. More silence. "Slade! Evelyn, come back!"

Nothing.

Miriel and Arnica followed him deeper into the trees as he continued his call. He remembered which direction they had been heading before being separated, so he followed that path as close as he could, hoping to overtake them, or at least find some obvious sign of them. Miriel attempted to help look, but she knew no more of tracking than Jack did. Arnica walked silently behind them.

Finally the cat said, "Time's up, scarecrow."

Miriel sighed. "You made an effort, Jack. Looks like they went on without you. Do you know where they were going, perhaps?"

"Yes," he said.

"We don't have time to follow them," Arnica said.

"They're going to see Raven. He can help you, too," Jack said. "We'll need some help solving the spell, and I can't think of anyone better suited to the task."

The cat and mage exchanged a look.

"Fine," Arnica said. "Lead the way."

JACK DIDN'T KNOW exactly where Raven's land was, though he knew the general direction. After admitting this, Miriel opened her pack and pulled out her stones, clearing a space on the ground and casting them down.

"You've met this Raven before?" Arnica asked.

"Yes," Jack said. "Have you heard of him?"

"Only rumors. Nothing to get excited about."

"I was told he could be a deity," Jack said. "Or at least a descendant of one."

Arnica laughed at that. "We'll see," she said. "So long as he can help us, I don't care if he's just another dreadlord, or a liar, or whatever he is."

"What sort of deity?" Miriel asked. She finished reading her stones and gathered them up again. Once she secured them in her pack, she pointed out their direction and they continued on.

"A bird god," Jack said. "Supposedly he created the world."

Miriel had pulled a ledger and quill out of her pack, an inkwell floating in the air alongside her. She scribbled rapidly as they walked, almost tripping over several rocks and branches. Somehow she always avoided them at the last second. More magic, Jack supposed.

"Interesting," she muttered, still scribbling.

"Probably just a powerful mage," Arnica said.

"Perhaps," Jack said. "You'll see him soon enough."

"He may be interested in helping bring more animal mages into the Guild," Miriel said. "Wouldn't that be something, Nica?"

"I suppose."

"He has his own ideas about the way things should work," Jack said. "But what do I know? Anything's possible."

"Has he mentioned any other gods?" Miriel asked. She didn't look up from her ledger.

"No," Jack said. "Not a word."

"Hmm..."

"That's a relief," Arnica said. "It's all rubbish anyway."

"What do you believe?" Jack asked. "About gods and the world, I mean."

"Me?" the cat asked. "I think if there are any gods, they certainly aren't sticking around down here. They gave us magic for a reason. It's our job to use it to help each other and stop those who would use it for harm."

"That's why you're going after the witch."

"Exactly."

They came across a creek—an offspring of the lake—and had to wade across. Miriel stowed her ledger and quill away and picked Jack and Arnica up, one in each arm. They managed to get across without incident, but Jack couldn't help looking back, thinking of the Hunter. It was probably waiting for them to return to drier land, unless it had found a way across since last they'd seen it. Fear that it had already captured Evelyn and Slade rose within him, stopping him entirely for a moment as he pictured the scene in his head...

Miriel's glance back got him moving again. He couldn't think about that. If the Hunter had found them, the best he could do for them was keep moving and find a way to save them. And Nadya...

The forest felt more alive than any of the other times he'd traveled through it. Perhaps it was the proximity to Raven, or the witch, or maybe this stretch of land was simply more magical than all the rest. Birds called and flew overhead, rabbits darted past, and squirrels scampered from tree to tree. The sky took on a deep blue tint, almost like it, too, was infused with magic. The wind hurried by, whispering the secrets of others but keeping its own. Anything felt possible.

"Do you feel it?" Arnica asked.

"I do," Miriel said. "This land is...different. Like all the mages in the world congregated in one place."

"Can't be anything good," Arnica said. "We'll have to stay on our guard."

Every tree they passed seemed to glow with unspent energy,

pulsing with vibrant light. The very air grew thicker, slightly warmer, hinting at summers long past. They passed through this for several more minutes until Miriel shouted, "I have it!"

"What?" Arnica said.

"This place: it's faeries. I'm sure of it."

The cat snorted. "Can't be. They're almost as elusive as witches."

"Well, what else could it be?"

"Maybe some other magical being? Didn't you study those at some point?"

"It *could* be," Miriel said, rubbing her chin. She began to scribble again, muttering to herself. The sparrow in Raven's land had mentioned faeries. They were all supposed to be far away, if Jack remembered right. He began to search the treetops for the slightest movement, the merest suggestion of tiny wings.

The land sloped downward, leading into a narrow valley, two high mountains towering on either side. The tops pierced the clouds, and maybe even the realm of the gods, for all Jack knew. The group descended quickly, the view of mountains soon lost behind the canopy of trees.

"We're still going the right way?" Arnica asked.

"Yes. It should be at the other end of this valley," Miriel answered.

"I just hope—"

A loud *boom* shook the ground, almost knocking the three off their feet. Birds cried and called, animals scattered and made a fuss, but the source of the noise remained hidden.

"I think it came from further ahead!" Miriel said, dashing forward.

"Wait, Miriel!" Arnica said, beginning to dash after her. She stopped and looked back at Jack. "Well, come on then!"

He quickly obeyed. They reached the bottom of the hill and kept going, the trees thick together. The *boom* sounded again, closer and louder than before. Flocks of birds took to the air, crying in panic. Jack almost stumbled over a rock sticking out of the ground, catching himself just before he lost his balance.

"We don't know what it is!" Arnica said. "Be careful!"

"Of course I'll be careful!" Miriel called back. "Who do you think you're talking to?"

Jack struggled to keep up, falling further and further behind. He would've simply stopped and let them leave him, but the cat continued to look back.

"Come on!" she said. "You're slowing us down!"

Leave me, then, he thought, but he didn't say it. He really had no desire to find out what was causing all the noise—it reminded him too much of the giant the witch had conjured—and it seemed like it would only be more trouble. He'd experienced more than enough of that.

The ground shook for the third time and Jack fell, landing face-first in a pile of leaves. They crunched and crackled as he lifted himself, and he watched as the mage and cat moved even further away. He flopped back down and sighed. What was the point anymore? He didn't care about them, or the noise, or the witch's spell. He just wanted to find his friends and rest.

Miriel sighed above him. "Come on, then," she said, lifting him out and brushing leaves off of him. She stowed him in her pack and ran off again, her stones and books bouncing around beneath him. Specks of light shone through the fabric, creating miniature constellations.

The *boom* sounded for the fourth time, the loudest yet, and Arnica cried, "There!"

They slowed considerably after that, sneaking up on whatever it was they'd spotted. Jack stood and pressed his head through the opening of the bag, which hadn't been secured. A clearing sat before them, two groups facing each other in battle: Slade and Evelyn stood to the right, a pack of wolves to the left. A bright glow appeared around Slade, rippling with energy before blasting toward the wolves with deadly speed. The blast hit some invisible barrier, creating another *boom* and shaking the ground.

"Give up!" one wolf called. "You're surrounded!"

More wolves emerged from the trees, creating a ring around the two. His friends glanced about, scowling at the wolves, but didn't give in.

"Tell your master he can send for me peaceably, but I won't be taken by force!" Slade yelled.

"What do you think is happening?" Miriel whispered. They had stopped just within the tree line, hiding behind the trunk of a large oak.

Arnica hissed. "It's that no-good fox. He probably double-crossed the wolves and they're out for vengeance."

"Those are my friends," Jack said.

"Those two?" Miriel said.

"That miserable scoundrel?!" Arnica cried, struggling to keep her voice down.

"Yes," he said. "Slade and I aren't the best of friends, but he's on our side, I promise. I'm guessing he wronged you in the past, and for that I'm sorry. He's betrayed me as well. But they need help. Is there anything you can do?"

"I won't shake a whisker to help him!" Arnica said.

"We probably should do something," Miriel said. "But what can we do against wolves...?"

Jack thought a moment, cringing as one wolf dove for the two, only kept back by an invisible shield Slade had erected. Heroic deeds filled his thoughts, images of him dashing forward, scaring the wolves back as Evelyn flew to his side, Slade following close behind. But he was powerless and he knew it. The wolves would tear him apart.

"Isn't there some magic you can do?" Jack asked.

"Maybe—"

"Don't do it!" Arnica said. "He doesn't deserve it!"

"And what of Evelyn?" Jack demanded. "You know nothing about her. The wolves could kill her!"

"Let the fox take care of himself," Arnica said. "He's capable."

"Enough, both of you," Miriel said. "It doesn't really matter if he can handle it himself or not, or if he's a horrible miscreant or not. They're the ones we've been searching for, and it'd be pointless to come all this way only to sit back and let the wolves have their way. Now stay here."

She put Jack on the ground next to the cat, followed by her pack. When she stood again, she faced the fight with a grim set to her mouth, her fists clenched at her side, like some ancient battle goddess. Or maybe a nature goddess who had been pushed one time too many. A wind rose about her, lifting her hair into snake-like strands around her head, her dress whipping around her ankles. She strode out into the clearing without a backward glance. The wolves attacked again, knocked back by Slade's shield and another blast of his magic. Then they noticed Miriel.

For a long moment they simply watched, eyes wide as she approached. Slade glanced their way, his eyes only narrowing further, as though it were simply one more issue to deal with. A second later, the wolves scattered in all directions, none brave enough to face the mage. The fox didn't even look at them, his focus entirely on Miriel.

Jack dashed out just as bright orange flames sprang up around the fox, serving as an added barrier.

"Stop!" Jack cried, waving his arms overhead.

"Jack?!" Evelyn called.

Slade ignored them both and sent a blast of fire toward Miriel. The flames spread out around and above her, blocked by her own shield. She stopped, arms raised to either side in peace. Slade's fire decreased in size until it was confined once more to his body. The two studied each other, the fox unwilling to trust.

"Jack, who is this?" Slade asked, still not looking at anyone but Miriel.

"A friend," he said. He hoped she turned out to be a friend. It seemed the best answer to get Slade to lower his defenses. "She's going to help us find the items for the spell," he continued. For a moment he worried that wouldn't be enough, that Slade would insist on fighting her.

The wind around Miriel abruptly dissipated and she lowered her arms. She bowed and said, "I am Miriel, a mage of the Guild. It is an honor to meet you, fellow mage." She paused to give Slade a chance to reply. He didn't. "Jack has told us of your problem with the witch. It is our desire to bind her so she cannot hurt anyone else."

"Us? Are there more of you?"

"Just me," Arnica said, appearing from behind Jack.

Slade's eyes widened, but he held his ground. "You," he said.

"We meet again," Arnica countered. "You want to drop that fire shield? My companion and I have not threatened you."

"I'll keep it up, thanks," Slade said.

"We're all friends here," Jack said. "Come on, Slade."

"They're not my friends."

"If they're here to help, I say we let them," Evelyn said. "Maybe they can decipher the spell."

"Unlikely." The fire blazed a moment longer, then sank back into the fox's skin. "So these are the two you abandoned us for?" he asked Jack.

"Not abandoned. We...crossed paths and they thought we could help each other."

"What do you have to gain?" Slade asked.

"That witch is dangerous," Miriel said. "As members of the Guild, it is our duty to seek her out and make sure she's contained."

Slade stole a glance at Jack, who quickly shook his head. No point telling more than they had to. If Miriel and Arnica found out about the other witch, it wouldn't be from them.

"We're grateful for the help," Evelyn said, catching Jack's warning.

"What was your name, dear?" Miriel said.

"Evelyn."

"Jack tells us you're actually human... What did you do to draw the witch's attention?"

Evelyn looked at the ground and mumbled, "I did this to myself. I made a deal with her." She looked back up, a spark in her eyes as she dared them to judge her. "It was completely voluntary. I tried to use her to escape my life, but it didn't turn out how I expected. She wouldn't undo the spell."

"You don't say," Arnica said.

"I'm doing everything I can to make things right," Evelyn continued. "She's enchanted my father as well, and my brother is missing. If you can help me, I will gladly be in your debt."

Miriel smiled and said, "We will do what we can."

"Now that we're all the best of friends, can we continue?" Slade said. "The wolves may still be nearby."

"He's right," Arnica grudgingly agreed.

"Well, let's be off then," Miriel said.

Slade took the lead, casting one more distrusting look at the mage and cat. Evelyn fluttered to Jack's shoulder and they fell behind the others.

"I was so worried," she said.

"I'm sorry," he whispered. "They wouldn't let me come back."

"Wouldn't let you?"

"Shh." He looked ahead where Miriel and Arnica were holding their own whispered conversation, the cat held in the mage's arms. "They're nice enough, but they have their own agenda. They're out for the witch, nothing more."

"Which one?"

Jack grinned. "I only mentioned one: Ferah."

"But what happens if we get all the ingredients and then have to return to Igraine? She still has to perform the spell to bind Ferah. They'll find out about her."

"We may think of something before then," Jack said. "Who knows? We may lose them. That seems to be a common occurrence."

"No. We just lose *you*." She chuckled as he pretended to be offended. "Well, it's true."

"It would help if I were a mage as well."

They entered the trees again, the light dimming even further. Ahead of them, Miriel shivered, pulling Arnica closer.

"It'll be winter soon," Evelyn said.

"If we're lucky, you'll be human by then."

"I hope so."

"Jack?" Miriel said, glancing back.

"Yes?"

She waited for him to catch up so that they were walking side by side. Arnica jumped down and walked a little way ahead.

"We didn't get a chance to talk about it before, but I wanted to see what I could do about helping you retrieve your memories."

The offer caught him off guard. He'd become used to the fact that he couldn't remember his life before, if there even was a life before. The chance to know, once and for all... He wasn't sure he wanted it.

"I'll need to cast a few spells to probe your mind," Miriel continued. "Maybe a few to encourage regeneration, but that will depend on the state of your thoughts."

"That's kind of you," Jack said.

She waved her hand dismissively. "If a witch did it, it's all the more reason to help. We have to stand against them."

Jack looked back at Evelyn, but she said not a word.

"Tell us the spell items again," Arnica said.

"The first was *tears of stone*," Slade answered.

"And this Raven guy will know what that means?"

"Perhaps."

"It better not be a waste of time," Arnica grumbled.

"A visit to Raven is never a waste," Slade said pleasantly, grinning back at them. Jack choked back a laugh and Evelyn giggled.

"What was the second?" Miriel asked. "Tree blood?"

"*Blood of leaves*," Evelyn answered.

"And *breath of the dead*," Jack finished.

"It seems familiar," Miriel said, rubbing her chin. "I can almost put my finger on it—"

The shrieks of birds filled the air around them, hundreds of them taking to the sky and flying swiftly away.

"What—"

"Hunter!" Evelyn cried.

For a long moment, time froze, all watching as Slade dashed out of the clearing and back the way they'd come. If Jack had a heart, it would've been pounding in his chest, thumping in his ears and drowning out all other sound. The spell broke and he followed after Slade, yelling, "Come on!" A quick glance back revealed the edge of the darkness seeping through the trees.

"What is that?!" Arnica yelled.

"Run!" Evelyn shouted, taking to the air after Slade and Jack.

The mage and cat finally moved, stumbling after the three. A low rumble built behind them, though whether it was the Hunter or something else, Jack didn't know. Slade stopped, increased his size, and allowed Jack to climb on his back.

"You won't owe me for this one," the fox said, taking off again.

"Shut up," Jack said.

🎋 23 🎋
DRYADS

They flew over the ground like a restless wind, like stars across the night sky. Jack gripped Slade's fur and leaned low over his back. Above him, Evelyn dodged through the trees, Miriel and Arnica running behind. Questions and fear wandered through their eyes, but the retreat prevented any words, so they ran on, unanswered.

Images of Nadya filled his thoughts and he clenched his eyes shut, guilt and shame rising within him once again. He would find a way to fix it. He *would*.

"Creek!" Slade shouted, bouncing into the water a second later. Miriel and Arnica hesitated, but one glance back and they jumped into the water as well, reaching the other side a moment later, spluttering and dripping.

"Stop!" Jack said. "He can't cross." The fox slowed, looking back until he was sure Jack was right. This time Jack watched as the Hunter came closer, blackening the leaves, the trees, the rocks, then stopping to consider them on the other side of the running water. A slender shape stood amidst the dark: thin, almost human. It raised an arm as though reaching for them, then dissipated, the shadows dissolving and leaving the land as it had been before, all sign of the creature gone.

The group stood there a moment, panting and shaking the water off themselves. Jack climbed down, his legs trembling just a little. Arnica was the first to speak.

"What in the name of all the hells was that thing?"

"A Hunter," Jack said. "Sent by the witch."

"And you didn't think to mention it before?!"

"It never came up!"

"Looks like you were right," Slade said. "Next time, I'll believe you. You're sure it can't cross?"

"Positive. But it will be back. It's only a matter of time."

"It's after me," Evelyn said. "I'm the one the witch cursed, so I'm the one it chases. Maybe it's better if you don't come with us. You'll be safer."

"Nonsense," Miriel said. "We're out here ready to track down a witch, at Arnica's urging I might add, so we're going to do this thing, no matter what comes up against us. It's only natural she should use some unusual magic. We'll just have to be crafty and employ our own."

Arnica stared at her companion as if she'd grown another head. "If I'd known going adventuring would have this effect on you, I never would've suggested it. I think I prefer you when you're timid and play by the rules."

"We can go for help," Jack said. "Anyone who knows anything about the spell will be a welcome addition."

"No, they won't," Slade said. "It would simply mean more people who think they have a say in how this is done. I already have my objections to these two. No use in adding to it."

"You think we *like* traveling with *you*?" Arnica said. "I'd rather dig my own grave!"

"Then do it," the fox suggested.

"Please, everyone," Miriel said, holding up both hands. "Bickering like this won't get us anywhere. So you two don't like each other: fine. You don't have to. As soon as the witch is taken care of, you can go back to pretending the other doesn't exist. In the meantime, we should continue."

"She's right," Jack said. "Let's just get to Raven and see what he can tell us. Perhaps after that, we can see what the Guild has to say. Every bit of knowledge is useful."

Slade snorted but gave no comment.

The fox took the lead again and Evelyn perched on Jack's shoulder, letting the others go ahead of them. Miriel wrung out her dress, splattering water on the ground, then moved on to her hair, which held even more.

"What a mess," she muttered, following Slade and Arnica as she wiped her spectacles on her upper sleeve, the only dry spot she could find.

"I'm glad you're all right," Evelyn said to him.

"I'm just glad I found you again. Just in time, too."

"We could've handled them."

"Perhaps. But then we wouldn't have gotten to see Miriel's performance. Makes me wonder what else she can do."

"How much do you know about them?"

"Only that they see it as their duty to track down this witch. Arnica didn't want to bother their superiors about it."

"So getting help from the Guild may not be an option."

"We'll see. But I'm sure Raven can tell us something."

Far overhead, a peal of thunder rumbled through the air, followed a second later by the spattering of raindrops through the leaves. The bright orange and yellow canopy above darkened and the distance transformed into a gray, shapeless blur. His feet would be ruined again, unless Raven's spell protected against mud.

"Good thing we already jumped in the creek, eh?" Miriel said, slowing to walk beside them. She took her spectacles off and tucked them into her pack, then passed her hand over her face, fingers splayed.

"Seems that way," Jack agreed. "Can you still see?"

"My eyesight's not *that* bad, but I cast a temporary clear sight spell. I can see perfectly right now. Should last through the rain."

"Why not use that rather than spectacles?" Evelyn asked.

"Too much wasted energy. My spectacles work just fine, and require no magic. Anyway, I wanted to speak more of retrieving your memory, Jack. I feel that it could help us. Call it a hunch, if you will."

The mage smiled, revealing teeth that had never known stain or disease. Unless they were magicked, which was entirely possible. Though Miriel didn't seem the type to waste magic on such trivial things as appearance if it didn't serve a purpose.

"What can you do?" Jack asked.

She shrugged. "Maybe nothing. But I have a few ideas."

"How would it help us?"

"Well," she said, looking ahead as they walked. "Let's say it was a witch who cursed you. Maybe by retrieving your memory, we can identify her as well. Every witch we stop makes the world just a slight bit better. Besides, if we know how she did it, maybe we can figure out how to reverse it."

"You could be human again, too, Jack," Evelyn said.

He looked at the ground, thinking back as far as he could remember. It was all sky and field. Except for the dreams... They'd been less frequent of late, but if they were true... It didn't seem like something that could actually happen. He was a scarecrow: always had been and always would be. He stole a glance at Evelyn, who watched him with a strange humor in her eye. If he squinted his eyes just right, he could imagine her long red hair framing her face, her skin pale in the autumn light. A raindrop fell in his eye, scattering the vision.

"All right," he said, wiping the drop away. "We can give it a try if you like."

"Excellent." Miriel smiled down at him. "We'll wait until we camp tonight. It's easier for me to be sitting still."

"Have you been doing this long?" Evelyn asked.

"Magic? Or memory retrieval?"

"Either. Both."

The mage laughed. "Well, I discovered I could do magic when I was very young. Maybe five or six. I never tried anything major. Just invisibility if I wanted to hide from my parents and siblings. The occasional vision in water, quite by accident. I only started studying memory retrieval in the last couple years. The basics are simple enough, but putting them into practice is still a bit of a challenge. But at least no harm can come of it not working."

"I've only just started studying magic," Evelyn said. "That's partly how I ended up like this. I wanted to learn more and my dad wanted me to get married."

"Who was your teacher?"

"Well..."

Whatever Evelyn had been about to say was lost as all of them stopped, a tingling sensation spreading across their skin. It was similar to what Jack had experienced before, only thicker, more present, in a way. He glanced around nervously, expecting anything and everything. Nothing could surprise him anymore.

"I don't like this," Arnica said.

"Be on your guard," Slade added. "We're not alone."

They watched the trees and shrubbery, the branches above, the ground beneath their feet, but nothing seemed out of the ordinary. It was simply an autumn wood in an autumn rain. Jack almost wished something *would* happen, just to end the anticipation. Evelyn snuggled closer to him, still scanning their surroundings for danger.

"May be those wolves," Arnica said.

Slade shook his head. "I don't think so. They're not the most magical creatures, and this definitely feels magical in nature. Besides, it's not their style."

"The Hunter?" Miriel asked.

"No. Maybe—"

Laughter, away to their right. All heads swiveled that direction, then it echoed again on their left. Shades darted between the tree trunks, out of sight a second before they could be sure they saw anything. More laughter.

"Stop playing games!" Slade shouted. "If you wish to speak with us, do it!"

"Don't anger them, Slade," Jack whispered.

"What do I care if they're angry? We have two and a half mages here; surely we can handle a little anger."

More laughter, this time shaking the leaves above and around them. The rain fell in greater waves, further obscuring their sight. Slade cursed.

"We need to get out of the rain!" Miriel shouted. "It's getting worse!"

Arnica shook herself and growled at their unseen foes. "Show yourselves!"

"It's no use," Jack said. "We should go, before..."

But his words hung unuttered in the air, right next to a face that pressed out of a tree and looked down on them, its ghostly hair a halo around its head. It wore an amused grin, its eyes squinched in wicked amusement. Its body shone a pale blue, but as it emerged from the tree, it slowly gained substance, becoming more corporeal with every passing second. When it landed on the ground, it was fully fleshed, all gold and brown and green, a tree woman with black eyes. When the rain touched her, it sank into her skin.

Slade and Arnica both growled, Slade crouching lower, prepared to spring.

"Don't, stop!" Miriel said. "She's not dangerous!"

"You know her?" Jack asked.

Slade didn't move.

"Not personally, but she's not trying to hurt us. Slade, stop, please! She's a dryad. Maybe she can help."

Slade stopped growling, but he didn't move from his crouched position. The tree woman—dryad—laughed, the sound like the grinding of wood. More faces appeared in the trees, but no others came down.

"She's a tree spirit," Miriel explained. "I've only ever read about them, but they're quite harmless."

"What do they want?" Slade asked.

They all looked to the dryad for an answer, but she only smiled at them and said nothing.

"Can they speak?" Evelyn asked.

"I'm...not sure," Miriel said. "I don't remember if any of the books mentioned speaking."

The dryad motioned for them to follow her, waving and pointing away in the trees.

"There's no way I'm following a tree spirit into the deep dark woods," Arnica said. "I came out here for a witch hunt, not to be eaten by a tree."

"They won't eat you, Nica," Miriel said, taking a few cautious steps toward the dryad. "Besides, I doubt you'd taste very good."

The dryad began to walk away, looking back now and then to make sure Miriel still followed.

"You do realize I won't come to save you if she decides you're dinner?" Arnica called after her.

"Come on, everyone!" the mage responded. "It's fine! I promise they won't harm us!"

Jack glanced at the others, none of them too keen on following.

"We can't let her go alone," Evelyn finally said.

"You're welcome to follow her," Slade said. "That would be the end of the quest and the end of my duty toward you, so be my guest."

Jack took a few steps forward, looking back at the group uncertainly. "Two and a half mages, right?" he said.

Slade sighed heavily, then laughed. "Yes, I suppose you're right. But if this goes badly and I have to waste my magic, I'm holding you responsible."

"I wouldn't want it any other way."

"Are you sure we'll be okay?" Evelyn whispered as Jack followed the quickly fading Miriel.

"No. But like you said, we can't let her go alone."

She nodded in response, eyes set firmly ahead.

Arnica sighed behind them. "Oh, damn it all, Miri. I'm going to regret this, I just know it."

They jogged after her, dryad faces smiling down at them from every tree, and the rain continued to fall.

THEY CAUGHT up with her fairly quickly, the dryad still beckoning them to follow. Miriel smiled when she noticed them behind her. "Glad you guys decided to join me. I thought I would have the adventure all to myself and get to boast about it later."

"When we get back home, you are not going out again until you're eighty," Arnica said. "What would Lirelin say?"

"She'd say, *My, Miriel, how much you've grown! Look how brave you were, chasing that dryad out into the rain!*"

Evelyn snorted and Jack raised a hand to cover his own laugh.

"And you were worried about *me* having too much fun," Arnica said, the corner of her mouth lifting in the slightest hint of a smile.

The dryad waved at them again, pointing ahead where a dark gray shape began to form out of the rain. A bit closer and a deep overhang emerged through the gray curtain, its back wall nearly out of sight. The dryad stopped and pointed, indicating they should go inside.

"A shelter!" Miriel said. "Just what we were wanting."

"Is there anything inside?" Slade asked. His fur hung limp at his sides and from his face, his bright orange coat dull and muddy. A crack of thunder boomed overhead, causing most of them to jump. The dryad stood immobile, still pointing. The rain fell faster, harder, one solid wall of water plunging to earth. The group hurried under the overhang.

The dryad smiled wide and disappeared, slipping into some tear in the air where they couldn't follow. The group began to shake themselves off, water pooling around them on the ground.

"Well, that was helpful," Miriel said. "Did you see how many there were, Nica? We shall definitely have to return to study them. We're still so behind in our knowledge of magical creatures!"

The mage wrung her hair out, spilling a large amount of water on the ground. Slade busied himself with gathering grass and twigs and leaves. Jack helped him and they made a pile near the edge of the overhang. Slade blinked and flame sprang from within the pile. Arnica lay down near one of the walls and Evelyn stood looking out at the forest beyond the gray curtain.

"Why do you think they helped us?" she asked.

"Who knows?" Slade said. "Maybe they were bored."

"Do you remember anything else about them from your books?" Jack asked Miriel.

"Not really," she admitted. "I think for the most part they are considered 'good,' but I don't know why they'd bother with us."

"Who cares?" Slade said. "We're out of the rain now, everyone's accounted for, and Raven is waiting. As soon as this rain stops, we can be off again."

They all looked toward the forest, the gray wall of water obscuring anything further than a few feet away. Jack sat next to Evelyn, absently wondering what the Hunter would do in the rain, or if the water had already destroyed it. Miriel sat on the other side of him, crossing her legs and pulling her pack into her lap.

"I think it's time we tried some spells," she said, pulling her stones and books out.

"May as well," Jack said. "We're not going anywhere."

"What are you going to do, exactly?" Evelyn asked.

"Oh, I'm sure I could do several things," the mage answered. "The hard part is choosing which ones."

She arranged the stones in a circle before her, alternating the colors so that none touched another like it. Then she grabbed a few leaves and sprinkled them in the middle of the circle, starting her own small fire that quickly consumed the leaves.

When all was ash, she moved one finger through it with eyes closed, drawing symbols and figures Jack had never seen before. She whispered a single word and opened her eyes, bending low over the circle to read what she'd written.

Jack and Evelyn looked at each other. He'd never seen magic like this. He was used to the instantaneous magic he'd seen Slade and Nadya perform, or even Olivarion and the witches. The use of stones and leaves seemed strange and mysterious in comparison.

"What do you see?" Evelyn asked after a moment of silence.

"Ash and rocks," Arnica said from the other wall. "That sort of magic is outdated."

"But effective," Miriel answered, her eyes never leaving the circle. "Leave me be."

"You'd have better results with one of Alexander's spells."

"Please, Nica."

"Who's Alexander?" Evelyn asked.

"One of the Great Mages," Arnica answered. "Dead a hundred years now. Most of the modern magic of the Guild is based off of his work."

Jack glanced at Slade, who feigned to not be listening to the conversation.

"Yes, and we still need to find his missing book," Miriel said, glancing up only a second.

"Wonder where it could be?" Arnica said, glaring at Slade.

The fox pretended not to hear.

"I thought you said the Guild is looking for it," Jack said.

"True," Miriel said. "But as Guild members, we're obligated to follow any leads we have."

"Well, too bad that scary dreadlord has it, eh?" Slade said, adding more debris to the fire.

"Yes, too bad," Arnica said. The cat glared at him a moment, then rested on her paws and let her eyes droop. "Wake me when something interesting happens," she said.

Miriel scowled at her companion, then looked back at her

rocks. "Well, I think this is a good start. It helps me to get the feel of you and explore what memories you currently have. Are you ready to go deeper?"

The mage looked up at him, her eyes peering into him almost like Raven's had. At that moment, he had no doubt that she knew everything about him.

"Yes," he said.

Evelyn leaned against him, offering silent encouragement.

Miriel looked back at her stones and ash, then bent low and blew the pile at Jack.

❧ 24 ❧

AGES PAST

The world disappeared and in its place rose a gray replica, a shadowy mirror. Jack glanced about, seeing no one else. "Evelyn?" he called. "Miriel?"

His voice echoed in the gray, swallowed up a second later to restore the silence. Trees surrounded him, thick and full, like they were in late spring. But no animals nestled in the branches, no birds filled the air with their song. No sound at all, in fact.

"Hello?" he called again.

Something moved away to his left. He hesitated, worried for a moment that it was the Hunter. Then he laughed and shook himself. This was supposed to be his memory; the Hunter wouldn't find him here. He followed after the figure.

It was like moving through deep water, every step a force of will. He waved his arms, pushing the air back to move faster, but he couldn't tell if it made much difference. The figure appeared through the trees again, walking leisurely.

"Hey!" Jack called.

The gray swallowed his words again. The figure didn't even look his way. Jack chased after it as fast as he could, finally catching up when it stopped to look up at the trees. A man, mid-twenties by the look of it, with a mop of curly hair. He watched the trees with a look of pure rapture, his face soft and peaceful. Jack knew that face.

The gray swirled around them, blurring into a whirlwind of shapes. When it came to rest again, they stood before a cottage surrounded by trees. A watermill churned a stream of water on the left side of the house. A garden sat on the right side. Inside the shelter connected to the mill were half-finished pieces of furniture: chairs and tables and benches. The man entered the cottage and Jack followed, noting the line of fish hanging on one wall. The man pulled one down and began to skin it. On the floor, a bear pelt stretched between the bed and the kitchen. Jack shuddered, images of snarling wolves flashing before his eyes.

"Can you hear me?" Jack asked.

The man didn't look up.

The gray swirled again, this time revealing a small village square filled with people. A peddler stood at the center of the crowd, his wagon packed with goods. Noise erupted all around Jack, startling him with its intensity. He could hear the birds in the forest singing their love song to the sun; the cries of the crowd as they pressed closer to the peddler, all impatient to be on their way; the snort of the horse as the man secured him to a hitching post. The man waited at the edge of the square and eyed the crowd doubtfully. Jack followed his gaze as it moved to the row of houses beside them, where a woman stood in a doorway, arms crossed. Her hair was long and dark, curly and thick, her every feature perfect, skin smooth and flawless. Even in the gray, her eyes twinkled with some inner brightness. On her face, a mask of indifference sat. That, and perhaps boredom.

The man hesitated, looking back and forth between her and the crowd. A moment later, his inner battle was decided and he approached the woman.

"Haven't seen you here before," she said.

"I live in the forest. My name's Alex."

Yes, yes. This is right.

"I'm guessing you're here for the peddler," she continued.

"Yes. My stock is running a bit low."

"You might want to come back later. This lot will keep him busy until sundown."

"I'll take my chances."

She looked back at the crowd, still smiling.

"Forgive me if I'm being forward, but what is your name?" Alex asked.

"Martha," she said, still not looking at him.

"It suits you."

She shrugged. "I suppose." She glanced at him again, brows furrowed in curiosity. "Why don't you ever come into the village? Aren't you lonely out there by yourself?"

"I never have time to be lonely. And the trees are generally the only company I seek."

She nodded and looked away again. "I would love to leave this place. I imagine I could do it, were I married, but that will be many years yet. Some more immediate solution is preferable."

"Why not just go?"

This time she sighed. "I don't think I'd get very far on my own. Besides, I can't leave my family with no explanation."

He nodded. In silence, they watched the crowd around the peddler and his wagon, all struggling to be the next in line.

"Well, I guess I better jump in while I can," Alex said.

"You should come around more often," she said as he turned away.

He smiled. "Perhaps I will."

Jack frowned, knowing he'd heard those words. This, all of it, was familiar, *so* familiar. Even with all the gray, he knew her hair was brown. Her eyes were blue. The gray swirled again, this time revealing the town square at some later time. The crowd and peddler were gone, though Martha still stood in the doorway. From down the street, Jack spotted Alex, walking toward them with a fast stride, his eyes on the ground.

"Alex!" Martha called.

He looked up, smiling at her and closing the remaining distance in a quick run. Everything swirled faster then, giving him glimpses of dinners, walks, conversations, kisses.

It slowed again to show Alex speaking with an older man inside a house.

"I'm sure you're already aware of my intentions with your daughter," Alex said.

"I am, but you probably won't like what I have to say. I think you should leave her be. Now, don't get me wrong. I think you're a fine young man. But she has dreams that don't involve a small village. If you marry her, she'll never be happy. Not so long as you stay here, anyway."

"I will certainly do my best to make sure she's always happy."

A vision of the wedding followed, Martha wearing a white gown and a crown of flowers in her hair. Jack knew that her mother had made the gown for her, that her younger sisters had gathered the flowers.

More visions then, faster and faster. Martha made clothes and Alex made furniture, they quarreled and dreamed, made love and explored the forest together.

"I want nicer dresses," she said. "When do you think we'll make a trip to the city?"

This repeated, over and over.

"You never do anything for me," she said. "I just stay here day after day. Don't you want to see the world?"

"These woods are big enough for me," he said.

"But not me," she muttered in response.

The visions after that were frequently of Alex alone, walking beneath the trees. Martha gave up her dressmaking and Alex made paper from the mill.

"Why did you even want to marry me?" she asked him. "It's obvious you don't care about me. So why even waste your time?"

"You know I love you," he said.

She laughed dryly. "Of course you do."

More swirling, then visions of Martha sneaking away from home. Alex returned to an empty house and waited for her.

"I got caught in the rain," she said when she returned. "Stayed at my mother's until it passed. I didn't think you'd miss me."

Dark fantasies rose in Jack's mind, knowing they were Alex's fantasies. *Just because she's unhappy doesn't mean she's unfaithful.*

A storm was coming, something momentous, evident in Martha's behavior, in Alex's denial, in the silence they shared.

"*Don't trust her!*" Jack shouted at Alex. But of course his words were swallowed.

Then it came: Alex emerged from the forest he loved and Martha waited for him at the door.

"I have a surprise for you, husband," she said.

"Oh?"

"Yes. First, you should know that I'm pregnant." She held up a hand to prevent him from speaking. "Don't get excited. It's not yours."

Jack's gut twisted at the stricken look on Alex's face. He knew this, had felt this pain before. Martha merely laughed.

"It's for the best," she said. "I don't need any lingering ties to you."

"Whose is it?" Alex asked, his voice low and barely contained.

Jack echoed him, wanting, *needing* to know.

"Honestly, I don't know," she said. "Let's just say it's mine. I've been very busy, raising the money I'll need to move to the city. You're probably wondering why I bother to tell you all of this, which brings me to the best part. There are some men coming today. I've arranged for you to be taken into the services of a kind old woman. She has...unique abilities, you could say. You'll be well taken care of, and quite incapable of following me."

"I'm not going anywhere!" Alex shouted. "And neither are you!"

"Oh, don't show emotion now, dear," she said, looking him straight in the eye. "The gods know I've tried often enough to get a reaction from you. I'm finally getting exactly what I want. You're a fool if you think otherwise."

Jack saw the men then, ambling up the road with their wagon and their ropes. Alex didn't notice them until the creaking of their wheels finally reached his ears. By then, one was already upon him, bashing him over the head with a club. Another man helped to tie him and lift him into the wagon. Alex swayed in and out of consciousness. Martha stood in the doorway, still smiling.

"Don't worry, sweetheart," she said. "I'll be just fine."

She waved as the wagon pulled away, blowing him a kiss as they entered the trees.

The gray swirled again, this time revealing a dirty, cramped room filled with other people, all bound. No one spoke. Alex lay against a wall, his face stained with dried tears. The men returned and pulled him from the room, dragging him up a flight of stairs and onto the floor in another room. The gray moved Jack with them, sitting him at the front of the room.

"Easy, now," a scratchy voice said. "No need to damage him."

An old woman sat in a chair by a fireplace, a blanket over her lap. Her smile was warm and kind, but her eyes were dark, hiding some cruel delight.

"Who are you?" Alex asked, attempting to rise.

"All you need to know is I am your new mistress. I seem to have too many servants of late, so I've come up with a better plan for you and the others. Something to amuse me. And bring in a little spending money."

"You can't sell us like slaves!" Alex cried, thrashing against his bonds.

"Not slaves," Jack whispered.

The old woman laughed. "I already have." She raised one wrinkled hand, lowering it slowly.

Jack could almost feel the tingling sensation, as if it had just happened. The rope around Alex loosened its hold, but he still didn't move. Instead, he stiffened, his features changing bit by bit. Jack remembered this, too, remembered the illusion that the old woman was growing, like some grotesque giant. When it was finished, Jack stared at a larger image of himself, frozen in immobility a few feet away.

"There, now," the woman said, her spell complete. "Such a pretty scarecrow. Please take him down to the wagon, boys, and bring me a cup of tea before you bring the next one."

THE GRAY RELEASED Jack and he collapsed to the ground, coughing and crying. Evelyn hovered over him.

"What's wrong? What happened?"

"What did you see?" Miriel asked.

Jack squeezed his eyes closed, wishing he could forget what he'd seen, could forget the feeling of betrayal that bloomed anew in his breast. He didn't want to remember, didn't want to know her name or her face or her touch...

He fled the shelter, ignoring Evelyn's worried cry, letting the rain pour over him unhindered. The trees were his refuge, always had been and always would be, and he sought them again. The gray rain curtain resembled the gray from the vision, but it let him be, revealing no horrors from his past. He sank against a tree, burying himself in the exposed roots until he was secure and safe in their arms of wood. And there he tried his best to forget.

THE RAIN CONTINUED through the night and into the next morning. It couldn't touch Jack. Weather, Hunters, gray worlds, none of them could reach him, couldn't trick him or hurt him or betray him. Martha still floated before him, a smiling ghost, laughing at everything he'd been through. He scowled at her, wanting with all his heart to hate her as much as she hated him.

But he couldn't do it. So much time had passed, and so much had happened since then. The most he could muster was disdain.

A vision of Evelyn appeared before him, her human form, red hair piled around her as she read from her book in his field. And then even she was gone and an ocean of stars surrounded him, filling him until all he felt was peace. He rested there until the others began to call for him, their voices echoing through the air. Stars above and stars below, and Evelyn's voice on the wind.

He returned to the shelter.

The rain drizzled to a stop and the sun halfheartedly tried to pierce the wall of clouds. Evelyn and Miriel watched him with brows furrowed, mouths turned down in worry. Arnica and Slade just studied him.

"Are you...okay?" Evelyn asked.

He smiled, and it was easier than he thought it would be. Comforting. Natural. His smile widened, filling his face and easing his heart.

"I'm fine," he said. "Are we ready to go?"

They walked in silence at first, the others still unsure of his state of mind. He couldn't blame them. He still felt unsure himself, as if at any moment the despair would eat him up again, maybe not release him this time. But it didn't come. When he closed his eyes, all he saw was the stars, and it was enough.

"I was really worried," Evelyn said after they'd been walking for a while. "I thought maybe you would leave us."

"Never," he said. "Nothing has changed."

"But...you remember now, right?"

"I do. But it was a past not worth remembering. The present is all that matters now."

She nodded, then as an afterthought asked, "So, what was your name? When you were human, I mean."

"Alex," he said, saying it aloud for the first time. "Hardly suits me."

She laughed. "True. But it's a nice name."

"I prefer Jack."

"Do you want to talk about it?" Miriel asked, slowing to walk beside them.

"No."

"You at least have to tell us who cursed you," Slade said, glancing back at them. "Don't leave us in the dark. It may be of use."

"I don't *have* to do anything," Jack said. Then, realizing the harshness of his tone, he added, "Another witch. An old woman. She turned us all into scarecrows."

"*Us?*" Arnica asked. "There are more of you?"

"I think so."

"How sad," Evelyn said. "They're probably trapped, just like you were."

"We don't have time to track down every scarecrow in existence," Slade said. "There's a Hunter after us, in case you forgot."

Jack didn't answer.

"Still," Evelyn said. "Just think of their families. Friends..."

"We can track them down later," Miriel said. "They should be fine for now. That witch, however, is another story. Any idea where she was?"

He shook his head.

"Pity."

The tingling sensation, which Jack had grown used to, abruptly stopped. The others glanced at each other, but no one commented on it. He hadn't seen any dryads that day, but he was certain they had left their lands behind, every step taking them closer to Raven's land. The sun disappeared again behind the cloud wall and the trees thinned. Birds called overhead. The forest once more became familiar, safe, inviting.

Evelyn rested on his shoulder and Miriel walked next to him, no doubt hoping he would speak more about his memories. It was almost funny. He'd spent so much of his life in a state of curiosity about his past, and now he remembered and only wanted to forget. He wondered if Raven would laugh about it.

"Not far now," Slade announced.

Evelyn took to the air, flying ahead to get the lay of the land. Jack's mind turned back to the riddle of the witch's spell. *Tears of stone. Blood of leaves. Breath of the dead...* Miriel smiled at him like she could read his thoughts.

"Let's hope this old bird knows his stuff, eh?" she said.

WHEN THEY REACHED the outskirts of Raven's land, Slade called a halt. "I really don't know if you'll be allowed in," he told Miriel. "You may want to consider waiting for us here."

"Are you kidding? And miss out getting to meet a bird god? I don't think so."

"He's right, Miriel," Arnica said. "We don't know what sort of magic this Raven can do. It may not be safe for you."

"It may not be safe for any of us, but I don't see any of you offering to stay behind."

"She'll be fine," Jack said. "Raven once told me it's the soul that counts, not the form you wear."

"See?" Miriel said.

Slade didn't look convinced, but he nodded. "Fine."

He led them further in and soon they heard the familiar, "Halt!"

The little stone gargoyle sat hidden just beneath a bush covered in bright red berries. Arnica swiped a few to the ground, apparently for the amusement of it, for she left them there and paced back and forth, her gaze locked on their path.

A few moments later a sparrow flew up and said, "Welcome back! Follow me."

They obeyed. Jack hoped the sparrow's disregard of Miriel was a good sign. Surely if there was concern, he would've said something.

"I hope this is worth our time," Arnica said.

"It will be," Evelyn answered.

The land sloped downward again and the valley that held the large pond and the guest suites and the ruin appeared before them, spread out and shining from the rays of sunlight that broke through the clouds as though to illuminate them specifically. Jack inhaled, savoring the air, which was thick with magic and welcome. It was everywhere, if you knew how to look. Peace descended on his heart and the pain he'd started to carry dissipated, at least for a little while. In Raven's land, it held no sway.

"Wow," Miriel breathed. "It's beautiful."

"Not bad," Arnica said. "Beats anything the dreadlords have."

For the third time, Jack entered that valley, his promise to come for a simple visit fresh on his mind. Couldn't be helped, but he would keep that promise someday. So long as he wasn't destroyed by the Hunter first.

"Raven will see you on the lake," the sparrow informed them, guiding them toward the large pond. "Are you here to report, fox?"

"In a way. I can take us from here, if you don't mind."

The sparrow nodded its acquiescence and flew away.

The sun sparkled off the water, so bright that they had to squint. Jack could almost forget it was nearly winter. Several birds floated in the pond, many more nestling on the banks. The group reached the water's edge, but the large bird was absent.

"This is the right place, isn't it?" Arnica asked. "Where is he?"

"I'll look around," Evelyn said, taking to the air.

"It's the right spot," Slade said. "For the moment, we'll wait here."

"All these birds serve him?" Miriel asked, sitting on the bank.

"And many mammals, too," Slade answered.

"Just wait till you meet him," Jack told her. "It'll explain a lot."

"What sort of magic can he do?"

"I'm not sure, really," Jack said. "Shapeshifting. Travel between worlds. Creation, if he's the Raven from the stories."

"And many more things besides," Slade said.

"Big deal," Arnica said, stretching out beside her mistress. "If he's so powerful, why hasn't he taken care of the witches in this area? There's practically an infestation!"

"Maybe he views them in another light," Slade said.

"In that case, why would he help us?"

"Friendship?"

The cat scoffed and rolled her eyes. Jack chuckled, but Arnica had a point. Raven had no reason to help them. He could even side with the witches, and then what would they do? Could they fight against a bird god? Looking at Slade and Miriel and comparing their magic to Raven's, he knew what that answer would be.

Evelyn returned a moment later saying, "He's out on the water! We'll need to get some sort of boat to get to him. He's not budging."

"Sounds like a real gentleman," Arnica said, rising and stretching.

Miriel stood as well and looked along the bank, her hand shielding her eyes from the sun. "I don't see any boats," she said.

Slade cursed. "Of all the foolish things," he muttered. "Very well. We'll have to make a boat."

"How?" Arnica asked.

Slade raised one eyebrow. "You're a mage's companion and you're asking *how*?"

"That's a large amount of magic," Miriel said.

"Good thing I'm skilled," Slade replied. The fox faced the water and closed his eyes. Jack noticed he scratched the same spot on his chest, near his ribs, over and over. Almost like he was using it in his spell...

"The fire-tamer," Evelyn whispered beside him.

"You think?"

"Positive. There's a shimmer of magic there. Faint, but there. He's hidden it well."

The air around the fox swirled outward, his fur sticking up across his body. The others shielded themselves with arms and wing and paw as the blast poured over them. Grass and branches and leaves flew to the fox from all directions, stitching together bit by bit until a small boat sat before them, just large enough to hold all of them. The air around Slade calmed once more and he slowly blinked his eyes open.

He smiled, swaying just a little as he took a step forward, but he quickly righted himself. "All aboard," he said.

25

CLUES

Once in the boat, they sped across the water, powered by more magic. Slade slumped just a bit, but straightened whenever he noticed Jack looking. Neither said a word. Jack didn't know if it was an effect of the fire-tamer or simply the consequence of powerful magic. He didn't remember Slade showing fatigue after using magic in Alibeth, but then maybe that didn't require as much energy. Either way, the fox betrayed no emotion, refusing to show weakness.

Raven came into view ahead, resting on something wide and flat. The giant bird glanced their way, then returned to his study of the clouds and birds flying over the pond.

"Hmpf." Beside him, Arnica narrowed her eyes, her tail swishing in agitation. "I don't like him," she whispered.

"We don't even know him," Miriel whispered back.

"Doesn't matter. He should welcome us, acknowledge us, *something*. Not this silent indifference."

"Shh. He may hear you."

"Good."

Raven sat alone on an impossibly large orange leaf floating in the water. Jack wondered if it was created by magic as well, or if in some other world such leaves actually existed. As they pulled up beside him, Raven finally looked their way.

"So. You've returned."

It was unclear whether he was speaking to Slade, or Jack and Evelyn.

"I have," Slade answered, assuming the former.

"What do you have to report, fox?"

"I have done as you ordered, but we've come up against a riddle. We hoped you could make sense of it."

Raven looked to Evelyn. "Still a crow, I see. And you haven't changed your mind?"

"No, sir," Evelyn answered.

"You reached your destination, yet cursed you remain. Does that not discourage you?"

"Quite the opposite."

"Hmm. And you've brought new companions. What is your purpose here, human?"

Miriel stammered a bit, each word fumbling over the next. Finally she took a deep breath and said, "My companion and I are representatives of the Guild. We've heard rumors of a witch in this area and have come to investigate."

Raven laughed. "Yet your superiors don't know you're here, or even why you came."

Red rushed to Miriel's cheeks and Arnica bristled beside her. "I assure you—"

"I don't care much about that. Tell your betters, or don't. It's all the same to me."

He looked to Jack then before Miriel could respond.

"Good to see you again, friend. You look a little worse for wear. Not here for a visit, I take it?"

"I'm afraid not," Jack said. "I had a run-in with...an enthusiastic village, as you can see. I haven't forgotten my promise, though."

"Good. I will hold you to it. Now, tell me about this riddle."

Jack relayed the item list the witch had given them, his hope sinking as Raven's brow furrowed. "You don't know?" he asked.

"It's very interesting," the old bird said. "I have not studied witch magic as closely as I ought, it seems."

"Do you know what it means?" Slade asked.

"I do. But—"

"No buts!" Arnica said. "We've all come a long way to stop this witch. If you know how to stop her, then do it!" Then, as an afterthought, she added, "Please."

Raven guffawed. "You're a feisty one, no doubt of that. I will give you clues, nothing more. This is still a quest you'll have to complete on your own."

Arnica hissed. "As a fellow mage and animal, it is your duty—"

"My *duty* is to my land and my flock. Do not mistake me as your peer: I have none. That is simply fact."

"Please, forgive her," Miriel said hurriedly, ignoring Slade's scowl. "We only wish to stop the witch."

"Everyone *only wants* something. It doesn't excuse rude behavior." Raven ruffled his feathers, preening and looking away, as if they weren't there.

Slade glared at Arnica, but the cat glared right back. "Should've left you on the shore," the fox said.

"You could've tried."

"Stop it, both of you," Miriel said. "This is ridiculous and we're wasting time. Raven, sir, we are grateful for whatever help you can give us. Jack has spoken highly of you."

"Has he?" Raven said, giving Jack an amused grin.

"Please, can you tell us what you know about the riddle?" Evelyn asked.

The old bird sighed. "If I do, it will be the last help I give you on this quest of yours. You young ones must learn to do things for yourselves. That is how you grow and learn and avoid similar mistakes in the future." He leaned close, as though he were imparting a great secret, his eyes twinkling in delight. The group leaned toward him in return, all waiting to hear his words.

"To acquire the first item, you must find another enchanted creature, a bit like yourself," he said, looking between Jack and Evelyn. "For the second, you must gain the trust of things you don't understand. For the third, you must face your fears and learn sacrifice." He leaned back then, smiling still. "And that, my friends, is the end of your audience. You are welcome to stay here as long as you like, but I have a feeling you're impatient to be off, yes?"

"That can't be everything," Arnica said. "That doesn't help us at all!"

"Yes, we'll be off," Slade said, glaring at the cat again. "Unless my sentence has changed?"

"It has not."

The fox bowed in acquiescence.

"Thank you," Jack said. "We appreciate it."

"Don't forget your promise, Jack."

"I won't."

Miriel bowed a goodbye and then Slade propelled the boat back toward the shore, Arnica cursing the whole way.

"HOW IN THE name of all that's holy is that supposed to be helpful?!" Arnica demanded. "We're no closer than we were before we came here!" They pulled up against the shore and filed out onto the bank. The boat fell apart behind them, becoming a pile of debris on the otherwise pristine pond.

"I thought it was quite enlightening," Slade said.

"Of course you did. At this rate, we'd be better off going back to the Guild. At least there we can use the library."

"We should probably spy on the witch first," Miriel said. "That was the whole point, anyway.

"Agreed," Arnica said.

They walked slowly, barely paying attention to their surroundings. Everyone pondered over the clues Raven had given them.

"We'd have to split up," Evelyn said. "I'm not going back to the village until I have everything I need to defeat her."

"I'm with you," Jack reassured her.

"No, sir. Someone has to guide us to the village," Arnica said.

"Ladies," Slade said, smiling. "Look, we're all impatient to be done with this. You want to stop the witch, same as Jack and Evelyn here. Don't split them up. That will only frustrate them, and believe me, Jack here will take any chance he can to ditch you and make his way back to her."

The fox winked at Jack, who shook his head. Sure, it was *true*, but Slade didn't have to make him sound so...willful. Selfish. Evelyn winked at him and he sighed. No point denying it.

"Now, that library idea of yours sounds promising," Slade continued. "It means returning to Alibeth, but as I am commanded to help you, I will go where you lead. If we hurry, I'm sure it won't take but a few days to get back to the city, find what we need, and be one step closer to acquiring the items. We'll just have to be extra careful to avoid the dreadlords. And with you two with us, I feel much easier about venturing into the Guild's territory."

"Waste of time," Arnica muttered.

"It sounds fair to me," Miriel said, casting an unreadable look the cat's way. "There are a few things I'd like to lear—"

"Jack! How are you?"

Jack glanced up just in time to almost be knocked over by a bird diving his way. She pulled up just in time, landing on the ground in front of him.

"Caerla!" Evelyn said. "How have you been?"

The hawk studied the mage and cat, unsure what to make of them. "Fine," she said. "Busy. Raven has set me on a new task, so I don't have long to talk."

"We were just leaving ourselves," Slade said, his voice thick with honey.

"You're still a crow," Caerla observed. "Intentional?"

Evelyn shook her head. "There are a few more things we have to find."

"Such is the way of life. And you, Jack? What happened to you?"

"I'm well," he answered, "despite my obvious appearance. It's not as bad as it looks. Just a bad situation."

The hawk cocked her head to the side but said no more about it.

"This is Miriel and Arnica," Evelyn said. "And this is Caerla," she added, turning to the pair. "She's helped us before."

"You're a mage?" Arnica asked.

"I am. So is your companion."

"Maybe you can help us bring more animals into the Guild," Miriel said. "We probably should've spoken with Raven about it, but—"

The hawk laughed. "We have no desire to join with the Guild, but we appreciate the thought. I'm sorry I can't stay longer, but I really must be off. Remember your duty, fox."

Slade narrowed his eyes. "I do."

She quickly disappeared into the forest, leaving the group looking after her.

"Are all the birds rude here?" Arnica asked.

"They just have...other concerns," Jack said. "They don't mean anything by it."

"Believe me, they do," Slade said. "Shall we be off?"

They set out again, heading west toward Alibeth, the sun sinking behind the trees.

"What did she mean about your duty?" Jack asked Slade as they neared the edge of Raven's land.

"Oh, she's just referring to the charge Raven's laid on me. My sentence. I don't need a reminder, believe me."

"What did you do that allowed him to boss you around?" Arnica asked.

"First of all, he can do it to any one of us simply because he wants to. No one argues with Raven. Second of all, it's none of your business."

They traveled in silence then, Arnica's a bitter, annoyed silence, Slade's a heavy, brooding silence, and the others' an optimistic, thoughtful silence. Jack and Evelyn hung back once more, this time in order to avoid the charged air between fox and cat. Evelyn rested on Jack's shoulder and sighed.

"What did you think of Raven's help?" she asked.

Jack thought a moment before answering. His encounters with the bird had always been pleasant, though mostly on a personal level. The most recent audience had left him wishing to flee like all the others, if only to escape the negative atmosphere. He would make sure to visit alone the next time. With the exception of Evelyn, of course.

"I think we're supposed to really think about this one," he answered. "So far, we've been told who to speak with and where to go. I believe Raven wants us to rely on ourselves for a change."

"And if we can't do it? If we can't figure out the spell and can't find anyone else to help...?"

"We'll figure it out," Jack said. "Have some faith in yourself."

"I'm afraid, Jack. The thought hadn't occurred to me before, but we could fail. My father could spend the rest of his life enthralled to a witch. I could die a crow. My brother could never be found."

"Yes," Jack conceded. "That would be bad. All of it. I won't deny that. But there could still be some good, even if everything you say comes to pass."

"How?"

"Well, the Guild is eager for more animal mages. You could join them, if you wanted. Seems a mite better than trying to live in Alibeth or Underbeth, or even the forest, for that matter.

You'd still be able to fly, which I imagine must be nothing short of exhilarating. We'd still have the friendship of Raven, so if the Guild wasn't an option, you could join him."

Her eyes twinkled and she looked away. "That...doesn't sound so bad."

"And I'll be with you, no matter what happens. You have my word on that."

She snuggled against his cheek. "I know you will. You have no idea how much that means to me. You've been a great friend, Jack."

He smiled in return. The land rose as they left the valley behind. Slade zigzagged up the hill to make the climb easier, but it still took them several minutes to reach the top. Miriel and Arnica stopped and panted for a moment, Miriel's hands on her knees.

"Not used to this sort of life," she said.

"You were made for your books and papers," Arnica replied. "For the most part," she added, winking.

"Just you wait. Soon I'll outpace all of you. I just need to find my rhythm."

"We should find a camp for the night," Slade said. "And we'll need to start taking turns at sentry duty. The last thing we need is the Hunter to overtake us while we sleep."

Arnica snickered. "You weren't worried about it before. What's changed?"

"Simple. We've left behind the wetlands. The way to Alibeth from here is completely dry. If water's the only thing stopping that monster, I don't want to take any chances."

"But what can a sentry do?" Miriel asked. "How would we even see it coming in the dark?"

"The stars," Jack said. Everyone looked at him. He cleared his throat and repeated, "The stars. They disappear, when the Hunter's nearby. His darkness swallows everything. And the animals, they all run from him."

"So we sit around to see if the stars disappear and some animals run by?" Arnica asked.

"What about a ward?" Evelyn asked. "We have two mages and a beginner here. Surely we can come up with something."

"That would still require a sentry," Slade said. "Someone has to maintain the ward."

"We should find a place to rest, at least," Miriel said. "Especially if we're walking all the way back to Alibeth. I can be the first sentry, if it'll ease your mind."

Slade nodded his approval and they continued on for another hour before making camp in a little clearing. After making a fire, Slade left to find food. Arnica left by another path while Miriel pulled more food out of her pack.

"What about you?" Jack asked when Evelyn remained with them.

"I'm not hungry," she said.

"You want to talk, don't you?"

She didn't answer right away. Instead, she picked at twigs and leaves and grass and bark to create a nest for herself. When that was finished, she sat herself in it and watched him, but she still didn't speak.

"I... Is there something wrong?" Jack asked, unsure what to make of her behavior.

"A lot of things," she whispered. "But I'm about to propose something that could be very dangerous, and I'm trying to find the courage to say it. Okay, it *is* very dangerous, but it needs to be done."

"Please, just say it."

She sighed and looked out into the trees. "We need to do something about the Hunter. I know, he could kill us very easily if we're not careful, but just think of all the animals who've been killed in his pursuit of me. Maybe humans too, I don't know. It's too much."

Nadya's face shot through his thoughts, her final scream echoing in his memory. He didn't think he'd ever forget it.

"And if you don't want to help me, I'll figure it out on my own," she continued. "If we defeat the witch, maybe that'll be an end to the Hunter as well, but there's no telling how long that will take. How many more will die in the meantime?"

An image of Martha rose to his mind then, the way she was before. There had been joy there, once. There had been love, even if she denied it. And he remembered the way he'd felt when he'd found out about her betrayal. A feeling of despair, pain, hopelessness. It was similar to what he felt at the thought of Nadya, of her loss, and in that moment the Hunter became the representation of every evil thing that could happen to a creature during its life. Every hurt, every sorrow, every death.

"I can't just sit back and do nothing," Evelyn said. "I need—"

"You don't have to convince me," he said.

"What?"

"I'll help you. You're right, it needs to be done. We should've taken care of him sooner, but we've been a little distracted, to say the least."

She grinned. "No argument there."

Slade returned and lay down beside the fire, watching them with narrowed eyes. "What are you two whispering about? Anything interesting?"

"Just noting how much nicer you are lately," Jack said.

Slade laughed. "I have to be. Part of the job now."

"Hmpf," Evelyn said. "And here I thought it was because you liked us."

"I like you well enough," he said. "But I refuse to let emotions affect my affairs. You understand."

Jack laughed and shook his head.

Miriel watched all of them with a furrowed brow. "I could almost believe you're actually friends," she said.

"I was born for the theater," Slade said. "Alas, cruel fate has stepped in and thwarted my plans. But maybe someday."

Arnica returned and Evelyn settled into her nest to sleep. Slade rested his head in his paws and watched the fire, lapsing into silence. Jack lay back with his hands behind his head and watched the stars. Visions of stone and leaves and death passed through his mind, back and forth and back and forth, lulling him finally to sleep.

THEY CAME in the deep dark of night.

Jack woke and saw Miriel rise and stretch, looking out into the black forest. Slade rose, too, whispering to the mage as she examined the surrounding trees, finally satisfied enough to lie down and let the fox take over. Jack listened to the even breathing of the females, Evelyn's a faint whistle, Arnica's a deep purr, and Miriel's a gentle snore. They were comforting sounds, peaceful, but they weren't enough to usher him back to sleep.

"I know you're awake," Slade said.

Jack sighed but didn't look away from the stars. "How do you think all this will end? Can we even do it, you think? Defeat the witch, I mean."

"Do you seriously want to know my thoughts on that?" the fox asked, voice thick with sarcasm. "*Don't worry, we'll figure it out. Good triumphs evil. Fate will see it done.* That's what you want to hear, and I can say it over and over if you like."

"No," Jack said. "I want *your* answer."

"Well, if we're being honest. I think we'll have to be damn lucky to figure out the witch's spell. Even if we manage to get back to the Guild and search the library, do you have any idea how many books they have? We could spend the rest of our lives looking for answers."

"No hope, then?"

"*There's always hope*, or something like that. Maybe one of the mages there has actually studied witches and can tell us exactly what the spell means. Maybe Raven will change his mind and explain everything. Anything is possible."

"You're still not saying what *you* think."

"Who cares what I think?" the fox said, his voice lowering to almost a whisper. "I will do my part, just like I always have, and when all is done, maybe I'll finally return home. I've been away too long."

Jack glanced over at him, pondering whether he should question Slade on his past, when the first howl echoed through the night. It was followed by another, and another, coming from every direction. The fire was only the faintest ember, but Slade extinguished it with a wave of his paw and stood, alert. Jack stood as well, shuddering as the howls joined together to create a single, eerie call.

"Damn it all!" Slade said. "Just what we need."

"What is it?" Miriel asked, lifting her head.

"Wolves," Slade said. "Better wake the others."

They appeared out of the darkness, their eyes reflecting the moonlight. Teeth snapping and throats growling, they surrounded the group, inching closer while they had the advantage.

Jack felt for Evelyn in the dark, lifting her into his arms as the closest wolf snapped at them. Two more appeared next to it, forcing them back until Jack nearly tumbled over Arnica.

"What is it?" Evelyn asked, her voice thick with sleep

She gasped as she noticed the wolves. A fire erupted around Slade, illuminating the clearing so that each wolf was clearly seen. Bright green magic appeared at Miriel's fingertips, her hair rising into the air.

"Come on, then!" Arnica said, taking her stance next to her mistress and hissing, her hair rising to mimic Miriel's.

"Give us the crow," one wolf said. "We won't be scared off by your sorcery this time."

"That's a foolish thing to say, especially for a wolf," Slade said. "Do you really want to test your abilities against mine?"

"And mine," Miriel added, her voice a thing of gray and rot.

"And mine," Evelyn added, freeing herself from Jack's arms to sit on his shoulder.

The wolves didn't answer, merely lunged as one, jaws snapping. Slade and Miriel released their magic and Evelyn cried aloud, their magic sending a blast of wind against the wolves. At least one wolf managed to avoid the blasts and grasped Jack around the waist, clamping hard and pulling him into the forest.

"Jack!" Evelyn cried.

Her voice and the noise of the fight were soon lost as his captor escaped into the dark trees.

26

WILD MAGIC

They left him in a dark cave again, without the stars to provide even the smallest bit of light. Two wolves stood guard at the entrance, and he had no desire to explore the cave further for another exit. There was no telling how deep and dark it was.

He dozed in and out of sleep, unable to rest long for the worry that gnawed at him. He woke once just as a wolf entered and tossed something toward him. The something groaned and he breathed a sigh of relief.

"Evelyn," he said.

"Jack?" she mumbled.

"What happened?"

"One of them must've knocked me out."

"What about the others?"

"I don't know. Slade and Miriel took out several wolves before... I'm sure they're fine."

They found each other in the dark and Evelyn nuzzled against him. He sighed and leaned back against the cave wall, drifting out of consciousness once more. Whatever the wolves wanted, they were taking their time about it.

"I'm so tired," Evelyn said, her voice fading to a whisper.

"Let's get some rest," Jack said. "There will be time to worry later."

✤

THEY WERE WOKEN ROUGHLY the next morning, one wolf shaking them until they opened their eyes and stood. "The High Wolf awaits you," she said.

"Ugh," Evelyn groaned. "I feel like I've fallen from a roof. Everything hurts."

"Ride on my shoulder," Jack said, helping her up.

"Hurry," the wolf told them. "He won't be kept waiting."

"What do you even want?" Jack demanded. "Why go to all this trouble?"

"You'll find out soon enough."

She refused to answer any more questions. With Evelyn secured on his shoulder, Jack followed the wolf out of the cave and into the gray morning light. Several wolves stood sentry around the opening, which sat atop a high hill. More wolves stood lower down, watching the forest.

"This way," the wolf told them, indicating they would climb.

Against him, Evelyn whispered, "I'm so hungry, Jack. I didn't eat last night—"

"It'll be okay. We'll find you something. Can you not escape? Fly out of here?"

"I feel so weak. And my head is pounding. I wouldn't get very far."

He nodded and followed the wolf to the top of the hill. The forest spread out before them, a patchwork of autumn colors. Far in the distance, a tendril of smoke snaked into the air. The trees seemed to go on and on.

Overlooking the forest sat Ardel, the new High Wolf. Jack didn't think the wolves had figured out he was the young bear they'd bargained for, but it wouldn't entirely surprise him. The

JACK OF CROWS   301

white wolf turned at their approach. "Ah, we meet again." Jack froze until he realized the wolf was speaking to Evelyn.

"What is it you want?" Evelyn asked.

"Simple. I want my storm-eater back. *You* are going to get it for me."

"That's impossible!" she said. "It passed on to someone else, and there's no telling where it is now! You can't possibly expect me to find it."

"I do."

"I'm not even the one who took it," she complained.

"Nevertheless, you were one of those who sought it. As for you, scarecrow," he said, turning to Jack. "Rumor says Olivarion will pay a pretty penny to anyone who delivers you to him. Not sure why he'd want you, all burned and bedraggled as you are. He wants your fox friend, too, of course, but my troops have as yet been unable to capture him."

"And you won't," Jack said. "He's too smart for them. Plus, he's under the protection of Raven. We all are. Unless you want to anger him, you'd be wise to let us go."

The High Wolf laughed. "Raven and I have no quarrel with each other. He minds his own business and I mind mine. If I abuse one of his subjects, I can always provide him another. Such is the way of rulers."

"He puts more stock in his subjects than that!" Evelyn said.

"Besides, we're not subjects," Jack said. "We're friends."

The High Wolf laughed again. "We'll see. In the meantime, you both have a long journey ahead of you. One of my captains will accompany you, crow, to ensure you retrieve the storm-eater and return it to me. If you fail, you will be executed."

"No!" Jack said, lunging forward out of instinct. His guard dove between them, showing her fangs and growling. Jack backed away, scowling.

"Don't worry, scarecrow. I'll give you and the crow a moment to say your goodbyes." The High Wolf looked out over the forest again, saying, "I'm not cruel, despite what you may think. I'm merely doing what I believe is best for my pack. That artifact can be used by our mages for protection, survival, battle. It did much to win us the war, before it was stolen."

"Why don't you get one of your mages to get it back, then?" Jack asked. "They'd have a better chance."

"They have other duties," the wolf said. "Now say your good-byes. You'll leave immediately."

Jack looked at Evelyn, fear plain in her eyes. "Fly," he whispered.

She just shook her head.

"Hurry up," their captor said. "We have a lot of ground to cover."

"Jack," she said.

"Don't worry. We'll find each other again."

"Let's go!" the she-wolf said, nudging Jack down the hill.

"No!" Evelyn cried. "I'm sick of others dictating my life!" A swirl of leaves spun around her as she lifted her wings. Her eyes blazed a fierce green, glowing brightly in the dim light.

The High Wolf growled. "Stop her!"

The she-wolf lunged for Evelyn, but she took to the air, eyes still blazing.

"You told me she was sedated!" Ardel said.

"She was!" the she-wolf answered.

Evelyn spun in the air, the whirlwind around her flying out from her body toward the two wolves. Jack raised his arms to shield himself, but the wind passed over him like a gentle breeze. The wolves were knocked sideways, nearly losing their balance and tumbling down the hill.

"Find one of the mages!" Ardel commanded.

The she-wolf fled, ushered along by the wind. The High Wolf glared at Jack.

"You!" he said. "Make her stop!"

Jack looked up at Evelyn, mostly hidden by leaves, then back at the High Wolf. Ardel growled and lunged for Jack, his jaws snapping inches from the scarecrow's arm.

Evelyn shrieked and stopped the whirlwind. A second later, the ground rumbled and vines erupted from the earth, wrapping around the wolf leader's legs and nearly tossing him to the ground again. He bit and snapped at the vines, cursing.

"Run!" Evelyn yelled.

Jack paused a moment, looking back and forth between the High Wolf and her, then he dashed down the other side of the hill. He looked back midway to see a flash of blue light erupt at the top, followed by a scream. It sounded like Evelyn. He started to turn back when he saw her fly after him, her eyes still bright green.

"Let's go!" she said.

"What did you do?" he asked, doing his best to keep up. He dodged trees and rocks and fallen logs, but she still outpaced him. He risked a glance back, half expecting to see the entire pack on their tails. Instead, he saw something far worse: darkness.

"Hunter!" he cried.

"I saw it!" she yelled back. "Keep running!"

He obeyed, pushing himself as fast as his feet would take him. He prayed to any spirits or gods who could hear him that they would find a body of water soon. Absently, he wondered if the wolves had all been consumed or if they'd managed to escape. Despite their treatment of him, he hated to think of them as victims of the Hunter.

"Clearing ahead!" Evelyn yelled. "Just keep running! Don't wait for me!"

Before he could respond, she whirled in the air and flew back toward the darkness.

"Evelyn!" he yelled, running a few more feet before stopping to look back.

"Keep going!" she yelled.

But he couldn't leave her. Nadya's face rose in his mind, her final cry a permanent echo in his ears, and he took off after her. The darkness spread quickly; it had almost reached the bottom of the hill now. Evelyn perched on a branch a short distance away from it, cursing when she noticed Jack following her.

"I told you to go! You're going to get yourself killed!"

"So are you!" he yelled back. "I'm not leaving!"

"Idiot!" She shrieked and faced the coming darkness, letting her cry echo as her energy grew. When she released it, the whole earth shook, leaves raining down at the force of her fury, rocks freeing themselves from the ground to tumble down the hill. Her blast struck the darkness and an explosion rent the air, almost deafening. Jack fell backwards, unable to stand in the wake of such power. The ground shook again and a large crack split the earth, widening the space between the darkness and them. A spring rose up, forming a large pool at first until the crack widened more and it escaped, becoming a gushing stream to separate them from the Hunter.

As the magic released her, Evelyn fell from the branch, plummeting to the earth. Jack dashed toward her, catching her just before she hit the ground. She lay unconscious in his arms, her breathing labored. Jack looked back toward the Hunter. The darkness approached the stream and stopped, thinning and dissipating as it sought another way around. Finally, all was as it had been before, the autumn foliage filling the land with color and beauty. Only a few random dark spots on the ground and trees marked the passing of the Hunter.

Jack sat down beside the stream, shaking and wishing he could cry. It was too close, much too close. And Evelyn... He had never seen her use such powerful magic. He didn't know what it meant, if she had simply learned more than she'd let on, or if she'd acquired some powerful item to enhance her abilities. Whatever secrets she held, he was both grateful and fearful of them.

He laid her beside the newly-created stream and flopped back on the ground, staring up at the gray sky and trying to empty his mind of the questions that flooded it. In that moment, Martha entered his thoughts, her words and tone biting, venomous. He tried to block her out, but he was simply too tired.

She keeps secrets from you, Martha said. *What else has she kept to herself? She doesn't trust you, not completely. One day she'll turn on you, just you wait. It's inevitable, Alex.*

"That's not my name!" he yelled, sitting up. "Get out of my head!"

Martha laughed. *Just you wait,* she repeated.

"Jack?" Evelyn said, her voice barely a whisper.

"I'm here," he said, bending over her.

She tried to speak, but lost consciousness again. He sighed. At least her eyes had resumed their own color. Martha didn't return, but her words echoed in his mind. He rose and ventured into the trees to find firewood, banishing the horrid thoughts to the darkest corners.

EVELYN AWOKE LATE THAT NIGHT, just as Jack was beginning to doze off himself. He had sat beside her all through the day, unsure which direction to go. It had seemed better to stay put.

"Ugh, my head," Evelyn said.

"That's what you said this morning. Can you sit up?"

"I think so." She rose slowly, groaning as she managed to sit up and look at him. "I feel even worse than before."

"I'm not surprised. Evelyn...what exactly happened? I've never seen you do anything like that. I haven't even seen Slade or Miriel do anything like that. Olivarion could do illusions, but you managed to actually change the landscape."

"It was...mostly a feeling," she said. "I've felt it before, like a whisper, but at that moment it roared to life and I clung to it. And I just...knew what to do."

Jack frowned. "That doesn't sound like magic. Or at least, not the spell kind."

She shook her head. "It wasn't. I'm not sure what it was. It wasn't like when I made the leaves move in the field, or when I lifted you in the air. This felt...wild. Like it could consume me, burn my body of every scrap of energy."

Jack shuddered. It sounded too much like the Hunter. "Well, whatever it was, it worked. I'm worried, though. Maybe you shouldn't use it again until we've spoken to the others. If we can even find them."

"We will," she said, fluttering closer to the fire. "I'll bet anything they're on their way to Alibeth. Even if they followed us, they would've caught up hours ago and seen the marks of the Hunter."

"You think Slade would agree to go on without us?"

"Maybe if he knew we got away? Where else would we go?"

He shrugged and sat beside her next to the fire. Crickets chirped in the distance and the soft hoot of owls echoed through the trees. A gentle breeze blew past them, and Jack thought he even heard the croaking of frogs. After a few minutes of this busy silence, Evelyn took to the air, saying, "I need to find food."

Jack sat alone by the fire, worried for a moment that Martha would return to harangue him. Instead, his thoughts drifted to the witch's spell. *Tears of stone...* He thought of water trickling over rocks, rain on city walls, liquids created from stone and earth. Nothing seemed right. He sighed in frustration and decided he'd try a different approach: think like a witch. *If I were a witch, tears of stone would mean...actual tears from rocks? But how can rocks cry? Maybe if the rock were sentient and could feel...then it wouldn't be a rock exactly, but a rock creature.*

The idea whirled around his mind, suggestive and playful. He imagined trolls and goblins, gnomes and dwarves, gargoyles—

"Aha!" he cried, standing and lifting his arms in victory. The gargoyles. Raven's gargoyles. That had to be it, though how they would get tears from it was beyond him. For a moment he watched the dark sky, anxious for Evelyn to return so he could tell her, but minutes passed and she didn't come. Finally, he sat back down, sighing. His excitement still flowed through him, causing him to fidget. He twiddled his thumbs, shuffled his feet, lay on the ground only to sit back up. But he also smiled. Even though they still had to find two more ingredients, they were one step closer to completing the spell.

Somewhere along the way he dozed off, because the next thing he knew, it was morning. Evelyn winked at him as he opened his eyes and looked around. She sat perched near the fire, adding more twigs and pine needles.

"Good morning," she said. "You were out when I got back. Must've been exhausted."

"I tried to wait up for you," he said, rising. "I've figured it out."

He watched her face, but she furrowed her brow in confusion. "You what?"

"The tears of stone! I know what it is!"

Her eyes widened. "You do?! What is it?"

"The gargoyles," he said, smiling. "Raven's gargoyles. That has to be it. Unless you know of any other gargoyles around here."

"Jack!" she said, rising into the air in excitement. "You're a genius!" He laughed and she landed on his shoulder, nuzzling against him. Then she jumped into the air again, flipping and twirling for joy. "Only two more ingredients!" she said. "Then I'll be free!"

"Well, we still have to figure out how to get the tears, but it's a start," he said. "Maybe the others will have some suggestions for that part. We should probably head out soon."

"You're right," she said, landing back on the ground. "I've already eaten, so I'm ready when you are." They put out the fire and Evelyn flew high above the trees to get their bearings. "I think we need to go that way," she said when she came back, pointing off into the trees. "If the sun's anything to go by, we're directly east of Alibeth."

"Any idea how far?"

She shook her head. "But surely it shouldn't take more than a few days at most."

"What about the Hunter?"

"I can take care of it, now," she said.

"Evelyn—"

"I know, I promised, but it's that or die. I'll only use it if that situation comes up, I swear."

He sighed, but he couldn't argue. The alternative was unacceptable. They started off, the sun still fairly low in the eastern sky. Jack could only tell it was there because of the orange and pink glow behind the clouds. The higher it rose, the more the clouds obscured it until there was only gray once more. At least the leaves still hovered above, fiery and vibrant.

A change had come over Evelyn, whether from Jack's discovery or some secret of hers, he couldn't tell, but she seemed happier. Almost like how she had been when he'd first met her, carefree and hopeful. He decided to think no more about it and just enjoy the journey with her.

They traveled all day, stopping every few hours for a short break. Every now and then Evelyn scouted ahead, reporting when she spotted a village or town so they could be sure to avoid it. Jack didn't want to take chances with any other revelers.

Evelyn dove back down after her latest scouting and said, "There's a cottage ahead. I didn't see anyone and it looked a little overgrown. Should we check it out? It could be a good place to rest for the night."

"We can look if you want. I'll stay back a bit, just in case."

When they reached the cottage, Jack hung back in the trees, hiding behind a trunk as Evelyn flew to one of the windows. She peered inside a moment, then flew to another one, then around behind the house. When she returned, she said, "All clear! Looks like it's been abandoned for a while."

Jack emerged from his hiding spot and entered the clearing that held the cottage, which was overgrown with bushes and vines. "You're sure?" he said.

"Positive."

"No witches? It seems like the sort of place a witch would live."

She laughed. "No witches. I would think we'd have been warned off by now, don't you?"

"I suppose." He walked up to the door and tried the knob, but it didn't budge. "Huh. Not sure if it's locked or rusted."

"Here, allow me."

He stood back as Evelyn concentrated a moment, extending her wings toward the door until he heard an audible *click!* The door swung open on its own.

"There!" she said, beaming. "Shall we?"

"After you."

They entered the cottage, coughing a bit as the dust stirred in the new air, filling their lungs.

"This place has definitely been empty a while," she said.

Ragged furniture filled the room, all coated in a thick layer of dust. Against the far wall sat a fireplace, a black pot still hanging above a pile of ashes. A bed rested to the left of it. There was a nightstand, a sofa, a bookcase full of rotting books. A sudden fear rose in Jack and he hesitated to look too closely at the bed, but he did anyway, exhaling a sigh of relief. Whoever had occupied the cottage no longer physically resided in it.

"Looks like it could've been a witch's cottage," Jack said.

"Maybe," she agreed. "Or simply a hermit. Those exist, you know."

"I know," he agreed, chuckling. "Too bad the books are done for."

"Yeah, would've been fun to see what they contained. Oh, well."

She flew to the shelf and cocked her head to the side to read the titles. Jack walked over to the sofa, wiping some dust off and taking a seat. The dust exploded into the air, setting her coughing again, and he decided they'd just have to pretend the dust wasn't there. He doubted they could get rid of it all even with magic.

On the walls hung a few rotting paintings, as well as a few odds and ends, dried flowers and odd symbols hanging from strings.

"You know," he said, "if you ignore the dust, it's a nice little place. Quiet. Secluded. Cozy."

She laughed and joined him at the other end of the sofa. "Sure. We should move in when we're human again."

"You mean when you're human."

She looked at him in confusion. "What did I say?"

"You said, *when we're human.*"

"Oh. Well, I don't see why you have to be left out," she said. "Surely if a witch did this to you, then there's a spell that can release you as well. We just have to find it."

He sighed. "I don't know if I'm up for another journey for a spell. At least, not for a while."

She laughed. "Fair enough. But think about it. Don't you miss being human?"

"I only recently remembered that I was, really and truly remembered. I think I can stand being a scarecrow for a bit longer. It's...familiar."

She just nodded in response, lost in her own thoughts. An image of Martha again rose to his mind and he pushed her back. She wouldn't ruin this.

"How do you think we should get the tears?" Evelyn asked a moment later. Jack smiled, appreciating the subject change. There would be time to think of being human later.

"I would suggest asking Raven, since the gargoyles are his, only he's expressly said he's done helping us on this quest," Jack said. "So...maybe we should try talking to it? What would make a gargoyle cry?"

"Do they say anything besides 'Halt!' you think?"

"Maybe. They kind of remind me of myself, before Slade gave

me mobility. They must just stare at the forest all day, occasionally issuing orders to passersby."

"Makes me feel bad for them."

Jack shrugged. "I was happy. If it's all you know, it's actually
kind of peaceful."

"I suppose," she said, unconvinced.

The light dimmed further, the interior of the cottage
becoming so dark that they had to squint to see each other.
Finally, Evelyn laughed.

"This is ridiculous," she said, lighting a fire in the hearth by
magic. The ashes burned as well as if they were wood. He
suspected she was using the other magic again, but he said nothing. What did he know of magic?

They spoke a little longer, but his mind was too preoccupied.
Finally, he bade her good night and curled up in the sofa and
dust. He could see Evelyn out of the corner of his eye, perched
on the other end and staring into the fire. She lifted one wing
and gazed at it a moment, seeing something only she could see.
Then he closed his eyes and pretended to sleep.

ASHES

Two days later, they were still traveling, though Evelyn assured him they were much closer. They hadn't seen the Hunter, though they'd passed a few animals, all heading the same direction. None of them spoke to the pair.

"I bet Slade is pacing a groove in the floor of the Guild," Jack said. "What do you think?"

"Probably," Evelyn agreed. "Do you think he'll come back out to look for us?"

"Possible. I guess it depends on how long it takes us to get there."

The sun shone bright for the first time in days, lighting their path as if in blessing. Birds sang in the trees overhead and the breeze blew swift and cool. It seemed a near-perfect day. They traveled quickly, their strength renewed from their rest. Evelyn's good mood continued and they passed conversation easily. Jack still avoided the subject of his past, but he figured he'd have to tell her at some point. He could see the questions in her eyes.

"We should probably be thinking about what the second ingredient could be," she said. "I'm guessing it must be something similar to the first, but that could be a number of things."

"I've seen Slade dissolve into a flurry of leaves," Jack said. "Maybe it's him."

She laughed. "I'd love to hear you suggest that to him."

"Maybe I will. Do you think he'd willingly donate blood for us?"

"If we were talking about the old Slade, I'd say no. No question. But the 'new' one? Maybe. It depends on whether he sees it as part of his duties."

Jack pondered that for a while. Above, the clouds gathered together, conspiring against the sun. The wind blew a bit stronger in anticipation before settling down for good. Evelyn kept her thoughts to herself, much as she always had. In some ways she was open, but in many others she was a closed book, and he hadn't yet figured out the spell to unlock her. Though on second thought, he supposed he was much the same way.

The closer they got to Alibeth, the more animals they saw, which seemed odd to him. He supposed they could've been driven there by the wolves, but he was only guessing. If they weren't in such a hurry, he would stop to ask, but most avoided their eyes anyway.

When they came upon a group of deer, Jack searched through them for a familiar face, but he did not see her among them. "I was hoping to find Islei again," he told Evelyn.

"Well, it's a big forest. There's no telling where she may be."

"Did you say Islei?" one of the male deer asked.

"We did," Jack answered.

"She is of our herd."

"I see. Is she here?"

"Islei has been sent on an errand by Raven. I can pass on a message, if you like."

"That's very kind of you," Evelyn said.

"Just tell her we said hello," Jack said. "We'd like to see her again soon, though preferably not when we're running for our lives."

"I'll pass it on," the deer said, giving them an odd look. "You two must live exciting lives."

"Only at the moment," Evelyn said, grinning at Jack.

"I had hoped to ask her a favor one more time," Jack said, "but it is no big deal. We'll manage on our own. We're so close to Alibeth anyway."

"That you are," the deer said. "It is just over the next hill. If you keep going, you should reach it by sundown."

"Thank you," Evelyn said.

"Are you fleeing the darkness as well?" the deer asked.

"You mean the Hunter?" Jack asked.

"Call it what you will. It's killed so many already. Most creatures are fleeing any way they can. Our herd is headed south."

Evelyn glanced at Jack, fear and worry plain in her eyes, but he just shook his head. No point revealing more than necessary. They were doing their best to stop it.

"Thank you again," Jack said. "In a way, we are fleeing it. We have business in the city first."

The deer nodded his head in acknowledgment.

They continued on, but Jack turned a second later and said, "I forgot to ask your name."

"Janus," he said. "And yours?"

"Jack, and this is Evelyn."

"Islei will be glad to know you thought of her. Take care."

They left the deer behind, eager to reach the next hill and have this leg of the journey over. The sun started its descent, but the clouds finally initiated their attack and soon hid all trace of it.

"I feel horrible," Evelyn said when she was sure no other animals were nearby.

"It's not like we chose for this to happen," Jack said. "If we stop Ferah, then we stop the Hunter. We're doing everything we know to do."

"There must be something else we can do. This is my fault. I started all of this."

"You didn't know she'd send the Hunter."

Evelyn just sighed.

At last, they crested the last hill and found Alibeth sprawled out once more before them. Jack pondered how often they'd entered its gates, and how many more times they would return before their journey was done. He wished Evelyn knew a spell to make him fly. Surely that would speed up their progress.

They looked at each other, both hoping they'd find the others there, that they'd find the answers they sought, that the key to the spell was within reach. Then they started down the hill, light as feathers on the wind.

AFTER SQUEEZING through the side entrance, Jack tried to avoid the alley where he knew Manus lurked. The last thing Jack wanted was to have to deal with the dreadlord again. The first few times had been quite enough for him.

But sure enough, as soon as he passed by, a voice said, "It's you."

He cringed, turning slowly, still half hoping he could flee and not be recognized. A rat stood there watching him, but it wasn't Manus.

It was Druselda.

"You're the one who helped me before. My, you've had a bit of a tussle, haven't you? Still, I know a face when I see one. I haven't forgotten what you did for me, sir."

"It's nice to see you again, too," Jack said. It was only partly a lie.

Evelyn perched on the rooftop, peering down to see what had stopped him.

"Because of you, I found the courage to venture topside, as we Underbethers say. It's easier to see my Manus this way."

"Is he nearby?" Jack asked.

"No, sir, he's gone on some errand or other. Should be back soon, if you're wanting to speak with him."

"That's all right. I'm supposed to meet a friend anyway." Jack turned to leave, waving over his shoulder. "It was great to see you again, though. Good luck to you."

He dashed out of the alley before she could respond. After a few minutes of ducking and hiding, Evelyn dove down beside him behind a stack of crates.

"What happened?" she asked.

"That was Druselda," he said. "She may tell Manus she saw us. He's almost certain to inform Olivarion. We may have some trouble."

"Damn it. I was hoping we could avoid the dreadlords this time around."

"Me, too. Maybe we still can, if we hurry. At least we have some of the Guild on our side this time."

She shook her head for answer. He wasn't any happier about it, but it couldn't be helped. On they went, Evelyn guiding his path from the air. He barely thought about dashing from hiding spot to hiding spot anymore; the numerous visits had shattered his fear. With the sun absent from the sky, the darkness descended quickly. He only regretted that the clouds hid the stars. As much as he dreaded running about in the snow, he looked forward to the clear nights of winter, the stars like a blanket of fireflies above the earth.

"We're almost there," Evelyn said the next time she dove down to check on him. "I can see the Guild ahead."

"Let's hope the others are there as well."

They reached a place where Jack had to cross the main thoroughfare. Most of the people began to head home for the night, so it was mostly clear. He ran across quickly, a small black shadow in the starless night. A few more turns and they came to a halt.

Dozens of cats blocked their path, waiting for them.

Jack stopped, unsure for a moment what he was seeing. Then he tried to turn back, but they had already surrounded him.

"So, the rat was right," one cat said, stepping forward. "We didn't think you'd be foolish enough to return."

"If this is about the artifacts—"

"You know it is. But it also goes beyond that. You've dared to offend Olivarion."

Jack glared at them. "Take me, then. But it won't bring the artifacts back."

"We don't care about that," another cat said, closing in. "But someone has to pay. Why not you?"

He found Evelyn circling above, watching. A few cats followed his gaze and many climbed to the roof. She flew off before they could catch her.

"She'll join us soon enough," his captor said.

"She's too strong for you," Jack countered.

"But you're not. She'll return for you; don't pretend she won't. And we'll be ready."

They bound him, using both rope and magic so he couldn't so much as twitch a finger. When they carried him off, he had to be held between two cats, his face to the ground. The trip took several minutes. He hoped desperately that Evelyn would find Slade and the others before attempting a rescue. He knew the cats were right; she wouldn't leave him. Absently, he wondered how strong Olivarion was without the artifacts. The illusion he'd shown Jack must have cost immense power, but was it his own?

Finally, they tossed him onto the ground. He rolled for a second, coming to a stop at the feet of not one, but *two* cats. Slowly, he looked up, expecting Olivarion's face, but not the second.

"Aww, they've brought us a present," Sitara said.

Olivarion simply stared at him, eyes narrowed to slits.

Sitara circled him, her tail swishing slowly. "I was extremely upset when no one returned after I helped you," she said.

Jack tried to speak, but the magic that bound him prevented even that.

Sitara waved one paw and his control of his jaw returned.

"But Caerla *did* return," he said. "After she left Slade with Raven."

"Days later," she said, walking back to Olivarion's side. "After I'd spent all my resources in keeping my group together, in securing Olivarion's trust by myself."

Olivarion raised an eyebrow at her, but said nothing.

"The hawk's thanks meant nothing to me, by then," she said, turning back toward Jack. "Yes, I have the protection of Raven. But what good is that here in Alibeth? Will the old bird rise from his forest to come to my aid if I need it? Doubtful. You see? I have learned to look after my own, without aid. I have secured the safety of my people by my own wisdom. You stole from Olivarion, and from me, in a way. That is not easily forgiven."

"If I'd known, I would've come back," Jack said, but even as he said the words, he knew they weren't completely true. They had chosen to continue the quest, to put Evelyn's need above all others. He *did* deserve punishment. "I'm so sorry, Sitara," he continued. "I don't say that to get you to spare me. Everything you've said is true. I wish I could take it back."

"Of course you do," she snarled. "Everyone's sorry when they're caught."

"My dear," Olivarion said, "how would you like me to punish our captive?"

The dreadlord's voice held a softness Jack had never heard in it before. And his eyes... Almost vacant. Like his will was gone.

"Let the soldiers have their fun with him first," she said, turning to walk away.

"What did you do to him?" Jack called after her.

She paused mid-step, all of them sitting in suspended breath as she slowly turned her head to look at him.

"Dear Jack," she said. "You of all creatures should know a man in love when you see one."

She departed, leaving him alone with Puppet Olivarion and her soldiers. They fell on him with a fury.

WHEN NEXT HE opened his eyes, the sky shone a pale rose, but whether it were dusk or dawn, he didn't know. They'd ripped both his legs off, and his arms. Though he didn't physically feel it, the sight of his limbs thrown about, black and burnt as they were, his straw flying all over, tore at his heart and crushed his spirit. He felt smaller than he ever had, even when the revelers had thrown him into the fire. If he could just escape somehow... reach the Guild and find the others... But no.

That was gone, too.

In his darkness, Martha appeared, smiling her cruel smile. *They've left you for good this time,* she said. *It was always bound to happen. What can a scarecrow do? Nothing. Not even scare crows. Useless, that's what you are. What you've always been.*

"Yes," he responded, his voice barely a whisper. "Everything you've ever said was right. I'm just a burden to the others."

It would be better if you died here.

The cats didn't hear his conversation. They continued their fun, setting fire to his severed limbs and watching as the ash swirled up into the sky.

"Yes."

Give up, Alex. Your body is long dead. You were never much of a man to begin with.

"Yes."

They brought the torch to set flame to his torso and Jack closed his eyes, welcoming the inevitable.

"No," Olivarion said, stopping them. "Not until Sitara gives the go-ahead."

A few grumbled, but they obeyed.

High above, a small group of stars broke through the clouds, shining pale, cold light. Jack tried to reach for them, remembering a moment later that he had no arms to reach with. His heart surged within him, longing to join them, to fly up and up, away from everything. A shadow passed over the stars, a cry like a person swallowed by darkness, and then a flurry of black wings. The cats hissed and snarled, swiping at the air, but none hit their target. Then there was a blast of bright light and a boom of thunder and the cats scattered, leaving Jack alone.

Evelyn landed on his chest. "Oh, Jack," she said, her voice catching. "I'm so sorry I didn't come sooner. I thought... It doesn't matter. I have to get you out of here."

"Leave me," he said. "They'll be back and they'll catch you. I couldn't bear for that to happen."

"Don't be silly. You're coming with me."

She lifted him by magic, hardly an effort for her now, and he rose in the air behind her, flying closer to the stars he longed to join. Then the clouds covered them once more and he closed his eyes, sinking into a deep sleep.

"Gods," someone said. "They were *brutal* to him."

"Something should be done. They shouldn't be allowed to do things like this, to *anyone*."

"The dreadlords are their own authorities. Especially Olivarion. To oppose them would start a war."

"So they can just do what they want?"

Jack cracked one eye open, finding Miriel and Arnica standing a few feet away. For a moment he was surprised he was alive at all. He had been so certain he would die, that the cats would burn him completely and he'd be only so much ash on the wind.

"We have to be smarter than them," Arnica said. "That's the only way we'll beat them."

"Is that your focus now?" Slade asked. Jack couldn't see him, his voice coming from behind him. "Will you stay here and fight the dreadlords while we finish this?"

"No..." Miriel said. "But you can't deny it's a concern, even if it's not our primary one at the moment."

"Not Olivarion," Jack tried to say. His voice came out hoarse and cracked, like an old man who hadn't spoken in a lifetime.

"He's awake!" Evelyn said, flapping to his side instantly. She peered down at him as if she could gauge his wellness by sheer will.

"What did he say?" Arnica asked.

Miriel lifted him to a sitting position, supporting his back so he wouldn't fall down again.

"Not Olivarion," Jack tried again. Stronger, but still whispery thin. "Sitara."

"Sitara?" Slade said.

"But why?" Evelyn asked. "She was on our side."

"She's controlling Olivarion," Jack said. "It may be a spell, but I'm not sure."

Slade smirked. "He's not as powerful without his artifacts. Before, he used his brute strength and will, but rely too heavy on magic and you forget how to do even that, after a while. Makes it easy to be overpowered."

"Do you think she planned it?" Evelyn asked.

Slade shrugged. "Possible."

"Well, we'll have to deal with all of that later," Miriel said. "Evelyn told us you figured out the first ingredient. We've had some thoughts, but we won't know if they work until we're actually by the gargoyle."

"In other words, more traveling," Slade said.

Jack looked down at his absent limbs. "How am I supposed to travel like this? I'd hate for Miriel to carry me the whole way."

"We have an idea for that as well," Arnica said. "But first, we have an audience with Lirelin."

Jack's eyes widened. "How did that happen?"

J.H. FLEMING

"A lot has happened since we were separated," Miriel said.

"These two wanted to continue to Alibeth right away," Slade said. "They were convinced you'd manage to get away on your own and meet up with us here."

"Look where that got us," Jack mumbled.

"They were right, weren't they?" Slade asked. "You lost some body parts in the effort, but you both made it."

Jack just shook his head. No use arguing.

"Anyway," the fox continued, "we traveled back here—no Hunter attacks, by the way—and Lirelin wanted to speak to them as soon as they arrived."

"We had to sneak him in," Arnica said, pointing at Slade. "If they knew he was responsible for the loss of the book, they'd string him up."

"Why haven't you told them?" Evelyn asked.

Slade scoffed in mock offense.

"We will, in time," Miriel said, looking carefully at each of them. "But for now, *our* main focus is the witch. Slade doesn't have the book anyway, and the Guild is already making plans for getting it back from the dreadlord. Telling them would serve no purpose but to see Slade punished. We need him right now, so it makes sense to keep it a secret."

Jack and Evelyn both nodded, thoughtful.

"So Lirelin sent for us right away," Arnica continued. "Seems our absence wasn't completely unnoticed, so we explained that we had reason to believe there was a witch in the area. As she was busy with other matters, we took it upon ourselves to investigate the authenticity of such claims."

"She didn't like it, but she wasn't angry, once we explained," Miriel said. "Just requested to be kept in the loop."

Slade grinned wickedly. "So, off we go to let mama bear know that all the cubs are back in the den and we're off to take on the Big Bad Wolf."

Miriel and Arnica narrowed their eyes at him.

"I guess that catches us up," Evelyn said. She flew over to the window and looked down on the city. But Jack wasn't going to let her off so easily.

"Not quite," he said. "There's still the matter of what happened when the cats caught me."

Evelyn shrugged. "There's not much to tell. I got away and flew to the Guild to find the others. They were closeted with Lirelin, so I went back out on my own. By then they'd moved you. It took me a long time to find you again, and I'm sorry for that, Jack. I shouldn't have left you in the first place."

He shook his head. "Nonsense. They can do what they like to me. I feel no pain, remember?"

"But they tore your limbs off!" she yelled, suddenly upset. "And then they burned them so they couldn't be reattached! I don't care if you can't feel it. That's a horrific thing to have happen to you."

Wisely, Jack didn't answer. He sensed there was something else she wasn't saying, something related to the secrets she was keeping, so he just nodded in agreement.

"We'll take care of it," Miriel assured him. "Despite what you believe about yourself, you *are* important, Jack."

"If we're all done comforting each other, I believe mama bear is waiting?" Slade stood by the door, tail swishing in impatience.

Miriel laughed. "Yes she is. Guess we better report." She picked Jack up and carried him under her arm. The others followed behind her, Slade leading the way down the hall.

Jack didn't speak, or complain about having to be carried. He just thought of everything that had happened, both recently and over the last several weeks, and of everything that still needed to be done.

28

RETURN TO THE MAGES'
GUILD

The Guild was even bigger than he remembered. He saw only bits and pieces of it, shadowy, forgotten places, odd corners and alcoves overlooked by the majority. They would pass a row of windows overlooking an overgrown courtyard, its fountain choked with vines and debris, or a garden full of mages, all encouraging the flowers to grow. Sometimes the windows were dark or gray, sealed up in times past, their secrets locked away.

Evelyn rode on Miriel's shoulder above him, but she didn't speak. He could hear her soft breathing, feel the weight of her unspoken thoughts on the air between them. More than ever he wished they could go somewhere alone where maybe he could coax the words out of her, like drawing poison from a wound. There was no doubt the words were eating her alive.

They arrived in Lirelin's chambers a few minutes later, the door closing firmly behind them. Miriel lifted Jack up and around so that he sat against her, looking out. Everything about the room suggested riches and position. Thousands of books filled the built-in shelves that circled the room. A dome-shaped window sat in the wall on the other side of the room, a long cushioned window seat below it, overflowing with pillows. In the middle of the room were three sofas, a short table, and a lounge chair. Wooden doors sat on either side of the room, both closed. Jack guessed they led to Lirelin's bedroom and possibly private dining room. Unless she had a magic room, like the one in Sitara's mage's house.

The thought of the dreadlord and her betrayal stuck like a knife in his gut. He put her from his mind.

Lirelin herself sat on the sofa facing them. She was younger than he'd expected, possibly late thirties, with golden blonde hair that was pulled up from her face in a loose bun. If he had to guess what faeries looked like, he would describe the features she possessed: high, sharp cheek bones, dark blue eyes, depths of intelligence in her gaze, and a pale, thin mouth. Her nose was slightly upturned, her chin showing the slightest point. He half expected her ears to be pointed.

She wore a silver robe, and it occurred to Jack that the robes the mages wore might be a symbol of rank, or perhaps area of study. He'd never thought to ask.

"So, you've returned," Lirelin said. "This is the scarecrow you spoke of?"

Even her voice was faery-like in its sound, silvery, like her robe. She sniffed as she looked at him, betraying her thoughts. He decided to take no offense. He really wasn't much to look at.

"It is," Miriel said.

The group remained standing, though there was seating enough for all of them. Jack noticed then that Slade was not with them. The fox must've disappeared before they entered the chambers, though where he'd gone was anyone's guess.

"And the crow, I see," Lirelin said, turning her gaze to Evelyn. "Both enchanted by a witch?"

"Yes," Miriel said. "They've discovered a spell that should reverse the enchantment on Evelyn, retrapping the witch in crow form. She should be easier to deal with at that point."

Lirelin laughed. "So you would think. What sort of spell are we talking about? Where did they find it? In case you'd forgotten, animals are quite capable of magic. Who's to say she won't be just as powerful in crow form?"

"She's limited," Evelyn said. "She won't be able to do any magic."

"And you know this how?" Lirelin asked, arching one eyebrow.

Evelyn hesitated, struggling with how much they should reveal, and finally said, "We found her sister, the one who cursed her. While in crow form, Ferah is helpless. She only regains her power if a human willingly agrees to switch places with her."

"You didn't tell us this," Miriel said.

"We didn't know if we could trust you at first," Evelyn responded. "You didn't care about me or my family. You only wanted to find Ferah."

"You could've told us later," Arnica said, scowling.

"I'm telling you now."

"So, we have a second witch to deal with," Lirelin said, rubbing her eyes with her fingers. "Perfect. The good news just keeps pouring in."

"I'm sorry," Miriel said. "If I had known, I would've told you sooner."

"The second witch has done no one any harm," Evelyn said. "She just wants to be left alone. And she trapped her sister, the one who is out cursing and seducing people. Doesn't that prove she's not a threat?"

"The very fact that she is a witch proves she's a threat," Lirelin said, standing and walking toward them. "My job is to train the mages of tomorrow, to encourage strong relations between human and animal mages, and to protect mages and non-mages alike from witches."

"Are you the Guild leader, then?" Jack asked, speaking for the first time.

"No," Lirelin said, turning her gaze on him. "There is no leader. Only the Circle. Each member of the Circle is assigned to a different area of expertise, and to mentor a select number of mages. Miriel falls under my guidance, which is why she has brought this to me."

"Why are witches so evil?" Evelyn demanded. "Yes, Ferah is a bad one, but so are many humans, and animals! Her sister isn't cruel like she is. Only selfish. Surely there are exceptions for everything?"

"In many cases, yes," Lirelin answered. "You're right. But witches are one area where we cannot afford to take chances. It only takes the one time for them to give into their selfish natures, to do something cruel or evil that sets them on a path that they cannot turn from. It's in the nature of their magic; they can't escape it."

"So you kill them?" Evelyn demanded, her eyes hard and cold. "Just for what they are?"

Lirelin frowned. "No, we don't kill them. We set our own spells over them to destroy or hinder their magic. It takes many of us, so many, but it is worth it. Then they are free to resume their lives."

"Without magic."

"Without *witchcraft*. Many witches are simply mages who have turned aside from pure magic. When the witchcraft is gone, the magic remains. Most of the time."

"Couldn't they return to it?" Jack asked. "Something drew them to it in the first place, I'm guessing. Couldn't it happen all over again?"

"In theory, yes," Lirelin said. "But with the spells we cast, that access is blocked. Even if they strove with all their energy, they could not break through it."

"With your permission, my lady," Arnica said, "why don't we do that to all new mages?"

"We do," Lirelin said, causing a gasp from Miriel. "That is how we've kept the number of witches to such a small number. It's part of the initiation rites, though they don't realize what we're doing. It's the rogues, the mages who never come to us, that cause the rarities to pop up."

None of them said anything for a moment, taking this in. It seemed none of them had known. A thought occurred to Jack and he asked, "What about animals? Can they turn to witchcraft?"

"Certainly," Lirelin said. "Many familiars are actually witches themselves. Different species, performing magic together... It's a strong combination. That's part of the reason we want to draw more animal mages to the Guild. Together, we can create something the world has never seen." She smiled at all of them, opening her arms and indicating the sofas. "Please, everyone sit. We still have much to discuss, and long talking goes better when it's tempered by a full stomach."

Miriel and Arnica glanced at each other before sitting side by side on the left-hand sofa. Evelyn fluttered over to perch on the armrest. Miriel placed Jack in the corner of the sofa so he could stay seated by himself. Immediately, servants entered the chambers with covered platters. They placed them on the small table before them and whipped off the tops. Steam and delicious smells rose into the air. Hot bread, fruit, eggs, sausage, gruel: all manner of things were there for the taking. The servants also brought Miriel and Lirelin goblets of some sort of red juice. For Arnica, they brought a dish of milk, and a small bowl of water for Evelyn. Jack shook his head as they attempted to bring him a goblet.

"This is very kind of you," Miriel said.

"Please, help yourselves," Lirelin said. "Despite my frustration with the situation, I appreciate what you've done, Miriel. You too, Arnica. I believe we can turn this into an advantage for ourselves, if we go about it the right way."

Jack watched them all as Miriel and Arnica helped themselves to food and Lirelin continued speaking. He only barely listened; instead, he focused on what Lirelin *wasn't* saying. She didn't take any food for herself, and only sipped at her juice. Her manner had gone from cold and firm to warm and friendly in a matter of seconds, and he still wasn't sure what the cause was.

He mused that perhaps she simply wasn't a morning person, but deep down he knew it was something more.

Evelyn also didn't touch any of the food, and after a small sip of water, she sat silently next to Jack.

"I want you to return to the forest," Lirelin was saying. "Finish finding the ingredients for the spell if you think it will help, but I'd prefer that you didn't engage with the witch just yet. Watch her, learn what you can, and then return here. I can send reinforcements with you at that time. The excitement from the loss of the book should have died down a bit at that point."

"May we browse the library before we go?" Evelyn asked.

All eyes turned to her, Lirelin's wide, as if she'd forgotten the crow was there.

"That's why we came here, after all," Evelyn continued. "We need help to figure out the rest of the spell."

"Right," Lirelin said, smiling warmly, her eyes crinkling to thin slits. "Why don't you go there now? It should be fairly empty at this time of the morning. I'll send for you again in a few hours and we can finish our discussion then."

Without another word, the servants appeared again and whisked the food away. Miriel and Arnica stood, almost mechanically.

"But first," Lirelin said, rising with them, "there's the matter of your limbs." She turned to Jack, her head tilted to the side as she gazed at him. "I think mechanical would be best," she continued. "Not as much magic involved, so they're a little easier to maintain."

"I don't understand," Jack said. "What are you going to do?"

"Replace your limbs, of course."

"How? And what would I owe you for this?" Jack asked.

Lirelin's eyes widened in surprise. "Why, nothing. This is a gift. A reward for your cooperation with the Guild thus far. All we ask in return is your continued help."

"I see." Jack stole a glance at Evelyn, but she kept her silence.

Two servants appeared again, this time bearing small hunks of steel in their arms.

"Our smiths have only recently devised these," Lirelin said. "You shall be one of the first to try them."

The servants knelt before Jack, extending the metal toward him so he could get a better look. They looked like swords, only dulled and curved into smooth shapes, then fitted together to give the appearance of legs and arms. Smaller pieces, rounded and shaped just so, attached to the ends to create fingers and shoes.

"Magic fuses it all together," Lirelin said. "With these, you will run faster than you ever have before, move with ease, and not tire easily."

"This is too great a gift," Jack said, looking up at the mage.

She laughed and shook her head. "Nonsense. Let's try them on."

The servants fit the limbs to the empty spaces where Jack's own arms and legs used to be, then Lirelin bent over him and a surge of magic poured from her hand, felt but not seen. The limbs knit themselves to Jack as if he'd been born with them, or created with them. Experimentally, he flexed his fingers, stretched his legs. They responded perfectly.

"They will need to be maintained every few months or so," Lirelin said. "Just come back here and we'll take care of it."

Jack nodded, too overwhelmed to say anything. His emotions oscillated from grateful to suspicious and back again. He said nothing.

"Peruse the library as long as you like," Lirelin continued. "I will see you again soon." She stepped back to clear their path to the door. Miriel rose and bowed, followed by Arnica. Jack stood too, completely on his own. The limbs were exactly the right length, so he stood at the same height he had before. He bent his knees and waved his arms about, familiarizing himself with the feel of them. The others were watching him, so he said, "Thank you," to Lirelin and then followed

Miriel to the door, Evelyn landing on his shoulder a second later.

"That was...interesting," she whispered.

"Yes," he agreed. "I'm still not sure if I like her or want to keep my distance. Maybe a bit of both?"

The door shut behind them and Miriel glanced back. "What did you guys think?"

"She seems...intense," Jack said. "Kind, in her way."

"She has a lot on her plate," the mage said. "We do what we can to help."

"Thus the secrecy," Arnica added.

Jack almost asked about the food, but changed his mind. If there had been anything magical about it, surely Miriel and Arnica were fully aware. They had to be. What would Lirelin gain by putting something in their food, anyway?

They traversed the halls quickly, passing other mages who gave him a curious glance before moving on. None attempted to speak to him. Cats and dogs and birds also passed by, though not as frequently. They also showed only the barest interest in the party.

"In here," Miriel finally said, pulling open a large, heavy wooden door. They stepped inside, welcomed by the sight of hundreds of thousands of books, filling shelves that covered the floor and the entirety of the walls, excepting the large floor-to-ceiling windows spaced evenly around the room. The ceiling stretched high above, covered in a mural depicting a castle, mages casting spells, the forest, and even a dragon. Ahead of them and above was a second floor that reached to only half the length of the lower floor. More shelves filled its space, a spiral staircase leading up on their far left.

"You made it!" Slade appeared from between two book-shelves, grinning wickedly. "While you guys were appeasing mama bear, I've been busy doing research."

"No one saw you?" Miriel asked.

"Of course not. And I ensured that anyone remaining in here

left, so we have the whole place to ourselves."

Arnica sniffed. "Hmpf. Well, find anything useful? And you're welcome, by the way. We didn't mention you to Lirelin, so I hope you're grateful."

"Eternally, I assure you. And yes, I may have found a few interesting tidbits."

They followed him to a row of tables beyond the first several stacks of shelves. He'd covered one table in open books and pointed the group toward one of them.

"That one's all about witches. Doesn't hurt to know as much about our enemy as possible, right?"

"Good thinking," Miriel said.

Evelyn sighed in Jack's ear, but said nothing.

"Despite what Lirelin said, we better be quick," Arnica said. "She'll expect us to be heading out again as soon as possible."

"Nica's right," Miriel agreed.

They each picked a book already open on the table while Slade approached Jack, nodding his approval.

"Nice new limbs," he said. "What do you owe for them?"

"They were a gift," Jack said.

Slade shook his head and clucked his tongue. "I taught you better than that. Everything costs you something, Jack. Especially when mages are involved. Or any sort of magic user."

"My cooperation, then," Jack answered. "So far."

"There you go," Slade said, nodding. "What else was said?" He glanced back at Miriel and Arnica and then pulled Jack and Evelyn between two stacks of shelves.

"A lesson on why witches are bad," Evelyn said. "Lirelin made her views quite plain on that topic."

"Do I detect some disagreement? Are you saying you think they're good?" Slade asked, brow furrowed.

"I'm not saying that," Evelyn said. "I just don't think they're as bad as she makes them out to be. The second witch we found didn't harm us in any way. She just wanted to be left alone. I've met more frightening and oppressive animals than witches."

"Can't argue with that," Slade said. "What about her manner? Did she do anything strange?"

Evelyn thought a moment, so Jack said, "The food. She had some food brought, but only Miriel and Arnica ate any of it. I wasn't sure if it was poisoned or laced with something, or maybe enchanted. I don't have the eye for such things. But they both seem to be fine, so maybe it was just my imagination."

"I had the same thought," Evelyn said.

"Could've been a truth spell in it," Slade said. "Or possibly tracking or some such. Couldn't know for sure without probing one of the ladies. That actually would be normal, for the Guild. They like to control everything. That's part of the reason most animals won't join with them, but good luck explaining that to them. In the eyes of its members, the Guild can do no wrong."

Jack nodded. The explanation made sense, but he still didn't feel that he could completely trust Lirelin.

"Have you found anything useful?" he asked.

"Not really," the fox admitted. "What we really need is a grimoire."

"What's that?" Evelyn asked.

"A witch's book of spells. Each has their own personal book with their favorites written inside. Sometimes a witch may have more than one, if she inherited or found the grimoire of another."

"Where in the world would we find something like that?" Jack asked.

"Probably in a witch's house," Slade answered, grinning.

Evelyn sighed. "Then we're back where we started."

"Well, we have this whole library to ourselves for some time," Slade said. "Why don't we make use of it? Maybe we'll surprise ourselves." They split up, searching through the stacks that Slade pointed out. "Those will be the useful ones," he said. "They're split up by category, so I narrowed it down for you. Wouldn't you hate to search this whole library?"

Evelyn rolled her eyes. While she took the stacks, Jack went back to the table where the fox had laid out the books. The sight of so much paper and ink was nearly overwhelming, but he picked one and started to read. After a minute of this, he began skimming, searching for any mention of witches, grimoires, or spells.

AFTER A FEW HOURS, Jack stood and stretched, admiring his new metal limbs once more. "Anything?" he asked the others.

Arnica grumbled in answer.

"Let's take a break," Miriel suggested. "A little refreshment should do us good."

"You do that," Slade said, opening another book. "We'll be here."

Miriel glared at him, then wandered off, muttering to herself.

"We're not getting anywhere," Evelyn said from her perch on a shelf above them. "Why don't we just ask one of the mages? I'm sure if you let the librarians back in, Slade, one of them could help us."

"No," he replied, not looking up.

Jack walked over to the window, looking down on the Guild grounds below him. Secret courtyards, gardens, and patios lay spread out beneath him, arranged in perfectly designed patterns. Mages and servants appeared and disappeared, going about their day with no concern about witches. That he knew of, anyway. Maybe one of them specialized in the study of them. Now *that* would be useful.

"Jack!" Evelyn called.

He turned at the sound and saw her swooping down from the shelf and over to him with great speed. She pulled up just as she reached him and landed on the windowsill, laughing.

"I figured it out!" she said. "I know what the second ingredient is." Before he could answer, she said, "The dryads. It has to be them. I was reading a passage that mentioned them and everything just clicked in my mind. *Blood of leaves.* What do you think?"

"Seems likely," he said, his own excitement rising. "That's two ingredients, if you're right. Only one more."

"You found it?" Slade called over, overhearing the last of their conversation.

"Yes," Evelyn responded. "The second ingredient is the dryads. Or their blood, I guess."

Slade snorted. "Good luck getting that. Are you just going to ask politely and hope their goodwill extends to cutting themselves open?"

Evelyn laughed at him, apparently in too good of a mood to fight. Jack couldn't blame her; he couldn't wait to get back to the forest.

Arnica stretched, yawning. "So long as it stops the witch, I don't care what we do."

"We'll probably need to find some way to communicate with them," Evelyn said. "Maybe—"

A loud *boom* thundered through the air and shook the building. Several books fell from their shelves. Jack managed to keep his balance, but Evelyn tumbled from the windowsill to the floor. Slade and Arnica staggered a bit but stayed upright.

"What was that?" Jack asked.

The fox rushed to the window and the others followed, peering down to find not an idyllic center for magic and learning, but dozens and dozens of cats. They crawled over the rooftops and into the courtyards, destroying plants and attacking anyone they found. On the far side of the Guild, sitting on the peak of a roof, were Sitara and Olivarion. Slade cursed.

"Just what we need," he muttered. "Okay, time to leave! What's the quickest way out of here?"

This last was directed at Arnica, who still stared out the window with wide eyes. "I..." She trailed off, unable to find the words. Slade snapped his toes, enhanced by magic to sound like a whip crack. She blinked and said, "I'd rather wait for Miriel. I can't just leave her here."

"In case you hadn't noticed, there's a cat army outside and two pissed off dreadlords. So unless you want to go toe to toe with them, we need to *go*."

Arnica scowled at him. "You have an artifact now. Why don't you just use your magic and take care of them? Besides, the Guild is full of mages. We can handle this."

"It only takes a few cats to find us, and soon the whole library will be swarming with them. Even with magic, it'll be tough to escape. And even I have my limits. I'd rather flee and not waste magic, if you don't mind."

"I'm with Slade on this one," Evelyn said. "We've figured out two of the three ingredients. We should get out while we can. A fight will just delay us. Could even get someone hurt again."

She didn't look at Jack, but he knew she was referring to him. He couldn't blame her. With his metal-magic limbs, he didn't have the same fear, but he didn't want to fight, either. The longer they stayed, the greater the chance of that happening.

"I told you, I'm not leaving without Miriel," Arnica repeated.

"Fine," Slade said. "Wait for her, then. We're out of here."

He ran toward the door, Evelyn following a moment behind. Jack raised his eyebrows at Arnica as if to say, 'What else can we do?' Then he followed after them.

"Wait!" she called, chasing them. "Just stop a moment!"

But Slade had already opened the door and was peering out, his head swiveling side to side. He darted down the hall to the right and they poured out after him, carefully looking all about for any sign of the cats.

"Do you even know where you're going?" Arnica hissed.

"Not a clue," Slade whispered back. "Though any help you can give would be appreciated."

She cursed but didn't offer directions.

The hall curved to the left and extended straight ahead for a long ways, doors opening on either side to private rooms. Jack briefly wondered if any of them were Miriel's. He didn't think hiding in one would help this time, though. They picked up speed in the long hallway, Jack's metal limbs clanking loudly on the stone. It couldn't be helped, though, unless Slade knew a spell to silence them. It'd be easier once they got to the forest.

They slowed at the end of the hall to make the turn and nearly ran into Miriel. She jumped back and Slade slid across the floor toward the window to avoid hitting her. Jack and Arnica had a bit more warning and were able to stop in time. Evelyn simply flapped her wings to stop and descended to Jack's shoulder.

"Gave me a fright," Miriel said, clutching her chest. "What are you doing?"

"Getting out of here," Slade said. "Do you know a way out that doesn't involve tangling with dreadlords?"

She thought only a moment, then nodded. "The old servant passages. They're rarely used anymore and extend far into the city."

"Take us," Slade said.

Miriel took the lead then, another *boom* pushing them to greater speeds. Whether they were using magic or some sort of weapon Jack didn't know, but he prayed they didn't run into them.

Finally, they reached a narrow corridor that ended in an alcove, a small statue of an unknown mage standing guard. A single door stood in the wall on the left. Miriel used magic to unlock it and pushed it open.

"I didn't know you could pick locks," Arnica said reproachfully.

"A remnant from my novice years," Miriel said with a grin. "Hurry, inside."

Slade didn't have to be told twice. He disappeared into the darkness beyond the door, followed by Arnica. Jack and Evelyn entered just as another *boom* shook the place. Miriel shut the door, the *click* of her relocking it echoing in the black.

29

TEARS OF STONE

S lade created a ball of light that hovered in the air above
them, illuminating their surroundings for a few feet on all
sides. Cobwebs hung from the ceiling, dust coated the floor, and
the smell of mouse droppings filled the air as though it were
some tomb only recently exposed to the light.

"Charming," Slade said.

"You're the one who wanted to come here," Arnica said.

"Hey, I'm not complaining. Beats facing the dreadlords."

"It should take us right to the edge of the market," Miriel
said, taking lead again. "Let's just hope they don't know any
tracking spells or they'll be on our tails in no time."

"I can mask us," Slade said. "You just keep walking."

She did, the rest of them following single file behind her. "I
just can't believe they'd risk an open attack," she said. "I mean,
taking the book was one thing. But this is almost an act of war."

"What did you expect from dreadlords?" Slade asked. "Especially from Sitara. She doesn't have the strategic mind that
Olivarion has. He would've found a more subtle way. Probably
would've been successful, too."

"You sound like an admirer," Arnica admonished.

"In a way, I am," Slade said. "He has a brilliant mind for planning. Shame we had to be at odds over this. We could've made a great team."

Arnica scoffed. "He's right back there if you want to join him."

"Thank you, but no. Sitara is another animal entirely. Nadya, now, she—"

He stopped speaking, no doubt remembering Jack's news. Her name caused him to catch his breath as well, rubbing a sore spot that refused to heal. The best he could do was try to forget. The others didn't press Slade to continue, and for several minutes they walked in silence, except for the loud echo of Jack's feet.

Evelyn finally broke the silence. "We figured out the second ingredient," she said.

"Really?" Miriel asked.

"It's the dryads. If we can communicate with them somehow, that one should be easy. That just leaves the gargoyles and the third ingredient."

"The best I can figure on the gargoyles is to use magic," Slade said. "Unless you guys know any sad stories you want to tell them?"

Miriel glanced back with a sardonic smile. "Sure, that'll work."

The tunnel began to slope downward, the air pressing closer. Evelyn shivered. "You okay?" Jack asked.

"Yes, just felt a draft. I'm ready to get out of this tunnel."

"We should be close now," Miriel said. "Just a little further."

A faint light appeared ahead, supporting her words. They quickened their pace and soon had no need for Slade's little ball of light.

"At last," Arnica said.

"Let me go first," Miriel cautioned. "We need to be sure none of the cats are around."

The tunnel ended in a set of stairs that led to a door-shaped opening covered by a metal gate. A lock secured it, preventing anyone from using it to sneak into the Guild. Anyone who didn't know how to pick locks, anyway.

"This is useful," Slade mused.

"What's that supposed to mean?" Arnica asked, glaring.

"Just what I said. Don't worry, I have no plans to sneak in and steal anything. Currently."

"Remind me to advise Lirelin to seal this," Miriel said to Arnica.

"Come now, it's a perfect escape route," Slade said. "No need to sacrifice that. The security just needs to be strengthened a bit."

"And I'm guessing you have a few suggestions for that?" Arnica asked.

"I do, in fact."

Evelyn giggled in Jack's ear and he couldn't help but smile. Say what you want about him, but Slade had a sense of humor.

Miriel approached the gate and looked carefully left and right through the bars. Satisfied, she unlocked it and pushed it open, motioning them to hurry. When the last of them were through, she closed and locked it again. They were standing in a clean but empty side street decorated with potted plants and flowers at each door. Further down, Jack spotted the edge of a fountain in a small courtyard. The other direction led to the market. Looking back toward the tunnel, Jack saw only a solid rock wall, no sign of the gate. Unless you could see the signs of magic and knew where to look, it'd be tough to find.

"This way," Miriel said, heading straight for the busy market street.

"Ahem," Slade said.

She stopped and he nodded down at himself and at Jack.

"Right," she said. "Don't you know any spells to make yourself invisible? What did you do when you were in the city before?"

"Stayed to the shadows," Slade answered. "Didn't venture into the busiest street in the entire city."

"What about an illusion?" Jack asked. "Like you did with me before." He didn't elaborate, not knowing how much Slade wanted revealed. Not that he didn't trust Arnica and Miriel, but they would be sure to tell Lirelin, and he for sure didn't trust her.

"It will require a little more magic," Slade said reluctantly.

"Can't you use your magic this one time?" Evelyn asked. "It's sort of an emergency."

Another *boom* echoed from behind them. A few people in the market looked around at the noise, but it was far enough away that they weren't alarmed by it.

Slade huffed. "I suppose I could," he said.

He waved his paw over himself, transforming into a tall, thin man with a bushy red mustache and short beard. Then he did the same to Jack.

"Dapper," Evelyn said. "Though he seems odd as a blond."

"You can change him yourself if you like," Slade said.

"No time," Arnica said. "Let's go."

Rather than ride on his shoulder, Evelyn flew high into the air above them, guiding their path. Jack suspected it was disconcerting for her to see him as a man. He couldn't blame her.

They walked casually out into the market street, just two men, a woman, and a cat. No one gave them a second glance. *Does this really cost that much magic to do?* Jack wondered. It would've made their earlier trips to the city much easier. Manus for sure wouldn't have recognized them the last time. He wished he had a mirror handy so he could get a glimpse of himself.

Miriel continued to guide them, but every now and then Evelyn dove down and whispered in her ear, suggesting a better path. Then the mage would change course and Evelyn would return to the sky.

"How do you feel?" Slade whispered to him. He had stayed back with Jack, giving Miriel and Arnica a little space.

"Fine, I guess," Jack answered.

The crowd thinned a bit, but most of the people stayed near

the edges of the street to browse the stalls anyway, leaving their path mostly clear.

"You haven't walked openly in front of this many people before," Slade said, arching his eyebrow.

The sight of the fox as a man gave Jack an odd feeling, like he'd woken up to find the sky yellow and the sun green. It was just...off. Short, curly red hair covered the fox's head, along with a trim red beard. His eyes were a bright green.

"True," he said, pushing back his unease. "I'm trying my best to not think about it. Honestly, the sight of you is much more unsettling."

"Me?" Slade asked, chuckling. "What, am I not handsome enough? Or is my manly physique intimidating?"

"It's just odd seeing you as a human."

"Hmm," Slade mused. "Maybe I'll start appearing like this all the time. Get you nice and used to it. Then randomly switch back when you least expect it."

Jack frowned. "Why go to the trouble?"

"Because you're fun to mess with. And we're friends, aren't we Jack?"

He put his arm around Jack's shoulder, squeezing him for a moment.

"Yeah, sure," Jack said, unsure how to respond.

They reached the city gate and he was spared from having to say any more. A bored-looking guard in full armor watched as people passed. No one else was entering or leaving the city at that time of day. The guard waved to them but didn't say anything. Another *boom* echoed across the city behind them, much louder this time. They looked back, seeing a cloud of gray smoke rising in the air.

Miriel gasped and took a few steps toward it. "They're going to destroy everything!" she said, looking as if she were about to run back.

"You have plenty of mages to take care of it," Slade said,

keeping his voice down and pulling her back through the gate. "Let them deal with it. We have other problems."

She nodded reluctantly, but that didn't stop her from looking back every few feet as they followed the road out of Alibeth.

"It'll be all right," Arnica told her when they were a good distance away from the gate. "Slade's right. The others can handle it. Lirelin gave us this assignment and we have to see it through."

"I know," Miriel said with a nod. "Still, I hate it."

"Me too," the cat said, looking resolutely forward.

The wind blew fiercely and Evelyn flew down to glide just above them. Jack looked up at the gray, cloud-filled sky. A few small flakes of white drifted about in the air, never quite deciding to fall to the ground and stick. Much more of this and they'd be traveling in the snow.

"Should we head back to Raven's land first?" Evelyn asked. "Or find the dryads again? I can't remember which is closer."

"That would be Raven," Slade said. "He'll not want to see us, though. One of his sparrows will show up, so leave the talking to me. I'll just give a quick report and that should do the trick."

They entered the forest, leaving the road for a more direct route to Raven. Jack paused, looking at the dirt road twisting through the forest until it disappeared around a bend. He wondered about the villages and cities on the other end, if another road branched off and led to the sea. At that moment, it seemed that he'd never find out, he'd wander the forest and the path from Alibeth to Raven's land for the rest of his life. However long that would be.

"Guess we don't need these anymore," Slade said, sloughing off his human appearance like a coat. He shook himself, his red fur bristling a moment in the cool air.

"I was beginning to like you as a man," Evelyn teased Jack, landing on his shoulder once more.

He laughed. "I didn't notice much difference, to be honest."

He'd seemed taller, he supposed, standing eye to eye with Slade. But that had been the extent of it.

Slade took the lead and Jack and Evelyn fell back, which allowed them to talk in private. Above and around them, the leaves were growing darker, dull, preparing for the fast-approaching winter. Many trees had already shed their leaves, standing stark and skeletal in the pale air. A carpet of brown and gold lay at their feet, crunching as they passed.

"What color was your hair before? Do you remember?" Evelyn asked.

"Brown."

"Ah. Just as I imagined. Did you have a family? And don't feel obligated to answer. I'm just curious."

"It's okay," he told her, feeling that it was mostly true. So long as he pushed Martha back to the furthest corner of his mind. "I had a little cottage. Was married. I thought I had everything I could ever want, but..." He trailed off, feeling her stiffen on his shoulder. He decided to tell her everything. "My wife betrayed me. Sold me to a witch, who turned me into a scarecrow. One of the last things she told me was she was pregnant with another man's child."

Evelyn gasped. He'd never said the words out loud, but somehow it didn't hurt like he'd expected it would. It was sore for sure, but there wasn't that gut-wrenching pain he had dreaded. Just a faint remorse, a sad memory. His life as a scare-crow had added so many years between then and now that he could look on his past almost as if he were examining the life of another man. He could see now that Martha had never truly loved him. And somehow that was all right, because so much had happened and he'd experienced so many amazing things. Maybe the witch's spell could make him human again, too. He thought he'd like another go at it. Make better choices this time.

"I'm so sorry, Jack," Evelyn said. "I had no idea. I shouldn't have asked—"

"It's all right, really," he said. "It was painful at first, but I'm better now. Promise."

"If you say so."

"What about you?" he asked. "What was life like before you waltzed into my field to practice magic?"

She chuckled. "Well, pretty boring, actually. I did chores, watched my little brother..." She paused a moment, no doubt wondering again what had happened to him. Jack hoped they could find him soon, after they reversed the spell. It'd be easier to look for him as a human. She sighed and continued. "My mother died a few years ago. Caught a cold that just got worse and never recovered. My father was pretty torn up about it for a while. I guess that's why he became so strict on me. He didn't know how else to be, without her there."

"I'm sorry," Jack said.

"It happens. That's life. Nothing turns out like it should."

The land sloped downward, the hill ending in a shallow creek. The trees grew close together just beyond it and Slade plunged right in. The sky grew ever darker, the hidden sun having already sunk behind the clouds. The thick canopy of leaves cast even more shadow.

"We'll have to camp soon, unless you want to go on by mage-light," Slade said.

Arnica gasped dramatically. "You'd be willing to use magic?"

"I thought Miriel might like to. You two are in such an awful hurry, after all."

"Oh, for goodness' sake," the mage replied. She created a light for them and they continued on, covering another hour's worth of ground before stopping.

That night, Jack dreamed of Evelyn, human again, calling to him from a long distance, but try as he might he couldn't find her, and her voice grew fainter and fainter until she was gone.

Jack awoke to darkness.

Not the gentle, peaceful darkness of night, but the oppressive, deadly darkness of the Hunter. It took him a moment to realize someone was screaming, which was what had pulled him out of sleep. He jumped to his feet and looked for Evelyn, finding her a second later standing face to face with the Hunter.

Jack had never seen it so close. Its humanoid features were more evident, but consumed by shadow. Slade was shouting behind him, and Miriel, but he couldn't force himself to move. He could only watch as a roaring blue flame erupted around Evelyn, creating a shield between her and the shadow. With a yell of fury and pain, she lashed out at the Hunter with a mighty force of power, knocking it back against the ground. Someone grabbed Jack then and he was pulled along, watching Evelyn get further and further away.

"No!" he yelled, struggling against his savior.

The strength of his magic metal hands forced them to drop him and he fell to the ground. A second later he was on his feet, running back to Evelyn. She sent another blast of magic at the Hunter, eliciting a cry from it this time. It sounded like nothing he had ever heard, like a mixture of every animal that had ever existed and the movement of the earth and the rotation of the stars and the crashing of the ocean all in one.

Then it was gone, the forest around them returning to its quiet morning routine. The sun hadn't even fully risen yet. Jack stopped several feet from Evelyn, watching her cautiously, like she was some new predator that may turn on him next. Then she looked at him, eyes full of pain and fear and longing and he couldn't help but close the distance between them and wrap her in his arms.

"It's okay," he said, over and over. "It's gone. It will be all right."

Slade and Miriel approached them, the crunching of the leaves beneath their feet echoing in the eerie silence left in the

Hunter's wake. Jack glanced up at them, finally noticing the tears in Miriel's eyes, the way Slade stared fixedly at the ground.

"Where's Arnica?" he asked.

Miriel collapsed then, her face buried in her hands as she wept.

Slade shook his head. "We were too careless. We should've gone straight through the night to Raven's land. Maybe then..." He shook his head again.

"It wouldn't have helped," Evelyn said, her voice full of steel and grit. "Its attacks are becoming more frequent."

"How did you even fight it off?" Slade asked. "I thought you said the only way to escape is to cross flowing water. So how did you do it?" His eyes narrowed and he looked at her like she'd just revealed she had three heads.

"I don't know, really," she answered. "It was just...a feeling. Like the forest told me what to do."

"You don't listen to it!" Miriel cried, tears still streaming down her face. She looked wild, her hair frizzing in a halo around her and her spectacles smeared from crying. "You never listen to it! That way leads to darkness. Evil." She dissolved into tears again, whispering, "Nica. Nica..."

Slade glanced at her, then back at Jack and Evelyn. "I think it's clear we need to get to Raven's land as fast as possible, before it attacks again. Especially if it's attacking sooner."

"But I can hold it back now," Evelyn said. "We don't have to worry anymore."

"For the gods' sake, Evelyn!" the fox said. "That thing is pure evil, plain and simple. We don't stand and fight. We run. I've been ordered to look out for you two, and I'll be damned if I let you get yourself killed by that thing."

"That's all we are then, huh?" she said, her tone mocking. "Just some charge Raven has given you. He could release you when we arrive and you'd leave us all to finish this on our own. Why don't you just go? We'll be better off without you."

She took to the air, flying off into the forest before anyone else could speak. Miriel continued to weep silently and Slade cursed and lay down on the ground next to her. Jack watched for Evelyn, but he knew he'd never be able to catch up with her. He looked helplessly between the trees and the mage and fox, knowing they should leave as soon as possible. A dark weariness seemed to lie on them, making any sort of action a monumental task. Jack couldn't fight it, so he sat on the ground next to Miriel and Slade and waited for the mage's tears to dry.

EVELYN RETURNED ABOUT AN HOUR LATER, when the sun was already well on its way in the sky. She said nothing of her outburst, or of the magic she had used, barely speaking even to Jack. Rather than ride on his shoulder, she flew just above them, silent and brooding. Slade didn't bring it up, either. Jack helped him coax Miriel into walking, keeping one hand on her arm to steady her. She walked mechanically, like a sleepwalker, or one of the dead. It was a silent journey, the songs of morning birds and rustling animals serving as a cruel reminder of life, of its indifference to the dead and grieving. Jack almost hoped the Hunter came back, if only to bring back true silence.

His heart sat heavy within him—or his equivalent of a heart, at least. Arnica's face flashed through his mind now, next to Nadya's. Martha appeared again, too, whispering from the corners that it was his fault. He should've been stronger, faster, more clever. He ignored her, too weary to argue.

When they reached the edge of Raven's land, he almost didn't notice. The "Halt!" of the little stone gargoyle shook him out of his reverie and he stopped with the others, his mind still wandering distant paths.

"I'll do the talking," Slade reminded them, his voice weary and lethargic.

When the sparrow arrived, he spoke to it quickly, in hushed tones. Evelyn had landed on a nearby tree branch and Jack almost went over to talk to her, but he couldn't bring his feet to move. He didn't know what he would say anyway.

The sparrow flew away a moment later, zipping through the trees with unmarred energy. "I guess I'll do the honors," Slade said, bending over the little gargoyle to study it.

Evelyn finally flew over, joining him while Jack sat down with Miriel. She hugged him to her, her tears dry but her eyes lifeless. He patted her arm and rocked gently, hoping it would soothe her a little.

"I should've put my foot down," she said a second later, so quietly Jack almost missed it. "I should've insisted we wait, speak to Lirelin before ever setting out. Maybe we wouldn't have caught up with you again. It would've taken us longer to find the witch, but at least she'd still be alive."

"I'm sorry," Jack said, knowing it was inadequate, but having nothing better to offer. "I would bring her back if I could."

Miriel sighed. "You're too nice for this sort of thing," she said. "You should've stayed in your field. Just look at you: burned and dismembered and passed back and forth by heartless creatures more powerful than you. You deserve better. *She* deserved better."

"There's nowhere I'd rather be than right here," he said, glancing at Evelyn and meaning it with every fiber of his being. "You're right; I would've been safer there, but then I would never have met you or any of the others, and I wouldn't have known the sorts of things I was capable of."

"But is it worth it?" she asked, looking up at the leaves sheltering them. "Is any of it worth it?"

"I think so," he said. "Arnica thought so. She wouldn't have come out here if she didn't."

She was silent a long moment. Jack listened as Slade chanted spells over the gargoyle, waving his paws about. Then Evelyn took a turn, doing much the same thing. They tried it together next, starting something new when that didn't work.

"You're right," Miriel said. "She'd want me to finish this."

She rose, setting Jack down and standing slowly to her feet. He followed her, unsure what she had planned. She walked over to Evelyn and Slade and bent next to them, adding her own magic to the mix, their combined strength so great that Jack felt a tingle run up his back. A few seconds later, a cry rent the air, and for a terrifying moment Jack thought the Hunter was back. Then he saw the little gargoyle on the ground beside the three, pale and moving and alive, its mouth open in a wail.

❧ 30 ❧

BLOOD OF LEAVES

Slade produced a little glass vial from the folds of his fur and held it beneath the gargoyle's eyes, catching a steady stream of tears.

Evelyn cocked her head at him. "Where'd you get that?"

"I thought it best to be prepared. I have another for the dryads."

The gargoyle hiccuped and tried to stop its cry, causing a few more little burbles to escape its lips.

"Why is it crying?" Jack asked.

"Could be a number of things," Slade said. "We forced it into this state, and we weren't very gentle about it. I would guess it wants to be returned to stone."

"Let's do it, then," Evelyn said. "I feel horrible leaving it like this."

"You're sure Raven won't mind?" Jack asked, looking to see if the sparrow or Raven himself were coming to investigate.

"So long as we put things back how we found them, I don't see why," Slade said. "Besides, he knew this was what it was. If anything, he expected us to come here." He turned to the ladies. "Shall we?"

They combined their magic again, reversing whatever spell

they'd done to wake the gargoyle. Its sobs subsided, disappearing altogether as its skin solidified and it returned to its former state.

"Poor thing," Evelyn said.

"It'll be all right," Slade said. "We got what we came for. I vote we head straight for the dryads' land now. The less time we spend moping about, the sooner we'll get the final ingredients and finish this thing. There's no telling when the Hunter will be back."

They all nodded their consent and followed Slade, who knew the layout of the forest better than any of them. Jack glanced back at the gargoyle, wondering if it could think and feel as they did. It was like him, in a way, or how he'd used to be: stuck in one place, forced to experience only a small portion of the world. He'd meant what he'd told Miriel; he was glad that was no longer his life, even if he longed for it sometimes. It was a longing for safety, for familiarity, but going back meant giving up everything he'd become. He thought back further, to his life before he became a scarecrow. No, he didn't want to go back. There was nothing for him there.

The landscape began to look slightly familiar as they walked. Evelyn rode on Jack's shoulder, with Slade leading and Miriel dragging behind. Jack felt horrible for her, but he couldn't think of what to say to her. How many words could you say to the grieving before they became meaningless? He slowed his pace anyway so they could walk next to her. It seemed better than letting her walk alone.

"It's almost over," Evelyn said. "Arnica believed in this, and she'd be so proud of you for seeing it to the end. I think she was proud of you already, for the way the journey had given you courage."

Miriel just nodded.

They walked in silence for a while, watching as more and more leaves fell to the ground in their final dance. Jack remembered what Raven had said about gaining the trust of things they didn't understand. That was his clue about the second item. They dryads had seemed so friendly before; maybe they'd already gained their trust.

"We need to talk about what happened," Miriel said a while later. They looked at her, waiting for her to continue. Her eyes were red, her face creased with worry. She sighed before going on. "What you did was dangerous, Evelyn. It could've cost us all our lives, not just Arnica's. Do you even understand what you were doing? Do you know where that path leads?"

"I have an idea," Evelyn said. "But what I did saved us. You saw for yourself: the Hunter was forced back. *He* fled from *me*. If anything, I think it's something to be further explored."

"You don't get it!" Miriel said. "You have great potential as a mage. I'd hate to see you lost to us. Please, promise me you won't use it again. When we're done with all of this, we'll go back to the Guild and you can go through the initiation rites, become a full-fledged mage. You're already so far along. I don't think it'd take much time for you to be promoted from novice to initiate."

Evelyn shook her head in frustration. "What if I don't want to join the Guild? What if I want to join with Raven, even as a human, or follow my own path? I'm sorry, Miriel, but I can't promise you anything."

"But—"

"Up ahead!" Slade called back.

They all looked forward, seeing a long line of animals crossing their path. There were moles, opossums, badgers, rabbits, squirrels, and several species of birds. The group reached them and asked a passing opossum where they were going.

"Leaving these lands," the opossum answered. "It's cursed now."

"Cursed how?" Evelyn asked.

"The dark one," the opossum responded. "It kills everything."

Jack and Evelyn exchanged a worried glance.

"What if we can stop it?" Jack asked. "If we can make it leave, will you come back?"

The opossum spit. "No use. It will kill you, too. If you're wise, you'll come with us."

It moved on, rejoining its family and the rest of the animals fleeing their homes.

"This is why I won't stop," Evelyn said, looking to Miriel. "I owe it to all of these animals. Who knows how many of them the Hunter's killed? Not just Arnica and Nadya. All of their lives can be laid at my feet."

"Your own life will be added to the list if you don't use caution," the mage said in return. "I won't pester you more about it, but I won't help you if you choose to go down that road. I cannot."

"Fair enough," Evelyn replied.

"Ladies, can't we all just agree that the Hunter is bad and we need to end this?" Slade asked. "What does it matter what methods we use?"

"It matters because her choices could mean the death of many more creatures," Miriel said. "I'm done arguing about it."

Rather than respond, Evelyn flew ahead. Jack figured she didn't want to upset Miriel further because of Arnica, but he thought he understood why she couldn't agree with the mage. He wasn't sure he agreed with her himself. The Hunter needed to be stopped, that much was clear. If Evelyn had found a way, he would support her.

They passed the next hour in silence, Evelyn staying out of sight. Slade tried a few times to joke and lighten the mood, but it did no good. The heaviness that hung over them like a funeral shroud was too strong.

As the sun began to sink, Slade made a light to hover over them. The shadows already cast their long arms across the ground, hiding rocks and small holes and tree roots.

"We should stop soon," Miriel said after a short while of this. "I can't keep going today."

Slade looked for a place to camp and Jack jogged ahead to join him. His metal limbs crunched even louder on the leaves. He didn't think he'd ever get used to them.

"She's in a bad way," Slade whispered as they searched about for suitable ground. "We'll need to finish this soon, or take her back to the Guild. I'd hate to come all this way just to have to take her back with the task undone."

"Will we have a choice?" Jack asked. "We still don't know what the third ingredient is."

"I guess we could always leave her with Raven until we've finished. At least he's closer."

"Somehow I doubt he'd be willing to hold her captive. We can try, though."

They found a small clearing with a great view of the stars and decided to camp there. Miriel immediately lay down and curled up on her side, not speaking a word to them or waiting for a fire. Jack and Slade set to work gathering leaves and twigs and pine needles.

"It's funny, I'm almost used to this now," Slade said. "On my own, I never made a fire, but now it's routine." He grinned at Jack, his eyes twinkling mischievously. "Perhaps I should start traveling about as a human. Seems I'm a perfect match for your species."

"I hardly feel like it's my species," Jack said. "Even with my memories restored, it seems distant. Dreamlike."

"Will you try to become human again after all of this?" the fox asked. "Seems like the logical thing to do, considering how close you and Evelyn have become."

"I haven't really thought about it," Jack said, embarrassed. "I'm tired of all the traveling about. Granted, I don't want to be stuck in one place like I was on my post. But staying in the Guild, or in Raven's land, where I can walk about as myself and not rush to be anywhere... It's tempting, I'll admit."

The fox just smiled and continued gathering fuel. Evelyn returned and helped get the fire started. Jack almost attempted to talk to her about what Miriel had said, but something in her eyes stopped him. Instead, he lay down on one side of the fire and looked up at the stars, the smoke curling through the air to make a transparent veil. He thought of the magical place Raven had taken him, of the never-ending stars all around them. Even if it was just a dream, it was so beautiful, so mysterious, that he was sure it couldn't have come from his subconscious. So either Raven had sent it, or he really had been there. Both thoughts were comforting.

He didn't remember falling asleep, or dreaming, and the next thing he knew, it was morning and the others were up and feeding themselves and putting out the fire.

"We shouldn't be too far away now," Slade said. "If we're lucky, we can get there, get the blood, figure out the third ingredient, and have Evelyn human again by sundown."

"Wouldn't that be something?" Evelyn said dryly.

Miriel pulled her stones out of her bag and tossed them on the ground, silently reading whatever they had to tell her. The others finished with the fire and waited until she nodded, satisfied, and stored them back in her pack.

The land sloped gently upward from there, and after another hour of walking, an intense tingly feeling settled on all of them, causing Slade's fur to bristle and Miriel's hair to frizz a bit more. Evelyn shook her head several times as though to dispel it.

"We're in the right place," Slade said.

"How do we get them to come out?" Jack asked. "Should we call for them?"

"They just appeared last time," Evelyn mused. "Perhaps we just have to go a bit further. They're each connected to specific trees, aren't they?"

Slade approached one, sniffed for a moment, then shot a bolt of blue energy out of one paw and into the trunk.

"Ah!" Evelyn cried. "What are you doing? You—"

A face appeared in the bark, staring at them with eyes slanted in curiosity. They stared back, unsure what to say or do now that the creature had appeared. Slowly, the dryad emerged from the tree, her body slender and transparent. She appeared to have brown skin, a smattering of dry leaves serving as scant clothing. Her hair was a web of vines and leaves. They backed away as she removed both legs from the tree and stood looking down at them. She must've been seven feet tall.

"Hello," Evelyn said. "I'm Evelyn. My friends and I need your help. You helped us once before, or at least, a dryad did. I'm not exactly sure which one, and we were hoping you would be willing to do so again."

Slade clapped softly. "Elegant."

She glared at him, then looked back at the dryad.

"One of your kind led me to a cave," Miriel tried. "To get us out of the rain."

The dryad looked between them, and it was unclear if she understood or not.

"This is getting us nowhere," Slade grumbled.

"Just give it a moment," Jack said. "Raven said we had to gain its trust."

"And how long until the Hunter catches up?" the fox retorted. "What happens if it shows up and all the dryads die? What will we do then?"

"Slade, calm down," Evelyn said. "It will be all right. I can handle the Hunter."

"Not this again," Miriel said with a sigh.

"I really don't want to argue about it," Evelyn said, her voice calm but full of firm resolve. "We're probably just confusing the poor creature right now."

The dryad continued to look between the four of them and a smile spread across her face, slowly, as if she were discovering a joke. Several more faces appeared in the trees around them, all looking down with laughter and curiosity. Soon the air was filled with the rustling of leaves and the tinkling bell-like sound of their amusement.

"What are they laughing at?" Jack asked.

"Us, probably," Slade said. "I'll bet they do understand us. Perfectly. They just don't want to help."

"We don't know that," Miriel said. "Maybe I can find the one who helped me before..." She searched through the faces, but Jack couldn't see how anyone could tell them apart. All female, all with slender, bark-like features. Impossible.

"I don't think you'll have any luck," he said. "Unless she chooses to come forward."

"Waste of time. Like I said."

"Oh, stop it, Slade," Evelyn said. "What else are we supposed to do? Use magic on them? Cut them against their will?"

"Now there's an idea."

"You're not serious."

He shrugged, grinning. "Who can tell?"

"Don't even joke about such a thing," Miriel said, scowling. She turned back to the dryad. "Please, if you can understand, help us. We're trying to stop a witch."

The dryad tilted her head to one side, but still said nothing. Other dryads began to emerge from the trees, their tinkling laughter echoing through the air. Jack wondered if they were actually speaking to one another, if the language of dryads was laughter and bells.

Soon they were surrounded by the creatures, a small space separating the two groups. They didn't attack or do anything threatening; just watched, and continued their odd laughter. Jack was almost convinced they *were* speaking to each other. Maybe if they could figure out how to speak that language—

"Are you ready to do things my way?" Slade asked. "We're getting nowhere."

The ladies ignored him, continuing their attempts to speak to the dryads. Evelyn fluffed her feathers in agitation and even Miriel ran her hand through her hair as the tree women stared at them. Jack was certain Evelyn would use her magic again, would reach out to that wild power in the forest. Maybe it would work and maybe it wouldn't, but the longer they stood there, the more he thought it might at least be worth a try. Evelyn seemed to think the same thing, because she rose into the air, landing on a branch above them and spreading her wings.

A high-pitched keening rent the air then, so loud they had to cover their ears. Jack followed the sound and saw one of the dryads, mouth agape, standing with arm extended, green ooze dripping onto the forest floor. Slade held a silver dagger and a small glass vial, which he used to catch the green ooze. The tip of the dagger was coated in the stuff.

"What did you *do*?!" Evelyn shrieked.

The other dryads joined in the odd scream, their faces contorting and twisting in anger, the sound like the cries of a thousand infants. The dryads reached for them, fingers growing to sharp points, their leaves blackening in their rage. Their eyes had become nothing more than black slits.

"Time to go!" Slade said, stoppering the vial and vanishing both it and the dagger. He transformed, resembling the ferocious fire fox he'd become at the festival. He roared and pushed through the dryads, creating a path. "Hurry!" he called.

They all hesitated a moment, but as the dryads began closing in again, they rushed through, shoving at any who got too close. Spear-like fingers clutched at Jack, tearing at his clothing, but he pushed them away and cleared the outer ring, Miriel close behind him. Evelyn flew overhead, cursing at Slade.

The dryads pursued them.

With his metal limbs, Jack was able to run faster than he'd ever been able to before, and he no longer had to worry about his feet wearing away. The fox ran ahead of him, dashing through the trees with lightning speed. The mage kept pace with him.

The dryads jumped from tree to tree, their snarling faces appearing through the trunks, fingers reaching for them. Their cries had deepened to a guttural roar, a primal rage that sought vengeance.

"Why the *hell* did you do that?!" Miriel screamed at Slade.

"One of us had to do *something!*" he screamed back.

Jack tripped and went sprawling, leaves and dirt filling his mouth and vision. Then something grabbed a hold of his leg, pulling him backwards. One of the dryads snarled at him, revealing teeth that transformed before his eyes, growing pointed tips. He kicked and slapped at it, his metal limbs doing more damage than he anticipated. Green blood trickled from wounds on its face and arms and it screamed, releasing him. He got to his feet and dashed after the others.

He didn't know exactly when they stopped following them, but the next time he looked back, the dryads were far behind, slowing to a stop and watching them continue their flight. Slade kept going, down a hill and across a creek, until the tingly feeling of the land was completely gone and the dryads were out of sight. Finally, they stopped to catch their breath.

"That was the most heartless, idiotic thing I've ever seen!" Evelyn screamed, landing on the ground beside them. "How could you do that?! Who knows what sort of magic they had? They could've killed us all! And they did absolutely nothing to provoke us! Nothing! They wouldn't have harmed a grasshopper!"

"Will you calm down?!" Slade yelled back. "We got what we wanted, so what's the big deal? And none of us were hurt or killed. If the dryads were powerful, like you're suggesting, I could've handled them. It's not like I killed anyone!"

"How would you know?!" Miriel shouted, joining in. "You didn't stay to find out! That poor creature may not be able to heal itself, or even bind the wound. It could be bleeding to death right now!"

"How else were we supposed to get the blood?" Slade asked, calming his voice. "You say it might not have been able to heal itself. In that case, this whole quest would be in vain because it wouldn't be able to give us the blood without dying. So how is that any different?"

"It's different because it would've been given *freely*," Evelyn hissed, also lowering her voice.

"I'm with the ladies on this one," Jack said, scowling at the fox. "What you did was cruel. Monstrous, even. We thought you had changed, that Raven's influence had done some good for you. Looks like we were wrong."

"You too, Jack?" Slade said, mocking him with another grin. "Look, I didn't expect all of you to agree to this, and if there's some sort of punishment or backlash, I'll take all of it. But I did what needed to be done. We have the blood now, and there's only one ingredient left. I suggest we stop wasting time on things that can't be changed and figure out how to finish this."

Jack scoffed, disgusted. "You're no better than the Hunter," he said. "Attacking without thought, without care."

"Fine. Don't accept the blood. You're welcome to go back and ask the dryads to kindly give you some, please and thank you. I'm sure they'll be thrilled to see you again."

Evelyn screamed in fury and took to the air. Jack watched her go, his own emotions a mix of anger, frustration, and disappointment. He wished he could fly off with her. At least they could vent their feelings to each other. Instead, he was stuck with Miriel and Slade and an awkward, tense silence.

By unspoken agreement, they took off toward Raven's land, wishing to put as much distance between them and the dryads as possible. It wasn't so much the dryads Jack wanted to escape as it was the horrific scene he had witnessed. If he could just put one foot in front of the other, keep Slade out of his line of vision, he could pretend it hadn't happened.

When they set up camp that night, they maintained their silence, mutely refusing to even look at each other. Miriel and Jack gathered firewood. Slade wandered off, either to find food or be alone, Jack wasn't sure. Miriel sighed frequently, but still said nothing. Evelyn finally returned but kept to herself, staring grimly into the fire.

Jack lay back on the ground, hands behind his head as he looked up at the stars. The tree canopy hid most of them, but a few glowed through. The moon waxed full and clear, the clouds having broken up for the evening. He closed his eyes, imagining the place Raven had shown him, remembering the peace he'd felt there. Even if it was only a dream, it helped calm him.

His thoughts turned to the Hunter, and to Nadya and Arnica. He regretted, only a little, comparing Slade to the monster, but he couldn't deny the truth. The Hunter was a creature of death, stealing the life of its victims, like snuffing out a candle with a breath of air, and Slade—

Jack sat bolt upright, the ideas fitting together in his mind like a puzzle. Miriel and Evelyn glanced over at him, eyebrows raised with questions, but he said nothing and lay back down. If he was right, he didn't think he should talk it over with them. They'd have their own opinions and would likely muddy the path forward. Right then, it was clear and obvious before him.

He knew what he had to do.

❧ 31 ❧

BREATH OF THE DEAD

They walked slowly the next day, continuing their silence. Jack figured the others were thinking over what Slade had done. Maybe they were thinking of what the third ingredient could be, but if so, they said no word. They couldn't keep it up for long. Eventually they'd have to talk it over because it affected where they went next. As it was, they were wandering aimlessly in the direction of Raven's land, but they knew they couldn't actually return there. They were merely putting off the inevitable.

Evelyn glided down and landed on his shoulder, still not speaking. When she sighed, he glanced up at her. Miriel currently led the way, Slade dragging a little behind. Evelyn whispered, "What do we do now, Jack?"

"We keep going," he answered. "There's still one ingredient left."

"We don't even know what it is. I've thought and thought and I can't figure it out. I'm almost tempted to just give it all up, to accept that I'll be a crow forever and join with Raven."

"And leave your father to Ferah? Your brother to whatever fate he's facing?"

"What other choice do I have? I'm so tired, Jack. So tired. I just want it all to be over."

"It will be," he promised. "Soon."

"How can you be so sure?"

"Just a feeling, I guess."

She rubbed her head against him, sighing again. "If I go to Raven, will you come with me, Jack?"

"Yes."

"Promise?"

"You have my word." He laughed then and said, "Who knows? Maybe we'll get lucky and Raven will change his mind and transform you himself. Surely we've done enough to learn whatever lesson he was trying to teach."

She laughed in return. "Maybe."

Miriel stopped and waited for them. When they caught up, she said, "We should probably start thinking about exactly where we're headed."

"Jack and I were just speaking of that," Evelyn said. "Do you have any ideas?"

"Not really," the mage admitted. "I'll consult my stones."

They halted, Miriel digging her stones out of her pack and casting them on the ground. Slade kept a respectful distance, no doubt feeling their remaining anger toward him. Jack said nothing of his discovery. If Evelyn knew, she would give up the quest for sure, no doubt, and he wanted to prevent that if he could. They'd gone through too much.

He sat on the ground and watched the gray clouds, which had returned with a vengeance. They shifted slowly across the sky, creating swirls and patterns with meanings only they knew. He thought of the stars beyond them, hidden by cloud and sunlight. At least he'd gotten to see them the night before.

Slade approached after a short while, stopping a few feet from Jack. At first he said nothing, just picked at his fur while Jack watched him. Evelyn flew off, no doubt still angry at the fox. Jack couldn't blame her.

"Despite what you may think, I only did what I thought needed to be done," Slade finally said. "I'm trying to help the two of you. You can disagree with me, or hate me, if you want. You'd be right to."

"We just wish you would've waited," Jack said. "We could've figured it out. That's how we've managed so far."

"Perhaps," Slade allowed. "Perhaps not. Guess we won't know now, will we?"

Jack didn't answer.

"Well, any idea about this *breath of the dead* business? A bit morbid, don't you think?"

"Sure," Jack said. "What else do you expect of a witch's spell?"

"Could mean we have to dig up a body, or steal a fresh one. Might have to use magic on it. The ladies won't like that."

Jack shuddered, thinking about it. No, they wouldn't like that. He almost revealed his plan, but held back. He didn't think Slade would try to stop him, but he wasn't sure the fox could keep his mouth shut. At least until it was too late for Evelyn to do anything about it. Better to not risk it.

Miriel cursed, grabbing up her stones and tossing them into her bag. "Vague, vague, vague. That's all I get."

"At least you tried," Slade said. Miriel ignored him.

"Should we head out again? Or talk it out?" Jack asked.

Miriel frowned. "Probably talk it out. Means staying put for a while, but we're not getting anywhere anyway." She searched the sky for Evelyn, whistling when she spotted her. Evelyn glided down a moment later, landing on a low-hanging branch.

"Anything?" she asked.

"No," Miriel said. "We're down to throwing ideas about, figuring out what sticks. I have a few, but I don't like any of them."

"Same here," Evelyn said.

They talked over various possibilities, ignoring anything the fox said. Jack offered a few ideas of his own, things he had thought before, but kept his secret idea to himself.

"I'm not exhuming a body," Evelyn said. "I'm drawing the line there. I'd rather stay a crow."

"And we're not killing anyone," Miriel said. "Just so we're clear." She looked pointedly at Slade.

"Wouldn't dream of it," the fox responded. "A detestable thought, to be sure."

Evelyn rolled her eyes.

"So what do we do?" Miriel continued. "We can't go back to Raven, and the Guild is out for now."

"The owl?" Evelyn suggested. "She may send us on a long quest again, but I'm out of other ideas."

Jack shrugged and Slade offered no better alternative, so it was decided. Slade led the way from there, since of the four he was the only one who remembered how to get there. The ladies kept their words to him short, just in case he thought they'd forgiven him.

Evelyn flew ahead of Jack, leaving him to his own thoughts as they walked. An image of Martha came to his mind, but she held no more power over him. He mentally smiled and waved at her, daring her to taunt him. When she disappeared, becoming a wisp of smoke and floating away in his mind, he knew it was for the last time.

Nadya and Arnica appeared in his mind then, staring at him in pain and longing. "Soon," he promised them. They left without a word.

They covered a lot of ground, putting several hours between them and the dryads. When the sun began to set, Slade created a floating ball of light without being asked. They continued on as the darkness deepened. Finally Miriel said, "We'll need to stop soon. I'll take sentry duty first."

They split up to take care of their nightly ritual of finding food and firewood. When he'd finished, Jack lay back on the ground and gazed once more at the stars, which had begun to peek out at the world as the clouds cleared. He was glad he had spoken to Evelyn, and had made some sort of peace with Slade. It was only a waiting game at that point, and he was content to watch and wait.

When the stars began to fade one by one, consumed by a darkness thicker than death, he rose slowly to his feet. The others hadn't noticed yet. Jack walked toward the deepening black, Miriel finally catching sight of it and yelling, "Hunter!"

But Jack didn't run.

Face your fears, Raven had said.

Breath of the dead.

The Hunter's slim figure appeared then, its eyes glowing a bright white in the darkness, like two rogue stars. Jack glanced up again, hoping to catch one final glimpse of the real ones, but they were already gone.

Behind him, Evelyn was screaming, no doubt preparing some magic to force the Hunter back. The sound of rustling leaves as someone ran toward him echoed through the air and he dashed the last few feet, reaching out toward the creature even as it reached for him. Slade's paw gripped his shirt just as his hand touched the Hunter's, and the dark consumed him.

THE BLACKNESS all around pressed in like an impenetrable wall, squeezing tighter until he thought he would explode from the pressure. He could even taste it, thick and cold and almost oily, a living presence all on its own. For a terrifying moment, he thought he would be trapped there forever, awake and lost in unending darkness, unable to see even his own hand in front of his face. Then, finally, the darkness thinned a bit, becoming almost gray, but nothing like the gray world Nadya had taken him through when she'd transported them. This was blacker, crueler, and there was nothing magical about it.

Twisted trees appeared around him, mere shadows. Perhaps

the place was a shadow image of the real world, but the more he looked, the less likely he thought this. Wherever he was, the landscape was different from where he'd been when the Hunter appeared. He stood on a hill overlooking a broad valley, a high, dark mountain beyond it. There wasn't a single shred of color.

For a long moment, he stared at the valley, wondering what he ought to do. He hadn't expected to have any sort of consciousness after the Hunter took him. At least he'd given the others what they needed: his last breath, given freely. Slade would've captured it, he was sure of it. Always practical, always prepared. He would make sure Evelyn kept going, that she returned to the witch with the ingredients and finished the whole thing for good. He had no regrets.

As he looked out over the valley, a light column of smoke rose in the air from the forest below, snaking through the dark air. He watched for a moment, then set off down the hill.

When he'd first come up with the idea, he hadn't been sure it would work. He hadn't known if he was even able to die, let alone provide a dying breath. But the more he'd thought about it, the more he'd been convinced it *would* work. He'd been a man once, after all. Miriel had answered that question for him. No matter what form he was in, it was the soul that mattered, as Raven had said. He could just imagine them, possibly grief-stricken, likely determined and angry, heading back to the witch as fast as they could travel. They would be all right.

He reached the bottom of the hill and plunged into the trees. His sense of fear had vanished. Difficult to fear anything if you were already dead. In a way, it was a relief. The quest was over, at least for him, and even if he wouldn't see Evelyn again, at least he could be assured she would finish it. That was all that mattered, really.

The trees grew thick together and hid the column of smoke, but he continued in the direction he remembered seeing it, figuring he'd reach it eventually. Just had to keep moving. It seemed to take a long time to reach the mysterious fire at the other end of the smoke. The light remained exactly the same, never brightening or darkening. Just a monotonous grayish-black. Not a single other creature appeared, though this didn't seem to him very odd. Who was to say what the afterlife was like? Maybe that was part of it, being alone.

He finally did reach the fire, only it wasn't a fire. Just a column of smoke pouring out of a broken tree. He looked and looked, but couldn't find a single flame. No one else stood about or came to investigate. Logically, he knew someone should've noticed, or started the thing, or *something*. And then he reminded himself that he was dead and things didn't have to make sense anymore.

For the first time since Slade had granted him mobility, Jack was free to simply sit and watch the clouds pass through the sky. No more running from Hunters or wolves or cats. No more worrying about witches. But strange enough, he was bored, unsure what to do with himself. He could explore, and it seemed the place was big enough to do that for a while. Maybe forever. Somehow this didn't excite him as it once might have, but the thought of doing nothing seemed even worse.

He picked a direction and started walking, wondering what would happen if he simply laid down and didn't move again. Would he become part of the earth, forever gazing at the sky? Would he ever see the stars again? From there his thoughts drifted to Raven and he wondered what the old bird would say when he heard the news. Jack had made a promise, but the bird-god would just have to understand.

Something rustled to his right and he froze, unsure what sort of creatures he might have to deal with. Were there things worse than death? Could anything else happen to him? He didn't really want to find out, but he couldn't actually bring himself to fear it, so he went to investigate. He didn't have to go far. Beyond a bush and behind a tree and there it was: a black fox. It whipped its head around at his approach, and at first he thought it had three eyes. Two glowed a bright white and the third was in a diamond shape on its forehead. He realized a second later it was just its fur, but the effect was still a bit unsettling.

"What do you want?" the fox asked.

Jack gasped. He hadn't thought he'd ever hear that voice again, let alone see her.

She backed up, her posture low and defensive, her eyes never leaving him.

"Nadya? Is that you?"

"Who wants to know?"

He chuckled at the absurdity of it. "It's Jack." He looked down at himself, noticing his black body. Even his metal arms and legs had been affected. He could only imagine what his face must look like.

She crept a little closer to him. "Jack?" she asked. "Is it really you?"

"It is. The Hunter got me as well."

She cursed. "Never thought it would end this way. Don't get me wrong, I expected to die young. No illusions of old age and pups for me. But I thought it would be on a job, maybe at Slade's hand. Is that what you called him? Slade?"

Jack nodded.

"He's still alive, isn't he? The Hunter hasn't gotten him?"

"Not before he took me. What happened after, I can't say."

"Did he... Did he miss me?"

Jack smiled. "Yes."

She sat upright, her apprehension gone. "Good," she said, smiling to herself. "Good."

Jack glanced at the trees around them, a shadow replica of the real world. "Are you just passing through here? Or is this your area, so to speak?"

"Passing through," she said. "I haven't stopped moving since it happened."

"We haven't, either. Not really, anyway."

"Tell me about it."

So he related everything that had happened, leaving nothing

out. She laughed in the appropriate places, gasped, huffed in anger.

When he mentioned Arnica, she pondered a moment. "I haven't seen anyone else here. You're the first. Doesn't mean she's not here, though."

"Should we look?"

"If you'd like. I have to warn you, though, this place is huge. She could be anywhere."

"It's not like we have anywhere else to be."

She chuckled at that, leading the way through the trees. They trekked uphill and downhill, across black streams and gray stretches of grass. The only sound was the noise of their feet in the underbrush. No birds, no wind, no rustling of other animals. Nadya shook her head when he mentioned it.

"There's nothing here," she said. "Just...this. All the time. Until you showed up, anyway."

"Are we going somewhere specific? Or just walking in the hopes we'll run in to her?"

"Mostly walking and hoping. There's a great ledge further on where we can see all around for a long ways. If nothing else, we can try there and see what we see."

"Does magic work here?"

"No," she said. "Believe me, I've tried."

He wondered how much that bothered her, if at all. Was it because the Hunter was created by a witch? Did that mean witchcraft would work, then? So many unanswered questions, and no one to answer them anymore.

"Do you ever see the stars?" he asked.

Nadya looked back at him, eyebrows raised. "No," she said. "Never."

He nodded. "I figured. I hoped, though..." He let his voice trail off. There was no point in hoping in such a place. Deep down, he knew they were looking for Arnica because it gave them something to do. It had been a miracle that he'd found

Nadya at all, when he thought about it. He thanked whatever
god may have been responsible for that.

"I felt horrible, when it happened," he said. "For the longest
time, I couldn't stop thinking about you. I wondered if there was
anything I could've done differently, anything that would've
made the smallest difference—"

"Don't."

He frowned, going silent.

"I chose this. All you would've done was get yourself killed
along with me."

He thought about that a moment, finally asking, "Why *did*
you do it, Nadya?"

She remained silent and he thought at first she wouldn't
answer. But finally she said, "You had this grand mission to save
your friend. And you'd been through so much, but you didn't let
it stop you. You were brave in a way that few people are
anymore. I couldn't just sit back and let that go to waste. Sure, I
may do questionable things from time to time, but I know a
good person when I see one."

"But why even care? Good people die all the time."

"Maybe I thought it was time one of them stuck around for a
while."

They reached the ledge and looked out over the vast forest
below. It was different from the overlook Jack had stood on
when he'd first arrived, and the view was even grander. Still
endless black and gray, but it was a diverse landscape. A large
lake spread out to his left, disappearing into the distance, and
the great mountain he'd seen before loomed even closer. No
more smoke columns, though.

He'd asked Nadya about it, but she hadn't had an explanation, either. Some things just happened there, and there was no
one around to explain them. You just accepted them and
moved on.

"Which way?" she asked.

Jack looked in all directions, knowing deep down it didn't

really matter. Still, nothing wrong with pretending. "Let's try the lake," he said.

She started down the hill in that direction and he followed. His mind wandered back to Evelyn and the others and he hoped they had stopped Ferah already. He no longer knew how long he'd been gone, how much time had passed in the world of the living, or if they were even on the same timescale. Then again, maybe there was no more time at all. Maybe that's why the light never changed and the stars never shone.

It seemed only moments later that they reached the lake, but that was more illusion. They could've been walking for hours, for all he knew. He stopped questioning it and focused on looking for Arnica.

The lake looked oddly familiar, but he couldn't quite say why. The water didn't even move, appearing to be a smooth black surface made of glass. He put one foot in, just to test it, and was relieved when the water rippled. Nadya found a narrow path leading up a small hill and he finally remembered: the lake where he'd run into Miriel and Arnica again. They were similar, if not exactly the same. Maybe other places in the living world were reflected there, too, but he wasn't sure he would recognize them. An image of an empty black and gray Alibeth and Guild castle rose to his mind and he shuddered. Maybe it was better if they weren't reflected there.

"Do you feel that?" Nadya asked, furrowing her brow.

"Feel what?"

"Shh. Listen."

He did, even closing his eyes to minimize distractions. Far, far away, something rumbled.

"I've never heard that before," she said. "It may be your friend. Want to check it out?"

No point in protesting. Nadya paused, letting the rumble move through her again in order to determine from which direction it came, then set out. Jack wondered if she was chasing anything now, even the smallest sound, just to have something to do. Not that he could blame her. He would likely end up doing the same, eventually.

But the further they went, the louder the rumble became. It was an unnatural thing in that world of silence and darkness, and all the more desirable for that. Jack couldn't even begin to guess what it could be. Maybe the Hunter itself, doing only the gods knew what.

"Are you afraid, Jack?"

"No."

"Me neither. I think we should be, but I haven't been since I came to this place."

"I've felt the same way."

She smiled at him, her white eyes glowing even brighter. "Do you think if we die here, we'll cease to exist? Just disappear? That thought used to terrify me, but now it seems almost...a relief. No more endless monotony."

"Peace at last," he agreed.

"Listen to me," she laughed, "going on about death and resting. Who have I become?"

"You're still you," he said. "Don't doubt that."

The rumbling grew so loud he began to feel it in the ground, just a slight tremor at first, but increasing steadily the further they went. Another hill rose before them and this time Jack took the lead, hurrying with something resembling glee.

"We have to be getting close," Nadya said. "How much louder can it get?"

Then they were at the top and below them was a valley empty of trees. In their place stood a great host of animals, all gathered together and crying as one. Rabbits, deer, badgers, moles, birds: all black, all victims of the Hunter. For whatever reason they had found each other and gathered together, or else they'd crossed into death together. Jack shuddered at the thought.

Nadya stared in shocked silence, no doubt wondering, why now? And then all sound ceased, abruptly and without explanation, and a deeper darkness appeared in the distance, growing quickly and headed their way.

"The Hunter," Nayda whispered.

They waited for it; there was nowhere else to go. All the animals below watched as well as their shared murderer approached. For a second, Jack thought he spotted a cat in the throng and he nearly called out, but then the Hunter was upon them. It floated above for a moment, then floated to the ground, speckles of white light covering its body, growing larger by the second, and it jerked its limbs as if in pain. It didn't seem as tall as it had before, nor as menacing. The animals took up their cry again, rushing the creature in united vengeance.

It broke apart before any of them could reach it, the darkness rising from it like ashes in the air. What was left was a human child, a boy, eyes closed as if he were sleeping. He rose into the air, whether by his own will or something else, Jack couldn't say. The force pushed him back until he lay flat and then they were all rising, the darkness leaving their bodies and leaving them as they had been before.

Nadya laughed, raising her face to the sky above, which had also broken open to let in the light. Jack felt himself pressed down, squeezed until he was no more than a single floating speck, all of them tiny particles of light rising to join the stars and light beyond the world.

Home.

Then he was jerked back, forced to watch as all the others continued their ascension while he plunged down, down, back into the heart of the world.

❧ 32 ❧

RESTORATION

"Jack! Jack!"

The voice was all around him, deep and familiar and persistent. As the darkness faded, he saw the forest once more, as though through a veil. Slade was there, and Miriel, and another woman, her hair a wild halo around her. They towered over him like he was still a tiny floating speck, no more than a particle of dust. The second woman reached out and grabbed him, leaves and thorns sprouting through her hair and skin.

Miriel was screaming and Slade was chanting something, but the woman didn't seem to even hear them. She held him in her hand for a moment, looking at him with a mixture of grief and love in her eyes. Then she thrust him at the fox, her words so loud and jumbled that he couldn't understand any of them.

Slade took him as Miriel charged the woman, a bolt of bright magic appearing at her fingertips. The woman blocked the magic, throwing her arm over her face and shrinking at the same time. In her place was a crow, and after one last look at him, it took to the sky and didn't return.

JACK FADED in and out of consciousness after that. Slade had put him in some sort of container, and most of the time he lay in darkness, though not the darkness of the Hunter. He didn't hear Miriel's voice anymore. At times it seemed the fox spoke to him, but he couldn't understand the words. A pale gray veil lay over everything, less oppressive than the grayish-black of before, but still enough to keep him from fully entering the world.

He thought of Nadya and the others, hoping they had escaped to a true afterlife, not a black imitation. The boy must have been Evelyn's missing brother, Mordecai, trapped in a shadow form and forced to hunt them. Hunt her. He couldn't figure out why they'd been freed, though. And Evelyn...

He pushed the thoughts from his mind, knowing they would only drive him mad. He should've been free with the others, not trapped in a gray half-world. For the first time in his life, he felt true loneliness, more than he'd ever felt with Martha, or as a scarecrow stuck on a post. Just one familiar face, one he could actually speak to. That was all he wanted.

When the air changed, he felt it deep within himself, like something old and powerful, unpredictable, had reached inside him and shaken him up. Slade pulled him out into the light and before him was the largest human he had ever seen, even as small as he was. Only it wasn't a human, it was a bird, and then a human again, only different than before.

"Jack," he said. "Would you like to come out of there?"

The voice was soothing and comforting, like that of a beloved parent.

"Yes," Jack said.

The man smiled and shrank, color slowly returning to the world. Only the man wasn't shrinking, Jack was growing, larger and larger until he and the man were the same size. He had limbs again, and not metal limbs or scarecrow limbs, but human limbs, real and warm, not illusion.

Slade stood behind him, grinning. "Hey, Jack," he said. He

sounded tired, as if he'd been ill, or dare he think, crying? Jack looked at the man again, who transformed into the familiar form of Raven, shrinking in comparison to Jack but still large for the species. Jack looked back at Slade, having to look down to see him. They were in Raven's land, right beside the large pond where Jack had last seen the bird. He lifted his hands in front of his face, real flesh and blood. It was too good to be true, too bizarre.

Jack ran to the water's edge to get a look at himself. Staring back at him was a narrow face, cream colored, with blue eyes and light brown hair that fell to his shoulders. Well, brown except for the hair right above his eyes and extending down the right side of his face. There, it was black as midnight. His clothes had changed as well; gone were the scarecrow garments, and in their place was a brown coat and an off-white undershirt. Dark brown shoes and pants completed his new attire.

"You probably have questions," Raven said from behind him.

Jack looked back at the two. "Many."

"But first, how about some food?"

It hit him then, the intense hunger he had almost forgotten in all his years as a scarecrow. A cool breeze blew across his face and he closed his eyes, relishing the sensation. He hadn't realized he'd missed it.

Raven's servants brought food: fruit and vegetables and bread and even a little meat, and all of it was wonderful to him, everything bursting with flavor. He didn't ask what the meat was, unsure if it would be rude or not. Slade ate as well, casting little glances his way with an amused grin.

Finally, with his hunger satisfied and his excitement over the whole thing starting to subside, Raven sent his servants away, leaving Jack and Slade alone with him.

"So, what happened?" Jack asked. "Where are Evelyn and Miriel?"

"After you sacrificed yourself to the Hunter," Slade said, "Evelyn... Well, she figured out what you had done and was smart enough to get the final ingredient while she could. Then she just...cast the spell herself. It was... It was unlike anything I've ever seen, and I've seen *a lot*."

"She cast it herself? I thought a witch had to do it."

"Exactly," the fox answered.

Understanding dawned on Jack. Of course. She was the one he'd seen, the one who'd pulled him from the shadow world while all the others had passed on. Deep down he'd known this, but what it really meant, he hadn't considered.

"So...she's a witch?" he said.

"A fledgling witch," Raven answered, "but a witch, nonetheless."

"When she cast the spell, she was restored to her human form," Slade said. "I can only guess that means Ferah is in crow form again. Then the Hunter just fell apart before our eyes. It was her little brother, you know, the one Ferah said had run away. She knew all along what had happened to him. Anyway, Evelyn cast more magic and the next thing we knew, she'd captured a small speck of light and insisted it was you. By that time, Miriel was furious and threatened her. Evelyn passed you off to me and fled. In crow form, I might add. I guess she can change at will, now."

"I...saw all of this. Sort of," Jack said. "You were all so large... It seems more like a dream, now."

"An effect of dying and rising again," Raven said. "The living aren't supposed to know what happens in death. I won't be surprised if you begin to forget some of what you experienced."

"Where is she now?" Jack asked.

"Your guess is as good as mine," Slade said. "Miriel had had enough by then and went in search of the village by herself. I pointed her in the right direction, but I don't think she'll find anything. Just crows and confused people."

"Which is what she wants, I suppose," Jack said. "Do you think she'll go after Evelyn?"

"Undoubtedly. She'll probably return to the Guild first,

though. Possibly bring reinforcements. Who knows? It's no longer my problem."

Slade looked to Raven as he said this and the old bird nodded.

"Yes, you've done your duty quite well," Raven said. "I release you from my service. You are free to come and go as you please."

Slade grinned. "Don't worry Jack, I won't leave you quite yet. I'll have to be off soon, though. I've been away too long."

A sudden realization dawned on Jack and he asked, "How am I able to understand you? I'm not a mage, and I'm no longer enchanted."

"That is my doing," Raven said. "As you've probably figured out, I restored you to your human form, with a few extra added gifts. The animal speech is just one."

"What are the others?"

Raven's eyes twinkled. "I'll leave that to you to figure out."

"Thank you," Jack said. "I owe you so much. Not just for transforming me, but for everything. It was because of you that I didn't give up, many times."

"Careful on admitting you owe him," Slade said. "He may hold you to it."

"You're one to talk."

They both laughed, and it felt good, really good. Like a huge burden had been lifted. He still worried about Evelyn, but at least the quest was finished. Her father was saved, she was human again, and Ferah had been stopped. They would figure out the rest.

"I have a job for you, if you want it," Raven said. "Tension between the wolves, the dreadlords, the Guild, and my own people have grown of late, thanks in no small part to your little quest."

Jack blushed, but couldn't deny it.

"I need someone to work as my ambassador, so to speak. I was content to sit back and let things fall where they may, but it's more than time for peace to reign once more. Since you played a part in this, I think it right that you help to fix it."

Jack glanced at Slade, who pretended to be captivated by a blade of grass.

"I don't really have a say in this, do I?" Jack asked.

"Of course you do," Raven said. "Though I can't speak to what may happen if you refuse."

"All right, all right, I get the hint. I'll do it. But how do you know they won't simply attack me? I'm sure they don't have any fond feelings for me."

"You will be working directly for me. They won't challenge that. And if they do, they'll be dealt with swiftly. And you won't be traveling alone."

Raven nodded, looking out toward the water, and a second later a familiar hawk flew across the pond to join them.

"Hey, Jack," Caerla said. "You look much better."

"I feel better, too," he said, smiling.

"You two will work as a team," Raven continued. "And I'll expect frequent check-ins."

Slade rose, swishing his tail. "It's time for me to be off," he said. "I'll be back to visit, though. You may need someone to get you out of trouble."

"That's what I'm for," Caerla said.

"Then you're doomed," Slade told Jack.

Jack laughed, following Slade a short distance away and kneeling beside him. He whispered so the others wouldn't overhear. "There's one more thing you should know. I saw Nadya, in the shadow world."

The smile left Slade's face as his eyes widened. "You did?"

"She was all right. When Evelyn freed us, her soul passed on to whatever afterlife there is. She was...happy, at the end."

Slade looked down, nodding slowly. "Good," he whispered. "Good."

Jack laid one hand on Slade's back, relishing the softness of his fur for just a moment. "Take care of yourself," he said.

"Same to you," the fox answered. He dashed away, disappearing into the trees without looking back. Jack stood there a moment, wishing he could chase after him. Despite the things he'd done, Slade was one of his only friends. He returned to Raven with eyes downward, thoughts racing through his mind.

"You can rest here for a few days," Raven said. "You've been through a lot. Four days from now, you and Caerla will depart for Alibeth."

The hawk bowed and took her leave, winking at Jack before she flew off. A sparrow approached to take Jack away, but he held back a moment.

"I want to find her," he said. "Evelyn, I mean. I know you want me to work for you, and I don't expect to get out of it. I just...need to talk to her again."

"I expected as much," Raven said. "And I promise you'll soon be free to do so. But this cannot wait."

Jack nodded, his heart torn but hopeful. When the sparrow led him away, he followed with no further protest. Many of the animals glanced his way, but none were curious enough to approach him. The sparrow left him in the same suite he and Evelyn had once shared, which only drove home how much he missed her. He could only imagine what she was doing then, what sort of thoughts she must be thinking. She had saved him, and he didn't doubt she'd want to find him. Would she recognize him? Would he recognize her? If she could change into a crow at will, what else could she do?

Exhaustion began to set in and he lay down on the soft grass, watching as the stars appeared one by one high above. He folded his hands across his stomach and breathed deeply, loving the cold air, his full belly, and the feeling of peace that infused Raven's land. It was hard to be upset for long, there.

This time when he dreamed, he was back in the place of memory, the stars above and below as they reflected off the water. Far into the distance they went, twinkling and enticing him with their pure light. He followed gladly, without fear, without worry, and without guilt. There, finally, he was free.

EPILOGUE

He had traveled all night without rest.

The villagers had told him there was an inn not too far ahead, if he could just find it. So easy to get lost once the sun set. It also didn't help that he was traveling by foot, but he enjoyed it, though it took him longer. He hadn't planned to stay out all night, but he was so sure that if he went just a bit further, he'd see the lights shining through the trees...

Eventually, he had to stop and sleep in the forest, starting again at dawn and finally finding the place in the morning. He decided to get some food in his belly and rent a room. He didn't know how long he'd be there.

The inn sat in a wide field, the forest continuing to the north and the ocean stretching away in the south. He hadn't expected it to be as loud as it was. He still hadn't gotten a proper glimpse of it, but he would wander down to the beach after breakfast. The inn's common room was sparsely occupied, but more people came down the stairs as he got the attention of the innkeeper.

While he waited for his first hot breakfast in days, he looked around at all the people. There were several men together in a corner, probably foresters, or farmers, perhaps. A few women were scattered here and there, all in groups.

It had taken him over a year to complete Raven's task. Every group had wanted their own way, and few were willing to negotiate. They had seen it done, though, he and Caerla. The first thing he'd done when it was completed was seek out Igraine, Ferah's sister. But when he'd arrived in the abandoned village, it had been truly abandoned, the witch's cottage empty.

He hadn't known where to turn after that. Miriel and the Guild continued their hunt for witches, but they no longer involved outsiders. Too many uncontrolled variables. He wouldn't find help there. Raven had been cryptic, urging Jack to find Evelyn in his memories. Whatever that meant.

The breakthrough came when he ran into Slade again. The fox had been in and out of Raven's land throughout the year, never staying long. But the last time he'd visited, he'd mentioned a rumor about a witch in a sea village. It was better than nothing.

The more Jack had thought about it, the more certain he was that it was her. They had spoken often of the sea, and she was the only other witch he knew of. So he went.

He finished his breakfast quickly, studying the faces of everyone in the room. He didn't really think any of them were her, but he looked anyway. As he traveled down to the shore, the wind picked up, blowing his hair back and chilling him. He still loved the feel of the air on his skin, the way goosebumps rose over his arms.

Seagulls flew overhead, crying their disapproval to any who would listen. More birds scavenged on the shore, running away from the water as the tide rushed in. Some cried out when they weren't fast enough. The light of the sun on the water reflected even more brightly to his eyes, forcing him to shield them with his arm. He turned his head away from it, squinting, and caught sight of a lone figure further down the beach.

She wore pants and a tunic, unlike most of the women he'd come across in his travels. Her red hair blew all around her as the wind picked up, making her look like some wild goddess. Jack's breath caught in his throat and he hesitated, unsure if it were really her, if she would even know him. Then she shielded her eyes and looked his way and he found his feet making the decision for him, moving him closer before he'd fully made up his mind.

She watched him approach with a look of curiosity and wariness, her stance guarded and prepared for flight. He used another of the gifts Raven had given him, one it had taken him a long time to discover: he turned into a scarecrow.

It lasted only a second and then he was a man again, but that second was all it took.

Her eyes widened and she cried out, covering her mouth with one hand. Then she was running and he was running, and the waves crashed against the shore, covering him with their saltiness and washing away the final doubt.

ACKNOWLEDGMENTS

A lot goes into making a book, and this one wouldn't have been the same without the help of Phillip Drayer Duncan and Kayla Larson, who read its earliest drafts and helped mold it into the book you now hold in your hands. *Jack* is one of my earliest novels—the fourth I ever finished—and has undergone significant changes over the years. Thank you both for being its staunchest supporters.

Thanks must also go to Aaron Moschner, who created the most beautiful cover I could imagine for *Jack*. Thank you so much for helping this dream to come true.

And thank you, dear reader, for picking up this book. None of this would be possible without you.

-J.H. Fleming

About the Author

J.H. Fleming is the author of the Music the Gathering series, The Call of the Fae series, *Rhythms of Magic*, and *Peter Pixie, Mayor of the Multiverse: The Black Wand*. Her work has appeared in anthologies by NewCon Press, Evil Girlfriend Media, Mocha Memoirs Press, Seventh Star Press, and Pro Se Productions, as well as New Realm Magazine and Visionary Tongue Magazine. She received her Bachelor's degree in Creative Writing from the University of Central Arkansas.

In her free time, she enjoys reading, playing video games, and learning other languages. She'd prefer to live in a library in the middle of a forest, and has so far collected fourteen hundred books toward that goal. Until then, she and her partner live just over the Arkansas-Missouri state line, where they keep buying more books than they have room for.

You can find her at www.jhfleming.net, as well as on Facebook, Instagram, Twitter, Tumblr, and YouTube.

9 798987 949528